SHERRYL WOODS

The Heart of Hill Country

mira

mira

Recycling programs for this product may not exist in your area.

ISBN-13: 978-0-7783-0930-7

The Heart of Hill Country

Copyright © 2019 by Harlequin Books S.A.

The Littlest Angel
Copyright © 1997 by Sherryl Woods

Natural Born Trouble
Copyright © 1998 by Sherryl Woods

Printed in U.S.A.

CONTENTS

This one is for all the readers
who've embraced my characters and stories
through the years. You've been such a blessing
in my life and I treasure the friendship you've offered.

THE LITTLEST ANGEL

1

Angela hadn't wanted to come home like this, with her belly the size of two watermelons, and not one single proud accomplishment she could claim. She'd always meant her return to be triumphant, proof that she could succeed on her own without relying on the Adams name that meant so much in one little corner of West Texas. She'd envisioned a banner across the porch and a barbecue in her honor in the backyard and her name in lights, if Grandpa Harlan had his way.

Instead, it was the dead of night and no one even knew she was coming. Until she'd driven down the last stretch of deserted highway, anticipation mounting with every mile, she hadn't known for sure herself if she would have the courage to face her family. The car had settled that for her. It had conked out less than a mile from home. She sat in the rapidly chilling air and shivered, wondering if fate was on her side this time or just out to humiliate her further.

Home. The word had always conjured up a barrage of images for her, some good, some bad. Over the last six years the bad ones had faded until only the special memories remained. With her birthday tomorrow and Christmas just a few days away, it was no surprise that it was the holiday memories that came back to her now in a flood.

The celebrations always began early and lasted through New Year's, with everyone—aunts, uncles, cousins—traipsing from home to home for one party or another, but always, *always* ending up at White Pines. Grandpa Harlan insisted on it. He claimed he could spoil his grandkids rotten in his own home on Christmas Day if he chose to, while anywhere else he might have to show some restraint.

Rather than feeling deprived that her birthday was so close to Christmas, Angela had always felt as if all of the holiday trimmings made the day more special than it would have been at any other time of the year. Other kids got cakes and a single party. Angela's celebration included a huge tree, blinking colored lights, endless music and nonstop parties that went on for days.

She'd missed that while she was away, missed it when she'd noted the occasion all alone in a college rooming house already deserted by students who'd headed home for the holidays. Last year she'd almost forgotten it herself. She was too caught up in love, too excited about sharing her first Christmas with a man who really mattered to her.

Now, though, the memories were as vivid as if she'd never left. Even from her stalled car way out here on a lonely Texas highway she imagined she could see the lights twinkling on the ceiling-scraping Christmas tree, smell the aroma of Consuela's fresh-baked sugar cookies and bread mingling with the scent of fresh-cut pine.

She could almost hear the sound of carols being played at full volume, while her dad chided her mom that she was going to deafen all of them.

She sighed as she remembered the angel of shimmering gold that was ceremoniously placed on top of the tree each and every year and the pride she'd felt when that duty had been given to her. At five she'd been too small to reach the top, so her father had hoisted her up on his broad shoulders so she could settle that frothy angel onto the tree's highest branch. Then and only then, in a room that had been darkened for the ceremony, did they switch on the lights, always too many of them, always so magical that she and her mom had gasped with delight, while her dad had grinned tolerantly. The same ceremony had been repeated at White Pines, where as the oldest grandchild she'd always been the one who'd put the angel on her grandfather's tree.

So many wonderful traditions, she thought now. How could she have run away from all the warmth and love in that house? she wondered in retrospect.

Rebellion, pure and simple. She had chafed at all the bright expectations and what she now suspected had been imagined pressures. Like all families, hers had only wanted what was best for her.

It was just that the Adams men, particularly Luke and her grandfather, had a tendency to think they were the only ones who knew what was best. No two men on earth could be more mule-headed once they'd charted a course of action, for themselves or someone they loved.

Ironically, they had rarely agreed on what that course should be. One plan would have been hard enough to fight, but two were impossible. Angela had wanted to decide her future for herself, and leaving—choosing a college far from Texas where the Adams influence didn't reach—had been the only way she'd seen to do it. She'd limited contact to occasional calls, an infrequent e-mail to her computer-literate father.

Now, with snow falling in fat, wet clumps and the roads turning into hazardous sheets of ice, she sat in her idled clunker of a car less than a mile from home and wondered if anything else could possibly go wrong. Even as the thought crossed her mind, she glanced quickly heavenward.

"Not that I'm tempting fate, You understand," she said wearily. "But even You have to admit my life basically sucks these days."

She was twenty-two, unmarried, unemployed and no more than a week or two from delivering a baby. She was virtually back on a doorstep she'd vowed she wouldn't cross again until she'd made something of herself and done it totally on her own without the Adams power and influence behind her. If she'd taken one thing away from Texas with her, it had been the fierce Adams pride, the determination to buck everyone and chart her own path.

She supposed, in a manner of speaking, that she had. She had made a royal mess of things. No other Adams that she knew of had gone so far astray. She'd skated through college with grades no higher than they had to be. She'd lied about who she was and run away more times and from more places than she could count. Rather than upholding the noble Adams tradition, she'd thumbed her nose at it. Oh, yes, she'd made something of herself, all right, but she wasn't especially proud of it, and this was hardly the triumphant homecoming she'd once envisioned.

The only thing she had going for her was the absolute certainty that the two people inside would welcome her back with open arms and without making judgments. Luke and Jessie Adams accepted people for who they were, flaws included. That went double for their only child, the daughter they adored. They would be relieved that she'd finally realized that her heart and her identity were all wrapped up with the tight-knit family who'd been patiently waiting for her all this time.

As she huddled in the rapidly cooling car, she recalled the oft-told story of the joy with which she'd been welcomed into the world twenty-three years ago tomorrow. She had been born in the middle of a Texas blizzard with no one around to assist her mother except Luke Adams, her uncle at the time and the man who became her father. Luke had been blind drunk that night, but he'd sobered in a hurry when faced with the immediacy of those shattering labor pains. He had risen to the occasion like a true Adams hero.

From an early age Angela understood that they both considered her to be their Christmas blessing, a miracle on a cold and bitter night. With her natural father dead, her birth had brought Luke and Jessie together, helped them to overcome the anguish and guilt they'd felt at having fallen in love even before her father's fatal accident. Just as her name implied, she was their angel. Living up to such a lofty label had been daunting.

Admittedly, though, their expectations for her probably hadn't been half as exalted as she'd imagined them to be. She hadn't done a lot of listening before breaking the ties with home. At the first opportunity, she had fled Texas, first to attend college, then to roam the country in search of herself. It was time, she had thought, to do something totally outrageous, to discover what she was truly made of. Being angelic was a bore. She wanted to be wicked or, if not actually wicked, at least human.

Unfortunately, even after four years at Stanford and a year on her own the answers still eluded her. Over the past few months she'd had plenty of empty nights to examine her past. She was human, all right. The very human mistakes were mounting up.

She'd made the worst miscalculation of all in Montana with a rancher named Clint Brady, a low-down scoundrel if ever there was one, she thought bitterly. Her mound of a belly was testament to that. She wasn't looking forward to the hurt and worry that her parents would try their best to hide when they saw her and realized just how much trouble she'd managed to get herself into. She hated the thought of the heartbreak she would read in their eyes.

She was less worried about the reaction of her incredible grandfather, Harlan Adams. When it came to family, he was thoroughly predictable. He would probably set off fireworks to celebrate the birth of his first great-grandbaby. If he had questions about the baby's conception, he'd keep them to himself.

For the time being, anyway, she amended. As meddlesome as he was capable of being, he wouldn't be silent for long. By year's end he'd probably have a lynch mob searching for the baby's father, assuming he could get Angela to name him, which she had no intention of doing. Not even Clint Brady deserved to face the rancor of the Adams men, once they'd been riled up.

In addition to Luke and her grandfather, there were Cody and Jordan. They might be wildly different in some ways, but they all shared the Adams gene for pure cussedness and family loyalty. Clint wouldn't have a prayer against the four of them. He'd be hog-tied and married to her before he could blink. She would have no more say in the matter than he did.

To her chagrin, just the thought of Clint and her wild and reckless behavior in Montana made her blood run hot. Until she'd met him, she'd had no idea that passion could be so overwhelming, so completely and irresistibly awe inspiring.

Nor had she known how quickly passion could turn to hatred and shame.

She was glad now that she'd lied to him, that she'd faked a whole identity so that she could pretend for just a little while that she wasn't Luke and Jessie Adams's little angel. It had been liberating to pretend to be Hattie Jones, a woman with no exalted family history to live up to, a woman who could be as outrageous as she liked without regrets.

The decision to lie had been impulsive, made in a darkened country-western bar where she'd stopped to ask about a waitressing job that had been posted in the window. Clint had had the kind of lazy smile and sexy eyes that made a shy, astonishingly innocent college graduate imagine that all sorts of forbidden dreams were hers for the taking.

The job had been forgotten as she'd succumbed to newly discovered sensuality she hadn't even been tempted to test with the boys she'd met at Stanford. By the end of the night they were lovers. By the end of the week, she had moved in with him. She supposed that there was yet more irony that after all her running, she'd wound up with a rancher, after all.

More than once in the blissful days that followed she had regretted the casual lie she'd told when they met. More than once she had vowed to tell him the truth about who she was and where she came from, but Clint had been the kind of man who lived in the here and now. He didn't talk about his own past. He never asked about hers.

As weeks turned into months, it seemed easier to live with the lie. She liked being devil-may-care Hattie Jones, who flirted outrageously and never gave a thought to tomorrow. She liked the way Clint murmured her name in the middle of the night, as if he'd never before heard a word so beautiful.

In Clint's arms she was ecstatically happy. His ranch was a fraction of the size of her father's or her grandfather's, the days were long and exhausting, but none of that mattered, not at night when they made magic together. She found peace on that tiny Montana spread and something she had thought was love.

Then she'd discovered she was pregnant, and all of the lies and secrets between them—most of them admittedly her doing—had threatened to come unraveled.

When Clint had reacted in stunned silence to the news they were expecting a baby, that famous Adams pride had kicked in with a vengeance. She'd shouted a lot of awful, ugly things and he'd responded in kind. Even now the memory of it made her shudder.

If he'd been that furious over the baby, she couldn't

imagine what his rage would be like once he discovered that she'd lied to him from the start. In her entire life, no one had ever made her feel so low. Nor had she ever before wanted to hurt a person so deeply that he would never recover from it. Words were their weapons and they had used them well.

Angela hadn't waited for tempers to cool. She'd loaded up her car and hit the road before dawn, determined to put Clint Brady and Montana far behind her.

That had been nearly seven months ago. She'd been in a lot of cities since. Few of them had even registered. She had no more than vague memories of cheap hotels and back-road diners.

She wasn't exactly sure when she'd realized that Clint was following her. It had been almost a sixth sense at first, a nervous knotting in the pit of her stomach, a prickly sensation scampering down her spine. She was too hurt, too sure that she'd been wrong to get involved with him, too ashamed of her age-old predicament to let him catch her. What was the point of one more argument, anyway? It was best to put him in the past, along with all the other mistakes she'd made. A fresh start beckoned from around every curve in the road.

To her surprise, Clint hadn't given up easily. He'd nearly caught up with her in Wyoming, cutting short the part-time waitressing job she'd taken to get gas money to move on. Warned about the man who'd been in earlier asking questions about her, she'd slipped out the diner's back door just as Clint came through the front.

The narrow escape had made her jittery for days. She hadn't felt secure until she'd managed to trade her beloved blue convertible in for cash and a sensible beige sedan so old she hadn't even been born the year it was made. No car that old should have been expected to survive the kind of journey she'd taken it on.

She had moved quickly on to Colorado, then doubled back north to Cheyenne, looped up to South Dakota, then headed west to Seattle, enchanted by the idea of living by the water.

In Seattle she'd found a one-room apartment in an area called Pill Hill for all the hospitals clustered together. For the first time she had searched until she landed a halfway decent job as a receptionist. She'd found a kindly obstetrician to make sure she was doing all the right things for the baby she'd already learned to cherish. She'd vowed that the baby would never have to pay for the mistakes she'd made. Oddly enough, though being Angela Adams had daunted her, being a single mom did not.

In Seattle she'd even made a few friends, older, married women who invited her over often for home-cooked meals and the kind of nurturing concern she'd missed since leaving home. She took endless walks along Elliott Bay, bought fresh produce and fish at Pike's Place Market, sipped decaf cappuccino in every Starbucks she passed.

Clint seemed to have lost her trail or else he'd just given up and gone home, satisfied that he'd made a noble attempt to find her. No doubt that enabled him to sleep well enough. By then, he was probably sharing his bed with some other woman. At any rate, she'd felt it was safe to linger in Seattle. Contentment seemed almost within her grasp. She couldn't bring herself to admit that she was disappointed that he had given up.

Maybe, if it hadn't been for the Seattle weather, she could have made it work. But as summer gave way to fall and then to a premature winter, all that rain and gloom had finally gotten to her. She began to miss clear blue skies and the kind of heat that baked the earth.

When she packed up and moved on, she told herself her goal was merely sunshine. The undeniable truth was, she was heading straight for Texas, toward home.

For better or worse, she was going back to become Angela Adams again. The spirited Hattie Jones had died in Montana. Like it or not, Angela Adams was a Texan through and through. Her baby would be, too. The heritage she had abandoned for herself, she had no right to dismiss for the baby. It should be up to her child to decide someday if being an Adams was too much of a burden.

Not that she ever sat down and listed all the pros and cons for going home. The choice was instinctive. She'd hardly even needed a map to guide her south along the Pacific Coast and then east. If she'd stopped to reason it out, she probably would have found a hundred excuses for staying as far away from Texas as she could.

She'd developed a bad case of jitters near the end and wound up in Dallas, bypassing the turn to the south that would have taken her home much sooner. For days she'd lingered, wandering around the stores that had been decorated for the holidays, pretending that maybe this would be the final destination. It was close enough to home for an occasional visit, but far enough away to maintain her independence.

This afternoon, though, she had gotten into her car and impulsively started driving, taking familiar turns onto back roads and straight highways that were unmistakably leading her back to Los Pinos. Her static-filled radio had crackled with constant threats of an impending blizzard, but she hadn't once been tempted to turn back or to stop. Not even the first flurries of snow or the blinding curtain of white that had followed daunted her. Home beckoned by then with an inevitability she couldn't resist.

It was ironic, of course, that it had been on a night very much like this that her mother had gone into labor practically on Luke Adams's doorstep, had delivered Angela in his bed, with his help.

That had worked out well enough, she reminded herself as she tried to work up the courage to leave the safety and comfort of the car for the bitter cold walk home. Their marriage was as solid and secure as a bank vault.

Maybe that was why Angela had run from Clint Brady, had kept on running even when she knew he was chasing after her, even when she realized that it was possible that he wanted her back. She had seen what it could be like for two people who were head over heels in love, who faced problems squarely and grew strong because of them. She wanted nothing less for her child. If she couldn't offer the baby that, then she could at least make sure there was a wide circle of family around to shower her son or daughter with love.

As if in agreement, her baby kicked ferociously. Boy or girl, she thought defiantly, the kid was definitely destined to be a place kicker in the NFL. She rubbed her stomach and murmured soothing words, then drew in a deep breath.

Exiting the car to face an icy blast of air, she shivered and drew her coat more snugly around her.

"OK, little one," she whispered as excitement stirred deep inside her, overcoming dread or at least tempering it. "This is it. Let's go home."

2

Clint Brady had always possessed the kind of charm that could get him out of jams and, just as easily, into trouble. It was a blessing and a curse. Recently, he'd spent a lot of time regretting that he'd wasted a single ounce of it on Miss Hattie Jones. She'd been nothing but trouble.

Drawn to her blue eyes and dark auburn hair, enchanted by her from-the-gut laughter, seduced by a body that curved and dipped like a Rocky Mountain road, he'd tossed aside common sense and set out to get her into his bed. There'd been half a dozen years age difference between them, but he'd dismissed that as if it had been no more than a minute.

Even when half of what she'd said hadn't added up any better than his books at the end of the month, he'd dismissed reason and run with his hormones. He should have been old enough and smart enough to know better, which just proved how wrong things could go when a man started thinking with something other than his brain.

Even so, for the better part of a year, he hadn't regretted his decision. That choice had set them off on one heckuva steamy ride. Hattie had been like no woman he had ever known before—sweetly vulnerable one minute, a wickedly sensuous vixen the next. His life had been filled with an incomparable mix of unexpected laughter and impromptu sex. They hadn't been able to get enough of each other. They'd learned to strip faster than a cook could shuck an ear of corn.

Yet for all of Hattie's spontaneity in the bedroom, she'd had a head filled with commonsense advice and straight thinking. He'd admired that almost as much as he had her generosity in bed.

For a man who'd never known the meaning of permanence, not when it came to relationships, anyway, he had actually started to think about forever. The prospect had scared him worse than the first time he'd crossed paths with a bear and twice as badly as dancing away from a rattler.

Right square in the middle of his panic, she'd dropped the news that she was pregnant. She'd stared at him over a candlelit dinner and said the words straight out, as blunt as a dare and twice as challenging. He figured there wasn't a man on God's earth that would blame him for being temporarily stunned into silence.

Women, on the contrary, obviously expected a more immediate and more joyous response. Before he'd been able to gather his wits, before they could have anything resembling a rational discussion of their options, Hattie had come completely unglued. She'd hurled a bunch of accusations in his direction, then added that she was no more interested in commitment than he was. She'd verbally blasted the hard life she'd had living with him and had followed that almost immediately with the intentionally cruel announcement that she'd be giving the baby up for adoption and that he'd be the last man on earth she'd allow to claim any child of hers.

Shaken by her venom, Clint had shouted good riddance as she'd flown out the door. The echo of car doors slamming had been as sweet a sound as he had ever heard.

Naturally as soon as she was gone, though, he'd calmed down and changed his mind. He hadn't been able to stop thinking about a little blue-eyed, red-haired girl or boy who'd grow up to take over the small ranch he owned in Montana. He'd finally have the family he'd always secretly longed for, but had convinced himself was out of reach as long as he was living such a hand-to-mouth existence. With a few hours of peace and quiet to soothe his frayed temper, the sound of wedding bells hadn't seemed nearly so discordant.

Unfortunately, Hattie was long gone by the time he came to his senses. He had been fool enough to figure that she would come back when she calmed down, that they would work it out. In all the months they'd been together, he'd somehow missed the fact that Hattie had a temper to match that red hair of hers.

By dawn he'd begun to realize that he'd misjudged the depth of her fury. By noontime, he was calling himself every kind of fool for letting her get away. By four he was on the road, chasing down a trail that was already growing cold. No one in town had seen her go. She hadn't even stopped for gas.

He spent two blasted weeks he couldn't spare playing cat and mouse with a woman who clearly didn't want to be caught. When she ducked out the back door of a diner in Wyoming just as he came in the front, he blistered the air with a string of curses that could have been heard clear back in Montana. It was pure luck he'd been able to get a grip on himself before the sheriff had shown up to check out the lunatic on the premises.

He told himself he'd had it, that she didn't matter, that the world would keep on turning if he never set eyes on her again. He no longer allowed himself to picture his baby at all. It hurt too much to think that he'd never even know if he had a son or daughter.

Back home with spring just around the corner, he worked the ranch every day until his back ached and sweat poured off his brow. He collapsed into bed each night, exhausted, but with his mind still alive with images of Hattie and his body aching for her touch.

Then, despite his best efforts to keep them at bay, the images of their baby flooded in, the child he would never know if he left things as they were. He'd grown up fatherless, the youngest in a long line of kids and apparently the straw that broke his father's back. His dad had left the day he was born. His own brothers and sisters had resented him from the beginning, had blamed him for their dad's leaving. Only his mother had cared that he was alive. She was the only one with whom he'd kept in touch. It was easier on all of them if he kept his distance.

No one on earth knew better than he what it was like to wonder, what it was like to yearn for a father's smile, for a sense of identity that only a father could give. No kid of his should have to go through that. No kid of his would ever have a minute's worry that he was unlovable, that it was his fault that his dad wasn't around.

And so he'd started the search all over again, picking up a clue here, another there, using a private detective when he could afford one, his own instincts when he couldn't. At least once a month he was on the road, following a lead, showing a snapshot of a smiling Hattie, sitting on a low-hanging branch of a tree, skirt hitched up to her thighs. That picture had grown faded and blurred from handling, but her smile was still enough to make his heart ache.

He was way past desperation now. By his calculations the baby was due any minute and there were times it seemed he was no closer to finding Hattie than he had been seven months ago. The trail of slim leads from the last detective had ended in Dallas where she'd been spotted at a cafe. It was a huge city with lots of nooks and crannies a woman could hide in, if she was of a mind to, which Hattie certainly was.

Depressed by the needle-in-a-haystack enormity of the task facing him, Clint took refuge in a diner, the sort of cheap, inconspicuous place he'd discovered Hattie was drawn to. The too-bright lights glared off yellowing Formica and scarred chrome that had been polished until it managed a faint sparkle.

The tired colored lights on a tiny artificial Christmas tree winked on and off erratically, reminding him that it was a season of joy and wonder. The place smelled of stale grease and fresh coffee. The jukebox mourned lost love. If crying had been in his nature, Clint would have wept.

"Hey, sugar, you look like a man who needs a drink

worse than he needs the kind of grub you'll get in this place."

Clint looked up from the laminated menu and found himself staring into sparkling brown eyes. Unruly blond hair had been partially tamed into a luxuriant ponytail. Lush, upturned lips, which would have made his pulse race a year ago, did little more than draw a returning smile now. The tag on her pocket said her name was Betsy.

"Betsy, are the burgers juicy and big?" he asked.

"Big enough to shut down half a dozen arteries before you can say bypass surgery," she responded.

"Is the coffee hot and strong?"

"Sugar, it'll make the hair on your chest curl," she said, her gaze pinned on that particular part of his anatomy as if she could see straight through his shirt.

Clint nodded. "Then I'm in the right place, after all. Two burgers and keep the coffee coming." He glanced around, assured himself that he was the only customer, then added, "And I'll double your tip if you pull the plug on that jukebox."

"What's the matter?" she inquired with a touch of feigned indignation. "You don't like country?"

"Under the right circumstances, I love country music."

Her expression radiated understanding. "It's just that you're so low-down, you don't want to be reminded of it."

"Exactly."

She silenced the jukebox and left him alone after that, except to bring his food and refill his coffee cup half a dozen times. The last time, as the clock ticked on toward midnight, she lingered.

"Sure you don't want to talk about it? I've got nothing to do tonight but listen."

Clint couldn't see the point in talking, but he couldn't much see the point to keeping silent, either. He poured out the whole sad tale, while Betsy clucked and sympathized.

"So, let's see this woman who has you all tied up in knots," she said eventually. "You have a picture of her?"

He dragged out the snapshot and pushed it across the counter. Expecting no more than a glib comment about Hattie's beauty, he wasn't prepared for the quick, indrawn breath or the suddenly cautious expression.

"What did you say her name was again?"

"Hattie," he told her. "Hattie Jones."

"No way," Betsy said, then clamped her lips together as if she'd already said too much.

"You recognize her, don't you?" Clint demanded, his hopes soaring for the first time in months. "Has she been in here? Did she work here?"

"Heck, no," she said as if the idea were totally preposterous.

The reaction startled him. He'd always thought Hattie was a high-class woman, but she surely wasn't above an honest day's hard work in a diner.

"What, then? How do you know her? What name's she going by now?" he asked. It would be no surprise to discover she'd taken an assumed name. Nothing about Hattie surprised him anymore, including the fact that she was quicksilver fast at slipping away from him.

"Her own, I imagine."

"And that would be?"

Betsy stared hard, straight into his eyes. "What'd you say you wanted with her? Give me the bottom line."

"I told you before, we have some unfinished business. That baby of ours needs a daddy and I intend to be one."

"You aiming to marry her?" Betsy prodded.

"That's one possibility," he conceded, though he wondered if that particular answer wasn't out of the question. Hattie had made her opinion of him plain as day by running from him time and again.

"And the others?" Betsy asked.

"We'll work something out about the baby." Clint offered up a full-wattage smile, the kind he'd been told was irresistible to women. "Come on, Betsy. I saw that book you were reading. You're a sucker for a happy ending, aren't you? Help me out here."

Betsy appeared to weigh his response before saying, "I hope to hell I'm not making a mistake."

"You're not," Clint reassured her, then held his breath and waited. He thought he'd won Betsy's trust, but he was equally certain that something about Hattie was making her hesitate. Did she have a new boyfriend the size of a Dallas Cowboys linebacker? Or had she simply sworn Betsy to secrecy? Whatever the explanation, he saw the wariness in Betsy's eyes give way to determination.

"Her name's Angie," she said evenly. "Angela Adams."

She said it without the slightest hint of uncertainty that would come with recent acquaintance. In fact, she said it with the confidence of someone who'd known her long and well. Better than he had, maybe.

"Angie Adams," he repeated, testing the name on his tongue. "You're sure?"

"Sugar, she and I went all through school together, first grade right on through graduation. Of course, that's when I quit, but last I heard Angie was going off to some fancy college in California." Her brow creased. "Stanford, maybe. That was five, no, almost six years back. She'd be out by now."

If Hattie had been to Stanford, then Clint had a degree in nuclear physics. She'd been looking for a job in a low-class bar the night they'd met. He doubted Stanford gave out degrees in waitressing.

"It can't be the same person," he insisted.

"Then Angie has a twin," she replied just as adamantly.

"You haven't seen her recently, have you?"

"Not since graduation. Seemed like she couldn't put enough distance between herself and home."

"What about her family? Are they here in Dallas?"

"Heck, no. They're over in Los Pinos. They practically own the whole town and most of the land surrounding it. Her granddaddy was the biggest rancher in the state till he turned the family spread over to her Uncle Cody. Her daddy's the second biggest. Her Uncle Jordan owns an oil company."

Hattie? Clint thought incredulously. Hattie, who'd been having a tough time scraping together food money when he'd met her?

Suddenly, though, dozens of tiny evasions began to make sense. Her familiarity with ranching, despite her claim that she'd never set foot on one, took on new significance. She'd pitched in with chores as if she'd done them before, but she'd sworn she was just a quick study. He'd been too glad of the willing help to cross-examine her. Now it seemed as if his tendency to live and let live had been a big mistake. He should have started asking questions the day she appeared in that bar.

If she'd lied about her name and her background, what else had she lied about? Who the hell was Hattie Jones, after all? Had she even been pregnant when she'd left or had that been just another in the series of lies? Maybe she'd just been testing the depth of his affections and he'd failed the test, so she'd moved on to greener pastures.

Then again, she was awful close to home. If she'd been avoiding it for all these years as Betsy claimed, what would bring her back if not the impending birth of a baby? An heir to all this Adams wealth that Betsy had been describing? There was only one way he could think of to get answers.

"Can you tell me exactly how to get to her parents' place?"

"Better yet, I'll show you," Betsy offered. "I've got a whole week off and I was planning on heading over to Los Pinos for Christmas as soon as my shift ends at one. My car's been conking out on me a lot lately, though. If I can hitch a ride with you, I'll take you straight to their front door."

She winked at him. "And just in case things don't work out, I'll point the way to my folks' place. It's not as fancy as theirs, but you'll be welcome."

Clint didn't want to give her any false expectations. Betsy was a nice woman, but she was no Hattie. Who knew, though? Once he'd decided whether or not to strangle the woman who'd walked out on him, a straight shooter like Betsy might start looking pretty good.

"Let's see how this turns out," he said. "If this Angie Adams is the right woman, I'll owe you."

"Sugar, it's not your wallet I'm interested in." Her expression turned resigned. "But a few bucks is all you're likely to part with, isn't it? You really do have it bad, don't you?"

He wasn't about to admit just how bad. He settled for offering a warning. "Betsy, you don't want anything to do with a man like me. Just ask your old friend Angie. I'm sure she'd be eager enough to tell you all my flaws."

"Sugar, working in a place like this, I learned a long time back to be a good judge of character. You look just fine to me. Besides, Angie never did know when she had it good. Wait till you see that spread she grew up on. If she could turn her back on that, she doesn't have the sense the good Lord gave a duck. You'd be better off with a woman who appreciates you."

There was a time, Clint thought, when no one had appreciated him better than Hattie had. It was his fault that that had changed. In one lightning-quick moment of frozen panic, he'd destroyed all they'd had together. He was willing to accept responsibility for that much, anyway.

Or was he entirely to blame? Maybe Hattie was just the kind of woman who had to keep on moving on, who'd instigate a fight so she could go. Maybe she was just a natural-born liar. Could be he wasn't the first man she'd run out on or the first one she'd lied to.

After months of feeling angry and lonely by turns, he was about to find the woman who'd tied him in knots.

He'd settle things with her once and for all. For the first time they would put all their cards on the table and decide where they stood. He'd find out if she was even capable of telling the truth.

He hoped so. He really did, because no conniving, lying woman would get the chance to raise a child of his. If he didn't like what he discovered, their baby would be going back to Montana with him. She could bet the whole fancy Adams ranch on that.

3

Coming home had been a hundred times worse than Angela had anticipated and a thousand times better.

She had seen first shock, then joy register on her parents' faces as they'd realized who was ringing their bell and waking them out of a dead sleep. If she'd kept her old key, she could have crept in unnoticed and greeted them over breakfast in the morning, when she had her own emotions under better control. As it was, she'd dragged them out of bed, stunned them first with her return, then dismayed them with a refusal to answer a single question about the baby she was so obviously carrying. The tearful reunion had taken on a confrontational tone very quickly.

"Dammit, I want to know who's responsible for the condition you're in," her father had bellowed loudly enough to raise the rafters.

"I am," she had replied quietly.

He glared at her. "Unless things have changed a helluva lot more than I realized, you didn't get pregnant on your own. Where's the father of this baby? Are you married?"

Angela regarded him in stoic silence.

"Luke, that's enough," her mother had said eventually, when it was clear they were at a standoff.

As always, her touch on his cheek was more effective at quieting him than her words. Angela had always envied them that, the ability to communicate with a touch, a glance.

"Can't you see she's worn-out and shivering?" her mother had chided. "It must be below freezing outside. Come into the kitchen right this second and let me make you some hot chocolate."

"I'd rather have tea," Angela said, casting a wary look at her father's grim expression as he followed them into the kitchen. "Herbal, if you have it."

"Of course I have it," her mother said as she filled the teakettle with water and put it on the stove. "Consuela insists we keep wild blackberry tea in the house just for you. It was always your favorite."

"How is she?" Angela asked, smiling, relieved by the chance to change the topic. "I thought for sure she'd be retired by now. She must be what? Eighty-something?"

"Eighty-two and as spry as ever. She wears me out and she flatly refuses to retire," her mother said. "She says she won't have someone else in her kitchen. She'll be over the moon in the morning when she finds out you're home. She's been baking your favorite cookies for the past week. She swears something told her you'd be back this year. Nothing we said could dissuade her."

Guilt rippled through Angela. Consuela had been far more than a housekeeper. She had been the grandmother Angela had never had. She'd taken a terrible chance not staying in touch with her. At Consuela's age anything could have happened and Angela would never have known.

"I'm sorry I haven't been in touch, especially this past year. I'm sorry I didn't let you know I was coming."

"Nonsense. It doesn't matter. You're here now." Her mother glanced at her father. "Isn't that right, Lucas?"

His stony expression softened just a fraction. "Of course we're glad you're home, angel. We've missed you."

Tears welled up in her eyes at the hurt she heard in his voice. "I'm sorry," she said, her own voice choked. "I'm sorry for everything."

"Oh, baby, you don't have anything in the world to apologize for. You may not believe it, but we both understood exactly why you felt you had to go. Didn't we, Luke?"

"That's true enough. We didn't like it, but nobody knows better than we do what it takes to be an Adams in these parts," he said, his expression wry. "I fought it in my way. Your uncles fought it in theirs. You just ran a little farther than the rest of us."

"The bottom line is we love you," her mother said. "And we are both very glad you're home again where you belong." She hesitated. "You are here to stay, aren't you?"

Angela wished she could claim that she was just passing through, that she had a home and a life of her own to get back to once the holidays were over, but she couldn't. "If you'll have me," she said, no longer able to control the tears that had been threatening ever since she'd crossed the threshold.

Her father reached over and brushed the dampness

from her cheeks. "There was never any doubt about that. Never."

Angela could feel their love warming her, chasing away all the fears and loneliness of the past few months. Once she had felt smothered by that love, choked by the overly protective nature of her whole extended family, from Grandpa Harlan and her strong-willed uncles right on down to the two people in this room. Not anymore. She realized now just how desperately she had been longing for this kind of unconditional acceptance. For the past couple of months her nesting instinct had been kicking in with a vengeance.

After her father's initial outburst, her parents had held their questions about the baby she was expecting. They had filled her with hot tea and thick ham sandwiches and a half-dozen Christmas cookies before sending her off to bed in the room that hadn't changed a bit since she'd left it behind. Consuela had kept it swept and dusted, but the old concert posters were still on the walls, and her menagerie of stuffed animals still tumbled across the bed.

She'd heard her parents' whispers as they'd gone off to their own room and known that the reprieve from questions wouldn't last forever. It wasn't in her father's nature to let one of his own be hurt without taking action to see that it never happened again. Even as he'd fallen silent after her mother's soft reproach, Angela had noticed the stubborn, determined jut of his chin. Her mother's intervention had only managed to delay the inevitable until this morning.

As Angela stood at the foot of the steps and tried to work up the courage to enter the dining room for breakfast, she braced herself for the new barrage of questions

that he'd been forced to hold back the night before. She
vowed to tell them as little as she could get away with.
She ought to be very good at evasions by now. She'd
been practicing long enough. She'd perfected the tech-
nique in Rocky Ridge, Montana.

She drew in a deep breath and stepped into the dining room. Her mother and father looked up when they
heard her, and smiles spread across their faces.

Before she could even summon up a returning smile,
she was enveloped in the arms of a plump Mexican
woman whose once-black hair had gone almost completely white. There were new lines carved into her
olive complexion, but her dark brown eyes sparkled as
merrily as ever.

"Ah, *niña,* you are home," Consuela murmured,
stroking Angela's hair back from her face as she had
when she was a child. A rapid stream of Spanish that
was part welcome, part chastisement followed until Angela laughed and pressed a finger against the housekeeper's lips.

"Despacio, por favor," she pleaded. "Slowly, Consuela. I've forgotten every bit of Spanish you taught
me."

"Then you must practice," Consuela said briskly.
"It will be good for the baby, too. He will grow up bi-
lingual."

"He?" Angela said, grinning at the assumption.

"Of course. I know these things." Consuela scowled
at Luke, who hadn't bothered to hide his skepticism.
"You laugh? Did I not predict the sex of every child
ever born in this family, starting with you and your
brothers?"

"That was easy. No girl had been born in the Adams clan for a hundred years," Luke teased.

"And what of Cody's daughter? Or your stepsister?" Consuela countered indignantly. "They were not so easy to predict, yes?"

"OK, OK, I surrender," he said. "You know these things."

"Indeed," Consuela said. "Now, *niña,* what can I fix for you? Waffles, eggs, a Spanish omelet, perhaps?"

"The omelet," Angela said eagerly, her hands on her swollen belly. She grinned. "And the waffle. For the baby."

"Of course," Consuela said, bustling off to the kitchen to work her magic.

Angela sat down opposite her mother, aware of the worried glances she kept casting at her husband. Apparently she was anticipating the flood of questions, just as Angela was. Only Consuela seemed willing to accept her condition as a simple fact of life and not cause for an inquisition.

"Where have you been for the past year and a half?" her father asked oh, so casually, in what for him was a dramatic show of diplomacy. "Aside from an occasional call to say you were OK, we haven't heard so much as a word from you since you graduated from college. You never gave us so much as a post office box, so we could contact you."

"I was traveling most of that time," she said. It was the truth as far as it went.

"Obviously you stayed in one place a little too long," her father retorted.

"Luke!" her mother said sharply.

He scowled. "Dammit, we have a right to know the truth."

"Only if Angela wants to tell us," her mother countered. "She's a grown woman."

The unfamiliar dissension between the two of them set her nerves on edge. Worse, she hated being the cause of it. "I can't tell you," she said with regret.

"What do you mean you can't?" Luke demanded, bellowing again. "Don't you even know who the father of the baby is?"

Angela stared at him in shock. "Of course, I know."

"Then is it asking too much to expect you to tell us?"

"It is if you're going to go ballistic and start making trouble," she shot back. "I'm here. The father's not. That should pretty much settle things."

"Nothing's settled, as far as I can tell. I'd say that trouble you're afraid I'll stir up is already here. I'm just trying to figure out how to clean up after it."

Angela trembled at the sound of barely contained rage in his voice. It was exactly what she'd anticipated, what she'd feared she would be stirring up by coming home.

"Maybe I should go," she said softly.

"Absolutely not," her mother snapped, adding in a rare display of temper, "Luke, that's enough. Let's everybody calm down."

Her father looked as if he were ready to explode. "Fine. You get the truth out of her, then," he said, throwing his napkin onto the table and stalking out.

"Don't mind him," her mother apologized. "He's just worried about you. We both are."

"There's no need to worry. I'm fine."

"Sweetie, if you were fine, you wouldn't have been on our doorstep, half-frozen in the middle of the night. I know you. You came home because you felt you didn't have anyplace else to go. You have too much pride to have come home otherwise."

The all-too-accurate assessment brought the sting of tears to her eyes. "Maybe I just missed you."

"Maybe you did, but that alone wouldn't have been enough to get you back here, not after you made such an issue of staying away," her mother said dryly. "Now you can tell *me* what's going on, or you can tell your father, or you can keep it all bottled up inside."

Angela grinned ruefully. "Those are my only choices?"

"Unless you'd rather tell your grandfather," her mother retorted. "No doubt he'll be on his way over as soon as he hears you're back. He's expected tomorrow, anyway. I doubt I'll be able to keep him away. He's been just itching to put a private eye on your trail for the past year and a half. When he sees you're pregnant, there won't be a place on earth the father of that baby can hide."

Angela thought of Clint's efforts to track her down. He was a pure amateur compared to her grandfather, but he'd done a pretty good job of it just the same. "He hasn't exactly been hiding," she admitted. "He's been trying to find me for the last seven months."

Her mother's gaze narrowed. "But you've been determined to elude him? Why? Did he abuse you?" she demanded, her voice barely above a horrified whisper. "If that man harmed you in any way—"

"No," she said hurriedly. "He never laid a hand on me."

Obviously relieved, her mother's expression softened. Her gaze fell on Angela's stomach. "Oh, really?"

"I meant he never hurt me, not physically."

"Why did you run then?"

"He didn't want the baby," she said simply.

"Are you sure about that?"

She recalled in vivid detail the humiliation of sitting across that candlelit table from Clint, praying for a whoop of joy, even a smile, only to see that stunned, blank expression on his face. "He all but said it when I told him I was pregnant," she said.

"He all but said it," her mother repeated with a sad shake of her head. "Darling, if he was so anxious to be rid of you and the baby, why has he been chasing after you all this time?"

"I don't know."

"Don't you think you should try to find out? Don't you owe it to your child?"

"It's too late."

Her mother looked skeptical. "Tell me one thing, then. Did you love him?"

"I thought I did," Angela admitted softly, then forced her gaze to meet her mother's. "I was wrong. I just want to put it all behind me."

For a moment it looked as if her mother was going to argue, but then she nodded. "Well, you've certainly always known your own mind. If that's what you want, I'll do my best to keep Luke and your grandfather from stirring things up."

"It's what I want," Angela said firmly and without

the slightest hesitation. Even as she spoke, though, a little voice deep inside shouted, "Liar." She'd heard that same accusation so often the past couple of years that she was able to ignore it one more time.

Four in the morning or not, if he'd had his way, Clint would have started pounding on Angela Adams's front door the minute he and Betsy got to Los Pinos, but she had persuaded him to wait until a more reasonable hour. She'd also promised to make a call to the ranch to see if the lady in question was, in fact, back home again. Small town or not, her parents hadn't heard any gossip about it yet, though there'd apparently been plenty of speculation over the years about Angela's disappearance.

A half hour ago, after he'd managed to catch a couple of hours sleep in a guest room at Betsy's parents' house, she had made the call. She'd quickly confirmed that Angela had arrived home unexpectedly just the night before. She hadn't dared to ask whether the prodigal daughter had arrived home more than eight months pregnant. Still, Clint couldn't help believing that he had found his "Hattie" at last.

Now he sat outside the gate to the ranch and tried to bring his temper under control. The sight of a decrepit beige sedan half-buried in a snowdrift a half-mile back only raised his hackles more. He'd lay odds that was the car she'd been driving.

He told himself repeatedly that there was no point in charging in and getting the whole family riled up. Betsy, who'd proved time and again to be one of the most sensible women he'd ever met, had convinced him that a man in his position didn't want the whole lot of Adams men squared off against him, especially on their home turf.

So he was cooling his heels and hopefully his anger. He'd spent the past couple of hours envisioning this confrontation, envisioning the way Hattie's eyes—no, *Angela's,* dammit—would widen with shock when she realized she'd been found out. He could hardly wait.

He put his pickup in gear and drove up the winding lane to the impressive house. It seemed to ramble forever, dwarfing his own ranch. Barns, stables, everything in sight was spit-and-polish perfect.

Hands jammed into his pockets, he forced himself to walk slowly up to the front door, fighting intimidation over his surroundings every step of the way.

His control wasn't quite strong enough to prevent him from leaning on the doorbell. He could hear the impatient chime echoing through the house.

"I'll get it, Mom," an all-too-familiar voice called out.

The sound of that sweet voice sent goose bumps chasing down Clint's spine. Up until now he supposed a part of him had been holding out hope that Betsy had been wrong, that Hattie was Hattie and that there'd been no monumental lie between them. Now there was no denying the truth. He'd been played for a fool.

After taking a look around at her daddy's spread, he could imagine just how pitiful his own ranch had seemed to her. No wonder she'd been so eager to put it behind her. What stumped him, though, was why it had taken her so long to hightail it back to her daddy's place.

When the door swung open, he got exactly the shocked reaction he'd been hoping for, but he doubted it was any greater than his own. Even though he'd known she should be in the final month of her pregnancy—if she hadn't lied to him about that, too—the reality of it stunned him.

With her formerly svelte body swollen with his baby, she was more beautiful than ever. Curves that had been intriguing enough before were lush and gloriously feminine. He couldn't seem to tear his gaze away from her stomach, where both of her hands had settled protectively. Instinctively he reached out to touch her, to feel this growing child she'd kept from him, but she jerked away and tried to slam the door in his face.

Fortunately she was a little too ungainly to be as quick as she needed to be to prevent him from slipping inside. He caught the toe of his boot in the crack of the door, then wedged it open until the rest of him could follow. He closed it securely, while she eyed him as warily as if he'd been a rattler already coiled for striking.

"Hello, Hattie. Looks like we have some things to talk about." To his everlasting irritation, his voice shook when he said it. She still had the power to make him weak-kneed and crazy with desire. He had wondered if she would, had prayed that she wouldn't. At best, he'd wanted to be consumed with hatred, at worst, ambivalent. He hadn't wanted to be practically struck dumb with longing. Add to that her ability to rile him, and it was a wonder he managed to get a word out at all.

"Not here," she whispered urgently. Her eyes pleaded with him. "Please, Clint. I'll meet you in town. Just give me an hour."

He shook his head. "I'd like to accommodate you, I

really would, but you have this nasty habit of taking off on me. I don't think I'll chance it this time."

Just then a woman who looked like an older version of Hattie came down the hall and into the foyer. She was tall and slender and radiant. She had the kind of self-possession and grace that attracted men and made women envious. Her glance shifted from Clint to her daughter, then back again. Apparently even she could sense the crackling tension in the air.

"Angie, is everything OK?"

Clint figured he'd let Hattie field that one. He fixed his gaze on her and watched the color bloom in her cheeks. Her shoulders sagged.

"Mother, this is Clint Brady," she said eventually. "The man I told you about."

Mrs. Adams's friendly expression vanished at that. "I think you should leave," she said, her voice stiff and formal. "You've caused enough pain."

"I swear to you that I don't want any trouble, ma'am, but I'm not leaving. Not until Hattie and I settle a few things," he said politely, but firmly.

His vehemence clearly took her aback. Apparently few people argued with her, confirming Betsy's description of a family used to being in control not only of its own destiny, but of most of the world around it.

She quickly regained her composure, then glanced at her daughter, her expression vaguely puzzled. "Hattie?"

Clint's lips curved as he observed Angela's unmistakable discomfort. "I guess you forgot to tell your mother some of the details."

"Clint, please," she begged.

Her mother took pity on her, even if Clint's patience was too far gone for him to.

"I think it's best if you go. You don't want to be here when my husband gets back," Mrs. Adams insisted. "He has a quick temper and these circumstances call for some preparation."

Clint shrugged. "I figure your husband and I probably want the same thing about now..." He looked straight at Hattie. "Answers. I'm not leaving here without them."

Hattie sighed. Resignation spread across her face. "It's OK, Mother. I'll deal with this."

"Are you sure? I can call your father."

Hattie shook her head. "It's not necessary." She stared at him pointedly. "Clint's no threat to me."

Her mother backed down with obvious reluctance, leaving Hattie to lead the way into a living room that was almost the size of his whole ranch house. The money spent on the furnishings would have kept his place afloat for a year. The holiday decorations were as spectacular as any he'd ever seen in a department store, all gold and glitter and candlelight even at mid-morning.

Clint and Angela stared at each other uneasily. He was trying to assess exactly where to begin. She looked as if she were girding for battle.

An older Mexican woman appeared almost at once, bearing a silver tray laden with coffee and freshly baked cinnamon rolls. There was also a cup of herbal tea, the wild blackberry kind he knew Hattie favored. Somehow he felt reassured by that small bit of evidence that she was still the same woman he'd fallen for in Montana.

"Thanks, Consuela," Hattie said distractedly.

. "Thank you, ma'am," Clint said. "That coffee smells mighty good."

"You need anything else, you call, *niña*," she said to Hattie, then gave Clint an assessing once-over. Apparently whatever she saw pleased her, because she left the room with a satisfied smile on her lips. It appeared he had one person in his corner. Judging from Hattie's lack of welcome, he probably ought to count himself lucky that no one so far had aimed a shotgun his way.

"How do you do that?" Hattie said.

"What?"

"Mutter half a dozen words and charm the socks off a woman? First Mother backs down and Consuela practically swoons."

"It's a gift," he declared. He tried smiling at her. "Used to work on you, too, as I recall."

She didn't bat an eye. "That was then. This is now. How'd you find me?"

"Pure grit, *Hattie*."

"Drop the Hattie," she said irritably. "Obviously you've figured out by now that it isn't my real name."

"OK, Angela." He regarded her speculatively. "Something tells me, though, that around here they probably call you Angel."

The flood of color in her cheeks told him he'd hit the mark, but she ignored the observation.

"Maybe the more important question is why did you bother?" she asked.

Her expression was a mix of curiosity and an even deeper resignation. She actually looked vulnerable, more vulnerable than he could ever recall Hattie looking when she'd been dancing up a storm and flirting with half the men in Montana.

"You're having my baby, unless you lied about that, too, *Angela*."

"That didn't seem to matter to you when I told you," she reminded him.

"That was then. This is now," he mimicked. "I've been trying to catch up with you since the day you left."

"I repeat, why?"

"Because no child of mine is going to grow up without a father," he said simply, his gaze locked with hers. A shudder seemed to wash over her, even as a spark of pure defiance lit her eyes.

"It's not your decision," she retorted.

"Yes," he said softly. "It is. As of this minute, I'm making it mine."

4

Angela had her hands clenched so tightly in her lap that even her bitten-to-the-quick nails were cutting into her flesh. Clint Brady was the most arrogant, the most infuriating, the most insufferable man she had ever had the misfortune to cross paths with. He was going to make a pest of himself. She could feel it. His words flat-out guaranteed it. She had run out on him, which perversely made him want both her and the baby.

The truth was, though, he hadn't wanted either one of them when she'd been right under his nose and more than willing to stay. This display was just male pride kicking in, nothing more. She couldn't allow herself to get caught up in an emotional tug-of-war, not when Clint would eventually tire of it and leave. She couldn't work herself up over his threats and taunts. If she did, she'd be an emotional wreck.

Reasoning that out made her feel marginally better, despite the grim glint in his eyes and the stubborn jut of his chin.

Unfortunately, she also had the awful, gut-sick feeling that once he got over his desire to throttle the man, her father was going to take to Clint the way bears took to honey. They spoke the same testosterone-laden language. Add to that their dedication to ranching and the two of them were like two peas in a pod.

It was ironic, really. She had run away from Texas to escape all that stubborn, macho nonsense. Until just this instant, with Clint scowling at her and insisting that he had rights here, she hadn't noticed that he was cut from the same cloth as all the Adams men she'd left behind. Just her luck.

"Go back to Montana," she pleaded one last time. "I'm home. I'm surrounded by my family. You don't need to worry about me or the baby."

"Maybe you should let me decide who needs worrying about," he said.

He said it in that sexy, laid-back tone she had once found incredibly seductive. Now it was merely patronizing and irritating. She wondered for a minute if his potent effect on her had finally worn off, but one long glance at him told her the emphatic answer to that. Her blood practically sizzled and she seemed to have no ability whatsoever to stop it.

Fixing her gaze on sun-streaked brown hair that needed trimming just to be respectable, blue eyes with a look of pure mischief in them and sensual lips capable of turning kissing into an art form, she knew she was far from over him. Just looking at him sent a jolt of desire slamming through her.

While she caught her breath, she realized that he was studying her just as intently.

"You look a little pale," he concluded. "Aren't you getting enough rest?"

"My color has nothing to do with exhaustion. I just keep getting an image of you with a bullet in your heart when my father finds you here," she said dryly.

"I had no idea you cared."

"Oh, for pity's sake, that wasn't a declaration of undying love. I'd feel the same about some poor, hapless animal walking past a hunter's shotgun."

He grinned. "Would you really? I guess that puts me in my place."

She glared at him. "Don't you dare mock me."

His expression sobered at once. "OK, I admit, we are getting a little far afield here. We have plans to make. Exactly when is the baby due?"

She saw little point in not telling him. It didn't take a genius in math to calculate the date with some degree of accuracy. Clint certainly ought to have the starting point pinned down well enough.

"Two weeks," she admitted grudgingly. "Though first babies are a little unpredictable, according to the doctor."

"Good, that gives us enough time, then."

She regarded him suspiciously. "Enough time for what?"

"To plan a wedding, of course."

Angie's mouth dropped open. If he'd suggested brushing up on his medical skills so he could deliver the baby himself, she wouldn't have been any more stunned. "A wedding? You and me? Have you completely lost your mind?"

He paused, his head tilted thoughtfully, then said,

"Nope. I don't think so. What kind of wedding do you want? Huge, I imagine, though it may be a little late in the day to try to pull that off. How about New Year's Eve? Something small and intimate. That ought to suit your sense of the romantic. Maybe right here in the living room, if your parents wouldn't object. The room could be lit with lots of candles." He glanced around deliberately. "We're already halfway there on that score."

Angela stared at him incredulously. He was serious. She recognized that stubborn glint in his eyes all too well. If she didn't stop him, he'd be ordering the rings and the flowers. Poinsettias in honor of the season, no doubt. The room would be a sea of red. She shuddered at the image.

Maybe if he'd said one single word about love, she would have catapulted herself straight into his arms. Instead, he'd set off warning bells. She saw the scheme for exactly what it was: a way to stake a legal claim on her baby. Well, she wouldn't be a party to it, and that was that.

If Clint Brady really wanted to be a father to this baby, then he was going to have to prove it, not with an impulsive wedding, but over time. Weeks, at the very least. Maybe months. As furious as she was, maybe even years.

"Forget it," she said softly. "No wedding. Obviously you've been sitting around the past few months with guilt weighing on your mind. That's OK. I always knew you were an honorable man. Now you've tracked me down and done the noble thing. You made me an offer of marriage, and I appreciate the gesture. I truly do. But it's not necessary. You can go on back to Montana and live your life exactly the way you want to with no commitments holding you back."

Before she could say another word, he had crossed the room and hauled her up off the sofa—no easy task, in her present condition. "Shut up," he murmured just before his mouth closed over hers.

His lips tasted like deep-roast coffee and felt like black velvet, sensuous and seductive, as they teased, then plundered. Clint had always known how to make a kiss memorable, and he was at his best this morning. Or maybe it was just that she'd been longing for another of his kisses for far too long. At any rate, this one was a doozy. Her resolve melted, right along with most of the muscles in her body. She felt like a limp noodle by the time he released her. A restless yearning had begun inside her, and she knew exactly where that was likely to lead unless she stopped this craziness. They'd be in front of a preacher by nightfall. Her father would encourage that notion right along.

"Oh, my," she murmured before she could stop herself. So much for a display of resolve, she thought irritably.

"At least that hasn't changed," he said with obvious satisfaction.

"No," she conceded because there seemed to be little point in lying about it. His arms were just about the only thing between her and collapse and they both knew it.

She looked him square in the eye. "But it doesn't matter."

"Oh, it matters," he taunted. "It seems to me it's the only thing that does."

"Of course, you would say that. All that ever mattered to you was the sex. OK, I agree. We had spectacular, fireworks-caliber sex. Time stood still. The world rocked on its foundation. Adam and Eve would have envied us our total lack of inhibitions. So what?"

"So what?" he repeated softly. "You think that's unimportant?"

"In the overall scheme of things, yes," she said defiantly, even though that kiss had been potent enough to prove otherwise.

"Liar."

Angela shrugged. "I've been called worse, especially by you."

Clint sighed and for the first time he looked the slightest bit guilty. "Look, I know I didn't respond exactly the way you wanted me to when you told me about the baby."

Months of nursing hurt pride kept her temper up. "That's an understatement, if ever I've heard one."

"You took me by surprise, that's all. We hadn't talked about the future. We hadn't talked about the two of us, much less about a baby. You knew—"

"Did you or did you not say that a baby was the last thing you wanted?"

"I did, but—"

"Did you or did you not say that marriage was out of the question?"

"I did, but—"

She was on a roll now and had no intention of pausing for any of his fast-talking rationalizations. She'd been stewing over that night for months now. It felt good to have another chance to throw in a few more digs at his lousy behavior.

"Did you or did you not mean every low-down, spiteful, mean word you uttered that night?" she demanded.

"No."

That single word, spoken with soft vehemence, slowed her down. She regarded him skeptically. "Oh, really?"

Clint sighed. "OK, yes, at the time, I meant it."

"I rest my case."

"I didn't know we were having a damned trial here," he practically shouted.

Two worried faces promptly appeared in the doorway. "It's OK, Mom," Angela said hurriedly. "You and Consuela don't have to stand guard. Clint and I are just finishing a discussion we started several months ago."

Clint's cheeks turned a dull red as he apparently realized that every word they'd spoken had been overheard, that more than likely their kiss had been witnessed by two very interested parties.

Good, Angela thought. She was on her turf now. Let him suffer a little embarrassment and humiliation. Let him suffer the tortures of the damned, for that matter. In fact, she would have welcomed the arrival of her father just about now. She might even load his shotgun for him.

Even though Angela thought she'd made her dismissal of their observers plain, her mother stepped into the room, followed by the housekeeper. Obviously nobody intended to listen to a word she said this morning.

"Maybe we should all sit down and discuss this rationally," her mother suggested, a worried gaze locked on Clint.

"If you would like a New Year's Eve wedding, *niña,*

I could have everything ready," Consuela offered eagerly. "It would be my joy."

Had everybody she knew turned deaf all of a sudden? Angela wondered irritably. "There is not going to be a wedding, not New Year's Eve, not ever," she said, her voice rising with each word. "Haven't I made myself clear? Clint will be leaving, going back to Montana, and that's final."

"I don't think so," Clint said quietly.

Consuela beamed at him, then chided Angela, "Maybe you should listen to him, *niña*. He seems very sincere."

"Oh, yes," Angela snapped. "He's about as sincere as a snake in the grass."

"Has she always been this stubborn?" Clint inquired as if she were no longer in the room.

Her mother smiled, clearly more than halfway ready to succumb to his charm, won over by his call for a wedding, even if it had come belatedly.

"Wait until you meet the rest of the family," she said. "She comes by it naturally. In fact, if you wouldn't mind a word of advice—"

That was it. That was the final straw. "Mother, I do not want you giving Clint Brady advice," Angela practically shouted, hoping that sheer volume would succeed, when nothing else had.

Her mother went on as if Angela had spoken in a whisper. "You might let her cool down a little, get used to the idea. I'm sure she'll be in a more receptive frame of mind in a few days. You could stay with us. You'll be able to meet the rest of the family. With the holidays coming, everyone will be here for a few days. And, of course, today is her birthday, so we'll be pulling together a last-minute party just for us, to celebrate. You can't miss that."

Clint Brady here, under the same roof? No way. Either her pragmatic mother was trying to make the best of an awful situation or she was getting back at Angela for running away from home in the first place.

"I do *not* want him in this house!" Angela insisted.

Despite the vehemence and shrill, escalating volume of her words, she had the distinct impression they were falling on deaf ears. Consuela leaped up and bustled off to ready the guest suite. Clint thanked her mother for the invitation and accepted without so much as a by-your-leave look in Angela's direction. She might as well have been invisible, she thought, thoroughly disgruntled by the turn of events.

Since no one seemed to give two hoots about what she thought, she hefted herself up off the sofa again and marched out of the room without a backward glance. If she hadn't been thoroughly exhausted from running, if she'd had anyplace else on earth to go, she would have fled the ranch and Texas and the overwhelming presence of Clint Brady.

Unfortunately, as she had all too recently discovered, there was apparently nowhere she could hide that he wouldn't find her. If there was going to be a grueling standoff, it might as well be where she could sleep in her own bed.

Luke Adams had the look of a man on a mission. Standing beside his pickup with his single piece of luggage, Clint observed Luke warily as he approached, hands jammed in the pockets of his jeans, a scowl etched in his rugged features and fire blazing in his eyes. He guessed it was going to be a tricky conversation.

They were about the same size and, despite the difference in their ages, probably equally fit. Ranching toughened a man at any age, and Luke had the look of a man who didn't leave the hard tasks to others. They had that in common, Clint thought optimistically. That and Angela, though he doubted her father would view the latter as a subject on which there could be much agreement.

"You're Brady?" Luke asked, regarding him distrustfully.

Clint offered his hand. Luke Adams ignored it. Clint guessed it was because he was scared to death if his hands came out of his pockets, one of them would land squarely in the middle of Clint's face. Clint couldn't blame him entirely for the reaction.

"I know this looks bad," he began.

"Bad?" Luke snapped. "Son, I figure you've got about thirty seconds to do some very fast talking to keep me from ripping you apart."

"I think I understand how furious you must be, but I swear to you that I am trying to get your daughter to marry me," Clint said. "I'm trying to do right by her and the baby."

"Shouldn't you have been thinking about that nine or ten months ago, before she wound up pregnant?"

"Nine or ten months ago the only thing on my mind was trying to keep my ranch afloat," Clint said honestly. "I figured I wouldn't have a whole lot to offer a woman, if it went under and I lost the land. Then Angela hit me with the news that she was pregnant and I panicked. I know I was wrong. Hell, I knew it even while we were still shouting at each other, but before things could calm down, she split. I've been chasing after her ever since, trying to put things right."

He realized that despite his anger over the discovery of all her lies, that was what he still wanted. He shook his head ruefully. "That woman moves faster than any oil slick and she's twice as slippery. Until now I've barely caught sight of her since the night she stormed out of my house."

Luke pinned him with a penetrating look. "Why'd you bother chasing her at all, if catching her was so much trouble?"

It was the same question Angela had asked, but Clint wasn't any more certain of the right answer now than he had been a few hours earlier.

"Because I wanted to do the right thing by her. Your daughter's a hell of a woman. And that baby, well, I may not have what you have here, but I am its daddy. I figure a child has a right to know the man responsible for bringing it into the world."

To his surprise something in Luke Adams's expression softened. The harsh, down-turned lines around his mouth eased up just a fraction. It was not quite a smile, but Clint felt relieved nonetheless. The tension in the air lessened. The first step toward a grudging respect had been taken—or at least he hoped it had.

"Even though she swears she wants no part of you, are you planning on sticking around?" Luke asked.

"Until I can talk her into marrying me," Clint vowed.

He hadn't thought much beyond that. His first goal had simply been to make everything nice and legal. He'd figured that would be tricky enough without worrying about what the next step might be. He wanted an honest claim on that baby, if the matter ever wound up in court. He kept that particular motive to himself. After what Angela had done to him, he figured he was entitled to one devious act. A gambler would call it hedging his bets. Luke Adams probably wouldn't see it that way.

As it was, his declaration drew a full-fledged smile from his prospective father-in-law. "It won't be easy," Luke informed him. "She seems to have made up her mind to do this her way."

"I can be very persuasive when I have to be," Clint said with more confidence than was probably justified. Angela had shown some evidence of being able to resist his charms. That had been an unexpected turn of events. He'd thought that breezing in here and staking his claim was going to be easy. He wasn't exactly disturbed to find he'd been wrong. He loved a good challenge as well as the next man. It kept life interesting, especially if a woman like Angela was involved.

"We'll work it out," Clint promised.

Luke seemed to find his self-assurance amusing. "Good luck," he said. He started toward the house, then turned back, his expression sobering. "Just one more thing. I don't know the details of what went on between the two of you in the past, but you hurt that girl of mine again and this time you'll be answering to me. Do we understand each other?"

The warning was as plain as a six-shooter pointed at the gut. Clint's respect for Luke Adams tripled in that instant. Here was a man who fought for what was his, who fiercely protected those he cared about. He was exactly the kind of man—the kind of father—Clint intended to be.

"Perfectly," he said quietly. "We understand each other perfectly."

The only problem he foresaw was getting the message through to Angela.

"Mother, how could you invite that man to stay here?" Angela demanded as she paced her room in pure frustration. She was already feeling claustrophobic just thinking about his presence, and this house was five times the size of the one she and Clint had shared in Montana.

"It seemed the sensible thing to do, dear," her mother said blandly as she calmly folded the laundry Consuela had done earlier in the day. "You don't want him roaming all over the countryside talking about this situation with everyone he happens to meet, do you?"

"So this is some sort of bizarre protective custody to keep him from damaging my reputation?"

"Exactly."

"I have news for you. My reputation is bound to suffer the minute anyone gets a good look at me." She regarded her mother warily. "Or do you intend to lock me up here, too, until I do the right thing?"

"Of course not. You're perfectly free to come and go as you like, but I would say a little discretion is called for. You need to think long and hard about how you want to handle all of this. If you're determined not to marry Clint, then you'll have to decide what you're going to tell people, starting with the family."

Angela sighed. "I am not ready to see the family yet." She figured she might not be ready until her baby hit puberty.

"Well, you'd better get ready in a hurry because everyone is coming here tomorrow for our annual pre-Christmas party," her mother retorted, severely cutting into Angela's preferred timetable. "Someone is going to have to explain what's going on."

"I could hide in my room," she said wistfully, but without much hope that her mother would agree to such a cowardly plan.

"And what do you propose I say about Clint?" Her mother's eyes twinkled. "Or were you planning on locking him in here with you?"

"Mother!"

"It is an interesting thought," her mother said, then added slyly, "He is a very handsome man."

"What does that have to do with anything?"

"I imagine that's how you got into this predicament to begin with."

"Mother!"

"Sweetie, he's gorgeous. You're carrying his child. It doesn't take a genius to figure out you were sleeping together."

"I do not want to discuss this with you," she said, flushing with embarrassment.

"OK," her mother said cheerfully. "But I saw something in your eyes when you looked at him that reminded me of another woman."

"Who?" she asked, curious despite the instinct that

told her to drop the subject of her very primal and unmistakable reaction to Clint Brady.

"Me. It was exactly the way I used to look when I caught a glimpse of Luke. I could no more help it than I could control the setting of the sun. It was plain as day to anybody who saw me. Jordan and Cody saw it. Luke saw it. Even your natural father was aware of it. I was the only one so deep in denial that I didn't recognize what was happening."

"My father knew about you and Luke?" Angela had always wondered about that, but it wasn't something her mother had ever discussed.

"Erik knew how we felt. He also knew we'd never acted on it and that we wouldn't. After he'd had his accident, when he knew he wasn't going to survive, he gave me his blessing. He was an incredible, generous man." She brushed away the tears dampening her cheeks, then smiled. "He would have loved you so much. And he would have been very proud of the gesture you made by studying education the way he always wanted to."

Neither of them mentioned her failure to follow through and actually go into teaching. "It seems so strange to me to think that Luke isn't my natural father," Angela said instead. "I've always known it, of course, but on some intellectual level. It never really registered in my heart."

"Because he's been there literally from the beginning. He adores you."

"Were he and my father very much alike?"

"Not at all. Your father was the quietest and gentlest of the brothers. He was never suited for ranching, but Harlan bullied him into trying. I'm not sure he's ever entirely forgiven himself for that. If he'd allowed your father to follow his own dream, Erik would never have been on that tractor the day he died."

She patted Angela's hand. "Enough sad memories for now. You have difficult decisions to make. I have only one word of advice for you."

"Only one?"

"OK, three. Follow your heart."

Angela knew the advice was well meant. She knew it was sound. The only trouble was that the last time she had followed her heart, she had gone and fallen in love with a man who didn't believe in happily ever after.

She knew, too, that even though Clint was trying to bulldoze her into marrying him now, he no more believed in love than he had on the night she'd walked out of his house. It reminded her of some sort of deathbed conversion to religion. Say whatever it took.

She didn't trust the turnaround. She knew better. If anything, Clint's view of love and marriage was probably more jaded now than ever before. He knew that their whole relationship had been built on one huge, gigantic lie. She knew something else, as well, and it terrified her. Clint Brady wasn't the kind of man who'd forgive that kind of betrayal easily. If he was proposing, there was a reason for it, and it for darn sure wasn't love.

5

In retrospect, her birthday dinner had been an extremely civilized affair, Angela concluded as she helped Consuela carry the last of the dishes into the kitchen. Clint had even sounded sincere when he'd joined in wishing her a happy birthday.

She smiled grimly. It might have taken him aback if he'd known what she'd wished before she'd tried to blow out the candles on the cake Consuela had baked. Not that it mattered a hoot now. One candle had remained stubbornly lit, so apparently even the gods were in on the conspiracy to keep Clint around.

At any rate, her father and Clint had gotten along better than anyone could have anticipated. They'd spent most of the meal comparing notes on ranching. No blows had been struck. No harsh words had been exchanged.

Every time Angela had been tempted to interrupt or to snap out a sarcastic retort, a warning look from her mother had silenced her. In the end, she'd left the table so frustrated, she'd been ready to spit.

"Your young man—" Consuela began as they entered the kitchen.

"He is not my young man," Angela retorted automatically, hoping to end that particular notion right now.

The housekeeper ignored her. Persistence was as ingrained in Consuela's personality as her smile. She'd had years of dealing with Luke and the other Adams brothers to practice.

"He will make a very good father," she said. Her defiant expression dared Angela to argue with her about that.

"You don't even know him. How can you be certain of a thing like that?"

"Because he treats you well."

"Excuse me? He all but threw me out of his house when I told him I was pregnant."

"No, *niña*," Consuela corrected gently. "I think you ran because you got insulted that he did not react as you wished. That is your way. You run from things rather than facing them, just as you ran from your home years ago."

The hard-truth assessment was a little too accurate, and Consuela did have the proof of Angela's rebellious departure from Texas on her side.

"Whatever," Angela said dismissively. "The point is, a few months ago he didn't even want this baby." Even as she said the words, she rubbed her belly soothingly as if to apologize to the baby for its father's reaction.

"There are many things men do not know they want until we show them," Consuela said. "Lucas could not admit he wanted your mother and you until he almost lost you both. Perhaps it was the same with your Clint."

"*My* Clint is just the kind of man who wants what he can't have. I guarantee you that if I said yes to this crazy wedding nonsense, he would take off before the ceremony."

"Care to test that theory, angel?" a taunting voice inquired from the doorway.

Angela whirled around to find herself face-to-face with the man in question. "I really wish you would stop sneaking up on me."

He grinned. "I came in to see if you and Consuela needed any help cleaning up. You shouldn't be doing dishes on your birthday."

"I thought you and my father were off somewhere discussing breeding or something."

"Breeding is a touchy subject around here these days," he said dryly. "We've been talking about water rights. It's a much safer topic."

"Very funny. I'm so delighted that you two are getting along so famously."

He regarded her with obvious amusement. "You don't sound delighted. You sound miffed. Why is that, I wonder?"

"I don't give two hoots if you and my father become bosom buddies," she said vehemently.

"You sure about that, angel? Weren't you sort of hoping that he'd blow my head off?"

"The prospect did hold a certain appeal, yes," she admitted.

"Niña!" Consuela protested, sketching a cross over her chest. "You should not say such a thing. A lady is always polite to her guests."

"He is not my guest. He's mother's. I didn't want him here, remember?"

Clint grinned at the obviously distraught house-keeper. "I guess the gloves are off."

"Oh, go suck an egg," Angela snapped.

Consuela regarded her with stern disapproval. "That is not the way you were brought up to behave, *niña.*"

She blushed at the rebuke, but she was too angry to let the matter drop. She stared at Consuela in disgust. "For goodness' sakes, isn't anybody around here going to take my side? Clint's been here less than twenty-four hours and everyone is treating him as if he were the prodigal son back from the range wars or something."

"Perhaps we just see what is not so plain to you," Consuela said. "Now go along. I will finish up in here. You two need to talk." She faced Angela. "And to listen," she added pointedly.

Angela sighed.

"Well?" Clint said, when she made no move to do as she'd been told. "Do you feel like going for a walk?"

"Not really," she said stubbornly.

He chuckled, then said, "It's snowing."

Immediately, just as he'd intended, an image of another night filled her head. They had left the bar where they had met and walked aimlessly through the small Montana town of Rocky Ridge. They had said little as they strolled along, thrilling to new sensations and content merely to have hands clasped. They had walked for an hour or more, both of them afraid to break the spell of unexpected intimacy that had captivated them.

Clearly uncertain of where things would go from there, Clint had walked her back to her car. Standing there, his hands on her waist, he had bent his head oh, so slowly and kissed her. It had been the sweetest, most innocent of kisses, but it had been the start of something incendiary.

As he pulled away, his eyes locked with hers, and she had felt the delicate touch of something cold and damp against her cheek. A snowflake. It had melted against her heated flesh practically before she realized what it was. It took another and another before it had registered.

"It's snowing," she had whispered, delighted, her face turned up toward the sky.

"Nothing's more beautiful than sitting in front of a fire and watching the snow fall outside," Clint had said. "Would you like to share that with me?"

The answer had been easy and as inevitable as that kiss. By dawn, in front of a blazing fire, they had become lovers. And outside, the ground had been covered with the first snow of the season, a fairy-tale dusting of white that had turned the world into a wonderland.

There had been more snow that winter, blizzards, in fact, but none had been as memorable as the one that had fallen on that first night she had spent in Clint's arms.

She gazed into his eyes now and saw that he was daring her to recapture that magic.

"I'll get my coat," she said quietly and started from the kitchen. She turned back, still defiant, but a little sad. "It won't be the same, you know."

His lips curved at her tone. "Maybe not," he agreed. "Maybe it will be better."

"Are you warm enough?" Clint asked. The minute they'd gotten outside, he'd started wondering if he'd made yet another foolish mistake dragging Angela out on such a bitter cold night. When he'd noticed the snow falling, it had taken him back to another time, another place, when things between them had been far less complicated. That night had been about discovery and beginnings. Perhaps tonight would be about a new beginning for the two of them, one built on a more solid foundation.

"I'm fine," she insisted yet again, her face turned up to the sky.

Snowflakes landed on her cheeks and melted in rapid succession. They caught in her eyelashes. She looked as ecstatic and as shatteringly vulnerable as if they had just made love. Clint wanted to kiss her so badly his body ached. He forced himself to hold back. Kissing had been the start of their problems. It wouldn't solve them. As the feisty Consuela had insisted, they needed to talk more than anything else at the moment. Unfortunately he had no idea where to begin. The emotions ripping through him were complex and conflicting.

He could start with his outrage over her running off. Or he could yell about the risks she'd taken traveling alone, especially these last couple of weeks with the baby almost due. Or he could demand an explanation for the monumental lie that stood between them. That last angered him more every time he thought about it.

Hattie Jones, indeed! Had she merely plucked the name out of the air on the spur of the moment? He imagined that more than one woman meeting a man for the first time in a bar might fib about her identity until she knew precisely with whom she was dealing. But wouldn't an honest woman come clean when the flirtation turned into a relationship? Why in hell had Angela perpetuated the lie until the day she'd left him? He had the feeling that any answer she had for that would only infuriate him more, would perhaps deepen his disdain beyond repair.

"Go on," she said, breaking the silence.

He regarded her blankly. "What?"

"Yell at me. Tell me what an idiot I was to run away. Tell me what a jerk I was for pretending to be Hattie Jones for all those months."

"I'm the one who feels like a jerk," he grumbled, hitting on what galled him most, his own stupidity. "Why didn't I see that you were lying?"

"What man would suspect that a woman he'd been sleeping with for the better part of a year wasn't who she'd claimed to be?" she retorted. "I wanted you to think of me as Hattie Jones. I wanted to be Hattie Jones, at least for a while."

"I just have one question, why? Why did you lie? Not that first night, but later. Why did you keep lying?"

For a minute he thought he was going to get a flip response, some quick and easy explanation that would diminish the magnitude of what she'd done. Instead, her expression turned thoughtful and the silence dragged on. He let it.

"I suppose I just wanted a chance to be somebody else," she said eventually.

He stared at her in amazement. "Why? What on earth was wrong with being Angela Adams?"

She closed her eyes and sighed. "I know it doesn't make any sense to you. Just look around. I grew up on an incredible ranch. My parents are the best. There was no possible way on earth for me to be dissatisfied, right?"

"But you obviously were," he said, trying to make sense of it. He would have given anything to have grown up in a place like this with a family like hers.

Instead, he'd had to scramble for every penny he'd earned. His dream of owning his own spread had seemed impossible once. He had made it happen. He didn't resent the difficulties he'd faced or the comparative ease of her past. It was just the way life was. A man could let it make him bitter or make him strong. He'd opted long ago for strong.

He saw that she was still struggling to put her thoughts into words and conceded that even though none of what she was saying made any sense to him, she was genuinely troubled. There was no mistaking that.

"Not dissatisfied," she said finally. "I felt smothered. There's a whole long story about how I was born, right here in Luke's bedroom, as a matter of fact. Luke isn't my natural father. His brother was."

Clint tried to hide his shock, but failed. The relationships here at least had seemed so straightforward, but obviously they were anything but. She shrugged.

"It's complicated," she said in what was an apparent understatement. "Anyway, everyone credits my birth with getting Luke and my mother together. I was supposed to be some sort of Christmas blessing."

She held out her hand and caught a snowflake, watching it melt before she spoke again. "It's weird growing up as part of some sort of family legend. I always felt as if so much was expected of me. The truth was, no matter how hard I tried, I would always be mortal, just another human being with lots and lots of flaws, when I was supposed to be an angel. Maybe if I'd had sisters named Faith, Hope and Charity, the pressure wouldn't have seemed so intense."

Clint chuckled, even though he could see that she

was half-serious. He'd had six brothers and two sisters. The pressures she'd felt as an only child were an enigma to him.

"Don't laugh," she said. "Just being born an Adams comes with all sorts of baggage. Grandpa Harlan figures because we carry the name, we're all destined for something important. He also figures he gets to decide what that will be. Just ask Luke. He was the first one to rebel. Then Jordan. Even Cody bolted for a while. Only my dad tried to please him by going along with Grandpa Harlan's divine plan. It killed him."

Clint was stunned by her words. "Killed him? How?"

"Granddad wanted him to be a rancher, so he tried, when what he really wanted to do was teach. He was always distracted. His head was always in some book. You know yourself, a rancher can't afford to be distracted. Too many things can happen in the blink of an eye. Who knows what he was thinking about, but the tractor he was riding here on Luke's ranch ran into a ditch and overturned. He died a few hours later."

She sighed sadly. "You would have thought Grandpa Harlan would learn from his mistake, but he's still as meddlesome and controlling as he ever was. So is Luke. They are the most wonderful, best-intentioned men in the universe, but I couldn't breathe under the weight of all those expectations."

"So you ran off and became Hattie Jones," Clint surmised. He'd heard of people moving, settling in someplace new to reinvent themselves, but a whole new name and identity? Wasn't that carrying it a little too far?

"Not at first. Actually, other than choosing Stanford instead of the University of Texas, my first act of rebellion was relatively mild. I studied English lit and education, instead of agriculture."

She smiled briefly. It seemed a little wistful to him.

"I meant to be the teacher my father had wanted to be," she added. "I messed up at that, too. I graduated from college by the skin of my teeth, applied for my first teaching job and got cold feet. I knew in my gut I had no business at all being in a classroom trying to shape little minds, not when my own was such a mess."

"Is that when you came to Montana?"

She nodded. "Rocky Ridge was the first town I'd driven through that appealed to me. When you see Los Pinos, I think you'll understand why. Ironically, the two places are very much alike. Anyway, I walked into that bar on pure impulse to apply for the waitressing job posted in the window and there you were. It wasn't just that you were the sexiest thing I'd ever laid eyes on. You looked dangerous, harder and tougher than the men I'd met at school certainly."

She reached up and touched his hair. "All that shaggy, sun-streaked hair and those devilish blue eyes. You were flirting outrageously with me, and I felt as if you were my first and best chance to be a whole new person, a woman who was exciting and sensual and wicked. With you I could be anybody I wanted to be."

Clint wasn't sure why, but the explanation chilled him. He didn't want to be anyone's act of rebellion. People who stuck together ought to bring out the best in one another, not the worst.

"I'm glad I could oblige," he said with a surprising edge of bitterness. "You played the game well. Hattie was a real sexy invention. We had some good times."

She frowned ever so slightly at his words. "You say that as if the good times were all in the past."

"I think maybe they were," he said slowly. He gazed into her eyes, searching for the woman who had once intrigued him so. A man would have to be a fool to try to perpetuate something that had only been make-believe. Sometimes it was smarter just to concede that the game was over and call it a draw.

"What are you saying?" she demanded.

It appeared to him that there was a touch of panic in her voice. A day ago that might have delighted him. Now it hardly seemed to matter.

He wanted to tell her that coming here was a mistake, that trying to convince her to marry him was a mistake, but that would ruin his long-range plan for getting custody of his child. "Just that you can't recapture the past," he said instead. "I thought you could, but I was wrong."

Her eyes darkened with hurt, but he noticed she didn't try to argue with him.

"Then you'll be leaving, after all?"

He thought he detected a blending of hope and despair in her voice, but he was too upset to figure out what was going on in that mixed-up mind of hers. He shook his head. "Not a chance, sweetheart. I meant what I said about that wedding. That baby of ours is going to have my name."

"Why? You can't possibly care about the child of a woman you despise."

Despise was too strong a word, but he didn't correct her. "I care about *my* child, though. Make no mistake about it, angel, this baby is mine."

Now there was no mistaking the genuine panic in her expression. "Meaning?"

"I will fight you for him," he declared, then amended, "or her."

He saw her shudder as the words registered and knew he had shown his hand too soon. He regretted that, but it wouldn't change anything. Maybe the fight would be fairer if they both knew where they stood. Fairness was a lot more than she deserved.

"You can't," she protested.

"Watch me," he said and walked away.

"You can't win," she shouted after him. "Not here. The Adams name means something here in Texas."

"And Jones?" he taunted. "Does the name Hattie Jones mean anything?"

That silenced her. He was halfway back up the lane toward the house when he heard the rustle of her coat against denim, the crunch of ice beneath her boots as she followed him. He wasn't sure why, but he waited for her at the door.

That was a mistake, he realized at once, when he saw the sheen of tears on her cheeks. Then he told himself that the dampness was merely snowflakes melting. A woman as coldly calculating as Hattie Jones—or Angela Adams—couldn't possibly be crying.

Angela was holding back sobs by the time she closed the door to her room behind her. She would not let Clint Brady see that he had hurt her. She would not let him see that she was terrified of his threat to take the baby. But behind that closed door, she let her fear and anguish flow unchecked. Still in her coat, damp now with snow, she huddled on her bed, clutching a pillow. She had botched things again. She had tried to be open and honest with Clint—albeit belatedly—and he had taken her words and twisted them into something ugly.

He would use them against her, if he had to. She had seen that much in his hard expression. She had watched his pride kick in and she had shuddered. Months ago she had seen that his pride was a more than even match for any Adams.

She knew exactly what would happen. He would go into court and portray her as a woman unfit to be a mother, a woman who had committed the ultimate betrayal by pretending to be someone else entirely. He would describe her behavior in Montana as something wanton and sinful and she would be helpless to deny it, because that was exactly what she had meant it to be. Hattie Jones had been outrageous and deceptive, because those were traits that Angela Adams had been forbidden in her nice, protected world.

What had she been thinking? That wasn't who she was, not really. Just look how quickly she had done the traditional thing and fallen in love with the man. Just look at the perfectly normal expectation she'd had back then that they would get married and raise the baby they'd conceived in love together.

In the end she'd even messed up being outrageous. Now everyone was going to know about her foolish mistake. Her parents. Grandpa Harlan. The whole damned world, if Clint had his way. She couldn't let that happen. She had to find some way to compromise with him, some way to win him back. She had to smooth things over until tempers cooled.

Only a few hours ago he'd been determined to marry her. He'd wanted the baby to have his name. Obviously he wanted to do things the traditional way, just as she had from the very moment she'd discovered she was pregnant with his child. He wanted to behave honorably, because down deep that was the kind of man Clint Brady was. She had recognized that in him from the beginning. Maybe it was why she had felt so free to behave as she had, because she had known she could trust him not to harm her in any way.

He'd never taken back his proposal, not even when his temper had flared. Maybe his motives weren't as innocent and pure as he had wanted everyone else to believe, but he hadn't retracted the words. She could use that to her advantage.

She got slowly out of bed and changed into her nightgown. She washed away the last traces of her tears. There would be no more, she resolved.

She smiled at herself in the mirror. She had learned a few tricks as Hattie Jones. It was time she made them pay off for her. Once, Clint hadn't been able to resist her. Whatever her name, she was still that same woman.

Before anyone knew that his interest in marriage was totally self-serving, she was going to make absolutely certain that they were walking down the aisle. She was going to protect her role in her baby's life…no matter what Clint had in mind for the future.

6

"So, where's my precious angel!"

Angela heard her grandfather's booming voice all the way upstairs and sighed.

"Not yet, please God," she whispered. She wasn't ready to see him yet, wasn't prepared to see even a hint of judgment in his eyes. She wasn't ready to explain the baby she was expecting. She certainly wasn't prepared to explain Clint, not with things so terribly unsettled between them.

Nor could she rely on her parents to smooth the way. It wouldn't be fair to expect them to give answers to so many difficult questions, when she didn't know the answers herself.

"Not yet," she pleaded again.

Apparently God had other ideas. She heard her grandfather's two-at-a-time tread on the steps, then the sharp, impatient rap of his knuckles against her door.

"You in there, darlin'?"

Resigned to the inevitable, she drew in a deep breath,

plastered a bright smile on her face and threw open the door.

"Grandpa," she said and felt herself scooped into an awkward, but exuberant bear hug.

After a minute he set her back on her feet and stepped back. "Let me get a good look at you." His gaze traveled over her mound of a belly, then came to rest on her face. His eyes were troubled, but his beaming smile never faltered.

"You look pretty as a picture," he declared. "Impending motherhood obviously agrees with you."

"You should have seen me the first month," she said, thinking of the nausea that had been a constant companion. There had been mornings she hadn't wanted to budge from bed, much less see herself in a mirror.

"I wish I had," he said at once, "instead of you being away in who-knows-where all by yourself."

Sensing the likelihood that a lecture was about to begin, she hurriedly said, "My turn now."

She quickly scanned him from head to toe. Other than a few more gray hairs and a slight stoop to his shoulders he looked as fit as ever. He was one of those men who wore his age well and would until his nineties, God willing. He was almost in his eighties now and barely looked sixty.

"You haven't changed a bit," she told him. "You're every bit as handsome as you were the day I left."

He winked at her. "Love," he confided. "I highly recommend it at any age."

Angela grinned at the allusion to the woman who'd turned his whole outlook on life upside down. "How is Janet?" she asked.

"Perfect. Wonderful," he enthused, eyes sparkling at the thought of her. "She's downstairs with your mama. She's as anxious to see you as I was, but she shows more restraint. She still says I haven't got a lick of patience or any understanding whatsoever of privacy."

Angela grinned at him. "I guess there are some traits not even love can change. Not in an Adams man, anyway."

His expression sobered. "So when are you going to make me a great-granddaddy?"

"The way I feel right now, it can't be soon enough. Another week or two is what the doctor told me before I left Seattle to come home."

He shook his head. "I can't believe it. Me with a child in her teens and a great-grandbaby on the way. Talk about a couple of curve balls. Life's thrown me some doozies. Not that I'm complaining. I wouldn't have it any other way."

She grinned at his expression of delighted disbelief. "How are my cousins?" she asked, referring not only to the teenager her grandfather and Janet had had together, but to Janet's daughter Jenny. It was Jenny's theft of Grandpa Harlan's truck that had brought them together in the first place. As a child, Angela had always thought Jenny's rebellious ways fascinating. She'd envied the daring teenager. In the end, it appeared she'd outdone her.

"Jenny's going to be teaching school soon," he said proudly, apparently oblivious to the irony. If his reaction to Erik's desires had been half so approving, perhaps Angela's natural father still would have been alive.

"As for Lizzy," he went on, "she is the most beautiful child ever born and the smartest."

"Don't you let Luke, Cody and Jordan hear you say that," Angela chided. "You'll hurt their feelings. They all think they were gorgeous and sexy from day one."

"Those three have hides like an elephant," he said dismissively. "My talk's not going to faze them. Besides, they were never as cute as Lizzy. She's her daddy's girl. Top of her class every year."

Amused by his bragging, she teased, "Don't you suppose just maybe she inherited some of her intelligence from her mother? Janet is an attorney, after all, and a very good one." In fact, Janet Runningbear Adams had built a national reputation for her work on behalf of Native American causes.

He grinned. "Much as it galls me, I suppose I can share some of the credit with her." He looped an arm around Angela's shoulders. "Come on down and see them. Jenny's not here yet, but the others are waiting. Lizzy was ecstatic when we told her about the baby. She's tired of being the youngest. Cody and Jordan should be turning up soon with their broods. You won't believe how grown-up all my grandbabies are."

The thought of facing them all made her palms sweat. Overwhelming uncles, rock-steady aunts and rambunctious cousins. It promised to be too much.

"You go on ahead," she suggested. "I'm not quite ready."

Ignoring her hesitance, he declared, "You look fine to me. Another touch of powder on your nose isn't going to make you one bit prettier."

"It's not that. I…" She gazed into his eyes, pleading with him to understand.

His expression softened at once. "You're scared, aren't you?" he said bluntly. "Or ashamed. Which is it?"

When she said nothing, he captured her face between his work-roughened hands and met her gaze evenly. "Darling girl, there's no need to be. Family's all that's important to us. Everyone here has made more than their share of mistakes. Everyone here loves you, no matter what. Don't you know that by now? All that matters to us is that you're home again."

She nodded, tears welling up. Maybe it was his words, maybe her wacky hormones, but she felt like bawling. "I'll be there in a few minutes, I promise. I'm not going to duck out the back door."

His eyes twinkled. "What about that tree by your bedroom window? You thinking of climbing down that the way you did when you were a girl so you could sneak off to see your friends?"

She laughed at the memory, as well as the impossibility of resorting to such an escape now. She patted her belly. "Like this? I don't think so. I'll be down to face the music, and I'll use the stairs like a proper, grown-up lady."

"You'd feel braver with me by your side," he said lightly. "Nobody's going to mess with my darlin' girl with me around."

She grinned at that. "You can't protect me from everything, Grandpa."

"I can sure as hell try," he said fiercely. "I love you, angel. Don't make any mistake about that."

She stood on tiptoe and kissed his weathered cheek.

"I love you, too. And I didn't realize until now just how much I'd missed you."

He cast one last worried look in her direction, then retreated downstairs. Angela stared after him for what seemed an eternity, trying to work up the courage to join everyone.

"Facing your family's harder than you expected, isn't it?" Clint said, exiting the guest room across the hall.

"Is it necessary for you to spy on me?" she snapped, then recalled that she was supposed to be trying to win the man back, not offend him. "Sorry. It's just that seeing Grandpa Harlan shook me more than I'd expected it to. He acts as if I haven't done anything wrong, when I know perfectly well he must be furious."

"More likely with me than with you," Clint suggested. "Want to go downstairs with me and protect me?"

She glanced up at him with astonishment and saw the sympathy and understanding in his eyes. She knew perfectly well he wasn't one bit terrified of her grandfather or any man. Despite their battle the night before, he was offering her his support. She thought she had never loved him more than she did at this moment. It really was too bad that everything between them had gotten so messed up. At heart he was a decent, sensitive man. Maybe if she'd remembered that and given him time to adjust to the idea of being a daddy, things would never have gotten so out of hand.

For just a moment she allowed herself to imagine the way it could have been. Arriving home as Clint's wife, their first baby on the way, would have turned the holidays into something unforgettable.

Instead, there was bound to be an endless amount of tension and strain as everyone tiptoed around the subject of their relationship. She didn't envy Clint his role as an outsider, not with everyone bound to feel especially protective of her. He had no idea what he had let himself in for by accepting her mother's invitation to stay on through the holidays.

"I wonder if he knows yet that you're here," she murmured thoughtfully.

"I doubt it. I haven't heard any explosions since he arrived, have you?"

"My father might have warned him."

"Oh, somehow I doubt that," he said with a wry expression. "Your father would probably be delighted if your grandfather took one look at me and ripped me to shreds. Luke can't do it himself because we declared a truce yesterday."

She studied him curiously. "I wondered about that. How did you win him over?"

"I didn't say I'd won him over, just that we'd agreed not to brawl. I'm on probation. He's waiting for me to make just one tiny mistake and then, I guarantee it will be his pleasure to chase me all the way back to Montana."

She regarded him impishly. "One tiny mistake, huh?"

He scowled at her. "Don't go getting any ideas, angel. I have no intention of treading on anyone's toes until I can claim my child."

She ignored the subtle reminder of his threat. She would deal with that when the time came. Instead, some thoroughly outrageous instinct, probably left from her days as Hattie, made her link her arm through his. Now was as good a time as any to start her scheme to win him back.

"Let's go," she said with a wink. "Let's see just how much trouble I can get you into, if I try."

There wasn't so much as a twinkle in his eyes when he met her gaze evenly. "That works both ways, sweetheart. You'd do well to remember that."

The deliberate taunt jangled her nerves, just as he'd obviously intended. It reminded her that she was playing games with a master.

At the top of the stairs, before Clint's quick retort had evened the score, her promise of troublemaking had seemed like a fine idea. She'd expected to sail into the midst of her family with restored confidence.

Instead, standing in the doorway to the living room with a circle of inquisitive faces staring at them, she realized she'd miscalculated. Walking into that room on Clint's arm hadn't been the masterstroke she'd anticipated. It had simply quadrupled the speculation and added to the pressure. Now it wouldn't be just her folks and Consuela anticipating a wedding, but this whole roomful of relatives. Why hadn't she seen that she should have locked the man in a closet until after New Year's?

Since she couldn't seem to find her tongue, it was Clint who worked his way around the group, introducing himself with an ease that she found thoroughly annoying. Why wasn't he feeling the same kind of intimidation that she felt? This was her family, after all. Right this second he seemed more at home than she did.

He slowed when he got to her grandfather. She saw the two men taking each other's measure. Everyone seemed to be holding their collective breath, waiting to see what Harlan Adams would do or say to the man who had gotten his grandchild into the fix she was in.

Her grandfather's expression was unreadable, but he was the first to hold out his hand. "Welcome, son. It's good to have you with us for the holidays."

The palpable tension in the room eased.

"Thank you, sir," Clint said with just the right amount of deference. "I've heard quite a lot about you. It's a pleasure to meet you at last."

Who's lying now? Angela thought bitterly. Up until the day before yesterday, Clint Brady hadn't even known this family existed, yet he was treating them all as if they were people he genuinely cared about getting to know.

Worse, they were falling for it, toppling like dominoes under the warmth of his natural charm.

She sighed and tried to be grateful for the fact that his presence had shifted some of the attention away from her for the moment. She was able to slip from the room and head for the kitchen to get her bearings before yet another carload of exuberant Adamses showed up.

She was surprised to find the kitchen deserted. There was no sign of Consuela, even though preparations for that night's feast were well underway. Expecting the housekeeper to return at any second, she filled a glass with milk and sank down into a chair at the table where she had spent many an afternoon as a girl talking out her problems, sometimes with Consuela, just as often with her mother. This room had heard a lot of secrets over the years.

When the door swung open, she glanced up and

saw that it was her step-grandmother who'd followed her. Angela's smile was genuine as she surveyed the tall, slim woman with the shoulder-length black hair and sparkling brown eyes. She had always admired the strong, feisty lawyer who'd stolen her grandfather's heart. Janet Runningbear Adams exuded the kind of quiet serenity Angela wished she could attain. It had taken a woman with amazing self-confidence to stand up to Harlan Adams strong will and become his partner in life, as well as his mate.

Janet rested a hand on her shoulder, when Angela would have risen to hug her. "Stay where you are. I know how difficult it is to get up and down at this stage of pregnancy. Are you feeling OK?"

"As well as any blimp could be expected to feel," Angela told her. "Did you come in here looking for Consuela? Or a snack, maybe?"

"Actually I came to see you."

"Oh?"

"It was your grandfather's idea that we have a talk. He got it into his head last night after he spoke to your father and heard that Clint was here. Naturally he practically shoved me out of the living room just now, instead of letting me wait a bit."

Angela regarded her warily. "What did he want you to talk to me about?"

"He thought you might need some legal protection."

"Legal protection? From Clint? You mean like a restraining order or something?"

Her incredulity made Janet smile. "Actually, I think he was thinking more along the lines of a prenuptial agreement."

"Oh." Given the lack of real wedding plans and her own financial circumstances, the idea struck her as just as ludicrous. Besides, she'd always thought that starting a marriage by figuring out the financial ins and outs of ending it showed a certain lack of faith in the relationship.

"Why on earth would he think I needed something like that?"

"I'm not recommending it," Janet said hastily, clearly reacting to the defensive note in Angela's voice. "Your grandfather and I had quite a few words over that very subject when we got married. We ripped up a lot of paper, but a prenuptial agreement does serve a purpose. It can protect what's yours or his."

"You may not have noticed, but I don't have a lot," Angela said dryly. "My savings account is virtually empty. So's my checkbook. As for Clint, his ranch is hardly the kind of place that needs protecting from my greedy little grasp."

"But you're an Adams," Janet reminded her as if that alone explained the need for such an agreement.

"He's hardly likely to try to steal my name."

Janet grinned. "No, but you stand to inherit this ranch. You have a sizable trust fund from your grandfather that will be yours in another couple of years."

Neither of those things had ever crossed her mind, maybe because she'd figured her parents and grandfather would live forever. "Clint not only doesn't know about that, he wouldn't care if he did," she said with absolute certainty.

"Are you so sure? I was under the impression that there was a time when he wasn't the least bit interested in marrying you or claiming his baby. Now he turns up here and does a one-eighty. Maybe that's honestly motivated," Janet said reasonably. "Maybe not, but you ought to be sure before you risk everything that will one day be yours."

Angela shuddered. "I don't know. That seems so cold and calculating. It's not like Clint at all. Besides, none of this ever mattered to me, anyway."

"Possibly not, but you should think about this baby you're carrying. You should protect what's yours for your child's future. Will you at least consider what I've said?"

Angela nodded reluctantly. Janet reached across the table and squeezed her hand. "If there's anything else you need to talk about, I'm available, not as a lawyer, but as a friend. Remember that. Sometimes it takes an objective outsider to help sort things out."

"You're hardly an outsider," she reminded her.

"I wasn't born an Adams," Janet said wryly. "In the end it makes a difference. An Adams is single-minded when it comes to family. On occasion I have to remind Harlan that there are two sides to most stories."

Angela grinned. "I imagine you do. Thank you. Maybe one of these days when I figure out what all the questions are, I'll see if you have any answers."

"Bottom line? There's really only one question and I think you already know what that is."

Angela sighed. "Do we love each other, I suppose."

"That's the one."

"Any insights?" Angela asked wistfully.

"I haven't seen the two of you in the same room long enough to tell yet." She winked. "Give me until tomorrow. I'll share my matchmaking insights with you, though to hear Jenny tell it, I'm really lousy at it."

That said, she left Angela alone again with her thoughts. All of the things she had to consider were beginning to give her a headache. If she'd thought she could manage it without getting caught, she would have slipped back up to her room and hidden out there until the holidays were over.

The distrust between her and Clint had just escalated to another level, fueled by Janet's suggestions that he had somehow discovered her potential net worth and decided that maybe being married wouldn't be so terrible after all.

At this rate, would they ever be able to rediscover the feelings that had drawn them together so many months ago? Or were they destined always to be at cross-purposes, always trying to second-guess motives?

Angela sighed heavily. She'd been exposed to a lot of very strong marriages over her lifetime. Jordan and Kelly, Cody and Melissa, her own parents, Grandpa Harlan and Janet. All of them had shown her the power of love. She believed in it with all her heart. She also knew that trust was at the core of each and every one of them.

Over the last few days the seeds of distrust had been sown between her and Clint, intentionally or inadvertently. It didn't really matter which. The point was, could any couple overcome that kind of obstacle? The sad answer, it seemed to her, was no.

Clint knew he was on display. Hell, he was on trial. So far he thought he'd managed to hold his own. Harlan Adams was an even tougher nut to crack than his son, but Clint thought he seemed at least willing to wait and see if Clint could prove himself worthy of an Adams.

The irony of it all wasn't lost on him. If he'd known

everything he knew now about her family on the day he'd met Angela, even he would have said he was out of his league. But he hadn't fallen for Angela Adams. He'd been caught up in a blazing romance with Hattie Jones, whose background had been kept a mystery and whose heart was as generous as any woman's on earth.

That was what made him crazy now. He kept remembering all of Hattie's best traits and questioning which of them existed in Angela. Had any man ever been presented with such a complex puzzle to sort out? If so, he'd like to meet him and discover how he'd done it without losing his sanity in the process.

When another carload of family members turned up—Cody and Melissa and their kids, if he'd gotten the names straight—he took the opportunity to slip away from the ensuing chaos and hunt for Angela. She'd vanished again, though he was pretty sure this time that she'd gone no farther than the kitchen. He'd noticed that she seemed to retreat there an awful lot. It must have always been some sort of haven for her. That suited him just fine, since the warm room and the sympathetic housekeeper drew him, as well.

Sure enough, Angela was sitting at the table, eyes closed, a half-empty glass of milk on the table, her feet propped up on another chair. He noticed that her ankles were swollen. Since she was either asleep or simply oblivious to his arrival, he slid into the chair closest to her feet and lifted them into his lap. He massaged them gently, regretting all the exhausting days she must have spent when he hadn't been around to perform this simple act of kindness for her.

Her sigh of pure pleasure sounded genuine. Slowly she opened her eyes and stared at him in surprise. "You?"

"Who'd you think it was?" he inquired, chuckling at her disconcerted expression.

"I don't know. Consuela maybe."

"I'm disappointed, angel. I thought for sure you'd recognize my touch."

"It's been a long time." Her gaze caught his and lingered. "A very long time."

"Some things a man never forgets," he said. "I guess it's different for a woman."

"Not really," she admitted softly.

The response and the hint of intimacy hovered in the air between them, too fragile to test. Clint was wise enough for once to keep silent. He contented himself with the sighs his ongoing massage earned him.

"I suppose I can't put it off any longer," she said eventually.

"What?"

"Joining the others."

"There are more here now," he advised her. "Your uncle Cody, I believe. I skipped out before meeting him and came to look for you."

She grinned. "Two Adams men didn't alarm you, but three began to seem like impressive odds, I guess."

"Something like that." He gave her a lazy smile. "Or maybe I just missed you."

"I wish I could believe that," she said almost wistfully.

"Then do. It's true."

She regarded him with blatant skepticism. "True or convenient," she muttered.

His fingers stilled against her soft skin. "Convenient?" he asked, his tone lethal.

There was a flash of pure panic in her eyes, but it quickly gave way to defiance. "Yes, convenient," she said firmly. "You're up to something, Clint Brady. There's not a doubt in my mind about that."

"Sweetheart, unlike you, I laid all my cards out on the table. I intend to marry you and give my child my name."

"And then?" she asked distrustfully.

"Well, I suppose we'll just have to take things as they come after that."

She scowled. "Now that's the part that has me worried."

"It shouldn't." He slid his hand up her leg, beneath her slacks. The skin was soft as silk and warmed to his caress. "We were always very, very good at improvising."

An obviously reluctant smile tugged at her lips. "Yes," she conceded eventually. "Yes, we were."

7

Clint had grown up in what he considered to be a large family, plenty of brothers and sisters to make holidays chaotic, if stressful, even a handful of cousins on his mother's side to fill up the house. He'd always thought that was one reason he'd moved to such a small town in Montana and chosen an isolated ranch. He'd longed for some peace and quiet.

He now knew with absolute certainty that the one thing he would never get with Angela in his life was peace and quiet, not on holidays spent in Texas, anyway.

By three in the afternoon he'd lost count of the number of people who'd arrived for the pre-Christmas party. Harlan Adams presided over the celebration with as much pride as any clan patriarch in a state filled with larger-than-life men. He commanded the respect not only of his sons, but his daughters-in-law and of all the grandchildren. They deferred to him in most matters, teased him unmercifully about others and always, always showed their love with every word and action.

Clint knew it took an incredible man to earn so

much adoration. He'd never had a male role model of
his own. He'd thought when he first met Luke Adams
that Luke might be the man to emulate. Now he realized that Luke was simply his father's son: a strong,
honest man shaped by a strong, honest father. Cody
and Jordan were, as well. Parenting such fine men was
a legacy Harlan Adams could be proud of.

Watching their interaction made Clint feel the kind
of gut-deep envy that he'd never before experienced as
child or adult. Sure, as a kid he'd wanted a dad around
for the simple stuff, a father-son dinner at school, a
game of catch in the backyard, an afternoon of fishing.
He'd regretted not having something that even his own
brothers and sisters had experienced. But he hadn't felt
this wrenching sense of having missed something powerful and meaningful in his life.

He had no idea what kind of man his father had become when he'd left them, but the fact that he'd gone
said quite a lot about his character. It was obvious to
Clint that his father hadn't come from the same sort of
stock that Harlan Adams had. Even if he'd stayed, his
influence on Clint's life probably wouldn't have been
as sharply defined as Harlan Adams's had been on his
sons.

It was rare for Clint to feel that he wasn't another
man's equal, but in this crowd he began to have his
doubts. His own code of ethics was decent, his own
brand of loyalty deep, but he wasn't at all sure it mea-
sured up to what he was witnessing at this family gathering.

Having doubts about himself always made him edgy.
As a kid he'd taken swings at anyone who'd suggested

he was less than they were. As an adult he'd learned to avoid situations that would put him at a disadvantage.

Now, feeling decidedly edgy, he retreated outside after Consuela's gargantuan feast. He figured it would be hours before anyone even noticed he'd gone. If they did notice, they'd probably be relieved since his presence had created more than one awkward, stressful moment.

Angela surely wouldn't miss him. She was finally and totally caught up in her reunion with her family, just as she should be. Whatever questions anyone had raised had been silenced, probably by stern admonitions from on high. In the absence of such probing, she had relaxed. Her smile had come more frequently, twisting his insides with the innocent beauty of it. He thought she looked happier than he'd ever made her. That made him edgy, too.

"Too overwhelming?" she asked, suddenly appearing at his side as if he'd conjured her up. Her hair was whipping around her face in the icy wind. That same wind had put patches of color in her cheeks. She was desperately tugging at her coat, trying to close the ever-widening gap over her expanding tummy, but it was a losing battle.

He smiled at the futile effort and drew a responding scowl.

"You try adding an inch a day to your waistline and see how long clothes fit," she grumbled.

"You shouldn't be out here," he said curtly. "The sun's about to go down and the temperature's dropping."

"I needed some air and a chance to let my face muscles relax."

He grinned at that. He'd felt much the same way himself. Still, he couldn't resist the urge to taunt. "Too much smiling?" he inquired. "Didn't I read somewhere that it takes fewer muscles to smile than it does to frown?"

She chuckled. "Have you been reading those beauty magazines I left behind?"

It was closer to the truth than he wanted to admit. She'd cluttered the whole darn ranch house with her romance novels and her magazines. After she'd gone, he'd felt closer to her when he'd glanced through them. Silly nonsense, for the most part, at least when it came to the magazines.

The books had been another story. Some of those writers could weave a fascinating story, and the steamy sex in a few of them had left him downright hot for days afterward. He'd regretted not peeking at them when Hattie had been around to satisfy the urges they stirred.

"You have, haven't you?" she demanded, laughing. "I don't believe it."

He feigned a scowl. "Don't let it get around, angel. You'll ruin my reputation."

She eyed him speculatively and he could see evidence of the insatiable Hattie in her expression. She had always been as eager as he to make love, as anxious as he for a stolen caress or a passionate kiss.

"Exactly what other tidbits of useful information did you pick up from your reading?" she asked.

Suddenly enjoying the game, he reached over and tucked a wayward curl behind her ear. He lingered to trace his thumb across her lower lip and felt the shock of his touch jolt through her. The flare of yearning in her eyes was unmistakable. Once upon a time he'd seen it often. That kind of longing was heady stuff for a man who'd always been odd man out with his own family. To have someone want him so desperately fueled his masculine ego and filled his heart. Only after she'd gone had he realized just how much he'd come to depend on it. Now she was openly offering him a chance to grab just a small taste of what they'd once shared.

"For starters," he said quietly, his gaze pinned on hers, "I learned that sometimes a kiss is more devastating than sex, that the brush of a finger across a woman's lips can make her toes curl." He studied her quizzically as he suited action to words. "Is it true, angel?"

She swallowed hard, but never took her eyes from his. The bold look further inflamed him as he waited to see if she'd respond honestly or lie.

"It seems to be," she said. "But I think one experiment is hardly scientific."

Smiling to himself, he traced the outline of her mouth, lingering at the dip in the top lip, then skimming the bottom lip lightly with his fingernail. She trembled.

"Two for two," he said with satisfaction. "Enough yet?"

"Not nearly enough," she insisted.

"The experimenting's getting dangerous," he warned.

"You scared?" she taunted.

"No, but maybe you should be."

"Nothing scares an Adams," she retorted.

He laughed. "That's definitely one part of your heritage you never denied. You were always game for any risk."

"So were you. Some said it was what made us a good match," she said.

"Still feeling intrepid?"

"Always."

He slowly lowered his head until his mouth hovered over hers. "Still?"

With her gaze pinned to his, she simply nodded.

The touch of their lips set off a familiar blazing heat. Clint was no longer aware of the biting cold of the wind. Inside, his body temperature shot up. Perspiration broke out on his brow.

When Angela settled into his embrace, her lips molded to his, he felt as if he could strip naked, make love to her right here and right now, and never even notice the frozen ground beneath them. She could make him hotter faster than a wood stove set on high. Always could.

"Hey, Justin, is there steam rising from Angie?"

Reality slammed into him at the comment. Angela went absolutely still in his arms. He guessed the whispered question came from young Harlan Patrick, Cody's son. He was twenty or so and had a smart mouth and a young man's fascination with sex. That much had been evident from the moment he arrived.

"Maybe we should douse them with water," Jordan's son, Justin, whispered back. "That's what Dad does to the cats when he catches them going at it."

"You do and you are going to be two very uncomfortable young men for the rest of your visit," Clint said. Angie shivered or so he thought. He glanced down and realized she was laughing and trying to keep her two cousins from catching her at it. She buried her face against his chest.

Justin and Harlan whirled to take off, but Clint released Angela with some reluctance and placed himself squarely in their path, one hand firmly on each boy's shoulder. He regarded them steadily. "Now here's the deal, guys. You keep very, very quiet about what you saw and I will keep my mouth shut about the cigarettes you were sneaking."

Despite being plenty old enough to smoke the two teens exchanged guilty looks. They knew how vehemently their grandfather objected. Harlan had gone on about it earlier.

"Are we agreed?" Clint asked.

"Oh, yeah," Justin said fervently. "Even at my age Dad would knock me from here to Dallas if he knew I was smoking."

"From here to Kansas," Harlan concurred. "We never saw a thing, Mr. Brady." He dared a glance at his cousin. "Sorry, Angie. We didn't mean to interrupt."

"Yeah," Justin said. "You guys go back to doing whatever it was you were doing when we showed up. Not that we noticed or anything."

"Later, guys," Clint said. "And ditch the cigarettes."

They took off running. Away from the house, Clint noticed with amusement.

"How'd you know they'd been smoking?" Angie asked when they were out of earshot. "I never smelled a thing."

"Guesswork," he admitted. "They looked guilty as sin when your grandfather was talking about cigarettes. My brothers and I used to sneak out and try to catch a smoke after some family gathering, so we could feel grown-up. It was my mother who caught up with us the second or third time we tried it. She was not pleased.

She threatened to shred the tobacco like a salad and make us eat it for dessert, if she ever caught us with a cigarette again. She said if we were going to put that foul stuff into our bodies, we might as well chow down on it. Said it would kill us quicker that way."

"Did she do it?"

"Never had to. We'd gotten the message."

She studied him, her expression thoughtful. "You never talked much about your family when we were together," she said.

"Neither did you," he pointed out.

"*Touché.* Maybe we should start all over again, pretend we just met."

He glanced at her protruding belly. "That's a little hard to do, don't you think?"

Suddenly she gasped and grabbed her stomach.

"What?" he demanded at once. "Are you OK? Sweet heaven, you're not going into labor, are you? It's too soon, isn't it? Have you even seen a doctor since you got here?"

"Whoa. Relax." She grinned. "Your kid was just making his presence felt. I think he's practicing for the NFL already."

"You're convinced it's a boy?"

"No, but Consuela is. She's almost never wrong." She regarded him shyly, then took his hand and placed it on her stomach. "Here, feel."

For several seconds he felt nothing at all, then suddenly he felt the *thump* of a very solid kick. The rush of feelings that came over him was mind-boggling. For the first time, the baby was a reality, not just part of some grand lie that stood between them.

"A field goal kicker, for sure," he said, feeling the unexpected sting of tears in his eyes.

He'd missed months of this. He'd been cheated of hearing his baby's heartbeat for the first time, of seeing Angela's body change to accommodate the child she was carrying. OK, so that was partly his fault, but she was the one who'd impetuously taken off. She was the one who'd kept on running.

"Damn you," he said softly.

She stared at him in shock. Her eyes filled with hurt and confusion at the harshness of his words. "What?"

"You've robbed me of so much."

Never one to take an accusation lightly, she scowled back at him. Temper flared in her eyes. "You had a choice," she reminded him stiffly. "You could have reacted like a man and accepted responsibility from the beginning."

It was the same old story, dragging them back to square one. Clint sighed. If he were entirely honest, he'd have to admit they shared the blame. There was more than enough to go around. Even so, he couldn't resist one last dig.

"Is that all you expected, for me to accept responsibility? I never questioned that this was my baby. Not once. I was always under the impression what you really wanted was for me to declare my love and marry you."

"It's the same thing," she said defiantly.

"Not quite, angel. And if you were being entirely honest, you'd admit that back then you and I were nowhere close to sorting out our feelings for each other. You didn't even trust me enough to tell me the truth about who you were."

Her lips compressed into an angry line before she snapped, "Don't talk to me about honesty, Clint Brady. You've never once owned up to what you're really doing here."

He went absolutely still at the unspoken accusation behind the words. "Meaning?"

"Just how did you find out who I was and where to find me? Was finding out that I came from a wealthy family enough to drag you down here after me?"

She had hinted at as much earlier, but Clint still couldn't believe his ears. The unfairness of her charge apparently never crossed her mind. Quick-tempered retorts came into his head, but he knew if he spoke even one of them, ugly words would start flying fast and furiously. Their tempers had always been their downfall. There was no such thing as a quiet, rational conversation between Hattie and him over even a small difference of opinion. They shouted whatever came to mind at full volume.

When the dust settled, there were always hurt feelings and fences to mend. He suspected it was the one area in life that didn't improve with practice. He suspected the cuts just went deeper and the fences grew harder and harder to mend. Maybe it was time to break the cycle and find a new way of getting along. Since he didn't have an imagination vivid enough to figure out how to do that on the spur of the moment, he decided some distance was called for.

"Go back inside, Angela," he said abruptly, backing away from her. "It's too damned cold for you to be out here."

"I will not," she said, digging in her heels literally

and regarding him with fire in her eyes. "You don't make decisions for me."

"Oh, for pity's sake, can't you do one thing because it's sensible and stop worrying about the fact that the suggestion came out of my mouth?"

With that he scooped her up in his arms and headed for the house. After a moment of stunned silence, she blistered the air with protests loud enough to wake the dead. Half the family was standing in the kitchen watching by the time he deposited her unceremoniously on her feet inside the door. Thank heaven no one laughed or she probably would have grabbed the carving knife lying in plain sight by the turkey and come after them.

He turned on his heel, then, and struck off for a very long walk. He glanced at the sky, hoping for signs of an impending blizzard. He'd figured no less than a foot of snow was likely to cool his temper anytime tonight.

He'd been walking for the better part of an hour, his face chilled, his hands jammed into his pockets, the wind cutting through his coat, when he saw Luke Adams walking slowly in his direction. He had the feeling Angela's father would either go or stay at a signal from him. He gave the older man a curt nod that was apparently accepted as welcome enough.

"I suppose you'll be wanting me to leave now," he said eventually.

He thought he caught a glimpse of Luke's smile in the moonlight.

"Not unless you want to," Angela's father said. "You're going to have to make up your own mind what the best solution is to this. You and Angela. If you decide to stay, we'll welcome you. If you decide to go, we'll look out for Angela and the baby."

"And hate my guts for the rest of your days," Clint concluded.

"Hating is a waste of time and energy," Luke said.

He said it with such passionate conviction that Clint stared at him. "You ever hated anyone?"

"Myself for a long time," Luke said candidly. "My father for a bit."

The response stunned Clint. If Luke could hate a man like Harlan Adams, then there was no word for the depth of his own feelings toward his father. "You hated your father? How'd that happen?"

Deeply felt sorrow seemed to etch new lines in Luke's rugged face. "I figured between us we killed my brother," he explained, echoing the story that Angela had told Clint earlier. "I also resented the hell out of the fact that he was trying to control my life. Jessie was the one who made me see that the only thing in life that really counts is family. When you love people, you work out your differences, no matter how difficult it is or how long it takes. I was never a big talker, so it was always harder for me."

"I know what you mean," Clint said. "I always figured actions ought to speak loudly enough."

"I'd say yours do," Luke said with a grin. "They were loud and clear earlier tonight."

"Sorry," Clint apologized again. "That woman can make me angry quicker than you can set off a rocket on the Fourth of July."

"So I noticed, but that wasn't what fascinated me so."

"Oh?"

"What I saw was a man who cared enough about a woman to make sure she was in out of the cold, even when he was mad enough to throttle her. That's the kind of man I could respect." He gave Clint a direct look. "It's something to think about, isn't it?"

Before Clint could respond, Luke headed for the barn and left him with nothing but his thoughts for company.

At least there was one member of the Adams clan that didn't think he was here with an ulterior motive, he concluded bitterly. Too bad it wasn't Angela.

Where she'd gotten the nut-brained idea that he was after the Adams fortune was beyond him. He hadn't even known she had a dime to her name when he'd traced her to Dallas and met Betsy. If he was an ambitious, money-hungry kind of man, would he have been scrambling to make ends meet on a broken-down ranch in Montana? There were far easier ways to make a buck.

He just happened to love ranching. He liked the exhausting work and the never-ending challenges and the intellectual stimulation of figuring out how to better his herd from year to year. It might never make him rich, but fulfillment was all he was after. It was enough to have something of his own, something he could take pride in. If Angela hadn't seen that much in their months together, then she hadn't really known him at all. And it was damned sure he hadn't known her.

"Well, that was certainly humiliating," Angela said, when she'd finally calmed down enough to speak. Most of the family had discreetly slipped away, leaving her in the kitchen with two of her cousins and Consuela.

"I thought it was romantic," Sharon Lynn said with huge eyes and an exaggerated sigh.

Sharon Lynn was less than a year younger than Angela, but she'd stayed in Los Pinos her whole life, surrounded by family, content with running Eli Dolan's Drugstore, where her mother had once worked and where her mother and Cody had carried on much of their highly irregular and high-volume courtship. Maybe that explained why she thought that Clint's he-man act was so romantic. She wasn't worldly enough or liberated enough to know better.

"You want him, you can have him," Angela snapped.

Her cousin laughed. "Not on your life. I'm not wasting my energy chasing after a man who's already hooked."

"Besides, she already has eyes for Kyle Mason," Dani said. She gave Angela a sympathetic look. "Are you OK?"

"Just peachy."

Dani, who was now a veterinarian in town, urged Angie toward the kitchen table. "Sit down. Your hands are like ice." She glanced around the kitchen until her gaze found Consuela. "Could you make her some tea, please?"

Angela accepted the tea and the solicitude. Dani hadn't been born an Adams. She'd been adopted by Jordan when he and her mother, Kelly Flint, had married. She was older than Angela by four years, but it seemed to Angela that something had changed in her cousin.

Angela studied her intently, trying to figure out what it was exactly. Once exuberant and outgoing, Dani now seemed shy and quiet, even as she managed to take charge of the situation. Obviously her veterinary training had enabled her to cope well with unexpected emergencies, but there was a vulnerability about her that was out of character.

When she handed the cup of tea to Angela, her worried gaze shifted away the instant Angela made eye contact with her. Angela put the cup on the table and caught her cousin's hand. "You OK?"

Dani's responding smile seemed forced. "Hey, you're the patient, not me."

"It must be nice having a patient who can tell you what's wrong for a change," she teased. "I'm just cold. It'll pass." She sobered and added quietly, "There's something else going on with you."

"Don't be silly. I'm perfectly fine."

Sharon Lynn stepped in and circled an arm protectively around Dani's waist. She met Angela's gaze evenly. "Let it go," she said quietly, but firmly.

Angela was taken aback by the fierce joining of forces. The cousins had all been close growing up. There'd been no way around it, with family gatherings as common as Texas bluebonnets in summer. They'd never taken sides back then. In fact, the girls had all been amazingly compatible, practically as close as sisters. Had things changed since she'd been gone? Was she now viewed as an outsider? Were there secrets that would never be shared with her?

"I'm sorry if I pushed," she apologized.

Dani gave her hand a quick squeeze. "Don't worry about it." Her expression turned briskly professional and her gaze warmed. "How are you feeling now? Better?"

"I'm warmer," she said.

"But still unsettled," Dani guessed. "Clint strikes me as the kind of man who could keep a woman unsettled."

"He is a royal pain in the—"

"Whoops," Sharon Lynn said with a laugh. "Don't get her started again. There won't be enough chamomile tea on earth to calm her down."

"Maybe you should go upstairs and rest," Dani said.

"No," Angela protested.

"A few more weeks and you'll be begging for rest," Dani warned.

"Not with me around," Consuela said. "I cannot wait to hold this child in my arms. Angela will have to fight me for a chance to take care of the little one."

"You're still spoiled rotten, I see," Sharon Lynn said to Angela, even as she reached up and squeezed Consuela's hand. She eyed her cousin speculatively. "Have you ever actually held a job?"

"Don't be mean," Dani said.

The familiar bickering made Angela smile, even though she was the butt of the teasing. "Actually, I've held quite a few jobs."

"Couldn't keep one, huh?" Sharon Lynn taunted.

"You just wait until this baby is born. I'll take over the soda fountain for you one day and my milk shakes will have the residents of Los Pinos weeping."

"Have you ever actually worked a soda fountain?" Dani inquired skeptically.

"No, but I worked a bar. How different can it be?"

"My customers are sober," Sharon Lynn pointed out. "They know what they're getting."

Angela grinned at her. "Oh, how I've missed you two. Nobody could ever put me in my place the way you do."

"Not even Clint?" Sharon Lynn asked.

The back door slammed open just then, caught by the wind as Clint tried to enter. "Not even Clint what?" he asked, his gaze fixed on her.

"Not a thing," Sharon Lynn said.

"See you," Dani said, dragging her cousin out of the room.

Consuela snatched up a silver coffee service and slipped out behind them.

"Et tu, Brute?" Angela muttered.

"I do not know this Brute," Consuela said, then leaned down to whisper, "Talk to the man, *niña.* Do not stop talking until you have reached an understanding. *¿Si?*"

Angela glanced up into Clint's stormy eyes and shuddered. She had the distinct impression that quiet conversation was the last thing on his mind.

8

"Are you planning to apologize?" Angela asked Clint, figuring that a preemptive strike was called for.

"Me? You were the one throwing insults around," Clint shot right back, his blue eyes as stormy as a hurricane-tossed sea.

"Maybe we should take turns," she suggested cheerfully. "I'll apologize for making disparaging insinuations about your character, and you can apologize for being a dyed-in-the-wool macho jerk."

His gaze narrowed at the deliberate insult. "You're not off to a very promising start with that apology."

"Sorry." She smiled. "Best I can do."

"Let me get this straight. Are you admitting that you know perfectly well that I'm not after the family fortune?"

She thought about that for a minute. It was apparently about fifty-nine seconds too long, judging by the increasingly furious expression on his face. His righteous indignation did carry some weight with her. He'd never been an especially good actor. His emotions were always right out there in plain view. If he'd ever lied to her, she was pretty sure she would have known it. Of course, he'd probably thought the same of her. Maybe both of them were just plain lousy at character assessment.

"OK, I admit it," she said eventually.

He regarded her skeptically. "Say it like you mean it, angel."

"I know you didn't come here because of my family's money," she said solemnly.

"Mind telling me who sowed that idea in your head in the first place?"

Now that was tricky turf. She didn't want him to realize that her grandfather had been speculating about his honesty. They seemed to have built a good rapport in a very short time. She didn't want to force Clint's pride to kick in. It would destroy that relationship before it ever got a decent chance.

She bit back a sigh. No matter how she fibbed to herself about wanting Clint to back off and leave, the truth was she liked having him here, liked seeing him slowly becoming a part of the family. Getting along with Grandpa Harlan was a huge part of that. Perhaps her grandfather had had his doubts about Clint, but she wanted to believe Clint could prove to him there had been no merit to those doubts.

"It was just the only thing I could come up with to explain your persistence," she told him, skirting the truth by a wide margin.

He studied her intently for some time, then shook his head. "I never thought I'd say this, especially given recent evidence to the contrary, but you're a terrible liar, angel. If you came up with that notion all on your own, then I'm Billy the Kid."

The irony of the remark wasn't lost on her. "I guess I used to be more convincing, huh?"

"Much more convincing," he agreed. "So, 'fess up. Who was it?"

She debated lying again, then decided there wasn't any point to it. He was the kind of man who'd nag at it and sooner or later, he'd figure out the truth. Maybe it would be better if she told him. She settled for an explanation that was true as far as it went and left her grandfather out of it.

"Janet, actually."

"Janet," he repeated, his expression more thoughtful than furious. "I should have known. Was she advising you to protect yourself from my greedy clutches?"

"Something like that."

"She was just thinking like an attorney, I suppose."

"Exactly."

His gaze clashed with hers. "Unless your grandfather was the one who put the idea into *her* head. Was he?"

"Does it really matter?" Angela asked hurriedly. "The bottom line is Janet was looking out for my best interests the way any good attorney would."

"Did she want you to insist on a prenuptial agreement?"

"As a matter of fact, yes."

"Not a bad idea," he said calmly enough, though his eyes were once again turbulent. "Did you agree?"

"We're not getting married so what's the point?" she retorted.

"Let's just say we were, would you want the agreement?"

"Yes," she said instinctively, then hastily retracted it. "No. Dammit, Clint, I don't know what makes sense."

"You really don't trust me, do you?" he asked, sounding more defeated than angry.

"Do you trust me?" she shot back.

His grin was rueful. "Maybe not, but there's one big difference, darlin'. I've never betrayed you the way you betrayed me. I may have been a fool back in Montana, I may not have responded to your announcement the way you'd been expecting, but I have never betrayed you or lied to you. I accepted you at face value. Apparently you can't say the same."

She swallowed hard against the tide of hurt that washed over her at his charge. She couldn't deny it, either. He was right. He had far more reason to distrust her than she did him.

"Where does that leave us?" she asked, suddenly exhausted by the tension of the past few hours.

He leveled a look straight into her eyes, a look filled with questions and regrets. Then he sighed. "I wish to hell I knew, angel. I wish I knew."

Clint left the kitchen feeling more hopeless than he ever had in his life. To her everlasting credit, his mother had raised a houseful of optimists. She had refused to blame his father for walking out on them. She had never said a harsh word about the man who had left her to cope with all those children and a mountain of debts. She had just taken his departure as one more challenge to make them all stronger.

All of them had grown up believing that with just a little effort life could be better than it had been. He wouldn't say his brothers and sisters were overachievers, but they were undaunted by a good challenge. They'd heard the old adage about turning life's lemons into lemonade so often, none of them could drink the stuff.

He'd been the same until today. He'd been fortunate enough to go a lifetime without being distrusted. Back home, folks knew the Bradys were honest, if poor. In Montana, he'd paid off every debt he owed, including the ranch. As of last month, it was his free and clear. If he gave his word, he kept it. No one had ever had cause to worry about the kind of man he was.

Now these people who didn't know him at all found his motives suspect. He supposed it was natural enough that they would worry about one of their own, that they would think first of protecting Angela, but the instinctive lack of trust in him cut just the same. Worse, he had no idea how to rectify it. Words weren't the answer. And actions, the kind of actions that would deepen respect and engender real trust, took time, time he didn't have.

Sooner or later he would have to head back to Montana. He had a good foreman there looking after things now, but he couldn't rely on Hardy Jenkins shouldering the burden of running the ranch forever.

As he trudged up the stairs, it seemed he carried the weight of the world. Maybe he'd feel better with a good night's sleep. Maybe in the morning he'd have the answers that eluded him tonight.

He was halfway to his room—it was a damn suite, actually—when the man most on his mind exited a room down the hall. Harlan Adams smiled, his expression totally open and free of guile. Maybe he was already overcoming his suspicions, Clint thought hopefully.

"You aren't sneaking off to bed at this hour, are you?" Harlan asked.

"I was considering it," Clint admitted. "I've got some thinking to do."

"Not when there's a poker game about to start downstairs in Luke's office," he insisted. "Son, that would be downright foolish. Nothing takes a man's mind off his troubles better than a game of cards. You haven't played poker until you've played with us. Before the night's out, one of us is bound to bet the whole damn ranch."

"With my luck, I'd win it," Clint muttered under his breath. That would really win the family over, he thought.

"Never can tell, you might," Harlan said, proving his hearing was as sharp as ever. He looped a powerful arm around Clint's shoulders and propelled him back downstairs.

"Almost lost my own spread to Janet once," he confided. "That woman can play poker. She's got a sneaky side to her nature. Jenny's the same way. They even won over old Mule, God rest his soul."

"Mule?"

Harlan grinned. "Cantankerous man, but the best danged card player in Los Pinos. Mule had vowed never to play cards with a woman, but those two changed his mind. He said the kind of gumption and daring they had with a lousy pair of deuces was downright scary."

"Will they be playing tonight?" Clint asked, trying to

imagine the fierce competitiveness of husband against wife and daughter. From what he'd observed of Janet and Jenny, it ought to be amusing.

"Hell, no," Harlan declared fervently. "I can't have the two of them showing me up in front of my own boys, can I? Besides if Jenny ever gets her hands on another share of White Pines, she's threatened to put a Bloomingdales on it. I can't have that, even if she does swear that without a few fancy department stores around she'll move back east one day, just so she can spend a decent day shopping."

"And you believe her?"

"Did once," he claimed. "I'm not so sure anymore. Not since she's discovered Nieman-Marcus. Of course, with Jenny you never know quite what to expect. She's a lot like her mama that way, lively and unpredictable."

To Clint's amusement, he actually sounded as if he considered it possible that one day Jenny would impulsively erect a huge store on his property just so she could shop. It also seemed as if it didn't bother him all that much. Before Clint could analyze how a man could be so blasé about losing his land, they reached Luke's office.

"Look who I've roped into joining us," Harlan announced as they entered.

"Ah, another lamb to the slaughter," Cody retorted. "Do you have any card sense at all?"

"I've played a game or two," Clint said.

"Which probably means he won half of Montana playing poker," Jordan assessed.

"It was blackjack, actually," Clint said, only partially

in jest. He hadn't won his land that night, but he'd won the down payment for it.

"Does everybody have their deeds tucked away in a vault back home?" Luke inquired dryly as he poured Clint a shot of whiskey and set it in front of him.

"Are you kidding? Kelly won't even tell me where she has ours for safekeeping," Jordan replied.

"Melissa either," Cody added.

"Janet and I don't have secrets," Harlan boasted. "I know precisely where the deeds are."

"Sure you do," Luke taunted. "In her office, locked in *her* vault."

"OK, OK, enough of this nonsense," Harlan grumbled. "Who's dealing?"

"We'll cut for it. High card deals," Luke said, shuffling the deck one last time.

Clint pulled a ten and figured that was the end of it. He waited for one of the others to come up with an ace or even a jack. Instead, the ten took it and Luke handed him the cards, along with a warning.

"We take this seriously, son. No fancy games and nothing wild."

"Except our manners," Cody said. "As the night wears on, we forget everything our mama taught us."

"We get drunk," Harlan translated. "One of us tries to stay sober enough to haul the others up to bed."

"Who's turn is it?" Cody asked.

"Yours," Luke and Jordan taunted, removing the tumbler of whiskey in front of him.

"I think Clint ought to do it," Cody protested.

"And have him see us at our worst and remember it?

No way," Harlan said. "We might end up with our faces on the front page of the Dallas papers."

Clint stiffened at the suggestion that he'd resort to blackmail. It was only part of the rowdy teasing he was sure went on all the time with these men, but it cut a little too close to the accusations he'd all too recently been discussing with Angela. Thievery, blackmail, what would be next?

He glanced across the table and saw that Harlan was observing him with a steady gaze. He thought there was a message in that gaze, but he was damned if he could read it.

"Five-card draw," he said quietly and dealt the cards.

Luke won the first hand, which had the rest of them accusing Clint of stacking the deck to win over his prospective father-in-law. When Luke won the second hand as well, a hand dealt by Jordan, the men went silent.

They played now with a fierce intensity, the same way they did everything else. They'd played for a couple of hours when the cards began falling Clint's way. The chips stacked up in front of him. He had a nice bundle, when Harlan glanced at his watch and declared the evening over.

"That's it, boys. It's after midnight and I'm getting too old for this nonsense."

"Janet got you on a limited budget?" Luke teased.

"Nope, I just know when a man's on a roll. If the rest of you can't see it, then stay here and lose a few more dollars. I'm going up to my nice, warm bed and my nice, warm wife."

"Ah," Luke said. "Now that's a concept I can embrace." He, too, stood up.

"I guess that's it, then," Jordan said. "Congratulations, Clint. Nice playing. I think I hear Kelly calling me, too."

"Melissa's been calling to me for the past hour, but you haven't seen me dashing off to bed," Cody protested. "Besides, you guys, what about poor Clint? He doesn't have a wife upstairs."

"He can rectify that anytime he wants to," Luke responded dryly.

"I wonder about that," Clint said sorrowfully. "Angela doesn't seem inclined to make an honest man of me."

"Are you asking for our advice?" Harlan asked eagerly, clearly ready to sit down again if called upon for some wisdom about the battle of the sexes.

Clint laughed at the four men who were poised to stay and help him out with courting Angela. "Thanks, anyway," he said. "I have the feeling you all would just get me in more trouble than I'm in already."

"You're probably right," Cody said. "Not a one of us can claim our courtships were smooth sailing."

"And none of us learned a darned thing from our mistakes," Jordan added. "You go with your own instincts, Clint. You're the one she's in love with. Even I can see the way she looks at you and Kelly claims I'm clueless on emotional issues. You must have been doing something right up there in Montana."

After they'd gone, as Clint made his way upstairs, he tried to remember exactly what he'd done to impress Hattie Jones. About the only thing he recalled with any certainty was seducing her on the night they'd met. It wasn't a tactic he could try with the woman eight and a half months pregnant.

Or was it? He paused at the top of the steps and stared at the closed door opposite his own. Was Angela lying in bed wide awake, tormented by thoughts of lovemaking the way he'd been night after night? What would she do if he slipped quietly into her room and settled himself into bed beside her, if only to hold her close until morning? How long would it take her to wake the household? He envisioned a whole line of very shaky guns aimed in his direction. Drunk as they all were when they'd parted, at least one of them was still bound to hit him if they accidentally fired.

Even with that image sharply defined in his head, he reached for the doorknob and quietly turned it. He stepped into the room and closed the door behind him, then waited, his heart thundering in his chest, to see if his movements had disturbed her.

"You might's well come all the way in," she said as if she'd been wide awake and expecting him. "What's the matter? Did you lose your way back to your own room?"

His eyes adjusted to the room's darkness and his gaze sought out the bed. Though the covers were tangled, there was no sign of Angela in it. Besides, even through his alcohol-induced haze, he grasped the fact that the bed was on his left and her voice had come from somewhere on his right.

"Angel?"

"Yes," she said, her amusement plain. "I'm over here, by the window."

He saw her then, seated in a rocking chair beside the huge bay window. A faint trail of moonlight shimmered over her. She had brushed her hair out of its usual care-less knot so that it fell in glorious waves to her shoul-ders. Against the creaminess of her skin and the stark white of her nightgown, her hair shimmered like a cas-cade of garnets, dark red and mysterious and sensual. Quite simply, she took his breath away.

"You truly do look like an angel," he whispered, awestruck as always by her beauty.

"And you look like a man who's spent the evening in a saloon," she retorted dryly. "You're weaving a bit, cowboy. Sit down before you fall down. Did you have a good time with the Adams card sharks?"

"I did, indeed. I won."

He thought her eyes widened a bit in surprise at that. "Really?"

He pulled his winnings from his pockets and allowed the bills to flutter into her lap. There was a satisfying heap of them when he was done.

"My, my," she said, fingering a fifty. "Must have been pretty high stakes."

"High enough," he agreed. "But nobody bet their ranch."

"You sound disappointed."

He regarded her sadly. "Not that again, angel. I don't want your money. I don't want your land. How many times do I have to say it before you believe me?"

She regarded him speculatively. "What do you want, then?"

"You," he said without hesitation. "Just you."

Moonlight caught the sheen of tears in her eyes. The sight of them distressed him. "Are you crying?"

he asked, kneeling in front of her. He brushed the dampness from her face. "Don't cry, darlin'. Please don't cry."

"It's OK. I just wish…" Her voice trailed off.

"You wish what?"

She reached toward him and her fingers sifted through his hair, then came to rest on his cheek. "I just wish you meant it."

"I do mean it," he insisted. "From the night we met, I've wanted you. There's never been another woman like you. You make me…"

"Crazy?" she supplied.

"Angel, angel," he protested, "where's your sense of romance?"

"Sleeping," she said briskly. "That's what we ought to be doing, too. Everyone will be heading out at the crack of dawn. And tomorrow we start all over again at White Pines."

Clint stilled. He hadn't considered the possibility that everyone might go off somewhere for Christmas. Where would that leave him? Was he expected to head on home? Maybe linger back here alone? Or were they automatically assuming he'd be coming along?

He wondered if he could convince Angela to stay right here with him. They could have their own private holiday celebration, maybe even sort out where they were going without all the well-meaning interference. He was about to suggest just that when he realized that she was describing the last Christmas she'd spent with the whole family.

"It was just like today, only better. There were tons of presents, because everybody has always gone overboard. Consuela and her cousin Maritza, who works for

Grandpa Harlan, fixed enough food to last for a month. Grandpa waited to put up his tree until we all got there, so we could decorate it together. We sang carols while we did it, then we all traipsed off to midnight services." She sighed. "It was wonderful. Year after year we had the exact same tradition."

"And you've missed it, haven't you?"

"More than anything else we do," she admitted. Her gaze caught his. "Will you come with us? Will you share it with me this year?"

The invitation pleased him more than he cared to admit. "If that's what you want."

"It is."

"Someday soon, though, you and I are going to have to sit down and talk, all by ourselves, without any interruptions or distractions. The baby's going to be here any day now and we have to get things settled."

"No," she said sharply.

He stared at her. "What do you mean, no?"

"I will not make any sort of a decision about anything just because we have a deadline staring us in the face. Whatever happens between us, whatever conclusions we reach about the future will be made when the time is right and not a minute before that."

Clint stared at her in frustration. "Dammit, I want this baby to be born with my name."

"That's what I wanted seven months ago, and you were in no big hurry to accommodate me."

He stood up and began to pace. "So this is payback? You're going to punish the baby, make the kid start life without his father's name, just because you want to get even with me? How can you be so cruel and heartless?"

"Of course that's not what I want," she snapped. "But I will not marry you just so the baby can have your name. I'll put your name on the birth certificate. You'll have your claim to paternity, but any relationship between you and me is going to have to be based on something else, something just between the two of us." Her flashing eyes clashed with his. "Is that clear enough?" she demanded.

"Oh, it's crystal clear," he muttered as he headed for the door. He paused to take one last shot. "Since you have Janet covering all your legal angles, maybe it's about time I found an attorney of my own."

He heard her sharply indrawn breath across the room. Good, he'd struck a nerve.

"Clint, no," she protested, sounding panicked by his impulsive threat.

He refused to back down. Meeting her gaze evenly, he said, "Good night, angel. Sweet dreams."

He closed the door softly behind him, even though he would have preferred to slam it shut. That would have awakened the whole household, though, and he was in no mood to explain the latest argument he and Angela had had.

It seemed lately as if every time they tried to talk, it disintegrated into some sort of name-calling argument. Hadn't he concluded not more than a half hour earlier that it was time for actions, not word? There was no time like the present to get started, with his ire roused and his inhibitions weakened by whiskey.

He threw open the door and crossed the room in three angry strides. She had risen from the rocking chair and stood halfway between it and the bed, her gaze startled. Without a word, he pulled her into his arms and delivered a kiss meant to take her breath away.

She gave a soft yelp of surprise, then a soft sigh of pleasure as he peppered kisses across her face. He found the hem of her gown and lifted it, his fingers sliding over silky flesh that had filled out into lush, provocative curves.

When he reached her belly, he slowed and the nature of his touch changed to one of awe. Her skin was stretched taut, and beneath the surface, he felt the stirring of his child. His mood altered in a heartbeat. All of the anger dissolved. Lust gave way to something tender.

With a sigh that was part dismay, part frustration, he rested his forehead against hers.

"I'm sorry," he said, his breathing ragged.

"No, I am."

"We can't go on like this, fighting until our nerves are raw. We'll end up saying something one of these days that we can't take back."

"I know."

"Maybe we should put some distance between us, think about this," he suggested.

"Not again," she said.

The fierceness of her reaction startled him. "No?"

"Absolutely not. You're not running and neither am I. We will settle this, Clint. Let's just take one day at a time. Let's enjoy Christmas and maybe the rest will take care of itself." She rested her hand against his cheek, then smiled. "After all, it is the season of miracles."

9

Angela wasn't sure what had possessed her to invite Clint along to White Pines. She was asking for trouble, no doubt about it. Maybe she'd been persuaded because she didn't think she could shake him any easier than a horse could rid itself of a burr under its saddle. Maybe it was simple politeness.

More than likely, though, it had something to do with sentiment. They had spent the previous Christmas together, and despite all her reminiscing the night before about past holidays with her family, Christmas with Clint in Montana had been one of the most incredible of her entire life. She smiled to herself just thinking about it.

They had gone out the day before Christmas, tromped through a foot or more of hard-packed snow until they'd found the perfect tree. Clint had chopped it down and hauled it back to the ranch, grumbling all the way about the size of it. He'd sounded exactly the way her father did every year, which had made her homesick. In some peculiar way, it had also reassured her.

Seeing similarities in the two men she cared most about suggested that her judgment wasn't all bad.

Since an earlier search of the house had turned up not one single strand of lights or an ornament, Angela had gone into town after the tree was up and gathered everything she could think of to decorate the ceiling-scraping monster of a pine. Clint had taken one look at the bags of cranberries, packages of popcorn and yards of ribbon and shaken his head.

"I don't know, darlin'," he'd said, his expression doubtful. "This is looking an awful lot like work."

"You just wait," she'd promised. "We are going to have the most spectacular, old-fashioned Christmas tree you've ever seen. Start popping the corn, OK? I'll get busy with the cranberries."

They had sipped hot chocolate and played carols on the stereo as they'd worked. They'd eaten as much popcorn as they'd strung, but by evening the tree was crisscrossed with strands of white and red. Colorful red and green bows added a festive touch. Clint had flat-out balked when she'd wanted to add candles in place of lights.

"Enough's enough," he'd declared. "I don't want the ranch to burn down in the name of having some Christmas decorations straight out of 'Little House on the Prairie.' I'll go get lights, if you insist on having them."

"The store's sold out," she said, disappointed by his reaction.

He'd leaned down and kissed her. "Trust me, Hattie. I never make a promise if I don't think I can deliver."

She had started cooking while he was gone, sure that this was one promise he wouldn't be able to keep. She'd consoled herself by making every dish she remembered from Christmas dinners back home: turkey with corn bread stuffing, cranberry relish, mashed potatoes, gravy and two gigantic pumpkin pies.

It was dark by the time Clint had gotten home and the house was filled with the familiar scents of pine and cinnamon and roasting turkey. He'd stood in the doorway, shaking the snow from his coat, and sniffed appreciatively.

"It smells like Christmas in here."

She had grinned. "It's true what they say, the sense of smell does bring back memories, doesn't it?" She eyed the bag in his hand speculatively. "Lights?"

He'd tossed it to her. "Enough to rival some big-city skyscraper at night," he declared.

Eagerly she had opened the bag and found a half-dozen strands of tiny white lights, six hundred in all. Her mother would have been in raptures.

"Oh, this is going to be wonderful," she'd said, already imagining it. "I can't wait to see it."

Putting the lights on after the fact had been tedious and at times hilarious as they'd gotten tangled up in popcorn and cranberries, but the results had been worth it. The tree simply glowed, sparkling like a night sky with a million stars.

"You really get into this Christmas stuff, don't you?" Clint asked, watching her.

"Sure. Don't you?"

He'd shrugged indifferently. She'd tried to question him about his own holiday memories, but he'd cut the conversation short and won her silence by saying that the memories they made together were the only ones that mattered to him now. The sweet remark had brought tears to her eyes.

Clint had reached in his pocket then and handed her a small, gaily wrapped package.

Surprised, Angela had stared at it. "What's this?"

Clint grinned sheepishly. "What does it look like?"

"A Christmas present? For me?"

"It is Christmas, isn't it?"

"Yes, but—"

"You thought I'd forgotten."

"Something like that."

"Aren't you going to open it? Or would you rather wait until morning?"

"No, no, now is fine." She hadn't been sure she would be able to stand the suspense until morning.

Her fingers fumbled with the ribbon, which had been so artfully tied it was evident that a store clerk, not Clint, had been responsible for it. "It's beautiful."

"If you're that impressed with the wrapping, I can't wait to see your expression once you get it open," he'd said dryly.

"At this rate I may never get it open. My hands are shaking."

He'd reached out and clasped them between his, stilling her efforts. "Hattie, it's not a big deal. It's just a present, a token really."

Eyes tearing, she had gazed at him. "It's a big deal to me. It's the first present you've ever given me."

"Are you worried about my taste?"

"No, absolutely not. Anything you picked out will be special to me."

He'd let her finish unwrapping it then. The flat velvet

box made her heart thump unsteadily and once again she was all thumbs as she tried to lift the lid. Inside, against a white satin pillow, rested a gold pendant, a tiny Christmas tree with winking jewels as decorations. A diamond sparkled at the top.

"I thought maybe it would remind you of our first Christmas together," he'd said, looking awkward and uncomfortable at the sentimental gesture.

"Nothing you could have gotten me would have meant more," she swore to him. "Nothing." Eyes shimmering with unshed tears, she gazed at him. "Help me put it on."

It was his turn to fumble as he tried to manage the small clasp. When the necklace was secure, she gazed at herself in the mirror. The emerald, ruby and sapphire chips twinkled gaily against the soft gleam of gold as the pendant rested against her bright green sweater. He stood behind her in front of an oval mirror, his hands on her shoulders, as she'd admired the necklace. Lifting her gaze, her reflected glance caught his.

"Merry Christmas, darlin'," he'd whispered.

"Merry Christmas."

Now, thinking of that moment and the love she had been so sure she had seen shining in his eyes, she reached up and touched the pendant resting against her skin. She had worn it ever since, no matter the season, because it had reminded her of the man she had fallen in love with one lonely winter in Montana.

Could they recapture what they had felt that night? Or could they only move on to create new memories? When the new year began, would they still be together or would they have resolved to go their own separate ways, connected only by the child they had conceived together?

Her baby stirred restlessly in her womb as if he, too, was anxious to know the answers to those questions.

"I want us to be a family," she murmured, admitting it for the first time in a very long time.

Whether that was possible, though, was up to Clint. If he couldn't love her after what she'd done, if he couldn't forgive her for pretending to be the mythical Hattie Jones, then she would have to let him go.

"And we'll be just fine," she promised her child.

The baby kicked in apparent protest.

"We will," she repeated fiercely, her hands on her belly. "But I won't give up without a fight, little one. I promise you that, too."

This was the first Clint had actually seen of the town of Los Pinos. It was miles beyond Luke's ranch and beyond the home where he'd spent the night with Betsy's family. Gazing at the quaint, unpretentious stores and homey restaurants, he felt immediately at ease.

There was nothing fancy about the Texas town. It was practically a mirror image of the one he'd left behind in Montana. No wonder Angela had gravitated toward Rocky Ridge and felt at home there.

"I know," she said at a look from him. "I see the resemblance, too. I saw it that first night I stopped in Rocky Ridge. Felt it, too. The people are the same, warm and friendly. I still don't know why you wanted to stop here, though, instead of going on through to Grandpa's."

"You said your family does Christmas up big. I want to contribute my share."

She regarded him with obvious puzzlement. "You mean like some champagne or a couple of pies?"

He chuckled at the suggestion. "Knowing your grandfather, I'm sure he has the food and beverages pretty much under control. I was talking about presents."

"That's not necessary," she protested. "You don't even know the family that well. There's no need to be buying presents. No one will expect it. I only picked up a few last-minute things before I left Dallas."

"I want to," he insisted stubbornly. "You can help me pick out the right things." He glanced at her worriedly. "Or are you too tired? If this is too much for you, you can settle down in one of the restaurants and wait for me. The Italian one looks nice. I can smell the garlic clear out here."

"You are not sticking me off in some restaurant while you shop," she retorted. "I love picking out gifts. I can get a few more myself. Where do you want to start?"

He glanced up and down the street. There weren't more than a dozen stores, all decorated brightly. "You pick. You know what they stock better than I do."

"Let's start at Dolan's," she decided.

He glanced across the street at the shop with a dusty, ancient display and a forlorn string of colored lights drooping across the window. "The drugstore?" he asked doubtfully. "I'm not settling for cheap perfume and some boxes of stale candy, darlin'."

"Don't let the window fool you. It's been that way since way before I was born. Eli Dolan never saw any need to change it. Sharon Lynn runs the place now and she's stubbornly stuck with tradition. But it has the best milk shakes I've ever had. Made from scratch with real ice cream."

"Angel, we're supposed to be shopping, not eating."

Her expression turned sly. "The baby's starved and milk is very good for his bones."

He grinned at the ploy. "Oh, in that case, we absolutely should have a milk shake."

A bell over the door tinkled as they entered and half a dozen people seated at the old-fashioned soda fountain turned to stare.

"You're on display, cowboy," she said with a wink as she led the way to the counter.

Clint endured the stares, nodded at the introductions and stewed when the stares transferred themselves pointedly to Angela's oversize belly. It was one thing for the family to be watching the two of them speculatively. It was quite another to have the whole darned town ready to spread gossip.

"Maybe this was a bad idea," he muttered, just as Sharon Lynn emerged from a back room with a beaming smile.

"Hey, you two," she said cheerfully. "I'll bet you're here for milk shakes."

"You bet," Angela said eagerly, "chocolate."

Sharon Lynn caught Clint's eyes. "You, too?"

Caught now, he gave in to the inevitable. "Absolutely."

"I thought you'd be over at White Pines by now. Janet called earlier. She said you were expected any minute."

"Mom and Dad probably are there. We got sidetracked by a little shopping," Angela said.

Sharon Lynn leaned over the counter. "I don't see any packages."

"Because this was our first stop," Clint said. "Sustenance for the ordeal ahead."

"Ah, I see. Then I'd better make these shakes double thick. The stores are jammed and everyone's patience is frayed. Christmas Eve shoppers tend to be desperate. You'll need your strength to compete with them."

One by one the other customers drifted away, either anxious to finish their own last-minute shopping or eager to spread the news that Angela Adams was back home with a mysterious stranger in tow and a baby on the way.

"Don't worry about them," Sharon Lynn told him when Angela had left them alone to use the rest room. "They're harmless. The Adams clan has been giving this town something to talk about for years now. It's practically a tradition."

"I should have thought about that before I subjected her to this, though."

"Forget it. We've long since learned to be thick-skinned, since we seem destined to provide so much entertainment. Angela's not upset. Why should you be?" She regarded him speculatively. "Unless you really care deep down about her feelings?"

"Of course, I do."

She beamed as if he'd confessed to something far more telling. "That's a start," she said, giving him a peck on the cheek before going to wait on a wide-eyed customer who was staring at them from the cosmetic counter across the store.

When Angela emerged from the back, he smiled at her ready-for-anything expression.

"You look as if you're preparing to charge into battle," he teased.

"Have you ever shopped on Christmas Eve before? It's full-scale warfare."

"Even in Los Pinos?"

"Especially in Los Pinos. One of the other traditions around here is that everyone waits until the last minute to shop, so they can brag about how insane it was. I've seen people kicking and shoving to get the last electric razor."

"That bad, huh?"

"Worse," she insisted, then grinned. "But you have an edge. Practically nobody will argue with a pregnant lady."

"I just knew you were going to come in handy," he responded, then held out his hand. He studied her intently. "You're sure you're up to this?"

"Lead on. I can't wait."

Clint had never shopped for quite so many people before, not when he had a decent amount of money in his bank account and a heart that was suddenly full of Christmas spirit. Nor had he ever been accompanied before by a woman with a zealousness for a good bargain and the taste of an aristocrat.

They made four trips back to his pickup to deposit bundles of leather gloves, silver money clips and enough silk scarves to perform the dance of the seven veils. On the last trip, he suggested once again that Angela take time out and wait for him.

"No way," she argued. "I'm just getting warmed up. There's a sale at Geoffrey's we haven't checked out."

"You misunderstood, angel. That wasn't a suggestion. That was an order. Go have another milk shake.

Rest. Gossip with your cousin. Geoffrey's, whatever that is, will wait."

"Geoffrey's is a dress boutique," she said distractedly. Her gaze clashed with his. "Why are you so anxious to get rid of me?"

"It's Christmas Eve and I'm shopping. Why do you think?"

Her expression brightened as his meaning finally registered. "Oh."

He saw her reach instinctively to her neck and guessed that she was wearing the pendant he'd given her the year before. He'd been wondering about that. He had noticed the gold chain and thought it was the same one, but he hadn't been able to detect whether the tiny tree was on it or whether it had been exchanged for something else. She always wore it carefully tucked beneath her blouse. Her unconscious gesture now was very telling. He gathered she hadn't wanted him to see that she was sentimental about anything connected to him.

Ah, well, let her have her secrets, he thought with a smile.

"Are you going to wait in the drugstore or in the truck?" he asked.

Her eyes sparkled mischievously. "Maybe I have shopping of my own to do."

"Then we'll meet back here in twenty minutes?"

"Twenty? You can pick out a present for me in twenty minutes?"

He enjoyed the fact that she sounded disgruntled. "I was thinking of grabbing the first suitable thing I came across," he teased. "Maybe a huge bottle of that perfume I saw Sharon Lynn selling to a customer earlier."

"I'm sure whatever it is will be lovely," she said as primly and politely as any child who'd ever anticipated a doll only to receive socks and underwear.

"I'll do my best," he said cheerfully. "Twenty minutes, OK?"

"Fine. Don't get all bent out of shape if it takes me longer."

He noticed that she pointedly headed off in the direction of the hardware store. He also noticed that she kept glancing back over her shoulder to try to see where he was going. He waited until she finally went inside, her expression grimly determined, before moving swiftly up the block himself and going around the corner to a store he'd spotted earlier. He'd deliberately ignored it then, preparing for this moment and hoping that Angela wouldn't guess his destination.

It took him only a few awe-struck moments to make his selection and to arrange for a delivery to the ranch. At the mention of White Pines, the middle-aged clerk became even more accommodating.

"This is for Angie, then? I heard she was expecting a baby any minute."

The grapevine hadn't wasted a second, he noticed. "True enough."

"So," the woman said, "are you the proud daddy?"

Clint figured it wasn't any big secret, not at this point. "That's right."

"You're a lucky man. Angie was always a doll. I taught her English all through high school. I just moonlight here during the holidays. She had a real gift for understanding literature. I always thought she'd teach one day. I heard that's what she studied at college."

Since she seemed to have more facts than he did about Angie's educational history, Clint kept silent. The clerk handed him his receipt. "You have a real nice Christmas and tell Angie I said hello. Mrs. Grayson. She'll remember. Tell her I'd love to see her if she gets a minute while she's home."

"I'll be sure and tell her," Clint agreed. "Merry Christmas."

He made one more stop en route back to the car and tucked that gift in his pocket. He was leaning against the side of the pickup in nineteen minutes. He noticed there was no sign of Angie.

He finally spotted her lugging an ungainly bundle down the block. She could barely see around it.

"What on earth?" he asked, taking it from her and hoisting it into the bed of the truck. It wasn't as heavy as he'd expected, but it was the most oddly shaped package he'd ever seen. His curiosity stirred, despite his long-standing disinterest in gifts of any kind. Except for the gathering of relatives, holidays hadn't been a big deal at his house. Gifts had been practical, not sentimental or lavish. He'd never even seen, much less received anything that looked quite like this.

"Do I get a clue?" he asked, eyeing the giant red package with its huge green bow.

She grinned. "Do I?"

"I don't think so."

"Then neither do you."

"Just answer one question, then. Is it likely to explode?"

"Probably not," she said, her expression thoughtful. "Not if you drive very carefully."

"You know, angel, you're a real cutup."

"So they say."

He thought about passing along the message from her old high school teacher, then thought better of it. If he mentioned Mrs. Grayson, it was entirely possible that Angela would know where she moonlighted during the holidays. She might have been doing it for years. He would pass along the greetings tomorrow.

"Are you finished now?" Angela asked.

He glanced at the mound of packages tucked behind the seats of the truck. "I think so. I have something for your parents, all the aunts and uncles, the cousins and both housekeepers. That should do it, right?"

"Unless you're into pet toys, yes."

"Pets?"

"Dani has managed to foist off several kittens over the years. The main house is crawling with them, because Grandpa Harlan has always been a sucker for one of her sob stories. Uncle Jordan set a limit of two at home and he claims he's not happy about that, but I notice every time we're over there that one cat or another is always in his lap. Fortunately Dani's animal hospital also sells pet supplies and toys, so we buy them wholesale."

He shook his head. "Forgive me, but I think I'll skip presents for the cats."

"I'll forgive you," she said readily, then regarded him slyly. "Dani's a whole other story."

He sighed. "Where's the clinic?"

She grinned. "Just two streets down to the left. She'll be thrilled to see us."

"How many cats are we talking about?"

"Hard to say. The little devils multiply like rabbits."

"You'd think she'd do something about that. She is a vet, for goodness' sakes."

"She's also a soft touch. Every kid in town knows they can get a free kitten from her that's up-to-date on all its shots. She's the town's own personal animal shelter. There's no need for a pet store in Los Pinos."

Following Angela's directions, he pulled up in front of a small white house with dark green shutters. An old-fashioned white sign hung from a wrought-iron pole. A half-dozen cats lazed in patches of sunlight on the sloping front porch.

"The clinic entrance is on the side," Angela told him. "We can go in through the house and catch her in her office. Judging from the number of cars along here, half the pets in town have been overindulging in Christmas goodies. The waiting room will be a mess. Besides, family does have its privileges."

A harried-looking Dani barely waved at them as they slipped into the back of the clinic.

"Shopping for the cats," Angela called over the racket of barking dogs, howling cats and an occasional protesting screech from what sounded like a parrot or maybe a myna bird.

"A lot of pets get boarded here over the holidays," Angela told him. "I tried helping out once when I was in high school and Dani was still assisting Doc Inscoe during vacations from veterinary school. I couldn't stand it. Too much commotion. She's in heaven, though, and that's what matters. It was the only thing she ever wanted to do."

She led the way into what struck Clint as a pet store boutique. It was filled with elegant little sweaters for puppies, outrageously expensive leashes, dog houses that looked like mansions and a more varied assortment of toys than he'd ever imagined existed.

"Dani tends to indulge her animals. She thinks everyone else should, too. It's her little eccentricity, but we love her, anyway."

While he was still gaping in amazement, she zeroed in on several inexpensive little kitty treats hanging from an artificial tree like decorations. She gathered up a supply.

"I'll total up the cost at home and you can pay her when you see her," she said, dumping her selections into a bag and handing it to him.

"Are you sure this isn't a setup to get me arrested for shoplifting?" he inquired as they headed back through the house without so much as a parting wave for the clinic's owner.

"She won't even remember we've been here," Angela assured him. "Your money will come as a huge and welcome surprise."

Clint shrugged. "If you say so."

He added this package to all the others, then helped Angela into the truck. "Is this it? Anything else you want to do here in town?"

She shook her head.

Clint started the truck, then glanced over and caught the faraway expression on her face.

"What is it?"

"It just sank in. You and I are actually going to White Pines. Together."

There was something in her eyes and in her voice that told him not to make light of that. "That means even more to you than me showing up at your folks' place, doesn't it?"

She nodded. "I can't really explain it. Our ranch is home, but White Pines is..." Her voice trailed off.

"Is what?" he prodded.

"Something special," she said eventually. "Our history, I guess. Just wait. You'll see. Grandpa's ranch is like no place else on earth."

Given the fact that her own family's ranch was pretty spectacular, that was saying something. "Big?" he asked, trying to pin it down.

"Our place is bigger actually. Luke was trying to make a statement. It's not the house or even the land. It's a feeling that comes over all of us there, a sense of our own history maybe. Home is home," she said, clearly struggling to explain so he would understand. "White Pines is our heritage."

Heritage wasn't something that had meant much to Clint growing up. He'd hoped to change that with his own small ranch. He'd envisioned it as a legacy he could pass on, one that would flourish and grow with succeeding generations. It was clear that Harlan Adams and the generations preceding him had already endowed Angela and the others with that kind of meaningful legacy.

For one fleeting instant of doubt, he wondered if he would ever be able to offer her anything that would compare to it.

10

Clint and Angela's belated arrival at White Pines was greeted with amazement. Most of the family had already settled in and started helping Consuela and Maritza with the final preparations for tonight's family celebration and tomorrow's traditional open house but they all came out to help with the bundles that Clint had managed to amass in Los Pinos, exclaiming over the sheer number of them.

"I told you you were going overboard," Angela told him.

"What'd you do, son? Buy out the stores?" Grandpa Harlan asked with a grin.

He shot a look Angela's way, then said, "We tried, sir. Angela wore out too quickly."

"Very funny," she retorted. "Everything's wrapped. The presents can go straight under the tree."

"Except for the cat toys," Clint reminded her dryly.

"Oh, no, you didn't," her mother protested. "Tell me you did not make Clint buy gifts for all of your grandfather's cats."

"What can I say? He was feeling generous."

"And you took advantage," her mother chided, regarding Clint with sympathy. "Shame on you, Angela."

"Just doing my bit to keep Dani's business afloat," Angela insisted nobly. "She'd give away the store unless she's changed drastically."

Silence fell at what should have been no more than an innocuous comment. To Angela's confusion her mother rushed to change the subject.

Angela put her hand on her mother's arm to prevent her from leaving. She let the others lead Clint inside. As soon as they were out of earshot, she asked, "Mom, what's going on with Dani? I sensed something the other day, but Sharon Lynn hushed me up. Now everybody here gets all quiet when I so much as mention the possibility that she's changed."

"Sweetie, she's had a rough year, that's all," her mother said, looking decidedly uncomfortable. "I'm sure she'll tell you about it one of these days."

"Why don't you tell me and save her the trouble?" Angela suggested. "It might keep me from putting my foot in my mouth over and over again."

"It's her story to tell or keep to herself."

"Someone hurt her," Angela guessed. "Badly."

Her mother sighed. "Yes. Very badly. She lost three people she loved very much. Now let it go. Christmas is not the time for Dani to be thinking about the past. The best gifts you could give her are your love and support."

"And no questions," Angela surmised.

"Exactly."

She relented and kept the burgeoning questions to herself. She followed her mother inside. The rest of the family was gathered in the huge living room discussing the best place for the mound of gifts Clint had bought.

"We can't put them under the tree," Jenny protested. "It's not even decorated yet. We'll be stepping on them." Her dark eyes glinted with mischief. "I say we open them now."

"Nice try, you little sneak," Angela teased. "You always did want to open something on Christmas Eve. Next thing we knew you had half your presents open. It's time you learned to wait until morning like the rest of us. You're supposed to be grown-up, the oldest of all of us. It's about time you set an example."

"What's the fun of being grown-up at Christmas?" Jenny complained, poking at a particularly lumpy package with evident curiosity.

"You get to discover the joy of anticipation," Angela told her, then glanced at Clint. His steady gaze stirred its own brand of anticipation deep inside her. Aside from a couple of stolen kisses and a few fleeting, if very promising caresses, he'd barely touched her in too many months now. She knew all about the slow build of anticipation. Judging from the hunger she saw burning in his eyes, so did he.

She wondered idly if they could sneak in a kiss or two if she showed him the way to his room now. Her grandfather promptly put an end to that idea by suggesting a tour of the ranch before dark. Angela knew when it came to a competition between her and a herd of cows, it was a real toss-up which one would win. Clint reacted with predictable enthusiasm. Naturally Cody and Luke had to go along. Jordan stayed behind to make business calls.

"On Christmas Eve?" her grandfather grumbled. "What's wrong with you, boy? Don't you ever take a vacation?"

"When I do, it won't be to sightsee on a ranch I grew up on," Jordan retorted, grinning to soften the remark. "I'll whisk my beautiful wife off to a deserted beach in the Caribbean. You go chase after your cows. While I'm sitting in here by the fire, I promise I'll think of all of you out there freezing your butts off for no good reason."

After they'd gone and the women had retreated to the kitchen once again, Angela was left with her uncle. She wondered if Jordan would be any more forthcoming about Dani's troubles than her mother had been. Tales of his bemusement at becoming the adoptive father of a precocious five-year-old when he'd married Kelly were part of family legend. It was evident to anyone, though, that Jordan had taken to fatherhood and to Dani with the same kind of dedication that had built his oil empire.

"Uncle Jordan, can I ask you something before you make those calls?" Angela asked.

He glanced up distractedly from the pocket-sized computer that held the numbers of his important business contacts. "Sure, angel. What's up?"

"I'm worried about Dani. She hasn't seemed herself since I got back."

Normally the most tranquil of her relatives, Jordan suddenly looked mad enough to wring somebody's neck with his bare hands. "Leave it be," he said curtly.

"But—"

"Dammit, I said leave it alone," he thundered. "She's been through enough without dragging it all up again,

OK? The holidays are going to be especially bad as it is, thanks to that fool idiot she fell for."

His fury stunned her into momentary silence. "I'm sorry," she said quietly, beginning to get the picture, though far from all of it. "I didn't mean to upset you."

His expression softened. "No, I'm the one who's sorry. I shouldn't be taking it out on you. I know you're just concerned about her. Please, please, just don't ask her about it. Can you promise me that?"

"Of course," she said at once.

To herself, though, she vowed to get at the bottom of Dani's troubles. The two of them had always been especially close. Four when Angela was born, Dani had prided herself on helping to care for her messy baby cousin. As they had grown up, Dani had always been as eager as she to get into mischief.

"You two are just natural-born trouble," her grandfather had said on more than one occasion. He'd always said it with more pride than venom, though. Grandpa Harlan admired spunk, even when it made mincemeat of the discipline their parents favored. They knew to save their most daring enterprises for visits to White Pines.

"What happened, Dani?" she murmured as she climbed the stairs to the room she'd always used on visits to White Pines. "What or who hurt you so?" Every instinct told her this went way beyond a simple broken romance.

For the first time since his arrival in Texas in search of Angela, Clint felt his old confidence soaring. Ranching was something he knew and loved every bit as much as the men who were riding over White Pines land with him. Like them, he appreciated the beauty of the land. Like them, he understood the complexities and hardships of the business and the excitement of mastering the daily challenges.

"You have an impressive operation here," he told Harlan and Cody.

"It wasn't always that way," Harlan told him. "My ancestors hadn't run the ranch the way they should have. It took a lot of time and hard work and pure cussedness to make it what it is today."

"You should have seen us trying to drag Daddy into the computer age," Cody said. "He still thinks those new-fangled machines will be the downfall of us all." He grinned at his father. "Am I quoting you accurately?"

"Pretty much," Harlan said. "I still say you're in a hell of a fix when the electricity goes out and everything you need to know about your operation is lost in some danged machine."

"That's why we have back-up disks and battery-powered laptops," Cody responded.

"More money wasted that could have been spent on a new bull for the herd," Harlan insisted.

"See what I mean?" Cody said. "He'd be happy if we still did the books in an old ledger."

"Come up to my place," Clint suggested. "I'm lucky if my receipts ever get entered into a ledger. By the time I get back to the ranch house at the end of the day about all I can cope with is falling into bed. You'd be in heaven."

"He would," Luke agreed. "What about it, Daddy?

Want to go and rough it at Clint's? You can reminisce about the good old days."

Harlan scowled at his sons. "Now the two of you are trying to run me off my own place. That's the trouble with sons, Clint. Now daughters," he said with a sigh, "they're something else again. They give a man comfort in his old age."

Luke and Cody exchanged a look.

"He must have forgotten about Jenny stealing his pickup and crashing it into a tree," Cody said.

"And the time she ransacked the tool shed and splashed paint all over it," Luke added. "Then there was Lizzy's nosedive from the barn rafters. Broke her arm in two places."

"Selective memory," Cody agreed. "I hear it happens a lot in old folks."

"You think your sisters were trouble, maybe we should start dredging up the grief you all caused me," Harlan shot right back. "Let Clint weigh that and see whether he'd rather Angela delivered a girl or a boy."

Luke's expression softened at once. "Girls are a blessing," he admitted. "Angela could always light up a room. I'd come home at the end of an exhausting day and one smile on that little girl's face would cheer me right up."

"Indeed," Cody chimed in. "Sharon Lynn has been a joy compared to that brother of hers. Harlan Patrick must take after Daddy. He surely doesn't take after me."

"Who are you trying to kid?" Harlan demanded. "That boy is all your own worst sins come home to haunt you."

Clint chuckled at the nonstop and obviously affectionate banter. "Do you all ever let up on each other?"

"Never," Luke said.

"Why should we?" Cody asked. "Daddy acts as if we've made his life a torment, but there's another side to that story we could share with you."

"Never mind," Harlan said hurriedly. "We'd better be getting back and cleaned up before the women get dinner on the table. We'll never hear the end of it if we're late for Christmas Eve supper."

"Who cooked the turkey?" Cody asked worriedly. "Maritza or Janet?"

"I'm going to tell Janet you asked that," Harlan swore. "You'll be lucky if you get out of here in one piece."

"When was the last time you ate anything she cooked?" Cody retorted.

His father grinned. "Not since I married her, I guarantee you that. When we were courting, I had to be polite. Fortunately, most of the time she had the good sense to try to sneak food in from some restaurant and pretend she'd fixed it."

"Now who's telling tales?" Luke asked. "Isn't a husband duty bound to gloss over all his wife's flaws in public?"

"This isn't public, Luke," Harlan declared. "Clint's practically part of the family."

"Well, I still say we should be setting an example for him," Luke protested. "The first time he gives away any of my daughter's little idiosyncrasies, I can just about guarantee there will be fireworks."

"Your daughter has idiosyncrasies?" Cody asked,

feigning astonishment. "Since the day she was born, you've had us believing she was perfect."

"She is," Luke said quickly, then grinned. "For the most part." The grin quickly shifted to a scowl when he faced Clint. "That's something I can get away with saying, son. You can't. Just a word of caution."

"Believe me, that's advice I won't have any problem taking. I've seen your daughter's temper at close range." He gestured to a tiny slash over his lip. "Have the scars to prove it, too."

"She hit you?" Harlan asked incredulously.

"With a skillet," Clint claimed, though the truth was even more humiliating. He'd actually walked straight into the danged thing while she was waving it around as a threat. "It pretty well ended the last discussion we had before she tore off and disappeared on me."

"You must have riled her pretty good."

Clint realized he'd just waltzed himself straight into a dangerous trap. Maybe they suspected the fight had been over Angela's pregnancy, maybe they didn't. It wasn't a topic he particularly wanted to discuss with them.

"The same way you all rile your wives, I suspect... by disagreeing with them," he said.

The response drew the expected laughter and the potentially tense moment dissipated. They were still laughing when they walked inside.

Angela looked up from the pie crust she was filling with pumpkin and promptly caught Clint's eye. She looked worried. He walked over and brushed a kiss across her lips, plainly startling her.

"There's nothing to worry about, angel. We were just doing a little male bonding."

"That's what worries me," she responded.

"Shouldn't you be sitting down to do that?" he asked, deliberately changing the subject. He reached for a chair. "Sit."

"It's easier if I stand."

They scowled at each other in a stubborn test of wills. Clint finally shrugged. "Suit yourself. I'm going up to shower and change."

"Supper's in an hour," she called after him.

"Then you'd better get upstairs, too. I've never known you to take less than that to get ready."

"Uh-oh," Luke and Cody muttered in unison.

"I'm out of here," Harlan said, patting Clint on the back as he passed. "Good luck, son. If you figure a way out of this one, let me know."

Their wives vanished right along with them, leaving Clint with only Consuela and Maritza to run interference. The two housekeepers took one look at Angela's stormy expression and muttered something in Spanish that sounded dire. Then they, too, retreated.

"Take it back," Angela said, advancing on him with a spoon covered with pumpkin.

"You wouldn't want me to lie now, would you?" he taunted, edging around the table and trying to keep it between them. He figured he was safe enough. She wasn't half as quick as she'd been the time she'd caught him off guard with that skillet.

"Who spends twenty minutes just polishing his boots?" she demanded. "And another twenty in the shower?"

"Do the math, angel. That still puts me ahead of you."

"We haven't even gotten to the amount of time you spend shaving and admiring yourself in the bathroom mirror."

"Are you suggesting I should grow a beard to save time dressing?"

"No. What I am suggesting, Mr. Brady, is that you are a bald-faced liar."

"Takes one to know one."

She paused at that. The spoon, which she'd been waving threateningly, drooped to her side. From across the room he couldn't be sure, but he thought there might be tears in her eyes.

"Angel?"

"What?" she asked with a telltale sniff.

"Don't cry."

"I am not crying, even if that was another particularly low blow."

He circled the table to reach her, ready to take her in his arms and kiss away the tears. She whapped him on the butt with that damnable spoon. When she would have done it again, he wrenched it away from her and pulled her into an embrace that stilled her frantic movements.

Gazing down into her upturned face, he saw that he had been right about the tears, but there were also glints of laughter sparkling in her eyes now as well.

"Got you, didn't I?" she said with obvious pride.

"Only because you're sneaky. Truce?"

She sighed and slid her arms around his waist and rested her head against his chest. "Truce," she murmured.

Clint felt a rare and unexpected surge of contentment steal over him as he held her.

"Think we can keep the truce through New Year's?"

"I doubt it," she said honestly.

He grinned. "Me, too."

She sighed again. "Clint?"

"Yes."

"Do you think that means we should give up on any idea of a future together?"

"Just because we can't go ten minutes without arguing?"

"Yes."

"I don't see why, as long as we have sense enough to stop and listen to each other occasionally. Some relationships are just plain volatile. It keeps the adrenaline pumping."

"Are you saying we're excitement junkies?"

"I suppose." He regarded her curiously. "Do your parents argue?"

"All the time," she admitted.

"Have you ever doubted their love for each other?"

"Never."

"See there," he said. "Maybe they'll tell us how they make it work."

"Sex," Angela said without hesitation, then blushed. "I mean I don't know this for a fact or anything. It's not something we discussed. Haven't you noticed, though, that they're always touching, always stealing a kiss when they think no one's looking?"

"Like us," Clint pointed out.

"At least the way we used to be," she said thoughtfully.

"You can't steal a kiss from someone who's run off to another state, angel."

She met his gaze evenly. "Point taken. No more running," she promised. "I swear to you that I will stay right here and try to work things out."

"You're making a commitment?" he asked, surprised by the renewal of the vow she'd made before coming to White Pines.

"A commitment to try," she amended. "It's not going to be easy, you know. There's a mountain of distrust between us."

"Our baby deserves nothing less than our best efforts," he responded. "He deserves to know that we've done everything possible to give him a real family."

"Everything," she echoed.

Clint pressed a kiss against her forehead. Anything more and neither one of them would have been ready for dinner on time. Of course, time wasn't the only thing frustrating them at the moment. This baby of theirs was a built-in warning to cool down.

As they went upstairs hand in hand, he couldn't help wondering, though, whether Angela would remember her promise tomorrow when she saw one of the gifts he had bought for her. Maybe he ought to give it to her now, when she was in such an amenable mood. In his experience it was best to capitalize on moments like these to pin her down about anything. A day from now, even an hour from now, the winds might be blowing another way entirely.

_11_

Male bonding, indeed, Angela thought irritably. They'd probably been out there conspiring to get her married to Clint with the least amount of fuss. They'd probably been indulgently listing all of her idiosyncrasies and giving Clint advice on how to cope with them. Men! Especially Adams men!

She hurriedly took her shower and rushed to get dressed in a half hour, just to make the point that she could move quickly when the situation called for speed.

She thought back over the conversation they'd just had. The truce she and Clint had declared was just dandy. It would make the holidays peaceful.

But, she resolved, that didn't mean she wouldn't put him in his place occasionally. After all, the women in this family had to take a stand once in a while or be completely run over by their stubborn, willful and thoroughly unpredictable mates.

Goodness knows, she would never have guessed that both her father and her grandfather would take such an immediate shine to Clint, despite their natural protectiveness of her. They seemed to understand the man who'd tracked her down all the way from Montana. They talked the same language—ranching and testosterone. Clint was becoming one of the family before she could spit. On the one hand, she could see the benefits of that. On the other, it was darned annoying.

To her surprise, Clint seemed to be settling in quite nicely. He was showing no inclination to duck out and run home, no matter how she infuriated him. He seemed to have made up his mind to stick this out.

In fact, instead of being scared off, he seemed to be endlessly fascinated with everything about her and her family. And, if the truth be told, he also seemed every bit as intrigued by her swollen body as he had been on the day they'd met, back when she'd actually had a figure to brag about. For a woman who was feeling especially ungainly that alone would have been enough to endear the man to her.

She was also beginning to understand just how deeply she'd hurt him by taking off as she had. His anger over having missed so much of her pregnancy appeared genuine. Her heart just ached, thinking about all they could have shared if she hadn't denied them the chance by running away. Every time she turned around she saw fresh evidence of the kind of devoted father he would be, the kind of father any child would be blessed to have.

In fact, to her very deep regret, she was beginning to weaken. She was beginning to recall just why she'd fallen in love with the man in the first place. He was kind and gentle and amazingly patient. For the most part, anyway.

His touches made her sizzle from the inside out. And his kisses could have ignited a bonfire in a soaking rain.

But that didn't mean she would marry him…if that was what he was after with this truce. He hadn't actually said the words, not lately, not since that impulsive declaration he'd made when he'd first arrived. His entire focus seemed to be on the baby she was carrying.

In the dead of night, when she was feeling restless and uncomfortable, she couldn't shake the very real possibility that his child was all he really wanted, that when the baby came he'd fight her for custody. He'd hinted at that often enough. In fact, he'd virtually threatened her with the possibility.

Still, in the past couple of days, aside from an occasional verbal dig, they had pretty much managed to put all her lies behind them. The truce had sealed their pact to leave the past in the past. It was either a terrific start or the greatest lie of all, made to lull her into a false sense of complacency. Was it possible he meant only to win her trust, then abandon her, as she had him?

As she ran a brush quickly through her hair and dashed on a hurried dusting of makeup, she wondered if the risks of this truce didn't outweigh the benefits. Maybe it would be smart to start building a wall between them, one that would protect her when the inevitable time came for him to go, and the fighting started over their child.

She wasn't sure she would be able to bear that kind of ugly battle. She feared, too, that when the whole truth came out about how she'd deceived Clint, her family would desert her and support him. They were all honorable people and Clint was bound to have their sympathy on his side.

She was an Adams, though, she reminded herself sternly. That still counted for something. Even if every one of her relatives disapproved of what she'd done, they would back her in any kind of struggle for her child. She had no choice but to believe that they would fight to claim an Adams heir, no matter the circumstances of his conception.

She looked at her watch and grinned. Forty minutes precisely. She cast one last glance in the mirror and nodded approvingly. The dark green velvet maternity dress she wore was the perfect foil for her pale skin and auburn hair. The pendant Clint had given her rested between her breasts, drawing attention to their new lushness. She concluded she looked about as sensual and provocative as it was possible for an eight-and-a-half-months-pregnant blimp to look.

She also squared her jaw and stiffened her resolve. She would maintain Clint's truce, because she had promised, but she would keep her own defenses squarely in place.

"Remember that," she said sternly as she reached for the knob to open her door with fifteen minutes to spare.

Confident that she'd done the impossible in getting ready so quickly, she hurried downstairs and walked toward the living room.

To her chagrin, Clint was there before her, wearing a well-tailored suit and silk tie that had her gaping. He was a handsome man in denims and flannel. In a charcoal gray suit with his hair tamed, he was devastating. She couldn't help wondering if he'd brought that suit along because Christmas was coming or because he intended it to be his wedding suit. Her pulse fluttered wildly and her determination flew out the window. It either proved just how weak her resolve was or how extraordinarily potent he was.

His gaze locked with hers and she gravitated toward him across the room as if he were reeling her in with some invisible line.

"You look incredible," she admitted. "I've never seen you in a suit before."

"There's not a lot of call to wear one when I'm out with the cattle." His gaze swept over her appreciatively. "You've never put on such a fancy dress before, either. The color becomes you. You should wear it all the time."

It was the longest and prettiest compliment he'd ever paid her. Another brick thumped out of her recently erected and still-uncertain wall of defenses.

"Would you like something to drink?" he asked. "Harlan's brought in some nonalcoholic champagne just for you."

"I'd love a glass," she said, hoping it would take him a very long time to pour it. She could spend the time gathering her composure.

"It's a good sign when you can get a man to wait on you," Sharon Lynn teased, coming over to stand beside her. "It means he's totally, thoroughly smitten."

"Does Kyle Mason wait on you?" Angela asked, then regretted it when she saw the sad expression on her cousin's face.

"He doesn't even know I'm alive," Sharon Lynn confessed irritably, then sighed. "It's humiliating. I've tried flirting. I've tried making him double-rich shakes when he stops by the drugstore. I've even considered asking him out, but my pride balks at that."

Glad to have her own relationship sidelined as the topic of conversation, Angela asked, "Who is he? He didn't go to school with us, did he?"

"No. He's new to the area. He turned up about six months ago."

"And just how often does this Kyle Mason come into Dolan's?"

"Every day or so," Sharon Lynn said.

"And where's his ranch?"

"About thirty miles north of Los Pinos. He bought the old Carlson spread at Cripple Creek."

Angela grinned. "Doesn't that strike you as a long drive to take so frequently if the man hasn't noticed you? Unless, of course, he's addicted to milk shakes," she added.

Sharon Lynn paused, her expression thoughtful. "I never thought about that. Do you think that's possible?"

"Likely, in fact. Maybe he's just shy," Angela suggested. "And the Adams name might be intimidating to a newcomer around here. Could be you're going to have to take the initiative. Call him right now and invite him to the open house tomorrow."

"I couldn't," Sharon Lynn protested.

"Why not?"

"Last-minute invitations are so tacky."

"Not to someone who's been waiting and waiting for you to make a move."

"He probably has plans."

"Stop making excuses, Sharon Lynn," Angela

chided. "You won't know unless you call. At least it'll signal him that you're interested."

Her cousin's expression brightened. "I'm going to do it," she said, heading determinedly for the privacy of Grandpa Harlan's office.

"What was that all about?" Clint asked, reappearing with the champagne.

"You didn't listen in?"

"Of course not. It sounded like private girl talk."

Amused by his sudden burst of discretion, she said, "It was. I was just trying to shove my cousin off an emotional bridge."

"Uh-oh," he said uneasily. "Are you sure there's going to be somebody underneath to catch her?"

"Pretty sure."

"What if she gets the wrong answer and it ruins her holidays?"

She scowled at him. "Do you always have to look at the dark side of things?"

"Just being realistic."

Before Angela could worry herself into a tizzy over having inadvertently set Sharon Lynn up for a miserable holiday, her cousin dashed back into the room, her face aglow.

"He said yes," she practically shouted across the room. Oblivious to the curious glances from her parents and everyone else, she threw her arms around Angela. "Can you believe it? He said he would love to come. He didn't even hesitate."

"Obviously he'd been hoping for this."

"I was so sure he would have other plans. I know of

at least three women in town who have been pursuing him like crazy."

"Other than you?" Angela teased.

"I have not been pursuing him," Sharon Lynn protested. "I have been very demure."

The thought of the exuberant Sharon Lynn as demure was enough to bring a smile, but Angela managed to keep a straight face. "Well, it looks as if that tactic has paid off, then," she said.

"Thank you for prodding me into doing something, anything, to get this relationship off dead center."

"Speaking of dead center," Clint interjected, his hand on Angela's shoulder. "Could I speak to you for a minute privately, before we go into dinner?"

She stared into his serious eyes and gulped. Either he was going to lecture her on interfering in Sharon Lynn's life or he had something much more personal in mind. She was well aware of the gaps already created in her defenses after no more than a few minutes in his company. A little time alone and she might as well kiss her resolve goodbye.

"Can't it wait?"

"Not really."

She heaved a sigh and gestured toward her grandfather's office. "Let's go in there. We'll be able to hear when the others start into the dining room."

With Sharon Lynn's fascinated gaze following them, they slipped away. Clint closed the office door firmly behind them. The soft click of the lock sent goose bumps dancing up her spine.

Vaguely alarmed, her gaze flew to his face. "What on earth was that for?"

"I don't want to be disturbed. There's only one way I can think of around here to manage that."

She instinctively backed up a step. "You're making this sound awfully serious."

"It is."

She saw him reach into his pocket, but even then his intentions didn't register. Not until he withdrew a small square package wrapped in gold did she begin to get an idea of what was on his mind. If he'd been determined to hit on a surefire way to destroy her resistance, this was it.

Angela swallowed hard and eyed that package as warily as if it were a rattler. "Shouldn't we wait until morning for presents?" she asked without much hope of him taking the suggestion. Obviously he'd planned the timing of this moment very carefully.

"Not this one," he insisted, holding it out in the palm of his hand. He grinned at her. "Take it, angel. It won't bite."

She plucked it out of his hand as gingerly as if it might explode. She fingered the curling gold ribbon, but made no move to untie it.

"Come on," he urged. "Open it."

She lifted her gaze to his. "I'm afraid to," she admitted candidly.

He regarded her with obvious astonishment. "Why?"

"I don't think I can explain it."

"Try."

"If…" She drew in a deep breath, then tried again. "If it's what I think it is, it will change things."

"Forever," he agreed.

She sighed and closed her eyes. "That's what I was

afraid of. Clint, we just declared a truce. It's too soon to ask for anything more."

He regarded her with amusement. "It's not as if we just met, angel. This day has been a long time coming. Too long, some would say, including you, I thought."

If only he had done this back in Montana, she thought, then chided herself for being unreasonable. She hadn't given him a chance to. That didn't change the fact that it felt all wrong now.

"I know what you're trying to do," she began.

"Oh, really?" he said wryly. "What am I trying to do?"

"Make things right. Be responsible."

"And that's so terrible?"

"Clint, the timing is all off."

"What the hell is that supposed to mean?" he demanded, amusement giving way to exasperation.

She struggled for an explanation, but none came to her, none that would make sense to him anyway. "I can't explain. I'm sorry." She held out her hand, the unopened present still resting in her palm.

After an endless hesitation, he reached for the package, his disappointment plain. "Maybe you're right," he said halfheartedly. "I just thought…"

"I know what you wanted to do," she said. "And it was a lovely gesture, something I'll remember every single Christmas Eve as long as I live." She smiled, a little too brightly, probably. "I'm sure you can get your money back. The stores in Los Pinos have very lenient return policies."

That familiar headstrong look was back in his eyes. "I'm not taking it back to the store, angel. Just so you

know, I'm going to do everything in my power to see
that you accept it sooner or later."

She shuddered at the grim determination in his voice.
If only he'd sounded like a man in love, instead of a man
on a mission, she thought wistfully. Then it might have
been almost impossible for her to say no.

Clint was disappointed, but not broken by Angela's
refusal to so much as look inside that box, much less
accept the proposal he'd been planning all day. Maybe
it had been premature. It was just that he was so blasted
anxious to get things settled once and for all. He wasn't
used to being so out of control, to having anyone tie
him in knots the way she did. He'd hoped to seize control back again.

Which, of course, was exactly the problem. They
both wanted to set the ground rules and determine the
pace of this relationship. What neither of them seemed
willing to admit was that a third person was really in
charge, that baby of theirs. If Clint had to hog-tie Angela and drag her in front of a minister, they were going
to be man and wife when that baby was born.

As soon as he and Angela had rejoined the others, he
realized that he'd made a mistake in asking for that moment alone with her. He should have caught up with her
upstairs or waited. Now he'd raised expectations that the
two of them would be making an announcement over
dinner. He could see the anticipation in Harlan's eyes
and the anxiety in Luke's and Jessie's. Jessie's gaze kept
drifting to Angela's left hand as if she were expecting
to see an engagement ring there.

"Dinner is ready," Maritza announced, saving him and Angela from the speculative glances.

"Luke, why don't you escort your daughter in tonight?" Harlan suggested. "Clint, you take Jessie."

Clint met Jessie's eyes and caught the spark of amusement.

"He wants to give me time to cross-examine you," Jessie said. "Subtlety is not Harlan's strong suit."

"You can always ask me anything. I'm an up-front kind of man. It saves wear and tear on the emotions."

"OK, then. Did you ask Angela to marry you tonight?"

"I did," he confirmed. "She said no."

Jessie sighed. "I thought as much. I just don't understand that daughter of mine. I can see perfectly plainly that she is crazy in love with you. She's just being stubborn, like a typical Adams. She got a double dose of it, too, with Erik's genes and Luke's influence."

"Being an Adams can't be all bad," Clint teased. "You signed on for it twice."

"True," she admitted with a rueful grin. "I suppose I'm every bit as stubborn as they are. I hung in there with Luke when he flatly refused to admit how he felt about me. I hope you'll do the same with Angela."

"I don't have a choice. She's carrying my child."

Jessie studied him worriedly. "Is that what you've been telling her?"

"More or less. Why?"

"Well, no wonder she turned you down," she said, regarding him with dismay.

"I want that baby of mine to have my name."

Apparently he'd raised his voice, because several of the others glanced their way.

"My father left us the day I was born," he said more quietly, but just as fiercely. "I grew up thinking it was my fault he was gone. I will not allow that to happen to a child of mine."

Jessie rested her hand on his. "I know you mean well. I can see that you're desperate to do right by your baby, but what about Angela? How do you feel about her?"

As he was about to respond, she silenced him with a touch of her finger against his lips. "Don't tell me. Tell her."

The message was plain as day and Clint wondered how he could have been so blind to the obvious up until now. Of course Angela wanted to know how he felt about her. The only trouble was, he wasn't sure of that himself.

Her betrayal loomed between them and no matter how hard he tried, he couldn't seem to get beyond it. He was still attracted to her. He still wanted her. He understood the importance of forgiveness, but he wondered if he was capable of it.

He was quiet through most of dinner, wrestling with his conscience and his heart. He could have been eating sawdust for all the attention he paid the meal.

Beside him, Angela was just as quiet. She spoke only when she was asked a direct question, and the others, sensing that she was in turmoil, asked her very little.

Fortunately, the Adamses were a boisterous crowd. They more than made up for the silence of two of the guests. Only when the time came to decorate the tree did they insist on sweeping Clint and Angela into the midst of the activity.

"I'm a little tired," Angela protested. "I'll just sit here and supervise."

"Not a chance," Justin said, hauling her to her feet. "You're the only one who likes as many lights as I do. The others would stop after a couple of wimpy strands."

Clint observed in amusement as Angela and Justin wrapped at least eight strands of brightly colored lights around the tree. Watching them reminded him of her excitement just one year ago when he'd managed to find all those lights for their first tree together.

"Plug it in," Angela commanded now. When the lights blinked on, her eyes lit up. "It's beautiful."

"It's blinding," Sharon Lynn declared. "We won't even be able to see to put the rest of the ornaments on."

Angela rolled her eyes. "OK, OK. Turn 'em off, Justin. Let's finish decorating before we have the final lighting ceremony."

Tall and awkward, with the stretched-out lankiness of adolescence, Jordan's son practically upended the tree as he reached for the plug.

As Clint grabbed the tree and righted it, his gaze caught Angela's. Suddenly they were connected as surely as if they'd hopped aboard a time travel machine and zoomed back twelve months. He could see the memory in her eyes. Her expression softened, her complexion glowed and her lips curved into the faintest suggestion of a smile. He remembered it all as if it were yesterday.

"Let them finish," he suggested softly, holding out

his hand. "Before one of them tangles a strand of garland around your neck and chokes you."

"Hey," Justin protested. "We're not that clumsy."

"Couldn't prove it by me," Harlan Patrick taunted. "Who dropped one entire box of ornaments when we were carrying them down from the attic?"

Justin shot back a rude remark.

"Maybe I'd better sit down," Angela said, taking Clint's outstretched hand.

Though there were plenty of chairs in the room, Clint led her to a love seat so he could sit beside her. As carols played on the stereo and the cousins bickered and laughed, he felt a longed-for contentment steal over him again. When he turned Angela and settled her back against his chest, she didn't protest. Instead, to his relief, she sighed happily.

"Glad to be home?" he asked quietly.

She nodded. "But I miss Montana, too."

"You do?" Clint asked, surprised by the admission.

"Just the two of us. It was magical." She gazed up at him, her expression wistful. "I thought we were starting our own traditions."

"I thought so, too."

"Who would have thought so much would happen to change everything?"

"It doesn't have to," he said. "We can have that again, if we want it badly enough. Do you?"

Before she could answer, they were surrounded by cousins.

"Come on, Angie. You have to put the angel on top of the tree. It's tradition," Harlan Patrick said.

She gazed at Clint, her expression clearly torn.

"Go," he told her. "Traditions are meant to be carried on."

He sat back and watched as the others handed her the gold and white angel for the top of the tree. She handled the obviously expensive, obviously old angel with such tenderness that it brought an unexpected sting to Clint's eyes. There had been no such traditions in his family, no such sentiment. His mother had tried, but there were often too many divisions and old hurts to make the holidays anything but stressful. He'd stopped going home after a while.

He watched nervously as Justin helped Angela up the small ladder at the side of the huge tree, then steadied her as she reached for the top branch. She settled the angel firmly in place, then stepped down.

Someone with a magician's sense of timing turned on the tree lights at precisely the same moment as someone else doused the other lights in the room. There were audible gasps of delight, then applause.

"The best tree ever," Harlan declared.

"You say that every year, Grandpa," Justin teased.

"And every year it is the best," his grandfather retorted. "This year's best of all because the angel's back on top."

Angela stared at her grandfather. "I don't understand."

"He wouldn't let us put it on while you were gone," Sharon Lynn explained. "He said it was your job."

"I begged and begged," Lizzy complained, "but Daddy said we'd just have to wait till you came home again to see the angel back on the tree."

"Oh, Grandpa," Angela said, throwing her arms around his neck.

"Now, don't go getting all weepy on me, girl. You'll mess up my suit before church," he protested, looking pleased just the same.

Clint fingered the ring box that was still in his pocket and tried not to feel an overwhelming sense of defeat. How could he compete with this much love, with this family?

He realized then that Angela's gaze had sought out his. Their eyes met and lingered. His heart thundered in his chest at the desire and longing he thought he saw in her face. For just that instant, anyway, it seemed that no one else in the room mattered.

Possibilities stirred to life again inside him. Confidence soared. He found himself smiling. After all, this was the season of miracles, wasn't it? She'd said that herself not so long ago. Maybe one really was possible for the two of them.

12

Angela hadn't been inside a church since she'd left home. It wasn't that she'd lost her faith; maybe it was just one more act of rebellion. At any rate, when she walked back into the small, candlelit church she'd attended for most of her life, she felt a sense of peace stealing over her. Subconsciously she reached for Clint's hand. The warmth of his grasp was even more reassuring.

Throughout the familiar Christmas Eve service, she was all too aware of the man beside her, his deep voice blending with hers as they sang the joyous hymns: "Silent Night," "The First Noel," "Joy to the World." Each one brought back memories of past holiday seasons; each one stirred thoughts of one particular Christmas in Montana.

Ever since that moment when their gazes had locked back at White Pines, she had felt as if she and Clint were caught up in a spell. It was as if some unseen hand were drawing them closer and closer, insisting that they search their hearts for answers to the dilemma they faced.

She wanted to love him again, as freely as she had in Montana, without so many complications.

But life was filled with unexpected and unalterable twists and turns. Coping with them, in the end, would make them and their love stronger. She couldn't go back to being Hattie Jones, no matter how desperately she wanted to recapture that carefree time in her life. She was about to become a mother, with all the responsibilities—and joys—that entailed.

It would be so much easier to share the demands with someone, she thought wistfully, so much more meaningful to share the joys.

She stole a glance at the man beside her. Every line in his face, every expression on his lips was as dear and familiar to her as if they'd spent a lifetime together, rather than a few short months. Here was someone who wanted to take on that duty, who was eager to be a father to his son or daughter. On that score at least, she had come to trust Clint without reservation over the past few days. He loved the baby she was carrying as deeply as she did.

Tell me what to do, she prayed. *Please show me the path to take.*

There were no blinding messages in response, no signals in the night sky as they made their way home again. Maybe, as she had accused Clint of doing earlier, she was rushing things, trying to force a resolution when the only real answers would come with time. Patience, never one of her virtues, was absolutely necessary with so much on the line.

At home, when everyone else climbed up the steps to their rooms, Clint lingered at the foot of the stairs, his steady gaze on her.

"Sit with me awhile," he suggested. "By the tree."

As tired as she was, she was unable to resist the appeal of the invitation, the draw of the man uttering it.

The lights were still on, blinking reds and greens, blues and golds, a magnificent display of shimmering Technicolor. Leaning back in his arms, she half closed her eyes to soften the effect into something reminiscent of an Impressionist painting.

"What is it about a Christmas tree that makes us feel as if we've been touched by magic?" she asked.

She could tell from his thoughtful expression that he took the question seriously, and she loved him for that. Some men would have laughed it off as romanticized nonsense. Clint had always taken her most whimsical statements seriously, though. He was also capable of wicked wit or off-the-cuff philosophy. Their conversations had never been boring.

"It takes us back to childhood, maybe," he said. "Back to a time when we were truly innocent and filled with anticipation."

"Back to a time when we were greedy little brats, you mean."

He laughed. "I was trying for a positive spin."

"Do you ever think about what our baby will be like?"

He seemed startled by the shift in topic. "You mean boy or girl?"

"No, I mean the kind of person he or she will grow

up to be. Does it scare you, thinking about what the world is like and how to protect him?"

"Or her," he reminded her. "Now, having a girl scares me more than a boy. I figure I won't want any daughter of mine to date until she's ninety for fear she'll run across a man like me."

"What's wrong with you?"

"You, of all people, have to ask?"

"You're strong. You're decent. You're intelligent. Any woman would be lucky to have you," she declared with feeling, then recognized the irony.

"May I remind you that a very short time ago you turned down my proposal before I could even get it out of my mouth," he said, obviously aware of the irony, too. "I'd rehearsed the darned thing, too."

"Want to say it now?" The suggestion was made only half in jest. A part of her wanted a chance to say yes, even if common sense told her to stay silent.

He studied her intently, then shook his head. "Not right this second, angel. I can't take being humiliated twice in one night."

"I'm sorry."

"Don't be sorry. I was being impulsive. You were trying to use good sense. Marriage isn't something to jump into for the wrong reasons."

He rested his hand on her belly, and Angela felt her pulse skitter crazily. His expression turned awestruck as the baby shifted inside her. When he lifted his gaze to hers, she was almost certain she detected the sheen of unshed tears.

"Though this is a pretty darned good reason for getting married, if you ask me," he said quietly.

It was, Angela agreed to herself. But it wasn't the one she desperately wanted to hear. She could have told him that, probably should have, but she didn't. She wanted him to recognize their love on his own, to admit to it without any prodding from her…if he could.

"I think I'll go up to bed now," she said instead. She stood up, then bent down to drop a kiss against his cheek. "Good night, Clint. Merry Christmas."

He captured her face between his hands and kissed her back, slowly, persuasively until her knees were so weak she could barely stand. If he'd meant to make a point, if he'd meant to remind her that the passion between them burned hot even now, then he had.

"Merry Christmas, angel," he murmured. "See you in the morning."

With her blood pumping fast and furiously through her veins, she regretted the decision to leave, but pride wouldn't let her turn back. That was the trouble with the two of them, she concluded. They both had pride to spare, but no one with whom to spend the night.

Christmas morning dawned cold and bright. Sun glistened on a fresh covering of snow that had fallen after they'd gotten home from church the night before. Clint had caught a glimpse of it when he'd finally gone up to his room.

He'd stood by the window for an eternity, staring out at the stark, rugged terrain of White Pines softened by its blanket of white. Oddly enough, he'd felt no envy. His own ranch might be smaller, less ostentatious, but he owned every acre of it free and clear. He could take pride in the work he had done to make it a thriving cattle operation, one that would grow over time.

Was it enough to offer a child, though? Especially a child who could have at least some small stake in all this someday? He didn't like the doubts that kept creeping in when he least expected them. He didn't want to think about going home without his son or daughter.

He didn't want to think about going without Angela.

It was strange. He had come to Texas in search of Hattie—or more precisely, the child he'd fathered—but he'd found a different woman entirely. Not just in name, but in demeanor and more. To be sure, her body had changed with the child she carried, but it ran deeper than that. Hattie had been flirtatious and loving and generous, but he'd never seen the strength in her that he saw in Angela. She was prepared to face the uncertain future on her own, if she had to, without him.

His own feelings had changed over the past few days, as well. He'd come after a child. His child. He'd stayed, at least in part, because of a woman. She intrigued him in ways that Hattie never had.

Only one thing had stayed the same; the hunger she could build in him with just a glance. The skim of her fingers across his flesh, the touch of her lips, and he was achingly hard and hot as a branding iron.

Those thoughts of permanence and forever were coming more and more frequently, buoyed by the notion that the foundation was more solid. His attraction to her had deepened into something that could last through time. And this time, he thought, they had the truth on their side. They had a fresh chance to get it right.

He thought about what Jessie had told him earlier

about a woman needing to know that a man wanted her for herself and not for the baby she carried. Maybe it was time he admitted that, put his heart on the line. Not doing so up until now had been a coward's act. When Angela had turned his proposal down she'd refused an offer only slightly better than a business proposition. If he told her he cared, if he confessed to loving her, it would be him she was rejecting. Little had ever frightened him before, but that did.

He'd had a lot of months to toughen his pride. He'd had that final scene between them to play over and over again. He'd had the night she'd given him the slip in Montana to reinforce all of his fears that the woman he was chasing didn't want him. Just as his father hadn't. Old insecurities that had festered for years came back to haunt him.

He had no proof, none at all, that her feelings toward him had changed. Not really. Oh, she had returned his kisses with a matching ardor. She had sent glances his way that could steam up a mirror two rooms away. That should have been reassurance enough.

But Angela was unpredictable in ways that Hattie hadn't been. Telling her how he felt still seemed risky. The knowledge she would have after such an admission would give her a certain kind of power over him, and he didn't like giving anyone around him an edge they could turn against him.

He'd wrestled with the dilemma most of the night. By dawn the answers were no clearer than they had been.

He could sense that others were stirring. He'd checked with Consuela the night before, and she'd assured him that his gift for Angela had arrived and been safely hidden. It would be under the tree by this morning. Just thinking of it made him smile.

He rushed through his shower, dressed in another suit and struggled with another damnable tie. He'd be glad when the holidays ended and he could go back to wearing comfortable denims and flannel shirts again. He'd noticed that the other men had been complaining good-naturedly about their own fancy clothes the night before. Except for Jordan. He was a man who looked as if he'd been born to wear pinstripes. He was as relaxed in Armani as the rest of them were in their Levi's and Wranglers.

He thought of that soft, green velvet dress that Angela had worn the night before. It had taken every bit of his strength to keep from caressing the fabric and the woman wearing it. He supposed wearing a fancy suit once in a while was a small price to pay to see the women gussied up in velvet and silk and diamonds. Seeing the pendant he had given her nestled between her breasts had made him smile.

Pausing outside Angela's door now, he listened for sounds of her stirring, but heard nothing. He realized why, when he got downstairs. She was in the living room with her grandfather, Justin and young Harlan. They were all dressed up and staring avidly at the mound of packages under the tree.

"Merry Christmas, everyone," Clint said, not even trying to hide his amusement.

"Merry Christmas, son," Harlan said. He eyed Clint hopefully. "Did you hear anyone else stirring up there?"

"Not really. I just heard you all coming downstairs."

Four faces reflected obvious disappointment. Clint

noticed that Angela's gaze was fixed on the huge, wrapped package tucked back in one corner. From its size, Clint guessed it had to be the one he'd bought for her. He picked out the huge, lumpy present she'd chosen for him, then returned his gaze to her.

"Curious, angel?" he inquired, taking a seat beside her.

"It's Christmas morning. Of course I'm curious."

"We could open just one package each," Harlan suggested. "Wouldn't be anything wrong with that, would there?"

"Grandpa, you know the others would kill us," Justin said. "The rule is we wait until everybody's up."

Harlan grinned. "Then the two of you go upstairs and raise a ruckus. Let's see if we can't get this show on the road."

When the two young men had raced off, Angela regarded him sternly. "Grandpa, you're worse than they are."

"There's nothing like the spirit of giving to perk up a man's day. I'm old. I have the right to indulge my kinfolk."

"Who are you trying to kid?" she teased. "You want to see what everyone got for you."

"Watch it, girl, or that present with your name on it just might vanish before we get to the unwrapping."

"He always threatens us like this," Angela told Clint. "The man threatened to take back my teddy bear one year."

"You told me the one you had at home was bigger. I figured you didn't need two. Also thought you needed to learn something about gratitude. You learned your lesson, didn't you?"

She grinned at him. "Yes, Grandpa," she said dutifully. "I think I'll go tell Consuela and Maritza we want to eat breakfast before we open packages. I'll suggest a nice, long, leisurely breakfast, pancakes, waffles, the works."

"Oh, no, you don't," he said, catching her hand when she would have sashayed past him. He turned his gaze on Clint. "Take her for a walk, will you? Keep her out of mischief until the others come down."

Clint glanced outside worriedly. "I don't know, sir. It looks awfully cold and slippery out there. There's more snow coming down, too."

"Traitor," Harlan taunted. "I guess I'll go up and see if my wife is awake."

"Let her sleep if she's not," Angela said. "Yesterday was a long day. Today will be, too."

"Then she can catch up on her beauty sleep tonight, not on Christmas morning."

When he'd gone, Angela shook her head. "He always was the first one up on Christmas morning. He said he loved seeing our faces when we sneaked down the stairs to see if Santa had come."

"Who was second?" Clint asked.

"Me," she admitted. "Jenny always tried to act blasé and Dani was a sleepyhead. I didn't get any real competition until Sharon Lynn was big enough to get down the stairs by herself."

"Which just shows that some things never change," the woman in question said, yawning as she joined them. "Has anyone made coffee yet?"

"There's a pot on the buffet in the dining room," Angela said.

"I'll get it," Clint offered. "I could use a cup myself. Angel, what about you? Is there decaf?"

"I already have my herbal tea," she told him, lifting the mug to demonstrate.

He left the two of them poking at packages. They were still at it when he returned with the coffee and a huge tray of freshly baked sweet rolls Consuela had told him were meant to tide them over until after the presents had been opened.

One by one the others straggled down the stairs, as Angela and Sharon Lynn waited impatiently. Harlan was grumbling when he returned, decrying Janet's determination to shower and dress before joining them.

"I've given that woman enough fancy robes to stock a lingerie shop. Couldn't she have worn one of them?" he complained.

"Maybe she figured that once this day gets rolling, she wouldn't have another chance. No woman owns a robe that's fancy enough for greeting guests. What time are people expected for the open house?" Angela asked.

"Noon, same as always."

"How many?" Clint asked.

"Not too many this year," Harlan said. "A hundred or so."

The whole town of Rocky Ridge wasn't much bigger than that, Clint thought. Yet Harlan was more nonchalant about entertaining for such a crowd than Clint would have been at fixing dinner for four. Of course, with Consuela and Maritza on the job, he probably had very little to do except stay out of the way.

It was twenty minutes before Janet came downstairs. A cheer went up.

"Finally," Harlan said, feigning exasperation. There was too much love shining in his eyes for the comment to have much bite to it. She settled on the carpet at his feet and rested her head against his thighs. His weathered hand settled gently on her head. There was no mistaking how they felt about each other, Clint thought, envying them.

Lizzy deemed herself Santa and parceled out packages with enthusiasm. For all of the insistence on waiting until everyone was downstairs, there was no organized system to the opening. Everyone shredded paper as fast as they could. Shouts were exchanged. Thanks were hollered back and forth. The excitement in the room was palpable.

Clint was startled when the first gift was pressed into his hands, stunned when several more were added. He was relieved that he'd insisted on shopping for everyone, including the cats who were getting tangled up in the scattering of ribbons as they chased wads of wrapping paper.

He saved Angela's present to him for last, then laughed aloud when he saw the huge teddy bear she'd chosen. "For me?" he inquired. "Or the baby?"

"It had your name on the tag, didn't it?" she responded, then grinned. "But I know you're the sort of man who'd want to share with his baby."

"We'll see," he said, settling the bear beside him in the crook of his arm. "I kind of like this guy. He snuggles up and doesn't talk back."

"Watch it," she warned, laughing.

Whether it was the gift's placement in the corner or Lizzy's unerring sense of the dramatic, Clint's present for Angela was the last one delivered. It took help from Justin to drag it across the room.

Angela stared from the huge box to Clint and back again. "What on earth?"

"You won't know until you open it," he teased.

She studied the package intently. "You didn't bring this home yesterday."

"Nope," he said complacently, amused by her perplexed expression.

"How'd it get here?"

"I had it delivered."

"From where?"

"Darlin', just open the thing."

"Yes," Harlan said. "Hurry up. We're all waiting to see what's inside."

Encouraged by everyone, she began enthusiastically tearing away the wrappings. As he'd instructed, though, the box was plain. It revealed absolutely nothing about the contents.

"Want some help?" he asked, moving to her side and taking his knife from his pocket. He opened it and cut through the tape that sealed the flaps, then sat back and waited for her reaction. The entire room had fallen silent, and all eyes were on Angela as she peered inside.

She lifted out sheets of recycled packing paper, one after another. Clint watched her face intently and knew the precise instant when she saw the gift.

"Oh, Clint," she whispered, eyes shining. "It's beautiful."

"What is it?" Harlan demanded, trying to peer over her shoulder. "Let me help."

He lifted out an exquisite hand-carved cradle and set it gently beside Angela. Made of cherry wood, it was intricately detailed and polished to a warm shine. A puff of yellow bedding with teddy bears lined it. Clint imagined that giant teddy bear Angela had given him standing watch over the cradle and his child. It was as if they'd been on the same wavelength in some way.

"Son, that's a mighty fine gift," Harlan said, clapping Clint on the back. "Mighty fine."

Just then Angela gasped and clutched her stomach.

"Baby?" Harlan asked, regarding her worriedly. "Are you OK?"

"Honey, what is it?" Jessie said, rushing over.

Clint hunkered down beside her. "Angel, what's going on?"

He didn't like the way she looked one bit. Her complexion was pale, her eyes stricken as she met his gaze.

"I could be wrong," she said, "but I have a feeling that cradle arrived in the nick of time."

Clint stared at her, his heart slamming against his ribs. "What are you saying?"

"Unless I'm very much mistaken, I am about to have a baby."

13

If she hadn't been quite so panicky, Angela might have been amused by the stunned reactions to her announcement. Clint went absolutely white. Her father and grandfather, normally the most unflappable men she knew, started barking orders, most of them contradictory.

Her normally calm mother finally shouted over the commotion. "Enough!"

Angela grinned as everyone fell silent and stared at her mother. No one in the room knew any better than Jessie about the unexpected arrival of a baby. She hunkered down beside Angela and smiled reassuringly.

"You OK?"

"Just surprised."

"It could be false labor," Kelly offered helpfully.

The suggestion was echoed by Janet and Melissa.

"Clint, why don't you get her a glass of chipped ice?" her mother suggested.

Visibly grateful at being given an assignment he could cope with, Clint practically raced from the room. He came back with a glass of chipped ice and two excited housekeepers. Maritza and Consuela arrived chattering in Spanish, aprons flapping and hands waving.

"Harlan, how are the roads?" her mother asked. "Can we get her to the hospital?"

"I'll check," he said promptly. "If not, I'll call the snowplow driver and have him clear the way ahead of us. I pay enough taxes to get a few special privileges."

Just then another pain ripped through Angela. She latched on to Clint's hand and cursed a blue streak. He stared at her in shock.

"Oh, don't look at me like that," she grumbled when she had caught her breath. "I swore I wasn't going to do this."

"Do what?" he asked.

"Have this baby close to Christmas, much less on Christmas Day. Good grief, we'll be celebrating everything at once. My birthday, Christmas, everything."

"You should have thought about that before you got pregnant when you did," her mother said dryly.

"I should have thought about a lot of things before I got pregnant," Angela said, then cried out with another pain.

"How close?" she asked, panting. "Damn, I knew I shouldn't have ignored that backache during the night."

"Three minutes," her mother replied. "Harlan, forget the hospital. She'll never make it. Let's get her into one of the bedrooms. Dani, you come, too."

"Me? Why me?" Dani asked, turning pale. She looked as if she wanted to flee.

"Just come, please," Jessie said.

When Clint had carried Angela upstairs and settled her into bed, her mother turned to the obviously wary Dani. "Honey, you've got the most experience delivering babies of anyone in this room."

Angela wasn't sure whose wail was louder, her own or her cousin's.

The last bit of color washed out of Dani's face. "Me? I've delivered litters of kittens. I've delivered puppies. I've even delivered baby bunnies. Under duress, I've even managed to help out with foals and calves, but I have never delivered a child," she protested. "I really, really don't think this is the time to start."

"I agree," Angela said emphatically. In fact, the very idea horrified her. It was ludicrous, insane, totally out of the question. Fortunately, Dani seemed just as appalled as she was. Surely her well-educated, professional cousin could make them see reason.

Sweat beaded on Angela's brow as her body was wracked with another labor pain. Panicked, she clutched Clint's hand and demanded, "Get me to a hospital, damn you. I am not having this baby with the help of a veterinarian, even if she is the smartest, nicest cousin on earth. The baby will wait, if I have to hold it in with both hands."

"I don't know," Clint said worriedly. "He seems a little impatient to me. The roads are an icy mess. Snow's still coming down. You heard what your mother said. Maybe we'd better play it safe."

Angie panted, trying to ease another pain. As soon as she had breath to spare she glared at him and at her cousin. "I want a real hospital and a real doctor. No offense, Dani."

"None taken. Nothing would please me more than to accommodate you and turn you over to a real doctor," Dani said fervently. "Maybe Grandpa can get his helicopter pilot to swoop in and take you."

"Not in this storm," Clint insisted. He squeezed Angie's hand. "Darlin', we have to be sensible."

"You should have thought of that nine months ago," she declared. "That was the time for straight thinking and protection."

Clint grinned. "Angel, that particular horse is already out of the barn. Let's deal with the crisis at hand, OK?"

"Maybe we should just get my father in here. He has more experience at delivering babies than any of you do. He brought me into this world."

"I'm not sure how much help he would be," her mother retorted. "The last time I saw him, he was sitting in a chair with his head in his hands muttering something about history repeating itself."

She gazed up and found Clint hovering a few feet away from the bed. He looked so worried and ill at ease that she would have shipped him off to join the others if she'd had the heart. Instead, she figured what he really needed was something to do.

Resigned to making the best of a lousy situation, she called out to him. "Clint?"

He was by her side in an instant. "What? Are you OK? What can I do?"

"Help me breathe," she said, thankful that she'd at least had the sense to take the Lamaze classes in Seattle before she'd left. Of course, the coach she'd planned on having was still in Seattle, too, but hopefully Clint would be a quick study.

"Here's the deal," she said, and explained what she needed him to do. The explanation took a long time because she kept having to stop for the increasingly severe pains.

After a particularly bad contraction, Clint said, "That's *it*. No more babies. I don't ever want to have to go through this again."

"You?" all three women protested in a chorus.

He grinned sheepishly. "OK… Angela. I won't let *her* go through it again." He gazed at her mother worriedly. "Are you sure this is the sensible thing to do?"

"Sensible or not, we don't have a choice," she said, then looked to Dani, who'd just returned after finally conceding defeat and going off to scrub up for the impending delivery. "Do we?"

"Afraid not," Dani said irritably. "I'd say this Adams is about to make an entrance, like it or not. Aunt Jessie, can you find a blanket and some towels? Sterilize some scissors, too. And hurry, for goodness' sakes."

"Of course. I'll be right back." She feigned a scowl at Angela. "Don't you dare have this baby while I'm gone. I want to be right here when my grandbaby comes into this world."

"Then I think you'd better hurry," Angela said, her voice catching, then altering into a muffled scream. She didn't know a lot about the duration of labor. What she'd read said first babies tended to take a long time arriving. Hers didn't seem inclined to play by the rules. Typical of an Adams.

"Pant," Clint ordered. "Pay attention, darlin'. You remember the drill."

Fortunately she did recall there was more to it than panting. Since it was obvious everything else she'd just taught him had flown out the window. He watched her intently, then nodded. He grinned sheepishly when the pain had passed.

"Now I remember," he murmured.

With the next contraction, Dani murmured, "Here we go. Push, Angie. Do it," she said more sharply. "Push now."

"I am pushing, you lousy, no-good animal doc."

"Don't knock the help, kiddo, or Clint will find himself in my place."

"Be nice," he said hurriedly. "Dani's your best shot at getting this baby delivered with professional assistance."

"Oh, I think you could handle it, just as well as she could," Angela shot back. "How many calves and foals have you delivered?"

"A few."

"More than a few," she reminded him.

"Then get down here and take over," Dani pleaded. "I have absolutely no ego here. I'll take whatever help I can get."

Clint released her hand and was about to move when Angela latched on to it again and let out a shout that shook the rafters.

"Oh, my," Dani murmured. "Come on, Angie. Once more with feeling. That's it. Come on. Do it *now!*"

Angela felt as if her insides were being torn apart. Then suddenly, barely an hour after the severe pains had started, it was over. She tried to lift herself on her elbows. Clint was on his feet.

"My baby," she whispered urgently. "I don't hear anything. Dani?"

Just as panic was setting it, she heard a feeble cry, followed by a lusty wail.

"That's more like it," Dani said triumphantly. She took one of the towels that Jessie had brought in just that second and wrapped the baby. Her expression triumphant, she walked to the head of the bed.

"Angie, Clint, may I present your son."

"A boy?" Clint whispered, gazing awestruck at the chubby, red-faced newborn Dani placed in Angela's arms.

"Told you so," she said, her eyes filling with tears. "Oh, Clint, he's beautiful."

"Handsome," he corrected, grinning. "Boys are handsome."

"Not ours. He is absolutely beautiful."

"He is, sweetie," her mother said. She turned and hugged Dani. "You were terrific. I'll never be able to thank you enough."

"We won't be able to thank you enough," Clint said.

"No problem," Dani said, then sank into a chair as if her legs had suddenly turned to water. "I don't ever, *ever* want to do anything like this again, do you hear me? I've never been so terrified of messing up in my entire life."

"Now she tells us," Angela teased.

She glanced at Clint. "I have an idea." She beckoned to him and whispered. Clint nodded.

Angela grinned. "OK, then. Don't fall apart now, Dani. Come here and officially meet your new godson," she said.

"Oh, sweetie, you don't have to do that," Dani said, but her eyes were bright with unshed tears. She rubbed the back of her fingers across the baby's soft cheek. "But I'm glad you did. Have you decided on a name?"

"I have," Angela said. "Clinton Daniel Adams."

"Brady," Clint amended, a determined scowl on his face. "Clinton Daniel Brady."

"Do you see a ring on my finger?" Angela asked, looking at her mother and her cousin. "Either one of you? Is there a ring here?"

The two women exchanged a look.

"Bye-bye," Dani said. "Glad to be of help."

"Call us if you need us," her mother said, brushing a kiss across her forehead. "You were great, sweetie."

"You're abandoning me?" she protested. "How can you do that? I just had a baby."

"Clint's here."

"Yes, but he has his own agenda at the moment. I want somebody who's on my side."

"We are," her mother insisted. "That's why we're going. You two need time alone with your baby."

It wasn't the prospect of being alone with her child that scared the daylights out of her. Clinton Daniel was the kind of miracle it would take a lifetime to study and appreciate.

No, what terrified her was the glint of pure cussedness she saw in Clint's eyes. He'd been possessive and determined enough before. Now there was no telling the lengths to which he'd go to claim his son.

For a long time after Dani and Jessie left Angela's bedroom, Clint couldn't form a coherent thought. He kept staring at the tiny infant, who was now wrapped in a huge yellow blanket. His son. Practically bald except for a few strands of soft blond fuzz, eyes as big as saucers staring solemnly back at him, a tiny pink bow of a mouth. He was in awe of him.

"Would you like to hold him?" Angela asked.

"I…um, I don't know," he said warily. "What if I do something wrong?"

"Are you planning to drop him on his head?"

He stared at her aghast. "Of course not."

"Then you'll do just fine," she said, holding the baby up in the air for Clint to take.

He gingerly accepted the baby and his tangle of blanket. His gaze locked on his son's face as if he were mesmerized.

"Hi, kiddo," he said softly. Everything else in the room faded into the background as he concentrated on this tiny gift from God.

"I'm your dad," he said. "You and I, we're going to have a great time together. I have this little spread up in Montana and one day it's all going to be yours. I'm going to teach you every single thing I know about ranching."

"You might have to wait just a bit for that," Angela said dryly. "At least until he can walk."

"You're never too young to know that there's a plan and what your part in it will be," he insisted. "It makes a kid feel secure."

"You never had that, did you?" she asked.

He glanced at Angela, surprised by her accurate guesswork. "My mother did the best she could. Besides, the past's over and done with," he said, his gaze never straying from the beautiful face of his boy. "This child right here, he's the future. He's all that matters now."

"You can't build your whole world around a baby," Angela argued.

Something in her voice, a surprising hint of testiness, alerted him that her mood was rapidly disintegrating and that he was the cause of it. Suspecting he knew why, he glanced at her. "You OK?"

"Just peachy."

"Did I forget to mention how you fit into this future?" he inquired, giving her a lazy grin.

"Don't try to charm me, Clint Brady. All you care about, all you've ever cared about is your baby."

The accusation confirmed his own guesswork. Her feelings were hurt by what she perceived as his priorities. "That's not true, darlin'. You've just given me the most precious gift on God's earth and you will always have a place in my heart for that."

"I didn't have this baby to accommodate you," she grumbled, reaching for their son. Staking her own claim, he imagined. Clint reluctantly put the baby back into her arms. Her expression softened at once.

"He is precious, isn't he?" she whispered.

"He is, indeed, though I have a feeling you and I had better enjoy him while we can."

"Meaning?"

"I think I hear a thundering herd on the steps. My guess is we're about to have company. That boy's going to get passed around like a football."

"Over my dead body," she said, visibly tightening her embrace. "They can look, but nobody's getting this baby out of my arms today."

Before Clint could stake his own claim in what was becoming a knee-jerk reaction of possessiveness, there was a hard knock on the door, followed by a muffled burst of excited chatter. He supposed they might as well give in to the inevitable.

"You ready, angel?"

Her expression was clearly torn. "Not really," she said finally, "but I suppose it's only right to share on Christmas morning."

Clint opened the door and found Jessie trying to hold off the entire Adams clan.

"One at a time," she said forcefully. Then at a plaintive look from her husband and her father-in-law, she relented. "OK, two. Luke and Harlan, you can go in."

Clint grinned at her. "You think you can keep control of this mob by yourself?"

"You ever seen a mother bear protecting her cubs?" she retorted.

"I get the picture. Call if you need backup."

"You call if you can't budge those two men out of there in five minutes."

Clint went back into the room just in time to see Angela handing their son up to her grandfather.

"Your first great-grandbaby," she said.

As he cradled the infant, Harlan's expression was filled with the kind of fierce pride and tenderness that Clint had once longed to see in his own father's face. He thought he saw Luke surreptitiously wipe a tear from his cheek before he took his own turn holding the baby. This was the kind of tight-knit family, bound by love and respect, that he'd always wanted. If Angela would only say the word, he would be a part of it.

"How're you feeling?" Harlan asked her.

"Like I've been run over by a truck," Angela admitted. "But I've never been happier. He's perfect, isn't he?"

"The most beautiful baby boy I've ever seen," Harlan declared.

"Grandpa, you say that every time there's a new baby."

He winked at her. "But this time I mean it." He turned and held out a hand to Clint. "Congratulations, son. He's a fine-looking boy. He'll do the Adams name proud."

"With all due respect, sir, he's a Brady."

Harlan shot him a look of understanding. "Well, of

course, he is. But he's an Adams, too, and we take pride in our own, no matter what name they carry." He turned back to Angela. "Now I don't want you fretting about not having this baby in a hospital. I've called the Doc and he'll be here in an hour or so to check him out. He'd already got his sled out to come to the open house, so he said he'd just start a little earlier."

"Thanks, Grandpa." She smiled at her father, who was totally absorbed in studying Clinton Daniel's perfect little face. "You know what, Daddy?"

Luke tore his gaze away from his first grandchild. "What, darlin'?"

"I'm glad I had him at home. Now I know what it must have been like for you and Mom."

Luke grinned. "Darlin', you don't know the half of it. Dani is the next best thing to an M.D., compared to me. She was also stone-cold sober. Your mama got a rotten bargain when she stumbled up to my doorstep that night."

Angela shook her head. "I don't think so. I think that's the night we really became a family, even if it did take you a while to accept the inevitable."

Luke put Clinton Daniel back in her arms, then kissed her. "I love you, baby. Now your Grandpa and I had better get out of here before your mother comes in after us."

"Could you ask her to give us a second before she sends in the next round?" Clint asked. "There's something I need to say to Angela."

"No problem," Luke said, giving his shoulder a reassuring squeeze. "You just let Jessie know when you're ready for more company."

After Luke and Harlan had left, Clint sat down on the

edge of the bed, hip to hip with the woman he wanted so badly to be his wife. He reached out and gently brushed a fingertip across his son's cheek. His skin was so soft, just like his mama's.

"Clint?"

Her expression was questioning. He looked directly into her eyes and for a moment he lost his train of thought. She could do that to him, rattle him so badly he'd be tongue-tied. He swallowed hard and tried to collect his thoughts.

"There's something I should have said before," he said eventually. His gaze strayed to the baby nestled in her arms, then back to her. "Thank you. Thank you for my son. Thank you for not giving him away, the way you threatened to do."

For an instant he thought he saw disappointment flicker in her eyes, but then it vanished.

"He's my son, too," she said quietly. "I know what I said in Montana. It was awful and it was cruel. I have no excuse, except that I was upset." She smiled, but it was clearly forced. "Just like you said, though, that was in the past. I can't change it. I just want you to know that I will always take very good care of him."

"We will, angel. *We* will take very good care of him."

"And just how are we going to do that with you in Montana and me in Texas?"

Clint wanted to declare flatly that she was going to marry him and come back to Montana with him, but the stubbornness he saw simmering in her eyes warned him off making that particular declaration.

"We'll work it out."

"I will not have this child bounced back and forth between two states," she warned.

"Neither will I."

"Which leaves us with what choice?"

"I haven't got all the details figured out just yet," he admitted.

"Well, do let me know when you think you have a plan," she snapped.

"Don't be sarcastic, darlin'."

"Go tell Mother to let the others in," she said through clenched teeth.

"Are you upset, angel?" he inquired sweetly, delighted with the reaction. If he could keep her stirred up and off-kilter just a little longer, maybe he could come up with a surefire way to get her to tumble straight into his arms.

"Upset? Me? Of course not."

"Then relax your jaw before you grind all your teeth to nubs," he advised. "Your family will get the idea that you and I are having a little squabble on what should be the happiest day of our lives."

"We aren't having a little squabble," she said. "I am trying very hard not to kill you."

"Shh," he whispered. "You don't want the baby to hear you saying a thing like that about his daddy."

She regarded him sourly. "My hunch is he'll hear a lot worse before all is said and done."

Clint turned away before she could catch him grinning. The new tactic was working very nicely, he thought, very nicely indeed.

14

Clint was sticking to her like a damned burr. He was about as annoying, too, Angela thought irritably.

Maybe if he'd looked at her once, really looked at *her*, she would have felt better. Instead, he couldn't seem to take his eyes off his son.

She told herself she was glad he was so enchanted with the baby, so taken with fatherhood, but it might have been nice if just once he'd kissed her or squeezed her hand or even run a fingertip across her skin the way he did across the baby's. Every time she witnessed that trembling, awestruck touch, she was so jealous she could spit. How pitiful was that?

She glanced up as he came into her room. His gaze skimmed across her, then aimed straight for the cradle beside the bed. When he realized it was empty, then and only then did his gaze settle on her.

"Where is he?"

"Grandpa's got him downstairs showing him off."

"Again? I thought most of the state was here yesterday for the open house. They got a look at him then."

"I'm not sure, but I think he's just showing Consuela and Maritza that he can already make the baby smile."

"Didn't your mother say that was just gas?"

"Try telling that to Grandpa. He's sure Clinton Daniel is very advanced for his age," Angela said with a grin. She waited for Clint to make up an excuse and go chasing after his son. Instead, he pulled a chair up beside her bed and sat down.

"How're you feeling, angel?"

"Better than I expected. I'd be downstairs myself, but everyone insists I should be resting. Another twenty-four hours of this and I'll be stir-crazy."

"Maybe you should be thankful there are a dozen people around who are eager to take the two a.m. feedings."

She regarded him skeptically. "Are you relieved?"

Clint grinned sheepishly. "No. I want to do it myself. I jump up the minute I hear him so much as whimper, and I run smack into a traffic jam outside your door."

Angela chuckled. "You'd think I'd have the inside track. After all, I am in the same room, but even if I get to him first, someone plucks him right out of my arms and tells me to get my rest."

"They wouldn't be able to do that if you were breast-feeding," Clint said thoughtfully.

Angela hadn't even had time to consider that. Too many people had been trying to take charge in typical Adams fashion.

"You know, you are absolutely right. Everything's happened so fast, I haven't been thinking straight." She glanced at her watch and saw that it was just about time for another feeding. "Will you go down and retrieve our son?"

His expression was so eager, she wanted to laugh.

"I'll be back in a heartbeat," he promised.

"Don't let anybody talk you out of this," she warned. "They'll try."

"I'll tell them I have my instructions," he promised. "Then I'll grab him and run like hell."

Angela wished like crazy that she could be there to watch Clint repossessing his son. Nobody stood in Clint Brady's way when he was after something.

Suddenly, though, her amusement faded. Would it be like that when he decided he wanted to take the baby away from her for good? That possibility slipped into her head when she least expected it. It had been frightening enough before the baby was born, but now that he was here, now that she'd held him in her arms, she wasn't sure she could bear the thought of losing him.

By the time she heard Clint coming in the door, tears were tracking down her cheeks. He was babbling nonsense to the baby so intently that he didn't notice at first that she was crying. When he did, he stopped dead and stared.

"Angel? What is it? What's wrong? Did something happen while I was gone?"

"My baby," she pleaded, holding up her arms. "Please, I have to hold him."

He gently placed the baby in her arms, then studied her with bemusement. "Darlin', are your hormones going wacky or is something else upsetting you?"

Unwilling to explain the fear that had suddenly overwhelmed her, she shook her head. "I'll be fine. Just leave me alone with the baby."

Clinton Daniel began to whimper. Nothing she tried seemed to soothe him, which sent more tears cascading down her cheeks. Obviously she didn't know the first thing about being a good mother. Clint wasn't blind. He would see that and use it against her. Even now he was scooping the baby up and rocking him gently. The baby quieted at once, more proof that Clint would be the better parent.

"Mind telling me what upset you?" Clint asked mildly.

"It's nothing. I'm fine," she said, blotting her tears with a tissue and fighting for composure. "Let me have him. He's fussy because he's hungry."

Clint studied her worriedly. "Are you sure? Maybe this isn't the time to change the routine."

"It's hardly a routine," she said testily. "He's only twenty-four hours old."

Clint ignored her and glanced at the baby. "He's asleep again," he said softly as he placed him in his cradle. When the baby was settled, he pulled the chair a little closer to the bed. "OK, angel, tell me what's been going on in that head of yours?"

She sniffed and cursed the combination of hormonal swings and genuine terror. "Nothing."

"Tell that to someone who'll buy it."

"Clint, just go away. I'm fine."

He studied her intently, then sighed. "You aren't, by any chance, panicking that I'm going to run off to Montana with the baby, are you?"

Alarmed that he could read her so easily, she tried to feign shock. "Why would you say that?"

"Wild guess."

"Well, you can just take your guesses and go fly a kite."

He nodded, but didn't budge. "That's a productive approach."

"Are you suddenly into soul baring?" she countered. "Since when?"

"Maybe I just wised up and realized it would be smart to put all the cards on the table so there'd be no room for misunderstandings."

"Did this epiphany happen overnight?"

He grinned at her sarcasm. "No, it's been coming on for a few days now."

"OK," she said agreeably. "You go first."

"I'm not the one with the attitude."

"Maybe not, but I have a feeling my attitude might improve if you just this once said what was really on your mind. Try it."

He squirmed uncomfortably and remained as tight-lipped as ever.

"It's not so easy when the shoe's on the other foot, is it?"

"No," he conceded. "OK, I will tell you what's on my mind."

Now that he'd made the commitment to open up, Angela got a queasy feeling in the pit of her stomach. Maybe this was a really bad way to go. Maybe she wasn't ready to hear what was going on in his head.

"I've been trying to figure out a solution to our dilemma," he said.

His response took the option of silence away from her. "Any luck?" she asked warily.

"OK…as I see it, we have three choices. Well, one of them really isn't an option, but I'll lay it on the table. We could get married, baptize our son and head back to Montana together," he suggested, ticking it off on his fingers as if it were as unimportant as an item on a grocery list.

"Or, two, we could go into court and fight over custody and wind up with some judge deciding which one of us gets to keep him. Or, three, I could leave him here with you, forget all about him and let you raise him as an Adams."

She knew with absolute certainty that this last wouldn't be an option he would ever consider. As for a custody fight, as painful as it would be, she might have gone for that if it hadn't been for the whole Hattie Jones debacle. If that came out, well, the outcome in court might very well be a toss-up. She couldn't take that chance and Clint knew it.

"Are you trying to blackmail me into marrying you?" she inquired.

"Of course not. If you have other options you'd like to throw out here, by all means go ahead."

She considered and dismissed a few that were so outrageous not even she could think of a credible way to explain them.

"OK, what if we just worked out our own custody arrangement and had a lawyer draw it up?" she suggested hopefully.

He shook his head. "Now, you see, here's where I have a problem with that. I want my son with me. I don't want him bouncing from state to state, especially now when he's just a baby."

"We could wait—"

"Until he's older? I don't think so. I'm not going to miss one single second of watching him grow up."

Nor was she. The path kept twisting right back to marriage, Angela realized. A loveless marriage. Well, loveless on his part, anyway. She might not trust him worth two hoots, but she loved him anyway, for reasons that would never make a lick of sense to her. She sighed.

"I'll think about it," she said eventually.

He nodded. "Don't take too long, angel. Time's running out."

At the warning, her temper flared. "Don't threaten me. I can always take the baby and run again. It took you eight months to find me this time. I'll make damned sure it takes longer next time."

Clint seemed startled by her threat and her vehemence. Then his gaze narrowed and his eyes darkened. "Now it seems to me that's how we got messed up in the first place, with you making wild threats and refusing to listen to reason. Don't even think about running again, angel. Something tells me this time I wouldn't be searching all alone."

"Meaning?"

"Meaning that your father and grandfather would be looking for you right alongside me."

"They'd never join forces with you," she protested, but without much conviction. They would and she knew it. Clinton Daniel was an Adams and they would never ignore his existence or do anything to keep his father— a man they clearly liked and respected—out of his life.

Besides, tough as they were, they were also a couple of old romantics. They believed in happy endings. For some reason they had evidently gotten it into their heads that she and Clint belonged together.

She sighed. If only Clint felt the same, she thought wearily. If only they could recapture the emotions they had felt when they'd first met. Now, though, whatever feelings they had were colored by betrayal and fear and distrust. She wondered for the hundredth time if even love could overcome all that.

Clint had found the entire conversation with Angela about their future unsettling. As casually as he'd tried to introduce the subject of marriage, he'd been feeling anything but casual. If he'd been hoping for a sudden acknowledgment of the inevitable, though, he'd been sadly disappointed. She wasn't about to give him an inch. He did have her thinking, though, and that was something.

He gave himself until the first of the new year to make good on his scheme for getting Angela to admit she loved him. After that, with her or without her, he was going to have to head back to Montana. The thought of leaving her or his son behind made his stomach churn. His plan had to work. He was counting on it.

After another two days of sly hints and devilish taunts, he concluded that he had to be losing his touch. Just when he was dead-on certain that Angie was weakening, that she'd say yes to a proposal, she slammed on the brakes and put enough distance between them to keep him in a constant state of frustrated arousal. The woman was driving him crazy. One thing was certain, a lifetime wouldn't be long enough for him to figure her out. Meantime the clock was ticking and he was fresh out of ideas.

He'd lain awake half the night trying to assess his progress. As near as he could tell, it pretty much added up to zero.

When he staggered downstairs at the crack of dawn for some of Maritza's potent, eye-opening coffee, he found Luke there ahead of him.

"You look like something the cat dragged in," Luke observed, his expression amused. "Coffee?"

"Please."

"Baby keep you awake?"

No, it wasn't his son who was responsible for his lack of sleep. It was the kid's stubborn mother. He shook his head.

"Angela, then?"

"Bingo."

"I don't want to meddle, but if you'd like to talk about it, I can certainly listen."

The only fathers Clint had ever known well were the ones in this family. Unless he'd very much misread them, meddling was their middle name. "Thanks, anyway, but I think I'd better handle this on my own."

Luke nodded and regarded him thoughtfully. "You told me when we first met that you intended to marry Angela. Is that still your intention?"

"Yes."

"Have you asked her?"

"I've asked her, I've told her, now I'm trying to torment her into it by avoiding the topic completely."

Luke grinned. "I'd say that's your best bet."

Clint regarded his prospective father-in-law hopefully. "Do you honestly think it'll work?"

"In this family, reverse psychology is about the only thing that does. From the time she was an itty-bitty thing, Angie has been dead-set on going her own way, just the way I did. She couldn't wait to get away from Adams territory so she could prove she was her own woman."

"But she came back."

Luke nodded. "Exactly my point. We just had to be patient and wait for her to realize this was where she belonged."

"And that took how long?"

"Six years," Luke admitted.

"I am not waiting six years to claim my son," Clint exploded. "Can you see me commuting from my ranch to here every blasted month just to get a look at them? How am I supposed to convince her of anything from hundreds of miles away?"

"Maybe your absence will do the convincing."

"We were separated for seven months. You've been around since I caught up with her. Do you see any sign that she's mellowing?"

"Seven months is a drop in the bucket. Like I said, Angie's stubborn. We all are." He smiled. "But I think she's worth waiting for, don't you?"

Clint muttered a curse. "Yes," he conceded eventually, "but I still think it's a lousy idea. She may decide she can get along without me just fine."

"That is a risk," Luke agreed.

Clint shook his head. "It's not one I'm willing to take."

"I do have one other idea," Luke said, "but I'm not sure how well it will sit with you."

"Try me. I'm a desperate man."

"You could come to work with me."

Clint stared at him. "Here? In Texas?"

Luke grinned. "That is where my ranch is."

Clint was shaking his head before the words were out of Luke's mouth. "That's very kind of you, but no, I can't do that. My place is in Montana. I can't let it fall idle, and I can't expect my foreman to go on running it by himself forever."

"Let him hire somebody to help, or let him buy you out."

"Not a chance," Clint said vehemently. "I've worked all my life to own a spread of my own. I'm not walking away from it."

"If you marry Angie, my ranch would be yours one day, anyway."

"No," Clint said. "It would be hers. I appreciate your offer, but I can't accept it," he repeated.

"Don't be stubborn," Luke said impatiently. "One of you has to break this impasse."

"And you think I'm more likely to bend than she is?" he asked with reluctant amusement.

"Experience would suggest it," Luke concurred. "Just don't rule it out. It might be the bargaining chip you need."

"You're giving Clint bargaining chips?" Angela asked from the doorway. She was clearly exasperated with the pair of them. "Who's side are you on, anyway, Daddy?"

"Just trying to get you two off dead center," Luke

said cheerfully. He stood up and dropped a kiss on his daughter's forehead. "Talk, darlin'. Nothing's solved by silence. I ought to know."

Angela sighed as he left, then shot a wary look at Clint. "Tell me about this bargaining chip."

"It's not an option," Clint said. "Are you sure you feel up to being downstairs?"

"If I'd had the baby in a hospital, they'd have kicked me out days ago. Obviously the greatest medical minds in the world don't regard childbirth as a debilitating illness."

"That isn't what I asked. Can't you ever give a straight answer?"

"My, my, you are testy this morning. Daddy must have struck a nerve."

"I could do without the dime-store psychology."

"There's a shrink in Los Pinos who charges more. Care to try her?"

"You know, angel, you are trying my patience."

She didn't appear worried about that. "So?"

"It's a very dangerous path to take," he warned.

"Really? What happens if I test your patience? Will you storm off to Montana?"

So that was her game. He regarded her with sudden amusement. "It's not going to work, angel."

"What?" she asked, her expression all innocence.

"I'm not going to blow a gasket and abandon you here, even though that appears to be what you'd like me to do. Nor are you going to goad me into a display of temper that will have your family taking your side against me."

"Oh, well," she said with a shrug. "It was worth a shot."

She began to load a plate up with waffles and fruit. When she would have skirted past him and taken a seat on the opposite side of the table, he snagged her hand. The gesture caught her off guard. It took only the slightest jerk to have her tumbling straight into his lap. He caught the precariously tilting plate in one hand and set it safely on the table. His other arm circled her waist and held her secure.

There was fire in her eyes, when he met her gaze.

"Clint Brady, don't you dare."

"Dare what?" he inquired lazily.

Color bloomed in her cheeks. "Whatever you were thinking of doing."

"I was thinking of doing this," he said quietly and slanted his mouth over hers, swallowing yet another protest.

She gave a token shove at his chest, then sighed against him. Her mouth opened to his. When the tip of her tongue grazed his lips, he almost exploded. He'd meant to seduce her, meant to catch her by surprise with her defenses down and remind her of what they'd once had together.

Instead, she had twisted things around the way she had a habit of doing. He was the one off-kilter. He was the one who couldn't seem to catch his breath, whose blood was thundering through his veins.

Mystified by how she'd done it, he stared into eyes full of mischief, eyes that reminded him of Hattie.

Suddenly he tired of the game, all of it. Carefully he lifted Angie and set her in her own chair, then gave it a less than gentle shove to put a few inches of additional space between them.

She looked startled, then confused, then hurt. He pushed away from the table and stood, as anxious as she for once to put some distance between them.

"I'm going…" His voice trailed off. He didn't know where he was going or what he intended to do. He just had to get out of this room.

"Clint?" she whispered, her expression suddenly worried.

He didn't answer, because for the first time in his entire life he was at a loss for words.

15

A cold, empty feeling settled over Angela as she watched Clint walk away from her. He'd sounded so final when he'd said he was going, as if he'd given up, as if he might be leaving for good.

Well, that was what she wanted, wasn't it? It was what she'd prayed for, that he would go and leave her and her baby alone. What did they say? Be careful what you pray for, because it could come true.

She sat at the table staring at her cold waffle and unappetizing fruit and tried very hard to convince herself that it was best that he was heading back to Montana. If he couldn't love her back, then what was the point of prolonging this agony?

But no matter how hard she tried to convince herself to let him go, a part of her kept envisioning the loneliness of a future without him. Seattle had been awful enough with her nights filled with dreams of the man she'd left behind and her days just time to be gotten through.

At least in Seattle she had known somehow that he

was still searching for her, and in some awful, perverse way that had been enough to keep her going. It had given her hope that he hadn't given up on her, that they would be together again someday.

OK, maybe she was a fool, maybe she didn't have a smidgen of sense, but she couldn't let him leave, not without telling him how she felt. If he still wanted to go, if he couldn't bring himself to ever trust her again, well, so be it. At least she would have tried. Not trying would doom her to a lifetime of what ifs.

She hurried to the stairs, cursing the fact that there were so many of them and that she was so darned stiff and sore. It seemed to take her forever to get to the top.

She rushed straight to Clint's room and knocked on his door. When he didn't answer, she ignored everything she'd ever been taught about privacy and threw the door open. He wasn't there. In fact, there was no sign of him at all. With her heart thudding dully, she peered into his closets and released a sigh when she saw that his clothes were still inside.

He hadn't left, then, but she was sure it was only a matter of time.

Where could he be, though? A smile touched her lips as she came up with the only logical answer. Closing his door gently behind her, she crossed the hall to her own room where she'd left a doting Consuela keeping an eye on the baby. She opened the door, then hesitated, immobilized by the scene before her.

Clint was there, in a rocker by the window, the baby cradled in his arms. Clinton Daniel looked so tiny against that massive chest, so tiny and so very safe and secure. The picture brought a lump to her throat.

Clint glanced up then and his gaze locked with hers. "Quiet, angel. I just got him to sleep."

She tiptoed across the room and sat on the edge of the bed. "How'd you get Consuela out of here?"

"I told her I was starving. She went to fix me a hearty breakfast."

Angela stared. "But you just ate."

He shrugged. "So, I'll eat again. I figured it was the safest bet for getting some time alone with my son."

Angela forced herself to keep a light note in her voice when she asked the question that had been plaguing her. "Are you saying goodbye?"

The question seemed to take him by surprise. He searched her face intently, then asked, "Would it matter to you if I was?"

She swallowed hard against the tide of vulnerability that washed over her just thinking about giving a truthful answer. There was no choice, though. She had promised herself she would deal with him honestly, something she should have done from the first.

"Yes," she said softly. "It would matter to me."

"Why, angel?"

This was it, then. It was time for the truth, the whole truth and nothing but the truth. "Because I'm in love with you."

A knowing smile began at the corners of his mouth and spread. "Oh, really?"

She nodded.

"Say it again," he prodded. "Your father's said it. Your mother's said it. Even your uncle's told me that, but I want to hear it again from you."

"Look, dammit…"

He grinned. "That's more like it. You were sounding a little out of character there for a minute, all docile and sweet natured."

She regarded him ruefully. "I'm afraid I will never be docile."

"Thank goodness."

"But I will be honest, Clint. I swear to you that there will never be another lie between us." She searched his face, trying to gauge his reaction. "Is that enough?"

"Enough for what?"

"Enough to make you stay, enough for you to trust me again."

He sighed. "Angel, trust will always come hard for us. We got off to a rocky start on that score."

Her pulse seemed to slow at his dire prediction. It was her fault, too. The unforgettable, unforgivable Hattie Jones fiasco would always stand squarely between them.

"I see," she said, defeated.

He reached over and tucked a finger under her chin. "No, darlin', I don't think you do. Just because you have to work at something doesn't mean it's bad. I've always worked for everything that's important to me. The way I see it, nothing's more important than our future. I'll do whatever it takes to see that we overcome every obstacle the past has put in front of us. What about you? Do you believe our family's worth fighting for?"

Angela blinked back tears. She tried to form an answer, but the words simply wouldn't come. Finally she just nodded.

"Was that a yes?" he asked.

"Yes," she said, then lifted her gaze to his. Tears blurred her vision, but her voice was firm when she repeated, "Yes."

He gave a nod of satisfaction, then grinned. "Angel, you never asked, but there's something I think you ought to know."

A fresh burst of trepidation had her heart skipping a beat. "What's that?"

"This isn't just about the baby. It never has been," he said quietly. "I do love you. I tried not to, but it was like trying not to breathe. If my arms weren't occupied at the moment, I'd show you just how much."

She grinned. "I could put the baby back in his cradle," she offered.

"And risk having him start fussing again? I don't think so."

Despite Clint's protests, she took the baby anyway and settled him into the beautiful cradle his father had bought for him. He didn't so much as stir.

"At least your son has his priorities straight," she said, slipping onto Clint's lap. "Now let's work on yours."

"There's nothing wrong with my priorities," he grumbled, but he didn't complain when she feathered kisses across his forehead, then sought out his mouth.

Angela kissed him with all of the yearning and passion she'd been saving up during their months of separation. She could feel the hard ridge of his arousal beneath her hip and the thundering of his heart where her hand rested against his chest. His heat and the purely masculine scent of him surrounded her, carried her back to another time and another place when the two of them had been all that mattered.

"I do love you," she whispered against his lips.

"I know."

"Always did."

"I know."

She pulled back and scowled at him. "You don't know everything, Clint Brady."

"Maybe not, but I know the only things that matter. You and me, that boy of ours, family, ranching."

"See," she said triumphantly. "Your priorities are improving already."

"That's because I have such an outstanding teacher. Your motivational skills are excellent. Anytime you'd care to give me another lesson, I'm up for it."

"Maybe we'd better wait for our honeymoon for the lesson I have in mind."

His expression sobered. "Darlin', I'm not so sure we can fit a honeymoon in just now. I've already been away too long."

She was sure he was prepared to offer a whole laundry list of reasons why their honeymoon would have to be postponed, so she silenced him with another slow, lingering kiss.

"On the other hand," he began, his voice husky.

"If you'd let me get a word in here," she said, "I think I have a solution."

"By all means."

"We could honeymoon in Montana. It's certainly the most romantic spot I've ever seen."

"You want to honeymoon on the ranch?"

"Why not?"

"For one thing it won't be much of a honeymoon with me working and the baby with us."

"Consuela can look after the baby and I can help you work."

"Darlin', far be it from me to turn down such a generous offer, but you do have a very strange notion of what a honeymoon ought to be."

"Maybe more people ought to start their marriages the way they intend to live them. Could be honeymoons just set up a lot of false expectations that get ruined when the day-to-day realities set in."

"An interesting philosophy, but won't you be disappointed years from now when our kids ask what we did on our honeymoon and all you can tell them is that we worked our ranch?"

She shook her head. "No, because that's how we're going to make it *our* ranch, with me doing my part from the beginning."

He still looked skeptical.

"I mean it, Clint. This is what I want."

"OK," he said eventually, "but on one condition."

"What's that?"

"For our fiftieth anniversary, when we've turned the ranch over to our kids, we go around the world. We will make love in every romantic spot you've ever dreamed about."

"The only romantic spot I've ever dreamed of is in your arms," she confessed.

"Then we're off to a good start, angel, because I'm never, ever letting you go."

It was amazing how many strings could be pulled when the Adams name was mentioned, Clint concluded as he watched White Pines being transformed into an indoor garden for a New Year's Day wedding. The same crowd that had shown up on Christmas Day, despite a blizzard, was scheduled to return today, despite the competition from football and New Year's Eve celebration hangovers.

A part of him felt guilty that he would be taking Angela and his son away from all this, but she had assured him over and over that Montana was where she truly wanted to be.

Luke had grumbled at the choice, but had finally agreed that he would send Consuela along with them to help with the baby for the first month, just as Angela had predicted he would. Since the housekeeper rarely let the boy out of her sight now, Clint wondered what would happen when the time came for her to return to Texas. What the heck. Maybe they could persuade her to stay.

He gazed into the mirror and tried to reconcile the image of the man in the tuxedo with Clint Brady. He was so spiffed up he hardly recognized the once-poor cowboy who'd never paid a lick of attention to his clothes, if the money could be better spent on feed for the cattle.

"You ready, son?" Luke called out.

Clint opened the door to his room and found his future father-in-law and Harlan pacing the hallway. They, too, seemed to be anxious to get out of these monkey suits and back into working clothes.

He met Harlan's gaze evenly. "Thank you, sir, for agreeing to be my best man."

"Son, nothing could have made me prouder. I know if your family'd been able to get here on such short notice, you'd have asked one of your brothers, but I'm glad to fill in."

"No," Clint said. "You deserve the honor. You've been more than fair to me from the minute we met. A lot of men in your position wouldn't have been. The same goes for you, Luke. I hope I'll never let you down."

"Just keep our gal happy," Harlan said. "That's all we ask."

"Did I hear someone mention me," Angela called out from behind her door.

"Don't you dare open that door, darlin'. It's bad luck for the groom to see the bride on their wedding day," Harlan said.

"According to family legend, that didn't stop you and Janet from having a little chat before your ceremony. The way I remember it, you walked down the aisle together."

"Don't live your life by my example, girl."

She opened the door. "I can't think of a better one, Grandpa."

Clint would have closed his eyes or turned away just because of the silly superstition, if he'd been able to. Instead, though, he couldn't seem to tear his gaze away from the lovely vision before him. She had opted for simplicity in a narrow dress of white velvet edged with satin. From the front it was as innocent and sedate as any bride's ought to be.

And then she turned and he caught sight of the back... what there was of it. A deep vee plunged practically to her waist, exposing an almost indecent amount of soft skin.

"Aren't you afraid you'll get cold?" he asked wryly.

"Not if you're doing your job," she said tartly, and sashayed down the stairs ahead of them all.

So, he thought as he followed her, the mischievous Hattie lived, lurking somewhere inside his angel. It ought to make the next fifty years or so damned interesting.

Epilogue

Angela sorted through the stack of mail Clint had picked up in town and seized the pale yellow envelope from home. She'd been waiting for days for a long, chatty letter from her mother. After all those years she'd spent away, knowing nothing, she could no longer seem to get her fill of news now that she'd been there at Christmas. Phone calls satisfied some of her curiosity, but she liked receiving mail. She could hold it in her hands and practically feel the bond with her mother. She could read it over and over. And, of course, her mother always tucked in snapshots from the latest family gathering. There had been a huge Memorial Day barbecue just the week before.

Sure enough, there were three or four pictures from the celebration. The one of her parents stealing a kiss, thinking they were unobserved, no doubt, made her smile. Another of Grandpa Harlan flipping huge steaks on the grill and waving Janet away had her laughing out loud. He would never trust her when it came to cooking. He'd always said she could ruin a hard-boiled egg without half trying.

"A letter from your mom?" Clint asked, pausing beside her to drop a kiss on her forehead.

"With pictures," she said, displaying them for him. "I'll bet Dad didn't know anyone with a camera was nearby when he planted that kiss on Mom."

"I don't think he'd care," Clint said. "Personally, I love seeing the affection between them. I hope we still have that when we're old and gray."

"We'd better," Angela warned.

"Then let's stay in practice," Clint suggested. He sat in an over-stuffed chair by the fire and held out his arms. "Come here and read the letter to me."

She went to him eagerly and, after snuggling into his arms, she began to read:

"Dearest Angie,
We all loved the picture of baby Clint on the horse with his daddy. He's so big for five months, and he's the spitting image of his father. Quite the little cowboy. Please bring him to Texas soon so we can all fuss over him.

"Life goes on here. Everyone misses you. Sharon Lynn and Kyle Mason are definitely an item. She still credits you with getting them out of limbo and into each other's arms. After all those years in Dallas, Jenny has decided to come home and teach in Los Pinos. Harlan Patrick and Justin are already studying college catalogues and Janet swears Lizzy will never, ever go away to school, if what she hears about college campuses these days is true.

"I wish you could have been here for the Memorial Day festivities. Your grandfather was in his glory, but I must say I think he's slowing down just a bit. I worry about what will happen when we lose him. He's the glue that holds all of us together."

Angela glanced at the snapshot again and looked for the signs of aging her mother had seen. It seemed to her that her grandfather looked as robust as ever. She continued reading:

"Harlan is such a remarkable man, please do make sure your son has a chance to get to know him. Maybe we can all be together again this year at Christmas. Of course with no babies due, it will probably be boring.

"Whoops, almost forgot. We think that Dani has met *the* man. So far, though, she is being stubbornly resistant to the idea. Typical Adams, though in her case at least I understand what's behind her reluctance. Maybe, if you come, you can give her a push.

Until then, much love,
Mom."

Angela sighed and folded the letter.

Clint regarded her sympathetically. "Homesick, huh?"

"I was so sure I would never, ever feel homesick," she said. "I have everything I ever wanted right here. You, our son, a home."

"I could try to make you forget about it," he offered, his hand closing over her breast.

She grinned. "I'll bet you could, too."

His fingers stroked and teased until the images of home almost faded. Then he sighed.

"It's not working, is it? Your body's with me, but your heart is back in Texas."

"Afraid so."

"Then we'll go home," he said. "Christmas? Thanksgiving? You pick."

She regarded him speculatively. He seemed to be in an indulgent mood. "The Fourth of July is just around the corner," she suggested hopefully. "We could take a long weekend. Grandpa would send the plane."

"You know, Mrs. Brady, you have absolutely no patience."

"Sorry," she said without much real contrition in her voice.

"And I have absolutely no willpower when it comes to refusing you something you want. The Fourth it is. You call and I'll start supper."

She wound her arms around his neck instead. "How did I ever get so lucky?"

She lowered her head and kissed him. She began working the buttons on his shirt, then slid her hands inside over heated flesh and solid muscles. Clint moaned as her caresses became more and more insistent. When she reached for the snap on his jeans, he covered her hand with his and looked directly into her eyes.

"I thought you were anxious to make that call."

She shook her head. "It can wait. Some things definitely take priority."

Clint stood up then and shucked off his shirt and

boots and jeans with an efficiency that still startled her. She grinned at him. "Afraid I'll change my mind?"

"Nope, just encouraging you to hurry up and get naked, too."

"Unlike you, I do think there are some things in life worth savoring. Stripping happens to be one of them. Why don't you just stretch out on the bed and I'll show you what I mean?"

"I don't think so," he said, already fiddling with the buttons on her blouse.

As clever as he was with his own, he fumbled with hers. She'd always found that endearing somehow, proof that she could rattle him when little else in life could. Once in a while a woman deserved to have an edge with a man.

He didn't wait for her to finish undressing before his hands were everywhere, caressing, probing, pleasuring. She was breathless long before they tumbled into bed together, straining toward a first climax before he even touched the moist, sensitive core of her. With a quick, skimming stroke, he sent her over the edge, then settled back to take his time and do it all over again.

Her breath was coming in ragged gasps, her body was slick with perspiration and fiery with need by the time he slipped inside her, filling her up, joining with her in a way that made her feel whole and never failed to amaze her.

His movements were slow, languorous, as if they had all the time in the world, when the rapidly spiraling of sensation inside her said otherwise. With his gaze fastened to hers, he seemed able to tell the precise instant when one more stroke would have been too much.

"Not yet, darlin'," he said and stilled inside her.

Frustration and need had her thrusting her hips up, searching for release, demanding it. If she could have, she would have flipped him onto his back and ridden him, exulting in the sensations that never failed to astound her.

But there was pure joy in this, too, in letting him control the pace, in delaying the sweet, sweet end for as long as possible. She settled back to wait, to prove that she could be patient when it counted, but one tiny movement of his hips, the touch of his lips closing over her breast pitched her right back to a physical intensity that was just shy of exquisite torture.

And again, he drew back. He touched a finger to her chin, stroked a thumb across her lips, drawing her attention. "I love you, angel."

"I love you."

He smiled at that, then rolled to his back without releasing her. "Why don't you have your wicked way with me, then?"

Settled intimately astride him, she said, "I thought that's what I was doing."

He linked his hands behind his head. "Not so's I noticed."

She laughed at the hint of challenge in his tone and the spark of pure mischief in his eyes. "Why, you low-down, rotten scoundrel," she muttered, tweaking the hairs on his chest until he yelped. She laved the same spot with her tongue and had his breath catching in his throat and all signs of teasing fading from his eyes.

When she began to move her hips, his gaze locked with hers.

"Now that's more like it, darlin'."

"I'm so glad you approve," she said, her voice husky.

And then she was lost again to sensation, to the rasp of his day-old beard against her skin, to the hitching sound of his breathing and the rush of his blood when she touched a finger to the pulse at the base of his neck. Then all she felt was the heat, his and hers, so much heat that she was sure they would be consumed by flames.

The slick friction of their bodies melding was as new and thrilling today as it had been on the night they met. Familiarity and commitment had only made it better, had only deepened the bond that was renewed each time they made love.

There was trust now, too, trust that would last beyond this moment, trust that would carry them through eternity. It had been slow in coming, but Angela felt it each time they looked into each other's eyes, each time they made love with an abandon that could only come with honesty and hard-won faith in what they had together.

"Come with me, angel," Clint whispered. "Come with me now."

Angela smiled as they reached the peak together, both of them rocked by shattering sensation.

She collapsed against his chest, breathing hard and feeling like a million bucks.

"I don't think I'll ever be able to move again," she said eventually.

"I'm afraid one of us is going to have to," Clint responded.

"Why?"

"Our son is calling. It's dinnertime. And he's clearly impatient."

Angela struggled to untangle herself from her husband and the sheets. "I guess I'm just going to have to teach that boy to cook."

"You might have to wait until he's old enough to reach the stove," Clint pointed out. He kissed the tip of her nose. "I'll cook. You call your parents and tell them we're coming home for the next big barbecue."

"Not home," Angela said, her hand on his cheek. "This is home. I'll tell them we're coming for a visit."

A slow smile spread across his face and lit his eyes. If she'd known how much it would mean to him to hear her say the word, she would have said it much sooner. Texas and White Pines would never be far from her thoughts. Her family would never be far from her heart. But this *was* home now. It always would be.

As for their son, though she vowed never to say as much to him, he was their littlest angel, the brightest one in the universe. He would grow up knowing how special he was, but she prayed he would never feel the inadvertent pressures of living up to expectations.

And this man, she thought in wonder, watching Clint as he retrieved his scattered clothes, he was far more than the father of her child. She could admit it now, to herself and to him. He was her heart and soul.

* * * * *

NATURAL BORN TROUBLE

1

The day had already been too long and it wasn't even noon.

Dani Adams sank down into the chair behind her desk and vowed to catch a quick nap before her afternoon appointments. She'd been up since three a.m. with an emergency, a dog that had been struck by a drunk driver on a flat stretch of Texas highway just outside of town.

The sheriff's urgent call, when he was already en route, had awakened her. Minutes later, he had brought the bruised and bloodied animal in, and she'd worked for hours trying to save it. The poor old thing was hanging on by a thread.

She probably should have put him to sleep, but every time she thought of his owner, eighty-year-old Betty Lou Parks, she balked. Betty Lou adored that dog. He was her constant companion, riding beside her in the rusty old car Betty Lou drove into town once a week to pick up groceries. Dani had heard the anxiety and choked-back tears in Betty Lou's quavery voice when she'd called to check on her beloved pet and that had been that. Dani had promised to do everything she could to save the old woman's precious Honeybunch.

Honeybunch, she thought, smiling. The poor dog was probably embarrassed every time his master called to him in public. Mostly proud German shepherd, he had just enough mixed blood in him to give him a slightly whimsical look. Dani knew better than to be fooled by his appearance, though. He was fiercely protective of Betty Lou, which was probably why her children hadn't insisted long ago that she move into town from the isolated house where she still planted a garden every single spring.

Dani suspected most of her fee would come from that garden. Tomatoes, potatoes, beans, squash, herbs. Betty Lou raised them all, more than enough to last her through winter and to barter for some of her other needs. She was as independent now as she had been fifty years ago when her husband had died and left her alone with three small children to care for. Dani admired her resilience. She could use a little of it now just to get her through the rest of the day.

Sighing when her mind kept whirling and sleep eluded her, she picked up the batch of mail her assistant had left on her desk and out of habit sorted it into neatly organized stacks. Bills went into one pile, junk mail into another, professional newsletters and magazines into a third. When she came to a cheap business-sized envelope addressed in childish printing, her heart skidded to a halt. Automatic and too-familiar tears stung her eyes.

She already knew what she would find inside, a crayon-bright picture and a precisely lettered note. She had a whole drawer full of them, all from Rob Hilliard's two girls, children who had almost been hers.

Even after two years, every time one of these envelopes came it tore her apart inside all over again. Walking away from Robin and Amy when things hadn't worked out with their father had been the hardest thing Dani had ever had to do. For a time the envelopes had stacked up, unopened, because to see these expressions of love and know that she would never be a parent to the children who created them broke her heart. Phone calls left her shattered for hours, sometimes days.

Had she and Rob been married, had she been a real mother to the girls, at least there would have been the kind of custody arrangements that came with divorce. The girls would be with her part—if not all—of the time.

As it was, she had no rights, no legal standing whatsoever in their lives, just the powerful bond of a love that had deepened over the four years she had been with their father. Four years, during which expectations of permanence had been raised. An engagement that had sealed that expectation. Wedding plans had consumed Dani's thoughts and enchanted the girls.

And then it had all come tumbling down. Rob had met someone else and broken the engagement just weeks before the scheduled wedding date. Dani had been crushed. The girls, understanding none of what was going on, had been devastated when Dani had moved out of the house and left town.

Now distance and the attitude of Rob's young and insecure girlfriend precluded even the most casual of visits. Tiffany thought the girls would adjust more readily if the break were clean. Tiffany thought... Tiffany thought... Dani hadn't seen much evidence that Tiffany even had a brain.

As soon as the sarcastic criticism surfaced, Dani chided herself for being uncharitable. It was hardly Tiffany's fault that Rob had no spine to speak of.

At any rate, contact had been limited to whatever calls and drawings the seven-year-old and five-year-old girls could manage. They'd been astonishingly ingenious about it, too.

Now, though, they were slowly adapting to the change. The vows to hate Tiffany forever and ever were less frequent. So were the calls and notes to Dani. The spaces in between almost gave her time to heal, but it took only an envelope like this one to rip the wound open all over again and leave her feeling raw and vulnerable. How did adoptive mothers stand it when courts ripped their children from their arms to return them to the natural parents? How did they survive the loss? she wondered. How did they make the love stop? Or fill the empty space inside their heart?

For a moment she debated leaving the envelope unopened, but there seemed little point to it. Sooner or later she would open it anyway. Like removing a bandage with a sudden yank, this would be quicker, if no less painful.

The sheet of paper inside was a piece of Rob's expensive, embossed business stationery, she noted with amusement. He would probably have a cow if he knew they'd gotten into it and used it for coloring.

She studied the page, her eyes misty. Amy had clearly done the drawing. It was as vibrantly colorful

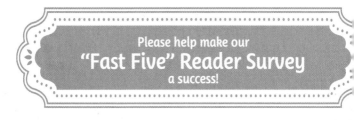

Please help make our
"Fast Five" Reader Survey
a success!

Dear Reader,

Since you are a lover of our books, your opinions are important to us... and so is your time.

That's why we made sure your **"FAST FIVE" READER SURVEY** can be completed in just a few minutes. Your answers to the five questions will help us remain at the forefront of women's fiction.

And, as a thank-you for participating, we'd like to send you up to **4 FREE BOOKS** and **FREE THANK-YOU GIFTS!**

Try **Essential Suspense** featuring spine-tingling suspense and psychological thrillers with many written by today's best-selling authors.

Try **Essential Romance** featuring compelling romance stories with many written by today's best-selling authors.

Or TRY BOTH!

Enjoy your gifts with our appreciation,

Pam Powers

To get up to
4 FREE BOOKS & THANK-YOU GIFTS:

✳ Quickly complete the "Fast Five" Reader Survey
and return the insert.

"FAST FIVE" READER SURVEY

1 Do you sometimes read a book a second or third time?   ○ Yes   ○ No

2 Do you often choose reading over other forms of entertainment such as television?   ○ Yes   ○ No

3 When you were a child, did someone regularly read aloud to you?   ○ Yes   ○ No

4 Do you sometimes take a book with you when you travel outside the home?   ○ Yes   ○ No

5 In addition to books, do you regularly read newspapers and magazines?   ○ Yes   ○ No

YES! Please send me my Free Rewards, consisting of **2 Free Books from each series I select** and **Free Mystery Gifts**. I understand that I am under no obligation to buy anything, as explained on the back of this card.

❏ **Essential Suspense** (191/391 MDL GNTC)
❏ **Essential Romance** (194/394 MDL GNTC)
❏ **Try Both** ((191/391 & 194/394) MDL GNTN)

FIRST NAME	LAST NAME

ADDRESS

APT.#	CITY

STATE/PROV.	ZIP/POSTAL CODE

as the little girl herself. A shaky American flag predominated, dwarfing two stick-figure children—Robin and Amy, according to the names neatly printed under them by the older Robin. Each child was holding what Dani assumed were meant to be sparklers.

"Happy Fourth of July" was printed across the top in red and blue letters. "We Miss You" had been added in bright pink and purple at the bottom. "Love, Robin" was as precise as a seven-year-old hand could make it. Amy's signature was twice the size of her sister's and bore little evidence of any understanding of capital and small letters.

"Oh, babies," Dani murmured. "I miss you, too." She stared at the picture for as long as she could bear it, then tucked it into the drawer with all the others. She would answer the note tonight, though she had no idea if the petty Tiffany allowed the children to see the occasional cards and letters Dani sent to them so they would know that she still thought of them and loved them, that she hadn't deliberately abandoned them.

The knock on her office door had her hurriedly wiping away telltale traces of tears.

"Yes, Maggie, what is it?"

Her nineteen-year-old temporary assistant poked her head in. She was clearly fighting a smile. "I'm really sorry to interrupt you. I know you need a break after the night you had, but we have an emergency up front."

"It's not Honeybunch, is it?" she asked, already pulling her white coat on over her slacks and short-sleeved blouse.

"No, no, it's nothing like that," Maggie soothed in a calming tone that proved what a good vet she, too, would make one day. "I think you'd better come and see for yourself."

Dani followed her assistant down the corridor to the reception area. Even before they got there, she could hear two voices. They were arguing. They were also very young.

"Told you not to take him out of the bowl," one was saying.

"I didn't," the other replied. "Not for long anyway."

Dani glanced at Maggie. The teen's lips were twitching with amusement again.

"I can't go back out there," Maggie said, drawing to a halt outside one of the treatment rooms. "I know I'll laugh and obviously this is a very serious crisis to them."

"Let me guess," Dani said. "We're not talking a puppy or a kitten here, are we?"

"Afraid not."

"A goldfish?" Dani guessed.

"You got it."

"Dead?"

"Oh, yes."

Dani closed her eyes and sighed. "You could have handled this, you know."

"Not me. I haven't even finished pre-vet school," Maggie said. "Besides, they wanted a real veterinarian. Said they could pay, too. Fifty cents."

"Terrific. Just terrific."

Plastering a smile on her face, she stepped into the reception area and confronted two boys, no more than eight, identical twins from the look of them. Both had spiky blond hair and freckles and the same front tooth missing. If she hadn't made up her mind never to let another child get to her, these two would have stolen her heart on the spot. As it was, she cloaked herself in a brisk, professional demeanor.

"I'm Dr. Dani Adams," she told them. "What seems to be the problem?"

"You're a girl," one of them said, eyes wide.

"Yeah, we wanted a real doctor," the other stated firmly. "Not a nurse."

Chauvinist little devils, she concluded, trying very hard not to bristle.

"I am a doctor. You can see my license, if you like. It's hanging over my desk."

The two boys looked at each other, seemed to reach a silent, joint conclusion, then nodded.

"I guess it's okay," one said with unflattering reluctance. "Show her, Zachary."

A smudged little hand emerged from a pocket. Zachary opened his fist to display a sizable, but very dead goldfish.

"We think he might be a goner," Zachary said, tears obviously threatening. "Can you save him?"

Dani hunkered down in front of them and took the patient. "I won't lie to you. It's serious, all right. Let me take him in the back and see if there's anything I can do."

The second twin regarded her suspiciously. "Can we come?"

"I think you'd better wait out here," she said. "I promise I won't be long."

Fortunately, she had learned long ago working for the last town vet to expect anything. She kept a drawer filled with suitable pet "coffins." In the back she placed the dead goldfish atop some cotton in an old jewelry box, waited a suitable length of time, then started for the front, struggling to keep her expression serious. Maggie was having no such luck, though she was trying to stifle her chuckles.

"Hush," Dani whispered as she passed.

Back out front she found the two boys once again trying to place blame. Worried gazes shot up when she returned. At the sight of the box, lower lips trembled and tears clearly threatened.

"He's a goner, isn't he?" Zachary asked pitifully.

"I'm sorry," she said quietly, handing the box to him. He took it gingerly, clearly more intimidated now that he knew the fish was indeed dead. "It was too late. There was nothing I could do. Goldfish really don't do very well outside their bowls."

The indignant owner of the goldfish poked his brother. "Told you, dimwit."

"Listen, Joshua Michael Jenkins, you don't know everything," Zachary said, punching his brother back and allowing the boxed-up goldfish to topple to the floor in the process.

Dani stepped between them and quieted them with a hand on each boy's shoulder. "Hey, you two, don't start taking this out on each other. It was an accident, I'm sure."

"It wasn't no accident," Joshua said, scowling. "He was jealous 'cause my goldfish lived and his didn't, so he killed it on purpose."

"Did not," Zachary said, trying to slip around Dani to throw a punch.

In his haste, he barely missed the box he'd dropped. Dani retrieved it. No telling what would happen if he squished his brother's fish on top of having killed it.

Dani hunkered down again and circled an arm around both waists, forcing them to remain where they were. "Were these your only pets?"

"Yeah," Joshua said. "Dad said until we could learn to be responsible and take care of a couple of goldfish, he wasn't getting us no puppy."

Dani winced at the appalling grammar, but figured someone better qualified than she was should be correcting that. "He's right, you know. If you own animals, it's very important that you take good care of them. It is a responsibility."

"We'll probably never get a dog now," Joshua grumbled. "And it's all your fault, dimwit. I coulda had one. It wasn't my goldfish that died, not until you killed it."

"Maybe there's a way you could change your father's mind," Dani said.

They eyed her skeptically.

"I don't know," Zachary said. "Dad's pretty strict. Once he lays down the law, he won't budge for nothing."

"How?" Joshua asked, clearly more willing to consider any option that would get him the puppy he wanted.

"Well, you see, I have a lot of kittens around here. People bring their cats by all the time, and I try to find good homes for them and their babies."

Joshua appeared mildly intrigued. "Kittens, huh? What does that have to do with us?"

"I was thinking that perhaps your dad might let you bring one home on a trial basis until I could find a real home for it. It would be temporary, of course. I know it's not a substitute for the puppy you want, but it would help me out and you two could prove to your dad that you are responsible enough for a puppy. What do you think?"

"Could we see the kittens?" Zachary asked.

"Sure."

Dani led the way through the clinic to the entry into her own living quarters. Francie III, a descendant of her own first cat, lounged under the kitchen table, where she had the benefit of the cool linoleum and a slanted beam of sunlight.

"Is that the one?" Joshua asked, eyes wide. "She's really, really big."

"She's expecting babies," Dani explained.

At the sound of her voice, more cats scrambled through the doorway, skidding on the waxed floor, then meowing plaintively for food as they wound themselves around her ankles. The cats gave wide berth to the two boys. Maybe on some subliminal pet network they'd heard about the goldfish.

Three kittens, not quite as fast as the adults, nor as discriminating, picked their way daintily toward two pairs of fascinating new sneaker-clad feet and sniffed.

The boys peered down at the scrambling, tumbling heap of kittens, two gray-and-white, one orange with white paws.

"I like the orange one," Zachary said.

"Me, too," Joshua said. "He looks like a tiger."

"It's a girl," Dani said.

"Does she have a name?"

"Not yet, but I'll bet she'd really like one. You two could name her, if you're interested."

"Mittens," Zachary said at once.

"That's a dumb name," Joshua protested.

"Is not. Her paws are white, aren't they?" Zachary bent down to pick up the kitten, but Joshua promptly nudged him aside.

"Don't even think about touching her," he said. "You'll probably squish her or something."

"Will not."

"Will, too."

"Hey," Dani protested. "If you two can't get along and work together to take care of her, then I can't suggest to your dad that he allow you to watch out for her for me."

"You're going to talk to our dad?" Zachary asked, wide-eyed.

"Of course. I can't send the kitten home with you without his permission. If you'd like me to, I'll call him right now."

"At work?" Joshua asked, then shook his head. "I don't think that's such a good idea. He's not in a very good mood when he's at work."

"Besides I don't think he'd like it very much if he knew Paolina brought us into town," Zachary added.

"Paolina?"

"She's our new housekeeper," Joshua explained.

"Yeah, and she's stayed a whole two weeks, longer than any of the others."

"I see." Dani hid a smile at the telling remarks. "You let me worry about your dad. I think he'll understand that this was a crisis. Do you know the number?" She picked up a nearby portable phone.

"Sure," Zachary said and recited it.

The familiar number had her pausing. "Your dad's in the oil business?"

"How'd you know that?" Joshua asked.

"I know someone who works there," she said carefully, not mentioning that the someone was her stepfather, nor that he owned the company. "What's your dad's name?"

"Duke Jenkins."

Ah, Dani thought, so these boys belonged to the mysterious Duke Jenkins, whose reputation in the field had been legendary. She'd overheard Jordan talking about how badly he hated the thought of losing him on exploration, but what an asset he would be anywhere in the company.

She'd also heard that the man was chafing at being chained to a desk. She suspected these two had something to do with his decision to take a safer assignment. Or perhaps his wife had demanded it. Then, again, hadn't she heard he was a widower? Or was he divorced? Either would explain why he and not their mother was making the decisions about their pets and why this new housekeeper was so important.

She hit speed dial for the company headquarters a few blocks away. Originally the company had been in Houston, but her mother had persuaded Jordan to relocate years ago. When the operator answered, Dani greeted her, then asked for Duke Jenkins.

"Don't tell me you've staked him out already," the young woman said with an audible sigh of regret.

"Actually, I'm calling on a business matter," Dani reassured her.

"Well, you're out of luck, hon. He's in with Jordan and last time I checked the rafters were about to blow straight off the building. I wouldn't buzz in there for the president of the U.S.A."

Donna Kelso was not easily intimidated, nor was Jordan the kind of man who tolerated much insubordination. Dani could only imagine just how explosive the meeting going on in her stepfather's office was. If Duke Jenkins was foolish enough to take Jordan on, he was either a very brave man or he operated on pure arrogance. If Jordan hadn't fired him in the first five minutes, then Duke Jenkins was a very valuable company asset. Dani knew better than to get caught in the middle.

"Never mind," she said hurriedly. "I'll catch up with him later. Thanks, Donna."

"You bet. You want me to leave him a message, say in a day or two when things cool down?"

"No, thanks."

She hung up and turned to see two very disappointed faces.

"I guess we don't get a kitten, huh?" Zachary asked.

"Not right away," she said. "But I will talk to your dad. I promise."

"When?" Joshua asked. "Tonight? He's always home by suppertime. You could come over. That would be best. Dad would never yell at a lady in person. He says it's not proper to hit girls and yell at them and stuff."

Dani wasn't at all sure she wanted to meet the formidable Duke Jenkins on his home turf, especially when his mood was likely to be surly. Still, she really did have to find a home for the kittens. She had a hunch a face-to-face chat with Mr. Jenkins was the only way these boys were going to get permission to bring one home. Besides, it might be interesting to see what sort of scars Duke Jenkins bore from his battle with Jordan. She'd known few men who dared to stand up to him and lived to tell about it, other than her uncles and grandfather, of course.

"I'll stop by as soon as I close up for the day," she agreed.

"Will you bring the kitten with you?" Joshua asked hopefully.

She shook her head. "That might be a tactical mistake, boys. I'd better talk to your dad first."

"He would probably like Mittens a lot if he saw her," Zachary argued.

"Trust me," Dani said, thinking that Zachary's tactical approach was very reminiscent of one she had used quite often at his age. Now she reacted with an adult's sense of caution. "We should get his permission first."

Let the man at least think he was in charge. It was a motto that made sense to her. It didn't mean he had to actually be in charge, as long as he thought he was. Being around a whole clan of master manipulators, most of them hardheaded males, had given her an edge on understanding the masculine thought process. She doubted Duke Jenkins veered too far from the same mold. In fact, Donna's report had just pretty much confirmed it.

"Dr. Adams?" Joshua asked, sounding suspiciously meek.

"Yes?" She noticed his gaze was pinned to the kittens again.

Blue eyes lifted and regarded her hopefully. "As long as you're going to talk to Dad anyway, do you think maybe you could see if we could keep all three kittens?" Joshua asked. "One for me and one for Zack and one for Dad."

"I don't know," she said. "Maybe we should start with just one. Besides, your dad might not want a kitten of his own."

"I'll bet he would," Zachary said. "He's kinda lonely now that Mom's gone."

Definitely another budding manipulator, she thought, fighting the salty sting of tears at the hitch in his voice. Probably a trait he'd picked up at his father's knee. That reference to his mom was definitely calculated to stir sympathy.

No problem, though. She was an Adams, by name and upbringing, if not by birth. When it came to manipulation, she had learned from the best authorities in the whole state of Texas, if not the entire world. Resisting Duke Jenkins and his sons would be a snap.

Then she recalled Donna's awestruck reaction at the mention of Duke's name. Maybe now would be a good time to start praying that she wasn't unwittingly about to start flirting with disaster.

2

Duke Jenkins was mad enough to bend a steel beam in two, preferably around Jordan Adams's neck. The man was stubborn, arrogant and, without question, the best oil man in the state of Texas. Maybe in the world. Duke figured he was no slouch himself, which suggested that maybe once, just once, Jordan ought to listen to him.

They were going to be wasting time and money drilling that new field. Every instinct he possessed told him that. He didn't give two hoots about the ream of geological surveys piled up on his desk. If he'd been able to get out there and look things over firsthand, run the dirt through his fingers, get a deep whiff of the scent of it, he would have been able to put some real strength into his arguments.

As it was, he was going with his gut, instinct honed by years of wildcatting. Jordan preferred cold, hard facts. Scientific facts, which in this instance Duke suspected had been doctored to someone else's benefit.

If he'd had somebody to look after the boys, Duke would have given Jordan all the facts he wanted. He would have been on a plane in a heartbeat, doing what he did best: finding oil and bringing it in, making them all richer.

Not that he cared all that much about the money. Most of his life he hadn't had a lot, hadn't needed much. Now he just wanted to insure that his sons would have a good future, a college education if they wanted it, though getting them through elementary school was proving to be challenge enough.

At any rate, he would trade the potential profits for the pure adrenaline rush of bringing in a new gusher any day.

Instead, he was surrounded by paperwork, mounds of it, most of which didn't matter a tinker's damn in the overall scheme of things as near as he could tell.

Oh, how he hated pushing papers around on a desk, he thought, staring irritably at the mostly untouched piles of it still awaiting some action or another. Well, today he'd had enough of it, he concluded, grabbing his jacket and heading for the door. If he hung around another few minutes, he might storm straight back into Jordan's office and quit, something he didn't have the right to do with two kids depending on him. The twins were the reason he'd made the move to Los Pinos in the first place. He had to give this major life-style overhaul a chance to work for their sakes.

Twenty minutes later, he had the top on the classic convertible down, the car radio was blaring a George Strait tune and he was curving down the winding driveway to the white, ranch-style house he'd bought on the outskirts of Los Pinos. There was a little dip in the land, then a rise. His house was nestled in that suggestion of a valley, surrounded by the pines for which the town had been named. A trickle of water that passed for a creek was the north boundary of the property. It looked like a picture-book image of what a home ought to be. He'd bought it at first sight because of that. It had triggered some sort of subliminal yearning within him.

Not that he had much experience with real homes. He'd bounced from foster home to foster home as a kid, a born troublemaker, according to those in the system who'd had to deal with his belligerence.

Used to being on the move, he'd seen no need to settle down once he'd grown up. Oil had been a way to stay on the go and pile up a decent bankroll.

Given his total lack of experience with lasting relationships, he probably never should have married, but Caroline had convinced him that they could make it work. When she'd been whispering in his ear late at night, when her magical hands had been busy moving over him, he believed almost anything that came out of her mouth.

Unfortunately, she hadn't counted on his refusal to quit wandering wherever the excitement took him. At first, she had gone with him, but once the boys had come along, she'd insisted on staying in one place. A few years of that and she'd gotten lonely and frustrated. When he was home, there had been more fights than loving.

A few months back, she had walked out, claiming that she'd had the twins to raise all alone for most of the past eight years, now he could see for himself how much fun it was. He could call her when he'd put in equal time and maybe they would work out a new arrangement.

Duke wasn't counting on it. He figured the divorce papers he'd received in the mail almost immediately pretty much countered any hopes he might have been harboring that things would eventually return to normal.

Even so, for a solid month he'd tried to pretend that nothing had changed. He'd convinced himself that he could go right on working crazy hours, taking off at the drop of a hat. Reality had slammed in when the fourth housekeeper in as many weeks quit in a huff.

Just in case the message wasn't plain enough, Zachary broke his arm and Joshua brought home a report card that suggested he hadn't cracked a book since his mother left. Even Duke had been bright enough to figure out that it was time to grow up and take responsibility for his sons, that parenting wasn't something a man could do in his spare time.

Not that he hadn't loved them all along. He had. He adored them. In fact, he was in awe of them. They were bright and mischievous and loving. He just didn't know a doggone thing about day-in, day-out caregiving. But he could learn, by God. There were books on the subject. He supposed there were even shrinks who specialized in that kind of stuff, not that he would ever be caught dead talking to one.

He did buy the books, though. A dozen of them the first week. When he caught the boys reading them, he figured he was never going to get an edge unless he worked at parenting full-time. With a sinking sensation in the pit of his stomach, he had hitched a ride in the corporate jet and had a long talk with Jordan Adams. Jordan came from a long line of men who understood about family. He'd offered Duke a vice presidency in Los Pinos on the spot. With it came the promise of stability.

Two weeks later, Duke had a new job and a new home. Moving in a hurry was something at which he excelled. It remained to be seen if he could get the rest of it right.

As he stepped out of the car in front of that appealing new home, the boys came barreling out the front door. It was a scene straight out of an old "Father Knows Best" episode and for a moment he allowed a feeling of immense satisfaction to steal over him. Not that it would last. His kids were irreverent little imps who would never be confused with anybody's angelic offspring for long.

"Don't let the screen door slam," Duke hollered just as it rocked on its hinges. He winced at the sound. He figured that door, the hinges and the frame would last a month, tops. Fortunately for all of them, he was reasonably handy with tools.

"Sorry, Dad," Joshua said unconvincingly.

"Yeah, sorry," Zack echoed.

Already stripped of his jacket and tie himself, he noted that they were looking a little more like normal kids again, with dirt streaking their faces and rips in their T-shirts. There had been one awful period when they'd been so neat and tidy he hadn't recognized them, just as he often didn't recognize himself in the business suits he was wearing these days. The boys' transition had been the fault of the second housekeeper. Or was it the third? Anyway, she'd had a very rigid outlook. She was the only one Duke had actually had to fire. She'd seemed to enjoy the challenge of turning his sons into proper young men a little too much.

"Hey, Dad, guess what?" Zachary said.

"Hush," his brother hissed.

"What?" Duke asked, suspicion aroused by the exchange.

Zack scowled at his brother. "We gotta tell him. She's coming right now."

"Who's coming now?" Duke asked. He glanced up the driveway and saw that, indeed, a four-wheel-drive vehicle of some kind was kicking up dust. "Okay, guys, what's up? What kind of trouble are you in?"

"We're not in any trouble," Joshua claimed. "Honest, Dad."

The last time Duke had heard that he discovered that they had broken a neighbor's window—his very large, floor-to-ceiling window. It had cost an arm and a leg to repair it. He would be taking the money out of their allowances until they reached puberty.

Since the truth seemed to be in short supply coming from these two, he decided to wait to see what the new arrival would have to say.

He studied the car as it came closer. Expensive and trendy once, it was little more than serviceable now. There was a layer of dried dirt, topped by dust over most of it, muting a dark green paint into something closer to muddy moss. For a man who took his cars seriously, this one was enough to make him shudder. He had an automatic hankering to rush for a hose and a can of his best wax.

The woman who emerged, however, had him shuddering for another, far more positive reason entirely.

She was a beauty. Long legs and skinny behind were molded by denim. The suggestion of very interesting curves lurked beneath a short-sleeved silk blouse that had been tied at a waist he could span with his hands. Blond hair, scooped into some sort of ponytail, escaped in curling tendrils to frame a face that was lovely even without makeup. He'd seen that face somewhere before, but for the life of him he couldn't remember where. As for the rest of her, he wouldn't have forgotten that in a dozen lifetimes, so apparently they'd never actually met.

A model, maybe? She was tall and thin enough. An actress? With that golden complexion and blue-gray eyes, she had a face the camera would love. Still, it didn't quite fit. Besides, Los Pinos, Texas, wasn't exactly crawling with the rich and famous. The town wasn't quaint enough to draw tourists. Nor was it home to any celebrities he'd ever heard of.

While his mind sorted through alternate possibilities, she crossed to where they were standing in three brisk strides. He wondered if she realized that the sway of her hips robbed her movements of the professional demeanor she was clearly after. She nodded at the boys, who were suddenly, inexplicably very quiet, then held out her hand.

"Hi, I'm Dr. Danielle Adams. Everyone calls me Dani."

Her voice was so low, so blasted seductive that her title and name barely registered. Duke took her hand in his and felt a jolt of pure electricity charge through him. He didn't feel much inclined to let her go, but she subtly wrestled her hand away from him. The reaction made him smile. So, he thought with satisfaction, she'd felt it, too. Hadn't liked it half as much as he had, though.

"Duke Jenkins," he said. "What can I do for you?"

"I'm the vet in Los Pinos," she said.

His gaze narrowed. Adams? A veterinarian? The pieces suddenly clicked into place and a sinking sensation settled in his stomach.

"You're Jordan's daughter," he guessed, remembering where he'd seen that face. It was very prominently displayed on his boss's desk, right alongside a much less interesting framed photo of his son and a family portrait taken some years back, when this woman had still been in pigtails.

"Yes," she said. Then, as if she were anxious to get past the subject of family ties, she rushed on with some convoluted tale of dead goldfish and kittens.

"I have all three of them in the car, if you'd like to take a look. I think the boys could really learn a lot taking responsibility for them, don't you?" she concluded, her eyes locked hopefully on his. He noticed they were more blue than gray just now as if some inner fire had sparked the sapphire in them.

Duke struggled to sort out the tale. When he had, he stared at her incredulously. "They killed two goldfish in less than a week, and you want me to let them care for three kittens? Doesn't that strike you as a bit risky?"

She gave him a winning smile that almost caused his heart to slam to a stop. Logic flew out the window. He wanted desperately to do as she asked, anything she asked.

"Really, it's not the same thing at all," she assured him. "Cats, even kittens, are reasonably independent and self-sufficient. And this would be temporary. I'm in a bit of a bind, you see. I have to find homes for

these three, plus two more that are too young to separate from their mother and then Francie III is expecting
again any day now."

Duke was astounded by the casual recitation. "Just
how many kittens are we talking about? I mean at your
house, not in the car."

"Well, of course, there's no way of telling for sure
with Francie, but I think there were five, maybe six others when I left, plus the mothers and a tomcat."

"You can't even keep track of the number of cats
living with you?"

"It changes, you see. Sometimes a neighbor's tomcat
will just wander in and make himself at home, which
probably explains why there are so many kittens in the
first place. And people find strays and drop them off
on my doorstep. I never quite know what to expect."

"You're a vet. Couldn't you stop this?"

"I would, but people know I love cats, so they're always coming to me when they want one. Sometimes
they're just not adopted as quickly as I would like, but
sooner or later they all wind up in good homes." She
smiled winningly again. "Like yours. This would be an
excellent opportunity for the boys to prove to you that
they can take responsibility for a pet, so you'd get them
the puppy they want."

"And how many puppies do you have around the
house?" he inquired suspiciously.

"None. I found they don't get along all that well with
the cats. I take those out to Uncle Cody. He's a real sucker
for a stray dog."

"And you think I'd be a sucker for three kittens?"

"Oh, no," she said, sounding genuinely horrified.

"I mean the boys did say you were lonely, but…" She winced. "Well, never mind. I just thought maybe you'd be willing to help me out for a bit."

Duke eyed his sons. Obviously they'd had a big day. They'd turned downright chatty with Dr. Dani. He would have to warn his latest housekeeper not to take them into town again until they turned twenty. Maybe then they would stay out of mischief and keep the details of his personal life to themselves.

"Look, it was really nice of you to come out here, but I'm afraid I'll have to take some time to think about this."

"But you have to at least look at the kittens," Zachary pleaded. "They're really cute."

"And they need homes," Joshua added. "Just like we did."

Duke scowled at Dani, annoyed that she'd put him in this position. The boys knew the rules. Apparently, they also knew he would never be able to resist Dani Adams. "Don't you want to chime in with your two cents?" he asked her.

She grinned. "No, they're doing pretty well on their own. I hate to oversell."

He surveyed her thoroughly just to watch the color climb in her cheeks. "Darlin', something tells me you could sell a man just about anything you put your mind to."

To his amusement, she blushed furiously at that, but held her ground.

"About the kittens," she persisted.

Duke recognized that he had been outmaneuvered and outmanned. Heck, he'd been sold when Dani Adams first opened her pretty little mouth. Besides, how much trouble could a kitten get into? "Okay, okay, I'll look at them. But we're just taking one. No more. Is that clear?"

The boys exchanged a look, but nodded dutifully.

Five minutes later, Dr. Dani Adams was tearing down the driveway kicking up dust again, and he and the boys were each holding one squirming kitten. For the life of him he couldn't remember exactly how that had happened. Something told him that a man would have to watch his step every single second around that woman or taking in stray kittens would be the least of his problems.

Back inside, he left the boys playing with the kittens, and headed straight for the kitchen where he could hear Paolina banging around pots and pans in time to the salsa music she was playing loudly enough to wake the dead. He hadn't decided if the woman was hard of hearing or just used the music to drown out his orders and the boys' complaints.

"Paolina?" he shouted over the din. When she didn't respond, he reached out and turned off the huge boom box on the counter. "Paolina?"

She glanced up at him in surprise. *"¿Sí?"*

"Did you drive the boys into town today?"

She tilted her head and regarded him warily as if trying to determine the politically correct response. *"Sí,"* she said eventually. "They ask to go."

"Because of the dead goldfish," Duke said.

She bobbed her head. *"Sí, sí, muy muerto."*

"Paolina, the next time the boys want you to take them into town, call and check with me first, okay?"

"Call, *sí, sí.* I will call."

He doubted she really understood a word he was saying, but he figured it was worth a shot. Paolina had been recommended by Jordan. She was related somehow to the line of housekeepers that had been working for their family for generations. A distant cousin, Jordan thought. Just here from Mexico. Very legal. All of her papers were in order. She just needed a job and a few basic language lessons, Jordan had promised.

Duke was quickly discovering, however, that if he hoped to have any kind of intelligent conversation with her, he was going to have to brush up on his Spanish. What puzzled him, though, was that she seemed to have no difficulty whatsoever comprehending the boys.

"*Gracias,* Paolina," he finally said with a sigh, hoping that at least some of his message had gotten through. She smiled brightly. "*De nada, Señor Duke.*"

He retreated to his study, only to find two boys and three rambunctious kittens there before him. The kittens had apparently been on his desk. Papers were scattered in every direction and one kitten, the one they'd informed him was his, was kneading whatever papers remained in his briefcase. Hopefully, it was the contract for those blasted mineral rights Jordan wanted to acquire. He could use the destruction of the paperwork as an excuse to delay the acquisition until he could get more facts to back up his belief that it would be a bad deal.

He nabbed the kitten as he sat down and allowed it to settle in his lap, where it purred contentedly. He found the sound soothing, even though his thoughts were in turmoil. Images of Dani Adams kept flashing through his mind. Those tantalizing flashes pretty much spoiled the head of steam he was trying to work up all over again at her father. He settled back and let the images linger.

She wasn't his type, not really. A little stiff, a little uptight and way, way too brisk and professional. He preferred women who were soft and cuddly and accommodating, the opposite of all those social workers and foster mothers who'd made his childhood a living hell. At least that had been his preference before he'd settled down with Caroline. Since the separation, he'd steered as far away from romantic entanglements as he possibly could. Maybe his type had changed.

Before he could spend too much time contemplating the likelihood of that, his phone rang. He didn't waste his breath trying to shush the twins, just grabbed the portable and walked through the French doors onto his patio.

"Duke? It's Jordan."

His shoulders tensed. "Yes," he said curtly.

"Look, I'm sorry our discussion got out-of-hand earlier. I put you into that position so I could take advantage of your expertise. I should be listening to you."

"With all due respect, yes, sir, you should."

"Still won't cut me any slack, will you?" Jordan said with a laugh. "Even when I'm trying to apologize."

"Sorry. I guess I missed that part."

"Maybe that's because I'm out of practice," his boss conceded. "Look, jot down some of your thoughts and let's go over this again in the morning, okay? Maybe clearer heads will prevail by then."

"Mine or yours?"

"Hopefully, both. My wife says I behaved like an arrogant, pigheaded idiot."

"You'll get no argument from me, sir."

"Kelly said the same thing about you."

Duke chuckled. "No argument there, either. I'll have my reasoning on paper in the morning."

"Good. Now, tell me. How are you and the boys settling in? I should have asked you that earlier today. Do you like it here? Is there anything you need?"

"The boys love it," Duke said.

"But you're still fighting the desire to get back into the field," Jordan guessed.

"Yes," he admitted, knowing that the older man would understand. At one time Jordan had been a wildcatter himself, trying to make a place for himself in a business vastly different from his family's cattle empire.

"You'll find this challenging enough in time," Jordan promised. "I'll see to it."

If Jordan didn't, Duke had a feeling his daughter could. "By the way, I met your daughter today," he said.

"Dani?" Jordan asked, clearly surprised. "How'd that happen?"

He related a condensed version of the dead goldfish saga that had his boss laughing.

"So how many kittens did she stick you with?" Jordan asked before Duke had even gotten to that part.

"Are you psychic or something? How did you know about the kittens?"

"Son, from the day I married her mother the house has been crawling with kittens, and I'm allergic to the blasted beasts. Dani has a way with her."

"I'll say," Duke muttered.

"Did she pull out the sob story about drowning them in the river if no one took them?"

"Good God, no."

"That's the one she used on me. Those big eyes of hers filled up with tears. She told me that's what Kelly intended to do to them unless I agreed to let them stay."

"And you believed her?" Duke asked skeptically.

"Of course not. Kelly's got the softest heart in the universe. But I had to admire Dani's ingenuity. My father bought it, though. She had cats all over White Pines by the time she was six or seven. Somehow over the course of twenty odd years she's managed to convince my father that it's a win-win situation. He saves the cats. The cats keep the mice away."

"Amazing," Duke said, thinking that Harlan Adams's legendary reputation did not include any reference to the notion that he was a soft touch.

"You could have told her no," Jordan pointed out. "You had no problem delivering news I didn't want to hear."

"This was different."

"Yes," Jordan said thoughtfully. "I imagine it was. Good night, son. We'll talk in the morning."

"Good night, sir."

After he'd hung up, Duke had the awful feeling that he'd revealed far more about his reaction to Dani Adams than he'd ever intended. And he didn't like that speculative note he'd heard in Jordan's voice one little bit. It appeared he was going to have to be on his guard about more than business when he went into work in the morning.

And he was going to have to stay the hell away from

Dani Adams and her cats. Even as he reached that conclusion, one of those blasted little kittens tried to crawl up the leg of his pants, its claws biting into his flesh even through the fabric. He heard the snag, even before he caught the plaintive meow. Looking down he saw that the kitten was caught partway up his calf.

"You're going to be nothing but trouble," he muttered sourly as he leaned down to disentangle the animal.

But even as he said it, he brought the soft, tiny creature up to curl against his chest.

"Nothing but trouble," he murmured again. This time, though, he was thinking of Dani Adams when he said it.

3

Dani was pretty sure she held her breath all the way back into Los Pinos. Duke Jenkins was the kind of overwhelming, purely masculine man who made a woman's toes curl without half trying.

With the notable exception of her stepfather, she'd spent her whole life around men whose fashion sense gravitated toward denim. Somehow Duke Jenkins had managed to make a perfectly respectable business suit and starched white shirt look as if he were only seconds away from stripping down to nothing. Her imagination had run wild. If a man like that put his mind to it, he could probably seduce a tree stump.

Of course, there was no chance of him trying anything with her. He worked for Jordan. More importantly, she was immune to his charms. He was a single dad, which placed him so far off-limits he might as well have been in Alaska with a barricade around him. With any luck she would never see him or his boys again. With better luck, she would never even hear his name mentioned.

Luck, of course, was never on her side, not when it came to matters of the heart, apparently.

No sooner had she walked into the house than her phone rang.

"I hear you met your father's new vice president today," her mother said without so much as a minute of small talk to disguise her prying.

"How could you possibly have heard a thing like that already? I barely left the man's house an hour ago. Do you have spies over there? Or can I blame this on Grandpa Harlan. I know he has them everywhere. He always knows what we're up to, half the time before we do. It's unnerving."

"You can't blame this one on your grandfather. Jordan spoke with Duke earlier on a business matter. He mentioned that you'd been there. He said you talked him into taking a few kittens off your hands," she reported with obvious amusement. "Jordan said he sounded a little bewildered by how that had happened."

Dani chuckled. "I'm sure Dad could identify with that."

"Indeed. I overheard him sympathizing rather sincerely. He told Duke to watch his step around you or his house would be crawling with all sorts of critters."

"I'm not that bad," Dani protested.

"You'll never convince Jordan of that. He wasn't the least bit interested in owning one cat, much less the dozens you paraded through here over the years."

"That was better than my brother's snakes and you know it."

Her mother laughed. "You bet. I'll tell Jordan to remind Duke of that when he's cussing about the cat hair all over the house."

She paused and all of Dani's self-protective instincts went on full alert. Her mother turned hesitant only when she knew she was about to tread on dangerous ground.

"So," her mother began a little too casually, "what did you think of him?"

"Who?" she asked just as innocently, determined not to be sucked into making an admission she could never live down. If she so much as hinted that she'd been attracted to Duke, even on a purely physical level, the meddlers in the family would turn that into an engagement before she could blink.

"Duke, of course."

"I didn't notice."

"Sweetie, a woman would have to be dead not to notice a man like Duke Jenkins."

"Okay," Dani conceded grudgingly, aware that nothing less than total honesty would satisfy her mother. She might as well get it over with. "If I were to have to give a totally objective description of the man, I'd say he's quite a hunk."

"An understatement, if ever I've heard one," her mother concurred. "He's gorgeous with all that thick, sun-streaked hair and those shoulders…" She sighed. "My goodness, those shoulders…"

"Mother!"

"Well, I can't help it. He reminds me of Jordan."

"Is Dad aware that you've fallen for his new protégé?"

"Very funny. The only man I've ever fallen for was Jordan and he knows it. Unfortunately, your father knew it, too. It took Jordan a while to figure out he felt the same way, but once he got the message things have worked out rather nicely."

As she spoke, Dani could imagine her mother's soft, nostalgic smile, the one that always came with any mention of Jordan Adams.

"Anyway, enough about that," her mother said briskly. "We were talking about Duke."

"You were talking about Duke," Dani corrected.

"And you were trying to avoid the subject. I was just going to say if any man on earth needs a woman in his life, he does."

Dani had been waiting for this particular hint. It was about as subtle as a swat with a riding crop. "Forget it," she said emphatically.

"Forget what?" her mother inquired innocently.

"I am not now nor will I ever be interested in Duke Jenkins."

"Because of his boys, I imagine."

"Of course, because of the boys. Mother, I really don't want to get into this again. Just forget it, okay? If you feel some sort of matchmaking force coming over you, give Jenny a call. She's older than I am. She's practically an old maid. Besides, she has Grandpa Harlan's tough hide. She could probably handle a man like Duke Jenkins, plus his sons without batting an eye. She needs a little romance in her life. I don't."

"Danielle…"

"Don't start with the *Danielle*. That always precedes a lecture and I don't need one. It's been a long day and I'm exhausted."

"But—"

"Bye, Mom. Good to hear from you. Love you."

"Danielle! Don't you dare hang up on me."

With only the slightest twinge of regret, Dani ignored

her mother's command and slid the receiver firmly back into its cradle. Francie III crawled into her lap, circled twice, then settled down, purring loudly as Dani automatically stroked her under her chin.

Jenny and Duke Jenkins. Now there was a combination to contemplate. Grandpa Harlan's adopted daughter was as potentially volatile as a high school chemistry lab. Unlike Dani, she would be a more than even match for a man like Duke.

Ironically, though, the thought of seeing the two of them together made acid churn in Dani's stomach. If she hadn't known better, she would have labeled the reaction as pure, gut-deep jealousy, which was ridiculous, of course. No single father would ever stir anything more dangerous than the quiet warmth of friendship in her ever again. She wouldn't allow it.

Famous last words, she thought a few days later when she went to White Pines for the annual Fourth of July celebration. There were Duke, Joshua and Zachary right in the thick of things. There was Jenny, beautiful, dark-haired Jenny Runningbear Adams, holding Duke's attention with her animated telling of some Native American lore. Dani wanted to strangle them both, which was hardly the reaction of a disinterested third party.

Everyone—with the exception of her mother and Jordan—claimed to be absolutely stunned that she and Duke had already met. Her grandfather's claim struck her as a little too hearty, a little too determinedly innocent. She didn't trust the man one iota, not when it came to meddling. How Harlan Adams could have heard about the whole kitten incident she had no idea, but she didn't doubt for a second that he knew every detail. Nothing in Los Pinos and especially with his own family escaped his notice.

Nor did she doubt that Duke and the boys were here at his personal invitation. She doubted he'd needed any coaching from her mother on this one. Grandpa Harlan was a romantic, and he wasn't about to rest until everyone he loved was settled down and as content as he was.

"Nice-looking family," her grandfather observed as if he'd gotten a look inside her head. Old as he was, he still moved with an agility and sneakiness that amazed her.

Dani stared straight into his eyes, hoping her unblinking gaze would persuade him that Duke Jenkins was absolutely the last person on her mind.

"Who?" she inquired.

He returned her gaze with a sharp look. "Don't play that game with me, gal. You know perfectly well who I mean. Saw you looking at them just a minute ago."

"I was just curious about what they were doing here," she insisted. "Usually it's just family here for the Fourth of July picnic."

"Can't tell around here anymore who's family and who's not," Grandpa Harlan grumbled. "Besides, your daddy's right fond of the boy. Thought I ought to take a look for myself. I have a lot of respect for a man who's all alone and trying to do right by his kids."

So did Dani. She just didn't want to be any part of the equation. As if he'd read her mind again, her grandfather squeezed her hand, then took off as if someone had lit a fire under him. When she caught sight of Duke heading her way, a can of her favorite soft drink in hand, she understood why.

He offered her the chilled can without explaining how he'd known it was the drink she preferred, then took a sip of his own beer. "I counted four cats in the barn when I was out there. How many more have you hidden around the place?" he inquired.

"Oh, I lost count ages ago," she said, even though she knew precisely. "How are the three I left with you?"

"Still alive, which is something to be grateful for, if you ask me."

"I knew the boys would take good care of them."

"The boys? Are you kidding? All three of those blasted kittens have taken up residence in my study. When they're hungry, they chase after me. I can't move from one place to another without tripping over one of them."

There was too much affection laced in with the grumbling for Dani to take his complaints too seriously. "Won your heart, did they?"

Duke scowled. "Even if they had, do you think I'd dare tell you?"

There was a teasing glint in his eyes that Dani found just a little too attractive. She opted for a quick change of subject. "I saw you talking to Jenny when I got here," she began.

"Keeping an eye on me, were you?"

"In your dreams, Mr. Jenkins."

"It's Duke, darlin'. Once you've given a man kittens, you need to be on a first-name basis."

"Okay, *Duke,*" she said with deliberate emphasis. "Isn't Jenny remarkable? Most men fall all over themselves when they meet her."

"Really?" He sounded genuinely surprised. "Guess I'm not most men. I prefer prim little blondes myself."

Dani felt her cheeks burning. "Even when they're unavailable?" she said tightly.

"Especially when they claim they're unavailable," he said. "Makes me wonder why they're hiding from life."

"I am not hiding from life," Dani protested instinctively.

Duke grinned. "Oh, did you think I was referring to you?"

"Go to hell, Mr. Jenkins," she snapped and turned her back on him. Infuriating, insufferable tease, she thought as she marched off, spine straight. She could hear his soft chuckle as she went.

The rest of the afternoon she did everything in her power to avoid him, but no matter where she went, no matter what she did, she could feel his speculative gaze on her.

"Don't look now, but you've made a conquest," her cousin Angela said when she found Dani sitting all alone in a swing on the front porch.

"If discussing Duke Jenkins is the only thing on your mind, go away," Dani retorted.

"Ah, so he's made one, too."

"Angela, I am warning you. If you say one more word about Duke Jenkins, at least in any connection whatsoever with me, I will leave this party right now."

Her cousin's gaze narrowed worriedly. "Are you okay?"

Dani forced a smile. "Just feeling a little pressured, that's all. Don't worry about it. Tell me about you instead. How's life in Montana? Are you happy?"

Angela sat beside her and set the swing into a lazy motion. "Deliriously happy," she confessed, beaming. "Clint's the most wonderful, sexiest, kindest man on earth. He's the best husband and father a woman could ask for."

Dani chuckled at the exuberant praise. "I seem to recall a time when you thought he was a sneaky, low-down, conniving son of a gun. Are we talking about the same man?"

Angela grinned. "You bet." She regarded Dani slyly. "Which just proves how quickly attitudes change. Never say never, when it comes to a man."

Dani stood up abruptly. "I have to go."

Her cousin nabbed her hand and held it tightly, preventing the escape. "Dani, I'm sorry. I was just teasing. You know how I am. I didn't realize it would upset you so."

"Never mind." She squeezed Angela's hand reassuringly. "It's okay. I'm too sensitive."

"Maybe if you or somebody would tell me what happened, I wouldn't be sticking my foot in my mouth every time I turn around. My mother, your father, Jenny, practically everyone has told me to leave it alone, but I can't. I care too much about you."

Dani sighed and sat back down in the swing, idly setting it into motion again. "It's not as if it's a big secret," she said finally. "Everyone in the family knows."

"And everyone tries to protect you by being tight-lipped about it, giving you your space," Angela guessed. "Maybe what you really need is to talk about it, scream, rant and rave, get it out of your system."

Dani grinned at the image of herself screaming, ranting and raving. It just wasn't the way she handled things. She kept her emotions all bottled up inside, unlike the rest of her far more demonstrative relatives. She had envied Angela for some of the shouting matches she and Clint had had. Blowing off steam had seemed to pave the way to healing. Maybe her way just allowed the wound to fester.

She'd said absolutely nothing about the broken relationship and shattered dreams when she'd come home to Los Pinos, after leaving Rob. Her family had seen her with him and the girls often enough to know exactly how much she had loved them all. They had come to adore Robin and Amy as well, though her father especially had always seemed to have reservations about Rob. At any rate, they had been able to guess the depth of her anguish and had left her alone to deal with it in her own way.

She glanced at Angela, saw the sympathy and concern in her cousin's expression and decided it wouldn't hurt to just tell her what had happened. Maybe it would put an end to these awkward moments that kept cropping up between them after so many years of being as close as sisters. She would keep the telling simple and dispassionate.

Once she began, though, the words began to pour out, words filled with far more rage than she imagined she had ever held inside.

"That beast, that terrible, awful beast," Angela said fiercely when Dani was done. "How could he do that to you, to them?"

"Relationships don't always work out," Dani said objectively. "I mean now that I think about it, I can see how wrong we were for each other. Marriage would have been a disaster."

"But what about those girls of his? Didn't he take their feelings into account at all?"

Dani found herself trying to defend Rob's decision to

go along with Tiffany's demand for a clean break, but she simply couldn't muster any conviction.

"The man was a bastard," Angela said. "Admit it."

"Yes," Dani said softly. "Yes, he was."

"A little louder. I didn't quite hear that."

"He was a lousy, good-for-nothing, son of a bitch."

Angela grinned. "Better. Want to try one more time?"

Tears rolled down her cheeks, but she shouted the words at full volume, adding a few more derogatory remarks for good measure. It was surprisingly cathartic, she concluded, laughing.

"I hope you weren't talking about me," Duke said, appearing out of nowhere at the end of the porch.

Dani couldn't seem to find her tongue, but Angela grinned at him.

"Is that how people usually refer to you, Duke?"

"Some do," he admitted.

"Well, you can rest easy. In this case, we were talking about someone else."

His gaze settled on Dani, his expression thoughtful. "I see."

Angela looked from Dani to Duke and back again. "I think I'll run along now. Clint's probably wondering where I disappeared to. He gets panicky when he thinks he's going to have to change a diaper."

Something that felt a whole lot like panic settled in the pit of Dani's stomach as well as she watched her cousin disappear and saw Duke striding up onto the porch. She hadn't realized she was holding her breath until she felt it slowly expel when he settled against the railing opposite her, rather than in the swing beside her.

"I've been looking for you," he said.

"Why?"

"Just looking for a friendly face."

"And you came looking for me?" she asked skeptically.

"Darlin', you're too polite not to manage a friendly face for a business associate of your father's. Besides, you want me to keep those kittens, don't you? You're not going to risk offending me."

"I'm sure Jenny—"

"I've talked to Jenny. I've talked to everyone here. I'd rather just hang out here with you for a while, if you don't mind."

"And if I do?"

"Then I'll leave."

Her gaze narrowed. "Would you really?"

"Absolutely." He grinned. "But I'd be back."

Dani sighed wearily. "Don't tell me you're the kind of man who only wants what he can't have."

"Are you saying you're not interested?"

"I believe I told you once today that I'm not available."

"Because of that jerk you were cussing out when I turned up?"

Oh, God, he had heard. "How much did you hear?" she asked, flushed with embarrassment.

"Enough to know you've been badly burned, that you're gun-shy."

She forced herself to meet his gaze evenly. "I've been around guns all my life. They don't scare me."

"Was that meant to be a warning?"

"Just stating a fact."

"Duly noted, then. Which brings us back to you and me."

"There is no you and me," she said impatiently. "Not today, not tomorrow, not ever."

He didn't seem impressed by her declaration. "Bet I could change your mind," he said.

"You'd lose."

His gaze locked with hers and made her tremble, proving his point. Hopefully, though, he hadn't noticed.

"Wanna bet?" he said softly.

Before she could guess what he intended, he'd clasped her hands and pulled her to her feet. In less time than it took to blink, she was in his arms and his lips were seeking hers.

When his mouth settled gently over hers, she thought briefly about struggling, about directing a well-aimed blow into someplace that would prove just how serious she was about being left alone. The thought vanished before she could act on it, lost to a sea of sensations so sweet, so wildly erotic that her knees went weak and all she could do was cling.

An aching need began to build inside her. Slowly she slid her hands into his thick, silky hair and opened her mouth to the endless, provocative kiss.

It might have gone on forever. She certainly wanted it to and Duke showed no signs of relaxing his embrace. It was the sound of voices nearby that forced them apart, both of them breathing hard and looking dazed. She was pleased to see that he looked at least as shell-shocked as she felt.

That was her ego talking, of course. When she managed to get her brain functioning again, she realized that she didn't want him getting any crazy ideas from that kiss. One kiss, well, that was just a kiss. It didn't have to lead to anything more. It couldn't lead to anything more.

If she'd doubted that for an instant, the sight of his sons barreling around the corner of the house at full throttle, shouting for him at the top of their lungs would have convinced her. They were cute kids, wonderful, exuberant kids. Duke was quite obviously a great father. There was no room for her in that mix. She wouldn't risk it for the boys. She didn't dare risk it for her own peace of mind, either.

"Dad, we've been looking everywhere for you," Zack shouted.

"And why is that?" Duke asked, his hand discreetly but possessively resting on her waist.

"It's time for the fireworks," Joshua explained, excitement sparkling in his eyes. "Can you believe it? They're going to have their own show right here. Grandpa Harlan—he said we could call him that—he said we could sit with him and the guy who sets them off and see how they work. Come with us, okay?"

"You run along," Duke said. "I'll be there in a minute. If they start before I get there, do not touch anything. Understood?"

"Okay," they chorused. The two boys regarded him worriedly. "You will be there in just a minute, right? Promise? I don't think they'll wait forever. It's almost dark now."

"I promise."

When they'd gone, Duke drew Dani back around to face him. "Come with me."

She shook her head. "No, you go. Share this with your boys. Obviously, they can't wait to see the fireworks with you."

"I don't think they'd mind sharing them with you,

too. In fact, once the show begins, I doubt they'll even know I'm around."

"Please," she said. "Just go."

He regarded her with concern. "Dani, do we need to talk about what just happened here?"

"Nothing happened," she insisted.

"If you believe that, we don't need to talk, we need another demonstration."

She held him off this time, just as she should have done the first time he bent toward her. To her relief, he didn't argue. He released her slowly, then trailed his knuckles gently down her cheek.

"Later, then," he said, proving that it was only a temporary reprieve from the storm of emotions he'd set off inside her. He tucked a finger under her chin and lifted it until their gazes were even. "No fireworks could possibly match the sparkle in your eyes, darlin'. Remember that, okay? Remember, too, that I'm the one who put it there."

Remember it? Dani thought it was quite possibly the most romantic, most dangerously seductive thing any man had ever said to her.

Her sigh was heavy and filled with regret. She was going to have to work very, very hard to pretend she'd never heard him.

4

Duke could still feel the tentative movement of Dani's mouth under his, could still feel the shudder washing through her body and the sweep of her fingers through his hair when she finally surrendered to that Fourth of July kiss. The memories alone were enough to leave him hot and cranky with frustrated longing.

He'd never experienced such an instantaneous response to a woman before, at least not one that posed so many complicated risks. Attraction was one thing. He appreciated a beautiful woman as well as the next man. But what he'd felt during that impulsive kiss had unexpectedly rocked him, touched him on another level.

The kiss had been a mistake, a terrible, dangerous mistake, he concluded. She was clearly vulnerable. She was his boss's daughter. He was in no position to, had no desire to, get serious with any woman. He was barely coping with a new job and being a full-time father. Adding a woman to that would just beg for disaster. The list of sensible reasons to stay the hell away from her went on and on.

Yet he knew himself well enough to realize that if the chance came, danger or no danger, he would take it again. She was as intriguing to him as a hint of oil beneath the earth, as alluring as the elusive scent of crude just out of reach.

He smiled at the thought. Dani might be a practical, no-nonsense kind of woman, but he doubted she would appreciate being compared to the search for an oil well. Yet for him nothing was more magnificent, more compelling than that particular hunt. Nothing got his juices flowing quicker than an oil strike.

Nothing except sex, of course. The thought of heated bodies and pleasurable sex brought him full circle, straight back to Dani. That totally uninhibited kiss had told him that Dani's prim facade would disappear in bed. He wanted to make that happen. He wanted to watch the transformation, the flaring of passion in her eyes, the hardening of her nipples, the restless writhing of her slender, normally controlled body.

"Duke?" Lizzy Adams peeked around the edge of his door. "Jordan's looking for you."

He shook off his daze and stared. He could feel a sheen of perspiration forming on his brow, but resisted the urge to mop it off.

"Why didn't you buzz me?" he inquired testily.

Rather than taking offense at his tone, she grinned. "I have been," she said. "For the past five minutes." She regarded him speculatively. "I guess you were lost in thought. Thinking about Dani, I'll bet."

Apparently, all of the Adams women were mind readers, he concluded, scowling at Harlan's precious daughter, who was also Jordan's baby sister. She was still in school and already so sexually precocious it was scary. She flirted with him outrageously or at least she had until she'd seen him with Dani at the family's Fourth of July gathering. All day today she had merely regarded him with very grown-up amusement.

As he tried to gather his composure, he told himself he would be very glad when Lizzy went back to school in the fall and he got himself a real secretary. An *old* secretary, he amended. He wasn't worried that the replacement would have as sassy a tongue. No one who wasn't an Adams would dare to take the liberties Lizzy did when it came to bullying her boss and meddling in his affairs. That particular trait seemed to come with the Adams genes.

"Tell Jordan I'll be right there."

"Already told him. That was five minutes ago, though. You're already late."

"Any idea what's on his mind?"

"Sure. He wants to know if you're interested in Dani." She shot him another unrepentant grin. "We all do."

"It's none of your business," he grumbled as he passed her. "Remember that."

She regarded him worriedly. "Can I give you just the teensiest piece of advice?"

"Can I stop you?"

"Don't try telling that to Jordan. He's just like our dad. They both figure it's their God-given right to meddle in everyone's life."

"Not mine," Duke said succinctly.

"Unless it happens to cross paths with Dani's," Lizzy pointed out, then shrugged. "I say go for it, though. She's been sad for way too long. She needs somebody to shake her up, make her forget about that creep who dumped on her. Something tells me nobody could do that better than you. There's not a woman on the premises who doesn't swoon when you pass by."

"I'm delighted to have your blessing," he said dryly. "Unfortunately, it appears that's not the one I need."

"It's a start," she retorted cheerfully. "Good luck."

Duke took his time walking down the short executive suite corridor to Jordan's office. If he had his way, they wouldn't have this conversation. Unfortunately, it appeared unlikely that he was going to get his way, which meant he'd better come up with some satisfactory answers for the questions Jordan was likely to ask.

In typical fashion, his boss didn't waste time on small talk. Duke was barely across the threshold when Jordan scowled at him and asked, "What's going on between you and my daughter?"

Duke took his time responding. He deliberately sprawled in a chair opposite Jordan, hoping that the casual pose would communicate in a way that words could not that he wasn't going to be intimidated. Eventually, he shrugged. "Nothing as far as I know. Have you asked her?"

Unfortunately, Jordan was too sharp a businessman to be fooled by Duke's tactic. "Oh, please, don't give me that," he shot right back. "I want a straight answer."

Duke sat up a little straighter. He met Jordan's gaze evenly. "I don't know what you've heard, sir, but that's the truth. We've barely met. She's made it plain she's not interested. What more is there to say?"

To Duke's astonishment, Jordan actually chuckled at that. "I don't suppose you see the contradiction in that, do you? According to your claim, you two hardly know each other, but already she's felt it necessary to tell you she's not interested. What do you suppose brought that on? You don't expect me to believe it's how she opens every conversation with a man, do you?"

He flinched at the direct hit. "I suppose not."

"Could it have something to do with you kissing her the other night?"

Duke stared. "How the hell do you know about that?"

Jordan almost looked as if he felt sorry for him. "Son, you were on the front porch of my father's house in the middle of a family picnic. The teenagers sneak around like budding operatives for the CIA. You can't keep a secret with this clan if you bury it in a cave a thousand miles away. How do you expect to keep anything quiet when you're right in the thick of things?"

"A good point," Duke conceded. "I'll have to be more careful next time."

Jordan looked positively hopeful. "Then there's going to be a next time?"

Duke gave up on the evasions. "If I have my way," he admitted.

Jordan gave a little nod of satisfaction. "Good." He studied Duke intently. "Dani's had a rough time these past couple of years ever since she broke up with her fiancé, Rob Hilliard. If I'd been more on top of things, maybe I could have done something to save her all that heartache." He sighed with obvious regret, then looked directly into Duke's eyes. "It won't be easy getting her to trust you, you know that, don't you?"

"Nothing worth having ever is."

"Yes, you of all people would know that, wouldn't you?"

"Then I have your approval to keep seeing her?"

"Would it matter if you didn't?"

Duke met Jordan's gaze with a steady, unblinking look of his own. "No, sir. With all due respect, it wouldn't."

"That's what I thought," he said, sounding pleased. "Just one thing, though."

"Yes?"

"Hurt her and there won't be a place on earth you can hide."

"Understood."

Contriving to see Dani again was a whole lot simpler than Duke had anticipated. He should have realized that a powerful man like Jordan wouldn't be content to sit on the sidelines and let things unfold at their own pace. Less than an hour after their conversation, Duke had an invitation to dinner the next night.

"Nothing fancy. Just the five of us," Kelly Adams told him.

"Five?"

"Jordan and I, you and Justin. And Dani will be here, of course."

Of course, he thought. "I'll give her a call and offer her a lift," he said. He cursed the eager note that had crept into his voice.

"I wouldn't, if I were you."

Damn, did everyone in this family meddle? "And why is that?" he inquired.

"She doesn't exactly know you're coming," Kelly confessed.

"And you think if she knew she'd find an excuse not to come," he concluded.

"I'd say that's a safe bet. You unsettle her," Kelly said. "I could see that at the picnic. Now me, I think that's a good thing. Dani wouldn't."

Duke didn't like it, but he could see the wisdom in taking Kelly Adams's advice. He doubted anyone knew Dani as well as her own mother. He supposed there was something to be said for the element of surprise. In fact, he couldn't wait to see the expression on her face when she realized they'd been thrown together again.

"I see," he said blandly. "Well, if you think that's best."

"I do. Of course, you could hitch a ride over here with Jordan," she suggested slyly.

"But then I'd have to get a ride home," he protested, then smiled. "Ah, yes, with Dani, of course."

"It was just a thought," Kelly said.

"A good one, too. I'll speak to Jordan and I'll see you tomorrow night."

Jordan didn't bat an eye the next morning when Duke asked for a ride. Duke didn't bother wasting time with excuses. They both knew exactly what the scheme was all about.

"I'll pick you up on my way home from the office," Jordan said. "Do you want a head start so you can change?"

Duke nodded. "A half hour ought to suffice."

"Perfect. I'll clean up some paperwork before I leave."

Duke knew Jordan well enough to realize that even a casual family get-together wouldn't mean blue jeans and chambray. The man had impeccable style and seemed happier in a well-tailored business suit than any man

Duke had ever met. Under the watchful supervision of the twins, he finally settled for a pair of slacks from the new wardrobe he'd been forced to acquire for his new executive position. He added a pale blue dress shirt with the sleeves rolled up and the collar open.

Joshua and Zachary surveyed him intently, then nodded their approval. They didn't seem the least bit disappointed at being left behind, which meant they'd probably cooked up some scheme for getting into mischief.

"You need some of that smelly stuff, though," Joshua advised. "Girls like that."

"I don't," Duke said.

"But, Dad—"

"I am not taking advice from an eight-year-old. You two go and do your homework."

"Can we stay up until you get home?" Zachary asked hopefully.

"Not a chance. I've told Paolina you're to be in bed by nine-thirty."

The twins exchanged a look that suggested they considered Paolina an easy mark. "And if I don't find the two of you in bed and sound asleep when I get back, you'll be grounded until you're twelve," Duke warned.

"Aw, Dad, you wouldn't do that," Joshua said.

"You wouldn't, would you?" Zachary asked more worriedly.

"Don't test me and find out," he warned, scooping them up one at a time for hugs. Moments like this made him realize how much he'd missed during all the times he'd been away.

"Tell Dani hi for us," they shouted after him.

"Tell her the kittens are really cool," Zachary added. "We might not need a puppy, after all."

"I'll definitely tell her that," Duke said just as he heard Jordan tap his horn out front.

To Duke's relief, they spent the ride discussing business and other impersonal topics. As always, Duke admired Jordan's quick intelligence and shrewd judgment. There was a rock-solid dependability about him that Duke envied. He hoped he could find some way to emulate it and give his sons the role model they deserved.

It took less than a half hour to reach Jordan's property. As they approached the house, Duke surveyed the small place with its colorful garden with some surprise. Huge pots on the porch spilled over with lush, vivid flowers. He had expected Jordan to own something far more pretentious than this tidy, homey farmhouse. Not even a fresh coat of paint could disguise the fact that it was quite old and had never been much more than a struggling ranch.

Only after he was inside did he see that first appearances were deceiving. When Jordan showed him around, he discovered that an addition in the back was spacious enough for an indoor pool, an office with book-lined shelves and a very private master bedroom suite.

Still, the original house was warm and cozy, compared to Harlan Adams's far more formal White Pines. Jordan observed his reaction.

"Not what you expected, is it?"

Duke regretted being so transparent. "Sorry, but no. It's lovely, but I thought you would live in something very modern."

"Modern and pretentious," Kelly chimed in. "He

did," she announced as she joined them with a tray of appetizers hot from the oven. "In Houston." She shuddered. "It was awful. Cold, sterile and big enough to house a family of twenty." She brushed a kiss across her husband's cheek. "I convinced him he needed a home, not a showplace."

"She was right, too," Jordan said. "As usual."

"This ranch had belonged to my family for years."

"Kelly single-handedly saved it from ruin after they were gone," Jordan said with obvious pride.

The sound of a car skidding to a halt out front interrupted their conversation. Kelly winced.

"Dani's here," Jordan guessed.

"She drives like you," Kelly complained. "She's going to get herself killed one of these days."

"I haven't," Jordan pointed out.

Duke gathered it was an old argument. He felt his shoulders tense as he waited for Dani to appear. The front door slammed, she shouted a greeting, then came to an abrupt halt at the sight of him. Her smile faded.

Kelly quickly hugged her and whispered something that had Dani managing a tight smile.

"Hello, again," she said tersely to Duke as she bent to give Jordan a peck on the cheek.

"You're looking especially lovely tonight," Duke commented, grinning at the blush that climbed into her cheeks.

"I just came from the Holcombe place. Their dog was having a difficult time delivering its pups. If I'd known there was going to be anyone here beside family, I would have gone home first to change," she said defensively.

"No need to gussy up on my account," Duke said.

"Well, there is on mine," Jordan said, wrinkling his nose distastefully. "You smell like a barn."

"Maybe I should just leave," she said, turning for the front door at little too eagerly.

"Of course, you're not leaving," Kelly said. "You have clothes in your room here."

Dani sighed. "Fine. I'll be back in a few minutes. Where's Justin, by the way? I need to talk to him about something."

"He should be home shortly. He's over at Cody's with Harlan Patrick. Or so he claims. I suspect they're in town chasing girls."

Dani grinned at that. "Having his sister working at Dolan's must really cramp Harlan Patrick's style."

"You should hear Justin on that subject," Kelly said. "He says Sharon Lynn is personally ruining any chance they have of ever getting a date."

"So Dolan's is the hangout for teenagers?" Duke asked.

"It has been for years," Jordan told him. "Not even the fancy new burger franchise that opened up outside of town can compete."

"Thank goodness," Kelly said. "I'm glad my kids didn't grow up with their social lives revolving around fast food and malls."

"If Jenny had had her way, we would have," Dani said. "She's still itching to get a Bloomingdale's close by."

"She just says that to get your grandfather stirred up," Kelly said, then turned to explain to Duke, "It's an old joke between them that she's going to put a mall on his land as soon as she inherits her part of it."

"We'll see," Dani said. She stared hard at Duke. "I suppose you miss all the fancy Houston stores."

"Afraid not. Shopping was never my thing. As long as I can buy a good pair of jeans, I'm a happy man."

Her gaze swept over his clothes, which were far more expensive than even a pair of designer denim pants. "Jeans?" she said skeptically.

"Darlin', even those of us who hung out around oil rigs know enough to get gussied up for dinner with the boss."

Jordan and Kelly fought unsuccessfully to hide their grins. Dani frowned at all three of them.

"Since I appear to be the one who's underdressed, I'll go now and spruce up," she said. "I had no idea we were standing on formalities around here these days."

"Just get the straw out of your hair," Duke taunted, chuckling when her hand flew up in search of the non-existent piece of straw.

Dani left the room with a scowl, but at least it appeared she didn't head straight for the front door. He glanced at Jordan just in time to see him exchanging an amused look with his wife.

"I think that went rather well, don't you?" Kelly said.

"The house is still standing, if that's what you mean," Jordan observed dryly.

"I gather Dani is not too keen on surprises," Duke said.

"Not if there's a man involved," Kelly told him.

"I can still skedaddle on out of here, so you all can have a pleasant, family dinner," Duke offered, albeit reluctantly. He doubted he would have made the suggestion if he weren't fairly certain it would be refused.

"No way," Kelly said. "I haven't looked forward to an evening this much in a long time."

"Me, either," Jordan said.

"I'm so glad to be able to provide you both with so much entertainment."

"Don't you worry about entertaining us. Just liven things up for Dani," Kelly said.

Something in her tone alerted Duke to the possibility that she and Jordan were putting a little too much trust in him. They had clearly assumed that his intentions were thoroughly honorable and that they would inevitably lead to something serious developing between him and their daughter. Was that what he wanted? He shuddered at the very thought of walking down the aisle again. He was far from averse to romance, but beyond that? No way.

Which meant, of course, that he was playing with fire here. Perversely, of course, the thought got his adrenaline pumping.

When Dani returned wearing a pair of snug-fitting pants and a cotton blouse, his pulse ricocheted like a bullet glancing off a fence post. She had scooped her blond hair into a careless knot on top of her head, leaving several wayward curls to skim her cheeks and shoulders. Duke felt an almost irresistible urge to tuck each one back into place…or to release the rest and run his fingers through the shimmering golden silk. It was a toss-up which way he'd go, if he had the opportunity.

Thankfully, he supposed, he didn't have to make the choice. Kelly announced that dinner was ready and they

all retreated to the dining room. Though Justin hadn't
come in, a place had been set for him, which gave Dani
the perfect opportunity to sit opposite Duke, rather than
beside him as her folks had so clearly intended.

As she slid into the chair, Duke grinned at her knowingly, bringing another of those easy blushes to her
cheeks. He discovered he could easily become addicted
to watching the color bloom on her pale flesh. Most
women he knew were way beyond such easy embarrassment. At the same time, Duke realized that Dani's
particular brand of innocence stirred an unfamiliar protective instinct in him. He managed to get through the
entire meal without deliberately baiting her.

He was less successful on the ride home. Dani was
clearly peeved about being forced to offer him a lift. Her
testiness aroused his contrariness. He settled back in the
passenger seat and studied her with blatant masculine
approval. There was no mistaking the unsettling effect
his gaze was having on her. She was shifting gears so
furiously that it was a wonder the transmission didn't
shriek to a complete stop in protest.

"Dani?" Duke said quietly after a particularly nasty
sequence of shifts.

"What?"

"If you don't settle down, we're going to end up in
a ditch."

"If you don't like the way I drive, you could always
walk."

"And have you feeling guilty for a week for leaving
me on a deserted stretch of highway in the middle of
the night? I couldn't possibly do that."

"I wouldn't feel guilty," she claimed.

"Yes, you would. Why don't you tell me what has you in such a rotten mood?"

"My mood is just dandy, thank you very much. If you don't like it…"

Duke grinned in the darkness. "I know, I can walk."

"Exactly."

"You aren't by any chance a little peeved that your parents didn't mention I was coming to dinner tonight, are you?"

"It's their house. They can invite anyone they want."

"True, but you're feeling as if you were set up, correct?"

She sighed. "Look, it's nothing against you, really."

"It's just that you're feeling cornered."

"Something like that."

"Why? It was dinner. It's not a big deal."

She actually gave a tight little laugh at that. "Maybe not to you, but believe me, they're hearing wedding bells. They hear them if there's an available man within a hundred-mile radius."

"Don't all parents want to see their children happily married?"

"Yes, but not all of them consider it their personal mission to make it happen. It's embarrassing."

"It shouldn't be," Duke consoled her. "I'm not feeling any pressure here. You shouldn't, either."

"Yeah, right."

"I'm not. Let's make a pact."

She glanced over at him, her expression wary. "What sort of a pact?"

"To stop worrying about what other people think and just see where things take us."

"*Things,* as you put it, aren't going to take us anywhere. I'm not interested."

"So you've said."

"You don't believe me?"

"No, darlin', afraid not."

She shifted gears with another screech, then sped up
to something close to eighty. Duke gathered she hadn't
liked his response.

"Are you planning on killing both of us just because
you don't like hearing the truth?" he inquired. "Or were
you just hoping to put the fear of God into me?"

She regarded him hopefully. "Are you scared?"

"Of you? Never."

"Well, you should be," she said testily. "One word to
my father that I find you reprehensible and you'd be out
of the oil business, not just his, but any oil company."

Duke laughed at the threat. "You think so?"

"I know so."

"Darlin', before you go spouting off idle threats,
maybe you should think again about whose idea this
little dinner party tonight was."

She fell silent at the reminder. After a moment, she
sighed. "Well, hell."

"Come on, Dani. It's not that bad, is it? Nothing has
to happen here that we don't want to happen. We're both
adults. I've been able to control my libidinous urges
for some time now. Something tells me you have, too."

"What's your point?"

"We shared one kiss. The world didn't come to an
end, did it?"

"I suppose not," she conceded grudgingly.

"We stopped with just one."

"Only because we were interrupted by your kids."

As soon as the words slipped out, she muttered a curse that had Duke grinning. Wisely, he kept his mouth shut about her very revealing remark.

When she pulled to a stop in front of his house, he made no move to exit. He held out his hand.

"Friends?"

She eyed his hand warily, then eventually reached over and clasped it.

"Friends," she agreed.

The minute her soft skin brushed his, Duke regretted suggesting something as uncomplicated as friendship. It would never work. He wanted her with a ferocity that startled him. If an innocent touch could set off such demanding need, he was in deep trouble. They both were.

He met her gaze and saw that she had reached the same conclusion. Her eyes had widened with surprise. Then, even as he gazed into them, they darkened with worry.

"Well, hell," she muttered, then carefully withdrew her hand from his. She squared her shoulders with just a touch of defiance.

"Friends," she repeated pointedly. "You promised."

He nodded and after one final look deep into her eyes, he climbed out of the car. Without a goodbye, she shifted very carefully into gear and drove away.

Duke figured he was going to have a lot of very restless nights in the future to regret that idiotic promise of his. His only consolation was the absolute certainty that Dani was going to be tossing and turning, too.

5

More than two weeks went by without Dani seeing any sign of Duke. Nor did she hear a mention of his name. In fact, everyone in the family was so careful to avoid so much as a whisper about Jordan's new employee and his sons that she guessed the silence was deliberate.

Her mother, who usually checked in every morning at some point, hadn't called at all the next day. She never had asked how their ride together the night of the dinner party had gone. Nor had anyone brought up the subject when she'd stopped by the following week or the week after that. It was almost as if they'd conceded that their plot had fizzled.

Of course, they were an incredibly sneaky lot. It was all probably calculated to pique her curiosity. She congratulated herself for not allowing the tactic to work, then sighed at the blatant lie.

The truth was she hadn't been able to get Duke off her mind since their first kiss way back on the Fourth of July. Nor had she been able to forget the feel of his lips on hers, the heat of his body or the purely masculine scent of him. And those sweet, sweet words, comparing the sparkle in her eyes to fireworks kept echoing in her head. It didn't seem to matter that so much time had passed since he'd paid her such an endearing compliment. She doubted she would ever forget it.

Of course, that memory was followed by an echo of his promise that they would become friends and nothing more. She couldn't seem to help feeling just a little disappointed that he'd taken her at her word that that was all she wanted. Why the heck hadn't he just swept her off her feet and made mincemeat of her ridiculous claim to be immune to him? They both knew what a lie it was.

Could it be that he was truly a rarity, an honorable man who stood by his word? Did he intend to back off and leave her completely alone except for chance meetings? That prospect left her feeling thoroughly disgruntled.

"Enough," she said sternly and marched herself into the animal clinic. Work had always been able to dull the most painful memories. Surely it could take her mind off of Duke Jenkins for a few hours. She had a half hour before regular office hours. She would spend it with Honeybunch.

Thankfully, the German shepherd was improving daily, though it would be another week or two before she felt confident enough of his health to send him back out to Betty Lou's. The old woman had hitched a ride with a neighbor every single day to check on her dog. Dani was fairly confident that it was the sound of Betty Lou's voice as much as her own medical expertise that had kept the dog alive through several touch-and-go incidents.

"Come here, big guy," she called softly. The dog's tail thumped once, and he struggled to his feet. He limped over to the edge of his pen and licked her hand. Dani hunkered down in front of him. "You feeling better? You know, you gave us all quite a scare the night the sheriff brought you in here."

Honeybunch's responding *woof* sounded creaky from disuse.

"No, no, don't apologize. It's not your fault that creep slammed into you," she said as she expertly ran her hands over his body checking his injuries. Everything seemed to be healing nicely. His stitches would come out tomorrow and then it would be mostly a matter of letting him get his strength back. His appetite was slowly returning, and he was regaining some of the weight he'd lost.

"Betty Lou is going to be very glad to get you home again," she told him. "She misses you."

The dog cocked his head at the mention of his mistress's name, then uttered a plaintive woof that had Dani smiling.

"Soon, boy. She'll be here soon," she promised.

"What happened to him?" a familiar male voice inquired, causing her to jump.

She glanced over just as Duke hunkered down beside her, his expression sympathetic as he allowed the dog to lick his hand. He seemed oblivious to the danger of getting dog hair all over his expensive suit. For some reason that pleased her deeply. Nor could she help noticing how strong his hands looked, yet how gently they moved over the injured dog.

"Hit by a drunk driver," she told him.

"Damn fool," he muttered, never taking his eyes off the dog. "I suppose he left the scene, too."

"Of course, but the sheriff caught up with him. A neighbor spotted the car and turned him in. He'd had his license revoked the month before."

"But he was still behind the wheel," Duke said with disgust. "Maybe sooner or later someone will start taking away their cars, instead of their licenses."

"My sentiments exactly," Dani said, standing up and giving Honeybunch a dog biscuit to chew on. She managed to inject a casual note into her voice as she asked, "What brings you by? And how'd you get past Maggie?"

"Is Maggie that perky young lady out front reading a veterinary medicine textbook?"

"That would be the one," Dani said. "Forget I asked. If Maggie was studying, she'd let Martians invade without batting an eye."

"I hope I am somewhat less formidable than Martians," Duke said.

Dani wasn't so certain, so she let the comment slide. "And you're here for?"

"Kitty litter and cat food," he responded easily. "Mittens and the others go through the stuff faster than the boys go through a gallon of milk."

Dani grinned. "Are you so sure that some of that milk isn't going into the kittens, as well?"

"Now that you mention it, no."

Since the explanation for Duke's presence was so patently flimsy, she couldn't help teasing him about it.

"You could have gotten the supplies you wanted at the grocery store, you know. They carry every brand you could want and their prices are much lower than mine."

"But then I wouldn't have had an excuse to see you," he admitted, his gaze settling on her face and lingering until her cheeks flushed.

It was what she'd expected, *hoped,* he would say, but she began a protest just the same. "Duke—"

"I know. I know. You're not interested."

"And you promised—"

"I promised we'd be friends, not that I'd avoid all contact," he pointed out.

"Is that why you've made yourself so scarce the past couple of weeks?" she asked without thinking of the implication of the question.

Naturally, though, Duke didn't miss it. His eyes lit with amusement. "So, you did notice. Good. Actually, I was out of town for several days on business. Jordan could have told you that if you'd asked."

"You've got to be kidding," she said. "Do you know what he'd make of my asking?"

"No more than I am, probably."

Dani scowled at him. "Well, don't let it go to your head. My curiosity was no more significant than if I'd been wondering about the absence of ants at a picnic."

"Lumping me in with other pests and nuisances?" Duke inquired.

Dani shrugged. "If the shoe fits…"

"A lesser man might be insulted by the comparison and give up. Is that what you're hoping? If so, you might as well save your breath. I'm a persistent kind of guy."

"Your persistence would pay off a whole lot faster if you picked somebody else to pester," she pointed out.

"Heck, Dani, surely you know that the chase is half the fun."

She frowned at the flippant words. "You see, that's exactly the problem," she said with gathering intensity. "It's all a game to you. You have two sons. You shouldn't be playing games. In the end they're the ones who'll get hurt."

His gaze narrowed. "Let me guess. You're talking from experience, aren't you? This has something to do with that jerk, doesn't it? And his kids weren't the only ones who got hurt. You did, too."

His guesswork was on the money. "It's not important," she insisted anyway.

"Tell that to someone who'll believe it, darlin'. Me, I just figure that gives me an extra obstacle to overcome."

She found his cavalier attitude exasperating. "Dammit, Duke, there you go again, turning it into some sort of contest. Maybe we can become friends, maybe not, but we sure as heck aren't becoming anything more. Have I made myself clear?"

"Abundantly," he said.

She didn't buy the easy capitulation. "There are a dozen women in this town I could introduce you to this afternoon, who'd be willing to play it your way, no questions asked. Give me the word and I'll call one right now."

"I don't think so," he said, his gaze locked with hers. "There are some obstacles to be overcome, but the fact remains that I've got my eye on you."

She returned his look helplessly. "Why?"

The simple question seemed to stump him as much as it did her. She had to give him credit for considering his answer before he replied.

"Chemistry?" he suggested eventually.

"Chemistry's a whole lot like fire," she warned. "You shouldn't play with it unless you know what you're doing. In this case, way too many people could get burned."

"You could be right," he admitted. "But I've always been a man who liked living on the edge."

"If it were only you and me involved, maybe it would be worth the risk," she conceded.

"It *would* be worth the risk," he retorted emphatically.

Heaven protect her from the male ego, Dani thought. "You and I are not the only ones involved," she reminded him impatiently. "That makes the situation intolerable for me. You're a decent man. Everyone says so. You're doing right by your sons under difficult circumstances."

"Don't make me out to be a saint," he protested.

She grinned at his irritation. "Hardly that." She deliberately reached up and touched his cheek, intent on keeping the gesture as casual as a handshake, as reassuring as a pat on the back. Unfortunately, even that simple contact sent a jolt of pure longing straight through her. She pulled her hand back and jammed it into her pocket, then started briskly down the hall, determined not to let him see how shaken she was.

To her relief, he didn't follow, but his softly spoken taunt did.

"It won't work and you know it," he called after her.

She hesitated, but refused to look over her shoulder. "What?"

"Pretending that there's nothing between us."

She turned then and met his gaze evenly. "There is nothing between us," she said flatly.

He shook his head, a smile on his lips. "Darlin', if you believe that, then I've got a spread of land smack in the middle of a swamp I want to sell you. In fact, I can probably convince you it's suitable for skyscrapers."

When she would have snapped out another retort, he held up his hand. "No, don't say something you'll just have to take back later. I've got time. There's no rush when it comes to romance. In fact, all the experts say slower is better."

He managed to imbue the words with enough seductiveness to set off a stampede of erotic images.

"What happened to friendship?" she asked, fighting the helpless feeling of being caught up in a whirlwind.

He shrugged. "It's a starting place."

"It's the beginning and the end," she insisted. "Accept that or stop coming around."

He shook his head. "There's that dare again, darlin'."

"It's not a blasted dare!" she shouted, then sighed. "Forget it. Obviously, you don't have a clue what I'm all about. Unfortunately, I can read you all too clearly."

"Can you really?" he said doubtfully. He covered the distance between them in three long strides. He framed her face in his hands and settled his mouth over hers before she could blink, swallowing her protest.

This time she did fight him. She planted her hands squarely in the middle of his chest and shoved. When that didn't work, she stomped down hard on his foot.

He stopped kissing her then, but he didn't release her. He kept his gaze fastened on hers until she was the one who finally sighed and looked away.

"I gather I made my point," he said softly, his thumb caressing her cheek.

"What point would that be?"

"That all the protests in the world won't convince me that there's nothing between us. The evidence says otherwise."

"Believe what you want to. It doesn't matter," she said, forcing herself not to evade his gaze or to react to his touch. "All that matters is that I do not want to become involved with you. Period. End of story."

"I'm sure as an Adams you're used to getting what you want in life," Duke retorted solemnly. "Knowing Jordan, it's probably a family tradition. But I'm afraid you've finally come up against something you can't control."

"Don't be absurd. Of course, I can control it."

"How?" He grinned. "By avoiding me completely?"

"That's one way."

"The obvious one," he said disparagingly. "I would have thought you'd be a little more original, maybe prove yourself under fire, so to speak."

Dani's gaze narrowed. "You are not going to trick me into spending time with you, Duke Jenkins."

He grinned unrepentantly and shrugged. "Ah, well, it was worth a shot. I guess I'll just have to rely on circumstances to throw us together."

"What circumstances?" she asked suspiciously.

"It's a small town. I work for your father. Your family

thinks we're a good match. I have three kittens. You're the town vet. Those circumstances."

"You're a manipulative troublemaker, aren't you?"

His booming laugh filled the narrow corridor. "Darlin', coming from an Adams, that sounds a whole lot like the pot calling the kettle black." He pushed open the half-closed door to the waiting room, then paused and winked. "See you around."

"What about the kitty litter and cat food you came in here for?" she blurted.

"Don't worry, darlin'. I'll be back."

A half-dozen speculative gazes followed Duke's exit. Dani figured it would be less than an hour before the news was all over town that she and Duke Jenkins had had some sort of a lovers' tiff right in the middle of her clinic. Her family would be thrilled.

She, to the contrary, was not thrilled. She was worried. In fact, she was very close to panic. She might not be the most experienced woman on the face of the earth, but she recognized temptation when it was staring her in the face. She was tempted by Duke Jenkins, all right. Trying to convince him otherwise was going to require all her wits and then some. She wasn't even going to bother wasting her energy trying to convince herself.

By the time the clinic closed at five and the last pet, except for Honeybunch, had been shuttled home by its anxious owner, Dani had almost managed to put Duke's visit out of her head. She closed up and wandered down to Dolan's to get a lemonade and a little friendly conversation with Sharon Lynn. Her cousin could always be counted on to brighten her spirits.

Big mistake, she realized when she saw her cousin's eager expression.

"You sit right here and tell me everything," Sharon Lynn said at once, automatically filling a tall glass with ice and lemonade and placing it on the counter in front of Dani.

"Make that to go," Dani said.

"Too late. Come on, spill it."

"The lemonade?"

"Very funny. What exactly happened when Duke came to call today?"

"Nothing happened."

"That's not what I heard."

"Gossip is very unreliable."

"Usually, there's enough truth in it to make it fascinating, though. So, tell the truth, did he kiss you again?"

Dani stared at her in astonishment. "How the heck would anybody know about that? The door was closed."

Sharon Lynn grinned. "So, he did. I suspected as much."

"Are you admitting that you didn't know that already?"

"Well, there was a fair amount of speculation. And Maggie peeked once. She seemed to think she had caught a glimpse of you in his arms."

"I am firing her first thing in the morning," Dani vowed.

"No, you're not. She needs the job and she's good at it. It's not her fault you and Duke decided to get it on in plain sight."

"We did not get it on, as you so charmingly put it."

"But he did kiss you?"

Dani sighed. "Yes."

"And you liked it?"

"No."

"Liar."

"Okay, I liked it, so what? It's not going to happen again. I have made myself very clear on that point."

Sharon Lynn tried unsuccessfully to hold back a grin. "Did you really? Did you by any chance make that same point out at Grandpa's a few weeks ago?"

"Yes, I did."

Sharon Lynn continued to smirk. "Guess he doesn't hear too well."

"He's a man, isn't he? Have you ever known one to listen to a blasted thing we say?"

"Actually, Kyle Mason hangs on every word I say."

"Oh, for heaven's sakes, stop gloating. We all know you caught the last decent man in the universe or so you keep reminding us."

"He is extraordinary, there's no doubt about that. Not that Duke is any slouch. He's charming and sexy and smart."

"How would you know all that? You've barely met the man."

"Not true. He comes in here with his sons all the time." She glanced up. "In fact, they're on their way in right now."

Dani flatly refused to turn around to look. "Please, please, tell me you are making that up."

"Why would I do that?"

"To drive me crazy."

"Not me," Sharon Lynn retorted. "But I'd say someone else is doing a pretty good job of it." Her smile widened. "Hey, Duke. How're you doing? Hi, Joshua, Zack. What's it going to be today?"

"Ice cream cones," Zack replied. "Dad said we could have dessert before dinner tonight. Isn't that cool?"

"Way cool," Sharon Lynn agreed.

Dani felt Duke's hands settle on her shoulders. A shiver skimmed straight down her spine even before he leaned down and whispered, "Told you so."

There was nothing to do but accept the inevitable. Slowly, she swiveled her stool around until she was face-to-face with him. Pure devilment was sparkling in his eyes. His gaze locked with hers and his expression sobered until an exquisite kind of tension shimmered in the air between them. Dani swallowed hard and forced herself to turn away. She smiled at Zachary and Joshua.

"So what's this about dessert before supper?" she asked.

Already licking his double scoop of chocolate ice cream, Joshua paused long enough to say, "Dad says as long as we cross our hearts and promise to eat every bite on our plates, we can do it this way just this once. It's 'cause Dolan's will be closed by the time he finishes fixing dinner."

"Yeah," Zachary chimed in. "It takes him a really, really long time to cook, 'cept when he zaps stuff in the microwave."

"I see."

"Can you cook?" Joshua asked. regarding her speculatively.

"Dani is the very best cook in the entire family," Sharon Lynn said before Dani could respond. "Her spaghetti sauce would bring tears to your eyes. As for her pot roast, well, let's just say that Maritza taught her and Maritza has been Grandpa's housekeeper for practically forever and he has gourmet taste."

Both boys' eyes widened hopefully. "Really? Maybe you could invite us to dinner sometime," Zachary suggested.

"Yeah, we really, really love spaghetti, especially if it doesn't come out of a can," Joshua added.

"Hey, guys, it's not polite to invite yourselves over to someone's house," Duke said.

"Oh, we don't stand on formality around here," Sharon Lynn said. "Do we, Dani?"

Dani gave her a sour look, then forced a smile. "Of course not. The next time I'm doing more than grabbing a sandwich for dinner, I'll give you guys a call."

Duke's eyebrows rose. "A sandwich? That's your idea of a healthy dinner?"

"Sometimes it's all I feel like fixing after a long day."

"Tsk, tsk," Duke chided. "You should know better. I propose that we all go out tonight. My treat. Since everybody's so keen on spaghetti, how's that Italian place? We haven't tried that yet."

"It's the best," Sharon Lynn enthused. "Dani loves their lasagna, don't you, Dani?"

"It's very good," she conceded. "Really, though, I can't. Not tonight."

Duke's gaze clashed with hers. "Busy?"

"Yes."

"Doing?"

She seized on the first thing that came to mind. "I have to keep an eye on Honeybunch."

"Who's Honeybunch?" Zachary asked as chocolate

dripped down his shirt. He was oblivious to the melting ice cream. Dani instinctively reached for a napkin and blotted it up, then wiped a streak off his cheek.

"Honeybunch is an injured dog I'm treating," she explained.

"Is he hurt bad?" Joshua asked.

"He's getting better," she conceded.

Duke shot her a triumphant look. "Then we can stop in and check on him on the way to the restaurant. That should put your mind at ease, right?"

She sighed heavily. She might as well give it up. There wasn't an excuse on the face of the earth that would work now, not unless she said flatly that she didn't want to go with them. There were two problems with that one: first, it was rude, second, it was a lie. A huge lie, in fact. She did want to go. Obviously, some part of her didn't care that a situation all too similar to this one had practically destroyed her.

"Why don't I go on ahead while you boys finish your ice cream," she suggested eventually. "You can meet me at the clinic when you're ready."

"Perfect," Duke said. "Fifteen minutes?"

"Yes," she said without enthusiasm.

Sharon Lynn grinned at her. "Have a good evening."

Dani nodded. "I'll speak to you tomorrow," she said, a deliberately dire note in her voice.

"Can't wait," her cousin said, clearly not the least bit repentant over her part in the night's turn of events.

Outside the drugstore, Dani briefly considered bolting, but dismissed it. It would be a cowardly thing to do, and no Adams had ever been a coward. Not that it was Adams blood flowing through her veins, but too many years of the family's influence had had an effect.

Ah, well, she only had to get through the next fifteen minutes of dread and what? Maybe another hour for dinner. An hour and a half, tops. That was hardly an eternity. Nor was it really long enough to feed this ridiculous attraction she was starting to feel toward Duke Jenkins. They would be chaperoned, too.

By ten o'clock she would be home, tucked in bed with a good book, just the way she had been on every single night of the past two years, except for those occasions when she'd been coerced into spending the evening with one family member or another.

The prospect reassured her. She was actually feeling reasonably upbeat when she heard the doorbell ring in the main part of her combination home and clinic. That optimism lasted until the moment she opened the door and saw, not Duke, but Rob, standing on the front stoop.

6

Dani stared incredulously at the disheveled man standing on her doorstep. It wasn't so much his identity that shocked her, as his appearance. Rob had always dressed impeccably. Tonight he looked as if he'd grabbed clothes from a laundry basket.

"What are you doing here?" she asked with an icy calm she was far from feeling.

"Can I come in? We need to talk."

"We do not need to talk," she retorted. "And no, you may not come in."

He blinked at her in obvious surprise. "What's the matter with you?"

His total lack of understanding of what he had done to her infuriated her as nothing else could have. Either he was blind or she had been so submissive that he'd anticipated being able to steamroll over her as if nothing had ever happened. Dani didn't like either explanation much. Both said things about her she would rather not have believed true. Well, then, it was about time she stood up for herself and made her feelings perfectly clear.

She stared at him coldly. "That's the problem, Rob. You never did have a clue about anything that mattered. It was always about what you wanted, what you needed."

When she would have slammed the door, he blocked it and for the first time she felt a niggling sense of unease. "Rob, please. Don't make a scene."

"Afraid that shining Adams image will get tarnished?" he asked sourly.

Dani was stunned by his bitterness. What the heck did he have to be bitter about? "Just go away, please. I'm expecting company." She spotted Duke and his sons strolling along the sidewalk less than a block away. "In fact, they're on their way right now."

Rob turned and followed the direction of her gaze. "Still looking for a built-in family, I see. You always were predictable."

Dani winced at the mean-spirited accusation. Any second now rage was going to overcome common sense and she was going to throw a tantrum that would set Los Pinos on its collective backside.

Fortunately, Duke had apparently picked up on the scene even from a distance. He spoke quietly to the boys, who stopped where they were without argument. Then Duke quickened his pace. Before Dani could say anything more, he was casually, but effectively sliding between her and Rob. He dropped a deliberate kiss on her forehead, then fixed an interested stare on her visitor.

"Hey, darlin', who's this?" Duke asked.

"Rob Hilliard. He's an old acquaintance from Dallas." Duke's gaze narrowed, which suggested he'd heard the name mentioned. Since she'd never told him the identity of the man who'd hurt her, she could only assume that someone else in the family had filled in the blanks she'd left in the story.

"Glad to meet you," Duke said. His tone was polite, but any reasonably bright man would not have found it welcoming.

"Rob was just leaving," Dani prompted, since he appeared not to have taken Duke's hint.

Neither man paid a lick of attention to her. They were squaring off like contestants in a championship boxing match.

Rob was no hero, though. Duke was at least four inches taller and twenty pounds of pure muscle heavier. Eventually her ex-fiancé backed down.

"I'll catch up with you later," he said pointedly to Dani. "Sometime when you're not so busy."

Duke shook his head. "I don't think that's such a good idea," he said. He studied Dani. "Is it?"

"No," she agreed. "It's not a good idea at all."

"Fine. Have it your way." Rob smiled at Dani, but there was little warmth in his expression as he added, "The girls send their love. They miss you."

Dani felt as if she'd been sucker-punched. She could deal with Rob. She could dismiss him as if he were no more than an inconvenience, but the girls... She couldn't pretend to be disinterested.

"Are they okay?" she asked.

Rob shot a triumphant smirk at Duke to indicate his belief that he'd bested the other man, after all. "They're unhappy."

"Why?"

"As I said, they miss you. They'd like to see you."

The offer was nearly two years too late. Dani didn't want to ask, but he'd left her no choice. "What about Tiffany? Won't she object?"

"We split up." Ignoring Duke's presence, he added, "They want you to come home. We all do."

The thought of holding Robin and Amy in her arms again, the prospect of reading them bedtime stories and drying their tears, all of it was almost enough to make her weaken. Duke's steady hand on her waist gave her the strength to shake her head. It reminded her that what she felt for those two darling girls was not nearly enough to compensate for the fact that their father was a weak, insensitive fool.

Steeling herself against his likely reaction she said coolly, "I would love to see the girls again, anytime you'd like to bring them for a visit. But we will never be a family, Rob." She met his gaze evenly. "Never. I'm surprised even you would be foolish enough to think it possible."

"But…"

"I think you heard her," Duke said quietly. "Now it's time you were on your way." He glanced at Dani. "Right?"

"Absolutely," she said.

Only after Rob had turned and walked away, did Dani feel her knees sag. Duke's arm circled her waist protectively. "You okay?" he murmured.

She nodded, unable to speak. There was too much emotion clogging her throat. This time she was the one who'd cut the ties to Robin and Amy, severed them beyond repair. Rob would never bring them for a visit, not now that he knew there was no place for him in her life. He'd been using those poor, sweet babies of his as pawns, just as he always had.

"Josh, Zack," Duke called to the two wide-eyed boys who were still standing where he'd left them. "Why don't you go into the clinic and spend a little time with Honeybunch." He looked at Dani. "Is that okay?"

"Yes," she said. "Just remember he's still hurt. Don't try to touch him."

When they were gone, Duke prodded her into the house. "Sit. Do you want something? Some tea? A stiff drink?"

"Nothing, thanks."

He studied her worriedly. "Are you sure you're okay?"

She managed a faltering smile for him. "Believe it or not, I'm relieved."

He stared at her incredulously. "Relieved? I'm afraid you're going to have to explain that one to me."

"All this time I've worried what would happen if I ever saw him again. At first I prayed that he would come after me, beg my forgiveness and take me back to be a part of his family again, just the way he did tonight."

"I didn't hear a whole lot of begging," Duke pointed out.

"For Rob, what you heard was close enough. Anyway, I imagined myself falling into his arms and going back. It's taken me a long time to realize that I was never half as much in love with him as I was with the girls. I adored his daughters. From the beginning I loved them as much as if they'd been my own."

She sighed. "And I worked so hard to win them over. I had Jordan's example to go by. Did you know he once thought he would be a terrible father? He was scared to death of me when he and mom were first seeing each other, but he made me a part of his life just the same. I wanted to make Rob's girls feel just as safe. Tonight when Rob asked me to come back, though, it was like a giant light bulb switching on. I realized I couldn't go just for them. Sooner or later their father and I would have split up and they would be hurt all over again."

"So all in all, this visit was a good thing?" Duke asked, his expression skeptical.

"I think so, yes."

He nodded slowly. "Okay, I'm glad, then. How the hell did you fall for a weasel like that in the first place?"

Dani grinned at his indignant tone. "He wasn't at his best tonight."

"An idiot in sheep's clothing is still an idiot."

Dani shrugged. "Much as I hate to admit it, maybe you're a better judge of character than I am, even if you do play havoc with old clichés. At any rate, Rob no longer matters. Let's eat. Suddenly, I'm starved."

"I do love a woman who has her priorities in order," he said approvingly. "Before we get the boys, though, one last thing."

"What's that?"

"If second thoughts about this Rob person start to sneak up on you in the middle of the night, don't call him," he warned. "Call me. I'll set you straight again before you go and do something rash."

At the moment, Dani couldn't conceive of having second thoughts. Nothing was clearer in her mind than the decision she'd reached just moments earlier to leave the past in the past.

"Promise," Duke insisted, when she hadn't responded.

"I promise," she said. "But—"

"No buts, darlin'. When it comes to love, second thoughts are a given."

"I don't love him anymore," she said with absolute certainty. Relief about that almost left her giddy.

"But you did once. Sometimes, in the middle of the night, that's enough to get you thinking crazy."

She regarded him speculatively. "You've been there?"

"Been there, done that. I don't recommend it."

"Will you tell me about it?"

"Maybe I will," he said. "If you ever make that call to me at three a.m."

Duke had been itching to plant his fist in that Rob person's face from the moment he'd walked up the sidewalk and seen him attempting to intimidate Dani. A thoroughly primitive, possessive instinct had flooded through him, startling him with its intensity. Only the certainty that Dani would have hated the resulting scene had kept him from following through on the urge. Something told him, though, that one of these days he'd get his chance. Men like Hilliard rarely learned their lesson the first time out.

All through dinner he kept his gaze pinned on Dani, watching for signs that she was already having those second thoughts he'd warned her about. She would, too. He'd heard enough to know just how much she'd loved those two kids of Hilliard's. Given the opportunity to have them back in her life, she wouldn't walk away without a single backward glance. The maternal instinct in her ran deep. He'd seen it in her reluctant interaction with Zack and Joshua. Not even past hurts could keep her from treating his sons with genuine warmth. Even now she was asking them about the day camp they were attending and showing the kind of genuine interest that could never be faked.

"Then the lifeguard at the pool said, 'Zachary Jenkins, you get out of the water right this instant,'" Joshua was telling her, his tone mimicking the teenager's precisely. "I said, 'But I'm not Zachary.' She didn't believe me. I got out of the water and five seconds later, Zachary swims smack in front of her. She turned real red and started to yell again, but then she saw me standing next to her. 'Told you so,' I said."

"And what did she do?" Dani asked.

"She said, 'Oh, never mind,' and walked away."

"Interesting story," Duke observed. "What exactly did Zachary do in the first place?"

"Uh-oh," Josh said, a guilty expression replacing the glee with which he'd told the story.

"Told you to keep your big mouth shut," Zack grumbled. "This is payback for the goldfish, isn't it?"

"Is not," Joshua insisted.

"Is, too."

"I'm waiting," Duke said, cutting off the exchange.

"It wasn't anything bad," Joshua said valiantly. "Not really."

"Maybe you should let me decide that," Duke said. "Zack?"

"I just dove into the water," Zack said, his expression totally innocent.

"A cannonball, by any chance?" Duke asked.

"Uh-huh," Josh said, nodding, his eyes alight at the memory. "A real whopper."

"And naturally someone was standing right beside the pool who didn't take kindly to getting splashed from head to toe," Duke guessed. "Who was it?"

"Some old guy," Zack said. "In a suit. Who'd wear a suit to a pool, anyway?"

"The mayor," Dani guessed, not even trying to smother a laugh. "He likes to stop by to see how things are going."

Duke stared at her. "The mayor? Terrific. My boys have been here less than six months, and they've already tried to drown the mayor."

Dani reached over and patted his hand. "Don't worry. A lot of people in town have considered doing far worse."

"Then why do they keep electing him?"

"No one else is willing to run."

"Why? Because everyone knows that it's Harlan Adams who really runs things?" Duke suggested.

Dani grinned. "Something like that. Grandpa Harlan does make his opinions known and people do tend to listen to him."

"Something tells me I ought to send the man a sympathy card," Duke said.

"No need to do that. He's heading over here right now," she told him, nodding toward the tall, silver-haired man striding purposefully their way. Even from a distance the water spots on his suit were evident.

"Ohmigosh," Zachary murmured, sliding down until he was all but under the table.

Duke latched on to his arm and forced him to his

feet as he rose himself to greet the older man. Dani's expression suggested she was finding the whole thing just a little too amusing.

"Danielle," the mayor said politely. "Good to see you."

"Good to see you, too, Frank. Have you met Duke Jenkins and his sons? Duke is a vice president at Dad's oil company."

If he hadn't been assessing the man so closely, Duke might have missed the subtle shift in his demeanor when he realized that Duke was tied very tightly to the Adams clan. His tone was suddenly deferential and whatever he'd intended to say about the incident at the town pool was swallowed. Duke refused to let his son off so easily.

"I gather you met the boys earlier today," he said. "Zachary, don't you have something you'd like to tell the mayor?"

Zachary looked as if he would rather eat worms, but he dutifully said, "I'm sorry for splashing you, sir. It was an accident."

"Yes, well, a little water never hurt anyone now, did it?" the man said. "Apology accepted."

"Dad, can me and Joshua go play the video games?" Zack asked, clearly anxious to get away before he caused any more mishaps.

"Yes," Duke said, just as eager to have them safely out of the way. He handed them the change he had in his pocket. When they'd gone, he added his own apology for their rambunctious behavior. "And please, let me pay to have your suit cleaned."

"Not necessary," the mayor said. "I just wanted to bring the matter to your attention in case you hadn't heard about it, but I see that wasn't necessary. Good day, Mr. Jenkins. Danielle, give my regards to your father and grandfather."

"Of course," she said, barely containing a chuckle as he walked away.

"What's so amusing?"

"He is. He really didn't have any business wearing a suit and standing beside a pool filled with kids. I swear I think he does it just to get his suit cleaned for free. Guilty parents are easy marks."

Duke stared at her. "This has happened before?"

"Once every week or two as far back as I can remember. I do believe Justin and Harlan Patrick were guilty of their share of infractions. Dad and Cody finally forbade them from swimming in the town pool. Naturally, that made it all the more fun to go there, even though there's a perfectly good pool at White Pines. They still sneak into town, but they've learned to avoid the days the mayor drops by."

"You could have told me that before I fell all over myself apologizing," Duke grumbled.

"I considered it educational," she retorted. "I wanted to see if you were capable of abject humility."

Duke chuckled despite his annoyance. "Did I pass the test?"

"You were very good. I believed you were very sincere."

"And the mayor?"

"Once he figured out you worked in an executive capacity for Dad, you could have told him to take a flying leap off the town hall roof and he would have done it and thanked you for suggesting it."

Duke regarded her speculatively. "You know, Miss Smarty-Pants, it occurs to me that if you hold such disdain for this man, perhaps you ought to run for mayor yourself. At least then the Adams pulling strings around town would be operating in an official elected capacity."

She looked horrified by the suggestion. "Me? You've got to be kidding."

"Why not? You're bright. Everyone in town knows and respects you. I think it's a great idea. When's the next election?"

"Thankfully, not for another three years."

"Just long enough to get your campaign funds lined up," Duke said.

Dani's gaze narrowed. "You're teasing me, aren't you?"

Duke shrugged. "A little, maybe. You've been looking a little too serious all evening, despite your claim that your ex-fiancé's appearance didn't upset you."

"It was just a shock, that's all."

"But you can't stop thinking about his girls, can you?"

She smiled sadly. "No."

"Then see them. He's opened the door."

"I can't," she said simply. "It wouldn't be fair to get their hopes up, when I know nothing will ever happen between me and their father. They're used to me being gone now. It's better if it stays that way."

Duke thought back to his own childhood. How many times had he prayed that his parents would suddenly come back to claim him? Even knowing that it was impossible, he'd harbored the dream in some tiny, secret place in his heart.

"They'll never get over losing you," he insisted. "See them. Let them know you still care, even if you can't be with them."

Obviously startled by his vehemence, Dani stared at him. "Experience talking?"

"It doesn't matter," he said. "Just trust me, kids never forget losing someone they love."

"Are you talking about Zack and Joshua? Do they miss their mother so terribly?"

Actually, that had been the farthest thing from Duke's mind, but it was an easier answer than revealing his own childhood traumas. "Of course," he said. "They ask about their mother all the time."

"And what do you tell them?"

"That she was very unhappy with me and that she needed to go away to find happiness."

"Does she stay in touch with them?"

"She did at first. She sent postcards every few weeks. It's been a while now since we last heard from her, though."

Dani reacted with visible anger. "How could a mother do that to her own children? How selfish can she be?"

Duke didn't have any excuses for Caroline, either. It didn't matter to him that she'd seemingly dropped off the face of the earth, but it hurt the boys. He understood that kind of anguish all too well. More than once he'd considered hiring someone to look for her, then dismissed the idea. If she didn't want to be a part of her sons' lives, then forcing her to go through the motions would be worse than letting them grieve and get it over with.

Though he understood its roots, he was still a little

surprised by Dani's indignation on their behalf. It reminded him of his very first impression of her. He'd
thought then, as he did now, that she would make a
terrific mother.

Earlier he'd caught Rob's sarcastic remark that she'd
gone looking for another ready-made family. Now he let
the idea simmer. It could be a solution for all of them.
She would have two boys to replace the girls she'd lost.
Joshua and Zack would have a mother's love again.
Goodness knew, the pair of them could use a gentling
influence.

And him? What would he get out of the bargain?
He'd already admitted that he was attracted to her. That
was definitely a start. The prospect of having her in his
life on a more permanent basis wasn't nearly as distaste-
ful as it probably should have been, given his avowed
determination never to marry again.

Years ago no one would have blinked twice at the
idea of such a marriage of convenience. Even now there
were lonely men in places like Alaska and elsewhere
who advertised for mail-order brides. Would this be any
different? He found that he was warming to the idea.

He glanced at Dani and saw her staring at the boys
wistfully. Yes, he thought again, it would work very
nicely for all of them.

"Why don't you go on over there and give them some
real competition," he encouraged.

She grinned. "You wouldn't mind?"

"No, indeed. They beat the pants off me. Let them
humiliate somebody else for a change."

"Not me," she said, flashing him a smile. "I grew
up with a bunch of very competitive relatives. I do be-

lieve if you check that particular machine, my record still stands."

Perfect, he thought as he watched her join his sons. Duke was the kind of man who trusted his instincts. He also made decisions in a rush and stuck by them.

For once in his life, though, he managed to curb his enthusiasm. Something told him he'd better have his scheme very well thought out before he presented it to Dani. She struck him as the kind of woman who might not be nearly as pragmatic as he was, even under her own currently vulnerable circumstances. She might prefer at least the pretense of romance.

He could manage that. Hell, she already made him hotter than asphalt in August. A little proper courting wouldn't kill him. Then he could spring the idea of marriage on her and everything would fall tidily into place.

Satisfied with the plan, he sat back in his chair, sipped his beer and observed her. Dani Adams was something, all right. The boys clearly thought so, too.

Now all he had to do was turn up the heat between them a notch or two and his troubles would be over by Christmas, maybe sooner.

All in all, he concluded, the move to Los Pinos wasn't turning out to be quite as miserable as he'd feared. His job might not be as exciting as oil exploration, but courting Dani Adams promised to make up for that.

When she turned toward him, he lifted his mug of beer in a silent toast. Anticipation sizzled through his veins like fine champagne. Yes, indeed, life in Los Pinos promised to get downright fascinating.

7

Getting Dani to fall in with his plans was trickier than riding a bucking bronco, Duke concluded after six weeks of her clever elusiveness. The woman had more unexplained social engagements than anyone he'd ever met. If he hadn't been a confident kind of man, he might have begun to wonder if she wasn't deliberately trying to avoid him. He concluded that he wasn't going to pull off this marriage proposal quite as easily as he'd originally anticipated.

He had surmised very quickly that simply calling and asking for a date wouldn't work. She was way too jittery to accept. She had claimed to be busy every time he gave her any sort of advance notice.

Stopping by the clinic for an impromptu visit was more successful, but he couldn't discuss the future while half her attention was on some kid's parakeet or gerbil.

Finagling invitations from one Adams or another was a snap compared to getting a minute alone with Dani once he was there. If he didn't know better, he would have sworn that she was onto him, that she'd read his mind that night at dinner and resolved to avoid him at any cost.

Of course, that was impossible, he thought as he observed her clean dive into the pool at White Pines on Labor Day. Her swimsuit, modest by current standards, clung to her in a way that made it seem practically indecent. He hadn't been able to tear his gaze away from her since he'd first spotted her emerging, soaking wet, from the pool. A second later she dove back in and remained submerged up to her neck as if to deliberately prevent him from getting another peek at her.

The woman swam like a porpoise and apparently enjoyed it just as much. She hadn't been out of the water all day. Neither had anyone else, which made the huge pool far too crowded for the kind of intimate conversation Duke was interested in having.

"Dani looks happy, doesn't she?" Sharon Lynn observed, perching on the edge of the chaise longue next to him, her expression a little too innocent.

Happy, wet and sexy as hell, Duke would have corrected, but discretion prevented it. He merely nodded. He'd discovered quickly that the only way to avoid prying around this family was to keep his mouth clamped firmly shut. Occasionally, they gave up and went away. Sharon Lynn, unfortunately, showed no such inclination.

"Are you responsible for that?" Dani's cousin inquired in a tone that suggested her interest ran deeper than casual curiosity.

The question might have amused him if it hadn't been so wildly off the mark. "Hardly. I've barely seen her recently." He couldn't help the cranky note that crept into his voice.

"I see," Sharon Lynn said thoughtfully.

"What does that mean?"

"I just thought…" She shrugged. "Oh, well, I guess I was wrong."

"Wrong about what?"

She hesitated as if she were debating with herself. Duke watched the visible struggle with fascination. He wondered what the devil she was hiding…or what she wanted him to think she was hiding.

"Sharon Lynn?" he prodded. "What made you think Dani and I were seeing each other? Has she said something?"

"Oh, no," she said. Again, there was a slight hesitation before she shrugged and said, "It's just that she's been into Dolan's with your sons quite a bit. Almost every afternoon, in fact. I just assumed that ever since you went out to dinner you two were something of an item."

Duke tried to absorb the implication. Dani had been spending time with Zack and Josh? That was news to him. How had this friendship between Dani and his sons developed without his knowledge? Was he that oblivious to the twins' activities or were they deliberately keeping mum about these little get-togethers? Probably the latter, especially if ice cream was involved.

Paolina took them to the town pool every day for swimming lessons, but he'd just assumed they'd gone straight home afterward since he'd all but ordered Paolina not to take them anywhere other than the pool without his specific permission. Naturally, they'd kept quiet about it. They'd known they were breaking the rules.

"What time have they been coming in?" he asked.

"About four, I guess. After their swimming lessons."

It was Duke's turn to mutter, "I see." A few weeks ago he would have grounded them for the infraction, but now he saw that their sneaky little visits could be used to his advantage.

Tomorrow the three of them would have company at Dolan's. Thank goodness school didn't start until the following week or he would have missed out on this opportunity to slip into Dani's schedule when she wasn't expecting him.

He was so busy making his plans, he completely missed the thumbs-up sign Sharon Lynn exchanged with Jenny Runningbear Adams as she strolled away.

"Can't you take a break tomorrow afternoon?" Jenny pleaded with Dani. "I only have a few more days until school starts. We haven't had a long chat since I got back into town."

Dani regarded Jenny suspiciously. "That's right, so why all of a sudden can't you wait to get together? I have a clinic to run, remember?"

"I know," Jenny said repentantly. "We should have done it sooner. It's my fault. The summer just got completely away from me. You know how I am."

That was the problem. Dani did know. Jenny was one of the most organized women she'd ever met. She didn't fritter away time. She had too much going on.

Like Janet, her mother, Jenny was involved in advocacy programs for Native Americans in addition to her teaching duties. Dani could believe that Jenny hadn't had a second to get together, but she wasn't buying this nonsense about time just slipping away from her. There was a reason for this sudden urgency.

Unfortunately, she couldn't quite figure out what Jenny's angle was. She tried one more time to get a fix on it. "Jenny, why does it have to be tomorrow afternoon? Make it six o'clock and we could have the whole evening. I'll even cook."

"That won't work," Jenny said a little too quickly. "Like I said, school's almost ready to open. I have all my teaching materials to get organized. I don't have another spare minute, especially in the evenings. I've been playing chess with Harlan then. He really looks forward to it."

"So the only time you have free is tomorrow precisely at four?" Dani asked skeptically.

"Yes."

"And I'm supposed to drop everything and meet you and Sharon Lynn at Dolan's for some girl talk? That's all? There's no hidden agenda?"

"Of course not. It'll be fun. I'll even treat."

Dani laid a hand dramatically over her heart. "Goodness, how can I resist an offer like that?"

"Then you'll be there? Four o'clock?"

Dani sighed. The only way she was going to find out what Jenny was up to was to fall in with her plans. "Yes. I'll shuffle some appointments around, and I'll be there."

"Wonderful," Jenny said, then glanced up. "Don't look now, but someone is staring at you. When are you going to give that poor man a break and go out with him?"

"It's not going to happen," Dani insisted.

"But you went out with him once. Didn't you have a good time?"

"That wasn't a date. It just sort of happened."

"Whatever," Jenny said dismissively. "You enjoyed yourself, didn't you? That's what Sharon Lynn said. Your mom said the same thing."

Dani sighed. "I'm glad everyone has been keeping you up-to-date on my activities."

"Were they wrong?"

"No, but I also had a little too much fun hanging out with Duke's kids. I won't take that kind of risk again."

"Because of Robin and Amy," Jenny said.

"And Rob," Dani reminded her. She had told no one about the painful scene over a month ago. She doubted Duke would mention it either.

"Sweetie, something tells me that Duke Jenkins is absolutely nothing like Rob."

Dani had made a similar assessment herself. That still didn't mean she was willing to take any chances with her heart or with his sons'. She'd seen enough of them over the past couple of months to know that they were endearing little devils. It wouldn't take much for them to make her go all mushy inside and then where would they all be when Duke packed his bags and took off for a new oil field? Sooner or later, he would. He hated being chained to a desk too much not to balk at it sooner or later.

"Forget it," she said succinctly.

"Then I guess you won't mind if I check him out," Jenny said.

Dani flinched at the suggestion but forced herself to shrug indifferently. "It's up to you. I have no claim on Duke Jenkins."

Jenny's stare was penetrating and disconcerting. "You're sure?" she persisted.

"I said so, didn't I?" she snapped testily.

"Okay, then. If we don't hook up again before I leave today, I'll see you tomorrow, right?"

Dani nodded and watched Jenny circle the pool in Duke's direction. Along the way she was waylaid by Sharon Lynn. Dani swore that the little whoosh of relief she felt had nothing at all to do with Jenny's failure to hook up with Duke. She didn't care who the man dated. He could go out with the entire female population of Los Pinos for all she cared, Jenny included. In fact, she was the one who'd first suggested they would make a good pair.

So why did the prospect still set off this odd little aching sensation in the region of her heart? she wondered. Lunacy, she concluded. Maybe exercise would restore the blood flow to her brain.

When everyone else headed for dinner on the patio, she remained in the pool. She swam laps, which had been impossible when it had been jammed. She was praying the exercise would wipe out the thoughts of the man who had been plaguing her for weeks now. She was running out of excuses to avoid him. She'd been so sure he would take the hint eventually, but he'd shown no signs of doing so. In fact, it appeared all she'd really succeeded in doing was increasing his fascination.

He had an absolutely inspiring mix of patience and determination.

Jenny would probably take care of that, she thought irritably. She was a little surprised to hear that Jenny was interested in Duke, but she probably shouldn't have been. After all, he was a gorgeous, bright, funny man. What sane woman wouldn't be interested in him?

Breathless at last, she swam to the side of the pool and clung.

"Worn-out?" an amused voice inquired from above her. She looked up into sparkling blue eyes and felt that strange little sizzle Duke managed to set off without even trying.

"Pretty much," she confessed. "How come you're not eating dinner with everyone else?"

"It'll still be there in a few minutes."

"Don't count on it. Uncle Cody and Uncle Luke have very hearty appetites. And Harlan Patrick and Justin are virtually grown men. Everyone knows they can clean off a buffet table faster than a butler with a hand-vac."

He grinned. "You worried I'm going to starve? Or just anxious to be rid of me?"

"Why would I want to get rid of you?"

"Good question. Care to answer it?"

"If I've given you that impression, I'm sorry."

"Said very dutifully and very politely. Why don't I believe it?"

"Believe whatever you like."

"Let me hazard a guess instead," he suggested. "I think you're scared to be alone with me. Look at you now, for instance. You're shivering."

"The air's cold," she said defensively.

"It's ninety," he pointed out. "And the water's not that cold, either, in case you were thinking of mentioning that next."

"How would you know? You haven't been in."

He grinned. "Keeping an eye on me, were you?"

"You know I could really grow to dislike you," she muttered.

He didn't appear to be horrified by the prospect. "Really? I don't think so. I think exactly the opposite is true and it scares you silly."

"You really are full of yourself, aren't you?" she said as a mischievous idea popped into her head. "Maybe you should cool off."

Before he could guess what she intended, she snagged his arm and toppled him straight into the pool. If he hadn't been off balance to begin with she doubted she could have managed it, but he was. He came up sputtering with a look of astonishment on his face. She might have laughed, if she hadn't noted the calculating gleam in his eyes. He wanted revenge.

She pushed off from the wall and swam for the opposite end of the pool. She was fairly confident of her swimming skill, plus she had the element of surprise on her side. And Duke was weighed down with shorts, a T-shirt and sneakers. She should have made it. No question about it.

When she felt a hand wrap around her ankle, she yelped with surprise and took in a mouthful of water. Strong hands spanned her waist and lifted her up. Her legs instinctively circled Duke's waist and her hands came to rest on his shoulders. At least his skin wasn't bare, she thought as desire slammed through her. If it had been, if she'd felt that muscled flesh beneath her fingers, it would have been all over. Her pretense of being unaffected by him would have vanished like a puff of smoke caught by the wind.

As it was, she doubted he could mistake the pebbling of her nipples beneath the scanty fabric of her bathing suit. Nor could he miss the catch of her breath or the way her own flesh was suddenly burning. She was surprised steam wasn't rising all around them.

When she finally dared, she looked into his eyes and saw that he appeared to be almost as stunned as she was. Lust had darkened his eyes. Dani suspected she would find that same passionate hunger reflected in her own eyes. She had never, ever wanted a man as desperately as she did this one. Right here, right now. The powerful force of it stunned her.

Abstinence and avoidance, it appeared, had been a waste of time. It had had exactly the opposite effect of the one she'd hoped for. Caught up against his body, she was feverish with need.

"You picked a hell of a time for this," he murmured, his voice husky.

"For what?"

"To tempt me to make love to you."

"I am not…" she began, but the protest died on her lips when she saw he would never believe a denial. She managed a halfhearted smile. "You ought to be grateful, actually."

"Why is that?"

"Given the circumstances, we won't make a terrible mistake."

"Would it be so terrible?"

Unexpected tears formed in her eyes and spilled down her cheeks, mixing with chlorine. Hopefully, that would disguise them.

"You know it would be," she said.

"I don't know any such thing, darlin'."

Before they could debate the subject, a voice called out.

"Hey, Dani, you out here?" Justin shouted. "Dad says you'd better hurry or there won't be any barbecue left."

"I'll be there in a minute," she called back, thankful that they were in the shadowed end of the water, invisible in the gathering darkness.

"Want me to get you a towel?" her brother offered.

"No, thanks. Go on back. I'll be right there."

She heard a muttered exchange, then a chuckle.

"Tell Duke to hurry up, too," Harlan Patrick called out. "Before Uncle Jordan decides to see what's taking you so long."

Dani chuckled despite her embarrassment. "There are eyes and ears everywhere with this family."

"Should I expect Jordan to meet me with a shotgun in the morning?"

"You never know."

He winked at her. "I'll take my chances. It was worth it."

"How can you say that? Nothing happened," Dani said.

"Sure it did. I just got all the proof I need that my instincts were on track the first time I saw you."

Her gaze narrowed. "Meaning?"

"I'll explain it to you another time. I think we'd better join the others."

"Duke Jenkins, what did you mean?" she said, scurrying after his retreating back.

Naturally, since she was more intent on catching him than on where she was, she managed to snag his soaking wet shorts just as he stepped onto the patio, right smack in front of her grandfather.

"Everything okay?" Grandpa Harlan inquired, not even trying to hide his amusement.

"Just peachy," Dani said and allowed the elastic waistband to snap back into place.

Duke grinned. "Better than that, actually."

"Good," Grandpa Harlan said. "I couldn't be happier."

Oh, sweet heaven, what was the family going to make of this? Dani wondered desperately. Not that the answer was all that difficult to figure out. They were going to assume whatever they wanted to. She could talk a blue streak for an entire year, and they would never believe that nothing had happened between her and Duke. For some reason, that didn't seem to bother him one bit.

She whirled around and scowled at him. "This is all your fault, you know."

"What's my fault?" he asked innocently.

If he couldn't see the hornet's nest they'd stirred up, she wasn't going to explain it to him. Let him find out for himself when her father cornered him first thing in the morning. She grinned vindictively. What she wouldn't give to be a fly on the wall when Duke tried squirming off the hook that he'd inadvertently managed to snag himself on.

"Are you making any progress?" Jordan asked Duke at their regular weekly planning meeting, which had been rescheduled for eight a.m. Tuesday because of the holiday.

"On what?" Duke inquired, feigning ignorance. He had a hunch they were not talking business. Jordan had taken to lumping the strategy for his personal life into the same sessions at which they discussed acquisitions and mergers.

"With my daughter, of course."

"You were at the picnic yesterday. You know as much as I do."

Jordan sighed heavily. "The girl's as elusive as a will-o'-the-wisp, isn't she? Just like her mother."

"Kelly was hard to get?" Duke asked. "For some reason I thought you two were childhood sweethearts."

Jordan grinned. "Depends on whom you ask. She claims she was always crazy about me, but I kept chasing after unsuitable women. When I finally woke up and decided the right woman had been under my nose all along, she turned me down. Again and again, in fact."

Duke was astonished. He'd never read an article about his boss in any newspaper or magazine in which some mention hadn't been made of the enduring love of his life. It was hard to imagine that theirs hadn't always been a fairy-tale love story. He had envied them that. It was something he never expected to experience.

"Really?" he asked. "Why didn't she accept your proposal?"

"She claimed she was only waiting for me to admit I loved her and Dani. Personally, I think she was paying me back for all that trial and error with those other women."

Duke found Jordan's revelations more disturbing than

he dared to admit. If Kelly had held out for an admission of love from a man she openly adored, would her daughter ever accept less from a man? Duke couldn't offer her love. He didn't have it in him.

He could promise her loyalty and faithfulness, companionship and friendship. He could offer her a family. Would that be enough to entice her to marry him? Or would she tell him to go hire a nanny, if all he wanted was someone to look after his sons? Unfortunately, he could practically hear her saying just that. Shouting it, in fact, at the top of her lungs.

Of course, he did have one ace in the hole. The attraction between them was powerful enough to singe asbestos. Some women confused sexual attraction with love. Few men did. He certainly didn't. He just prayed that Dani was one of the women who would never sleep with a man she didn't fancy herself head over heels in love with. Then, once he'd made love to her, he would be halfway to getting her to marry him.

Of course, he still hadn't even succeeded in getting her to go on a damn date, but he would rectify that this afternoon at four at Dolan's. The rest would follow.

He hoped.

8

"Hey, sweetie," Sharon Lynn said, when Dani walked into Dolan's promptly at four on Tuesday. "Lemonade? Or are you going to splurge on a milk shake? You haven't had one in a while."

"Since Jenny's buying, I was thinking of a hot fudge sundae," Dani said, already imagining the taste of the thick, warm chocolate drenching the chilly, creamy vanilla. If she had any vices, this was it. It had been weeks since she'd last indulged herself. There were a hundred and one reasons she deserved that sundae. Putting up with—no, surviving—Duke Jenkins was at the top of the list.

Aware of Dani's recent restraint, Sharon Lynn grinned. "Sure thing," she said and began scooping vanilla ice cream into a deep, old-fashioned glass dish before Dani could have second thoughts.

Dani glanced around the deserted drugstore. "Where's Jenny? I thought she'd be here on the dot since she was so insistent on me being here at four."

"Oh, she probably got caught up in something out at

White Pines," Sharon Lynn said without meeting her gaze. "You know how Grandpa Harlan is with his little projects. He loves having Jenny home so he can try to boss her around."

"Try being the operative word," Dani said, smiling. "No one ever succeeds in getting Jenny to do anything she doesn't want to do, Grandpa included."

"Much to his chagrin," Sharon Lynn added, handing her the sundae.

"She was a rebellious fourteen-year-old when he married Janet and adopted Jenny. You would think he'd have figured out by now that she's not going to change."

"Grandpa is the most optimistic man on earth. You know that," Sharon Lynn said. "Plus he managed to manipulate all but one of his stubborn sons into doing what he wanted. He's a master of reverse psychology. Why should he give up on Jenny?"

"That's not quite right," Dani countered soberly. "Even Uncle Erik followed Grandpa's wishes and became a rancher. We all know what a tragic mistake that was. He died because of it. You would have thought that would cure Grandpa of meddling."

Both she and Sharon Lynn fell silent. She had only very dim memories of Erik Adams. Sharon Lynn hadn't even been born when the accident on Uncle Luke's ranch had happened. Still, they both had heard of the heavy cost Grandpa Harlan had paid for pushing Erik into a career for which he wasn't at all suited. Maybe every member of the Adams clan was destined to make one huge mistake in a lifetime. Hopefully, Rob had been her one and only disaster.

Then again, maybe there was another terrible calamity on the horizon, she thought as she heard Duke's cheerful greeting to Sharon Lynn. The spoon almost slipped out of her suddenly shaky grasp when she felt his fingers skim her shoulder in a light caress as he slid onto the stool next to her. Yes, indeed, disaster was definitely right around the corner.

"Hey, darlin'. Fancy meeting you here," he said. "Sharon Lynn, how about a cup of coffee and a piece of lemon meringue pie?"

Dani slowly swiveled around until she could look directly into his eyes.

The glint she detected seemed an awful lot like triumph. Duke had never struck her as the kind of man who'd be tempted to play hooky in the middle of a workday. Nor was Dolan's so close to his office that he would be likely to pop in for take-out coffee, not when Jordan maintained a fully stocked snack bar for his employees and a dining room for executives.

Besides, Duke wasn't even dressed for work. He'd taken time to go home and change from a business suit into chinos and a T-shirt that emphasized the breadth of his chest and the muscles in his arms. She should be used to the fact that he was devastating no matter what he wore, but she wasn't.

Since he was very much here in the middle of a workday, there was only one conclusion she could reach. He had to be up to something and the something was related to her.

But how the heck would he have known...? One look at Sharon Lynn's expression answered that. Guilt was written all over her face. Dani turned back to Duke.

"Why aren't you at the office?" she inquired suspiciously.

The corners of his mouth tilted into the beginnings of a smile. "Is this an official inquiry or casual chitchat?"

"Whichever will get me a straight answer."

"I'm all caught up on my work," he said as if he were a kid swearing that all his homework was done. "Jordan gave me permission to take the rest of the day off."

Dani regarded him skeptically. "You asked?"

"Of course. I always play by the rules."

"Oh, please," she protested. "You don't expect me to believe that one, do you?"

He grinned. "It was worth a shot," he said and took a bite of his pie.

"It failed. Now try the truth. Why are you here?"

He took his own sweet time about answering. First, he tried another bite of the pie Sharon Lynn had set down, then a couple of swallows of coffee. Dani was fighting exasperation by the time he met her gaze.

"Actually, someone mentioned that this would be a good time to catch up with Josh and Zack," he said turning a pointed look on Sharon Lynn, who was suddenly very busy counting out little piles of napkins on the far side of the U-shaped counter. "Have you seen them today?"

"No." Dani watched her cousin trying to slip unobtrusively into the storage room. No question Sharon Lynn was in this—whatever *this* was—up to her eyeballs.

"Are you expecting them?" Duke asked.

Dani's gaze narrowed. "Why would I be expecting them?" Suddenly the whole convoluted plot began to come clear. She stared at her cousin, who'd almost made it into the safety of that back room. "Sharon Lynn, get back here. What do you know about this?"

"About what?" her cousin asked defensively.

"Me being here? Duke turning up? What's the deal?"

"Deal? There's no deal," she insisted, not coming one step closer. "I have no idea what you're talking about."

"Why you little…" Duke began, then suddenly grinned. "You're good. You know that. You are really good."

Sharon Lynn blushed.

Dani stared from one to the other. "Would one of you tell me what's going on?"

Since Sharon Lynn's lips were clamped firmly shut, it was Duke who answered. "We've been had, darlin'. Set up. Manipulated. Meddled with."

That pretty much confirmed Dani's own suspicions. After all, Jenny was nowhere in sight, either. Their scheming left her momentarily speechless.

"Let me guess," Duke suggested. "You were lured here to meet…?"

"Jenny," she supplied with a sigh.

"Any sign of her?"

"No." She scowled at her cousin. "Sharon Lynn?"

"Yes?"

"What are you two up to?" she asked again, though by now the answer was fairly obvious.

Fortunately, for her cousin, the phone in the storage room rang.

"Sorry," Sharon Lynn said, not sounding the least bit sorry. She made a relieved dash out of sight.

"That's probably Jenny now," Duke speculated. "Checking to see how things are progressing."

When Sharon Lynn was gone, Dani regarded Duke apologetically. "I'm the one who's truly sorry. They shouldn't have put you in this position."

He grinned and popped the last bite of pie into his mouth. "The way I see it there's nothing wrong with the position I'm in. The pie was great. The coffee's the best in town. The company's not bad. What about you? Enjoying your sundae?"

Dani considered lying, but decided it was a waste of time and good hot fudge sauce. "Yes," she admitted.

"Then eat up." He leaned closer. "Then we'll sneak out without paying. That'll serve 'em right."

She grinned at his notion of revenge. "I don't think the cost of a hot fudge sundae and some pie and coffee is going to teach those two a lesson. For that matter, they can probably get Grandpa Harlan to ante up for it. I detect his fine hand in here somewhere. I can just see the three of them in his den out at White Pines plotting and scheming."

"Maybe we should give them something to think about," Duke suggested, a worrisome glint back in his eyes.

"Such as?"

Even as she spoke, she realized she should never have asked. Those two words were as good as asking for trouble.

Duke swiveled her stool around until their knees were touching. His gaze locked with hers. Dani felt the sizzle of that look all the way down to her toes. If hot fudge was a vice, this was pure sin, she concluded.

She told herself she was going to look away any second now. She was going to move away from the graze of chinos against her knees and the lure of Duke's body heat. Any minute now, she promised herself.

Her breath caught in her throat. This was a dangerous game they were playing. In fact, they were flat-out flirting with disaster. If it could be called flirting, when the man looked as if he were one heartbeat away from scooping her up and hauling her off to bed, she amended. They were way beyond flirting.

When his callused fingertips skimmed along her cheek, her pulse zoomed straight into the stratosphere. When his thumb brushed over her lower lip, she felt the jolt in every cell from head to toe. She swallowed hard and willed herself to look away, move, get up and haul butt out of there.

Instead, she seemed to sway toward him, just when his head was swooping in and his lips were taking dead-on aim for hers. The kiss, which she was so sure had been the last thing on her mind, turned out to be as inevitable as breathing. Soft and sweet and tender, it left her feeling cherished in a way that she'd never, ever felt before.

"Oh, boy," she whispered, when he had pulled away. She was in trouble, hip-deep and sinking fast.

"Nice," Duke assessed. "But I'm thinking that's not enough to convince them we don't need their help."

"Hmm?" she murmured, too dazed to follow his thinking. She blinked as he slowly rose to his feet, gasped softly when he lifted her until she was standing toe-to-toe with him, close enough that his heat surrounded her, beckoned to her.

His fingers tunneled through her hair. His breath whispered against her cheek. And then his mouth covered hers again.

This time there was nothing soft or sweet or tender about the kiss. It was demanding and hungry and possessive. And it took her breath away. It dazzled her. In fact, in her personal range of experience, this was the mother of all kisses, the kind that could lure a woman into thinking she was in love.

That four-letter word slipped into her consciousness even as Duke deepened the kiss to a whole new level of bone-melting bliss. Love. *LOVE?* Whoa, baby.

Dani felt the emotional brakes slam on. She spun away from Duke so quickly she left both of them off balance and shaky. Clearly surprised, he regarded her intently.

"Dani, talk to me."

Embarrassment flooded over her. She had practically come apart in Duke's arms right in the middle of a public place. It was the kind of behavior that started rumors and caused pain. All they needed was for Joshua and Zachary to get wind of the incident. They were clearly eager for a new mom. One whiff of this and those fertile eight-year-old minds would start manufacturing all sorts of happily-ever-after scenarios that just weren't going to happen. She forced herself to look directly into Duke's eyes.

"This is never going to happen again," she said bluntly. "Never."

Apparently, her tone was more convincing than usual because for once he didn't argue, didn't make some teasing remark or offer up a challenge that would have turned her vow into a joke. In fact, he nodded solemnly as if he'd gotten the message loud and clear.

"Never," he echoed.

"Promise me," she said, just to be sure.

"This will never happen again, I swear it," he said.

He sounded sincere enough, she supposed, but for some reason she trusted him about as much as she trusted Sharon Lynn and Jenny at the moment. She glanced at his hands, checking for crossed fingers. If she could have she would have checked his toes as well. Nope, there were no overt signs that he was intentionally lying through his teeth.

"I'm taking you at your word," she said. "My father says you're an honorable man. I'm counting on it."

That seemed to make him uneasy, but again he nodded dutifully. "You can count on it, darlin'."

He said it so easily that she was vaguely insulted. Didn't he want to kiss her again? Had it been awful for him? What the heck was the matter with him that he was giving up so easily?

No, what was the matter with her that she wasn't taking his promise at face value and hightailing it back to the safety of the clinic? Hormones evidently played havoc with logic.

She stiffened her spine, picked up her purse and inched away from Duke, careful not to brush against him. She was being absurd. It wasn't as if the man was going to grab her and throw her on the counter and have his way with her. He'd just promised he wouldn't even kiss her again, for heaven's sakes.

Of course, there was no guarantee that she wouldn't be the one doing the throwing and the having. Maybe that was why it was very wise not to come within a mile of Duke Jenkins for at least the next forty or fifty years. Maybe by then her hormones would be in check. If they weren't, it would probably be some sort of medical miracle and they could go on TV on some X-rated sex channel for seniors. The thought of it made her smile.

"Dani?"

She blinked and met his gaze, fully aware that color was flooding her cheeks again. She had blushed more in the past few weeks than she had in her entire life before meeting Duke. "Yes?"

"Want me to walk you back to your clinic?"

"No," she blurted at once, then winced at the rude tone. "I mean, really it's not necessary."

He regarded her doubtfully. "You seem a little wobbly."

"I am not," she said emphatically. "Once I'm out in the fresh air, I'll be just fine."

"It's a hundred degrees out there."

So what? she thought. It had to be darned close to that inside when they were in the middle of that kiss. In fact, she probably ought to speak to Sharon Lynn about fixing the thermostat on the air conditioner. It was way too hot in Dolan's. In fact, she was tempted to pick up a menu and fan herself right now, but she could see how Duke might misconstrue that and turn it into some sort of admission that he affected her.

"The heat doesn't bother me," she insisted, backing away an inch at a time as if she were trying to slip away without him noticing.

"If you say so."

"I do."

"Then I guess I'll see you around."

"Right."

"Bye."

"Bye."

"Have a pleasant evening."

"You, too." Dani sighed. Much more of this polite leave-taking and she was going to throw up. Before she added that to the list of her most embarrassing moments, she bolted for the door.

The blast of humid heat should have slowed her down. She barely even noticed it as she practically ran all the way back to the clinic. She headed straight for her own part of the house. She'd left the air conditioning set at a pleasant seventy-five degrees. She turned it down to sixty and went and stood in front of a register and let the cool air blow over her.

Even when her body was shivering and the cats were trying to crawl under an afghan on the sofa, she still felt hot. Only then did she admit to herself that as long as Duke remained at the center of her thoughts it wouldn't matter if she bathed in ice water. She'd still be burning up.

Duke didn't glance away from the door through which Dani had exited until he heard a whisper of sound behind him. He turned to find Sharon Lynn regarding him warily. After a moment, she bravely forced a smile.

"More coffee?" she inquired cheerfully.

"I think maybe I'd better switch to iced tea," he said. "With lots and lots of ice."

"I noticed it got pretty warm in here," she said.

"I'm delighted we were able to provide the entertainment. Now maybe you can tell me something."

"What?"

"Exactly what were you and Jenny up to? It's fairly obvious to me that Dani does not want a new man in her life, especially not one who's a single father, right?"

"That's what she thinks."

Duke's gaze narrowed. "Am I missing something? Isn't what she thinks important?"

"Not if it's different from what she feels," Sharon Lynn explained patiently. "This afternoon proves what we suspected all along. She's attracted to you. She's just scared to death of doing anything about it. That's understandable, of course. But you can't stop living just because you've been burned by an idiot, right?"

"I suppose."

"Let me ask you something. Are you interested in Dani? I mean beyond a quick roll in the hay or something?"

"Isn't that an awfully personal question?"

Sharon Lynn shrugged off the implied criticism. "I'm an Adams," she said as if that were explanation enough. "We're nosy, especially when it comes to one of our own. Now stop avoiding the question. Are your intentions serious?"

Duke shook his head, amused by the persistence, if not by the prying. "I think Dani's the only one who deserves an answer to that question and she's not asking it."

"She won't, either. It's up to the rest of us to protect her."

"Would she appreciate you doing that?"

"Of course not," Sharon Lynn conceded airily. "But she'd expect it just the same. When it comes to providing backup, we're better than the Texas Rangers."

"I see. Well, let me give you just a little bit of advice from an outsider's perspective. The game is underway. Stay on the sidelines from here on out and watch. I think Dani and I can take it from here."

Sharon Lynn grinned. "Yes, I imagine you can do just about anything you set your mind to."

"I'll take that as a compliment."

"Of course you will," she said. "And I will stay out of it, unless I think you're getting out of line. Then I can pretty much guarantee someone in the family will call the foul."

He regarded her with amusement. "And the penalty?"

She returned his look solemnly. "You don't want to know."

Duke shook his head. "Your uncle Jordan said practically the same thing."

She grinned. "As long as you've gotten the message."

"Loud and clear, sweetheart. Loud and clear."

But the only signals he was really worried about were the ones Dani was sending him and those were very, very mixed.

9

Duke was constantly revising his strategy where Dani was concerned. After that last kiss, he concluded that she needed time to think about it, lots of time. He made himself so scarce that the only people who saw him regularly were his sons, Paolina, Jordan and his secretary. September eased into October, then November. Let Dani start to wonder what he was up to. Maybe it would force her to admit she was intrigued by him.

At least that was his theory. In practice, he was the one going stark-raving nuts. The boys weren't doing especially well with the forced confinement, either. They'd been plaguing him daily about going out to White Pines to see the horses or into town for ice cream. They were getting to be almost as restless and cranky as he was. He might not be experienced at this parenting business, but he sensed that something was going to have to give very soon.

Sitting in his study, he tried to focus on the paperwork he'd brought home from the office, but his mind wasn't on it. He was downright ecstatic when Joshua came to stand in the doorway, regarding him solemnly.

"Hey, son, what's up?"

"Are you busy?"

"Not too busy for you. Come on in."

Joshua bounded across the room and to Duke's astonishment climbed into his lap and burrowed his face against Duke's chest. His narrow little shoulders heaved with barely contained sobs. Duke had never felt so helpless in his entire life. He wrapped the boy in his arms and held on tight.

"Josh, what's going on?" he asked eventually, when the crying had abated somewhat.

"Nothing," Joshua replied, sniffing.

Duke smiled, grateful that Josh couldn't see it. "That's an awful lot of tears over nothing. Did something happen at school today?"

"No."

"What then?"

Joshua pulled back and looked straight into Duke's eyes. His little face was streaked with tears. "Dad, how come Mommy doesn't love us?"

Oh, boy, Duke thought, biting back a sigh. "What makes you think she doesn't love you? We've talked about this before, remember? It's me she's mad at, not you guys."

"I don't think so. I think she hates all of us. Me and Zack, too."

Duke began to get a sneaking suspicion about the cause of the tears. "Did she call here today?"

Josh hesitated, then sniffed and nodded. "She told us

not to tell you, Dad, I didn't mean to break the promise, honest."

"That's okay. Some promises should never be made in the first place. You should always be able to come to me. If someone tells you not to, always ask yourself why. Now tell me what your mom said that upset you so much."

"Zack and me asked her to come home. We told her we missed her a whole lot, but she said no." Fresh tears welled up in his eyes. "She said she was never, ever coming back."

Duke mentally cursed Caroline for being so blunt with the two boys, then swearing them to secrecy. Did she expect them to keep all the hurt bottled up inside? Or were the secrets just meant as payback for him?

He wiped away Josh's tears and tried to coax a smile from him. "Now you listen to me, half-pint. We're getting along okay, just the three of us, right?"

"Yeah, but it would be nice to have a mom again," Josh said wistfully.

Duke immediately thought of Dani. She might not be able to replace Caroline in their hearts, but she could fill an obvious void in their lives. It was time to move on to the next step in his strategy. If nothing else, this conversation with Josh had proven that it was time to start courting Dani in earnest.

Duke had given Dani so much space she was about to spit. Not even reminding herself a hundred times a day that she had asked for it seemed to help. Work took up most of her time, but there were always a few hours late at night when she had nothing to do but think and remember the way she had felt in Duke's arms smack in the middle of Dolan's.

That kiss was the most impulsive, uninhibited thing she'd ever done. Naturally, she couldn't get it out of her head, she consoled herself. It had nothing to do with Duke *per se*. It was the outrageous risk she'd taken that was plaguing her.

So why did she glance hopefully at the door to her office every time it opened unexpectedly? Why did she spend a solid hour primping before every single family gathering on the chance that Duke would be invited? Why was she so disappointed when he never turned up?

Perversity was one possibility. Insanity was another. Admitting that she was falling in love with the man despite her best intentions was not an acceptable explanation. A few breath-stealing kisses didn't amount to a hill of beans in the overall scheme of life. She would forget all about them soon enough. She just had to concentrate on other things.

"Such as?" she muttered testily to herself.

"Such as what?"

The masculine voice, which surely she had conjured up, sent a shiver dancing down her spine. Obviously, the attraction hadn't worn off, she thought glumly as she glanced up at the man filling the doorway to her office. He was back in a business suit and more devastatingly handsome than ever. Just the sound of his deep, husky voice was enough to make her pulse skitter crazily. If anyone took an EKG right now, it would land her in the hospital. She forced herself not to drag in a deep breath, sigh, swallow or otherwise indicate that he'd rattled her by popping up when she least expected him.

"Just talking to myself," she said, pleased with her calm, casual tone. "What brings you by?"

"An emergency. Well, two emergencies, actually."

Her professional mode kicked in. She was on her feet and halfway around her desk, when he put out a hand to stop her.

"Whoa! I didn't mean medical emergencies. Sorry."

She frowned at him. "It's not a word we take lightly around here."

"I know. I should have realized that."

"There are no half-drowned kittens, then?"

He grinned. "Nothing like that. The cats have gotten very adept at avoiding Joshua and Zachary. They seem to have a sixth sense when the two of them are up to no good."

"That's the beauty of cats," Dani agreed. "They're pretty good at fending for themselves."

"Like you," he suggested lightly.

She wasn't entirely sure if he meant it as an insult or a compliment. "I suppose," she agreed. She regarded him expectantly.

"Actually, I've been meaning to call," he began, but Dani cut him off.

"You don't need to explain. We agreed that we wouldn't see each other again."

He seemed surprised by the statement. "Is that what we agreed?"

There was that worrisome gleam in his eyes again. "Of course, it is," she said hurriedly. "I told you—"

"Specifically that I was never to kiss you in the middle of Dolan's again."

Dani's gaze narrowed. She thought she detected an

opening there for other kisses in other places, when nothing could have been further from her intentions. Explaining that, though, might be considered an over-reaction since he'd shown no particular inclination even to see her again lately.

"More or less," she said. She decided there was prob-ably safer conversational turf for them to be on, espe-cially since Duke seemed to be staring at her as if he hadn't been near a woman in a hundred years and des-peration was setting in. Since her own level of yearn-ing had reached a fever pitch, they were heading for trouble unless one of them changed the topic to some-thing a little less sexual.

"You still haven't explained about the so-called emergency," she said hurriedly.

He blinked at the reminder. "Yeah, right."

"Well?"

He glanced around her office. "Do you think maybe we could have this conversation someplace else?"

"Why?"

He regarded her with amusement. "Because I asked nicely?" he suggested. "We could go out for pizza. That wouldn't be too dangerous, would it?"

Dani winced at the suggestion that she found being alone with him dangerous. She had hoped he would in-terpret their last parting as a lack of interest on her side. Obviously, he'd reached just the opposite conclusion.

"Duke, please..."

"It's not a date," he assured her. "It's just that I'm starved. It's around dinnertime. Why not have it to-gether so we can discuss things."

"Things?" she repeated. "What things?"

He grinned. "I'll explain over pizza."

"Duke!"

"Please."

She could turn him down. She could manufacture other plans, but the honest to goodness truth was, she didn't want to. One sight of him standing in the doorway to her office and she'd reacted to his presence the way a parched man would to an oasis. Just because she didn't want to get involved with him didn't mean they couldn't be friends, did it? Perhaps that was all he was offering, she told herself, though the unmistakable heat in his eyes said otherwise.

"It will have to be a quick dinner," she said. "I need to drive out to Betty Lou's and take a look at Honeybunch."

Duke stared at her with obvious surprise. "I thought he'd be fully recovered by now."

"Actually, he is, but Betty Lou is lonely. She got used to me dropping in when I first took Honeybunch home."

Duke grinned. "The truth is, you miss that dog, don't you?"

"Well, he was around the clinic for several weeks," she said defensively. "Besides, it's more than that. Betty Lou has some terrific stories about Grandpa Harlan when he was a boy. I'm recording them all so I can blackmail him if the need ever arises."

"Now that does sound like a reason to keep calling," Duke agreed. "Mind if I tag along? We can drive out there first, then eat."

"I thought you were starving."

"I won't die from it."

"Okay, if you're sure. I'm warning you, though. Betty

Lou is liable to make a pass at you. She considers herself to be quite a femme fatale."

Duke returned her teasing gaze evenly. "I can hardly wait. I've been worried I was losing my touch."

They found Betty Lou fixing fried chicken and mashed potatoes, enough for an army. She invited them in without any evidence at all that she was surprised by their arrival.

"Betty Lou, this is Duke Jenkins," Dani said.

Betty Lou batted long, thick, mascaraed eyelashes at the man in question. "Oh, honey, I know who this is. Not a woman in town hasn't been speculating why a handsome catch like this is still on the loose." She looked Duke over from head to toe, then gave a little nod of approval. "How do you feel about older women?"

To his credit, he managed to keep a straight face. "I'd say that depends. If they're as beautiful as you, I'd say my mind is open."

"Then sit right down here. Dani, you, too," she added as an afterthought. "You're staying for dinner."

"But we intended to go out for pizza," Dani protested.

Betty Lou waved the long fork she was holding in a dismissive gesture. "You can have pizza any old time. I've got mashed potatoes, corn and a peach pie to go with this chicken. Now tell me you can turn down home-cooking like that."

"Not me," Duke said, eyeing the pots on the stove avidly. When his gaze reached the huge peach pie with the golden crust, he practically salivated.

Dani decided to save her breath. She would just have to wait until after dinner to discover what had been on

Duke's mind when he turned up in her office. Besides, they were probably better off with a chaperone, especially one who had her own designs on Duke.

"Dinner sounds lovely," she agreed. "Where's Honeybunch, by the way?"

"Out chasing squirrels last time I checked. He'll be dragging back here any second looking for something to eat."

"He's doing okay?"

"Better than okay," Betty Lou said. "He's taking full advantage of that new lease on life you gave him. I don't know how to thank you."

"You've already thanked me," Dani said. "A hundred times, in fact."

"Maybe so, but I know you would have put any other dog in that condition to sleep," Betty Lou said. "Maybe I should have, too, but I just couldn't bear it. He's been my companion for too long now. I expected to go to my grave long before he did. You can bet I gave that drunk driver a piece of my mind when I caught up with him down at the jail. It was bad enough that he hit the dog to begin with, but to just leave him in the road like that was a real heartless crime."

"The judge sentenced him to volunteer in a hospital emergency room for six months once he gets out of jail," Dani said. "The judge told him he wants him to get a good, up-close look at the victims of traffic accidents before he gets behind the wheel again."

Betty Lou shrugged off the justice. "The man's trash," she said. "He won't get the message. He'll end up dead sooner or later, which wouldn't bother me a bit, if it weren't for the guarantee that he'll be taking some innocent soul out with him." She shook her head. "Enough of this. You two didn't come all the way out here to listen to me go on and on."

"Actually, in a way we did," Duke told her. "Dani said you have some great stories about her grandfather."

"Harlan?" Betty Lou said with a chuckle. "That old coot and I go way back. Not that he likes to admit it. Ever since he married that young attorney, he pretends he's shaved a couple of decades off his age. Let me get all this food on the table and I'll tell you a thing or two about Harlan Adams."

For the next hour she regaled them with stories from her own school days. Grandpa Harlan seemed to play a pivotal role in most of them.

"Did you, by any chance, have a crush on my grandfather?" Dani teased.

"Heavens, no. Now that brother of his…"

Dani stared at her. "Brother? Grandpa Harlan had a brother?"

"Well, of course, he did. Henry Adams. Everyone around here called him Hank. Now there was a looker."

Dani was stunned. She had never once heard anyone in the family mention that name. "Did he die or something?"

"Not as far as I know," Betty Lou said. "There was some kind of falling out. He left town when he was quite young, maybe sixteen. He was quite a few years younger than your grandfather. He just took off. As far as I know, no one's heard from him since."

"Well, I'll be," Dani murmured.

A half hour later with the dishes done and Betty Lou openly yawning, Dani and Duke made their ex-

cuses and left. When they had climbed into his car, he
glanced over at her. "I gather you've never heard of this
great-uncle Hank."

"Never. Apparently Grandpa Harlan is even better at
keeping secrets than he is at prying into them."

Duke considered that, his expression thoughtful.
"Maybe you should leave well enough alone," he said.
"If he hasn't mentioned his brother in all these years, it
must have been a bitter feud. It might really upset him
to bring it up at this late date."

"I suppose," she said disappointed, but unable to
argue with his logic. She would ask her father about
Hank Adams, though. Maybe he or Luke knew something about the man.

At the moment, though, there was another secret she
needed to get to the bottom of. "When are you going to
tell me what brought you to my office this afternoon?"
she asked.

"Invite me in for coffee when we get to your place,"
he countered. "This isn't something we can discuss in
the car."

"Why?"

"Because I need to get a clear look at your face when
I bring it up."

She stared back at him nervously. "Uh-oh. I don't
like the sound of that."

He grinned. "It's nothing to fret over, darlin'. You'll
either say yes—" his gaze settled on her mouth "—or
no."

Dani's heart thumped unsteadily for the second time
that day. Yes or no? People said yes or no to proposals.
Marriage proposals. Surely, if he'd gotten the message

about kissing, then he would understand that it stood to reason she wouldn't be interested in marriage, right? Or had he just capitulated easily on the kissing, knowing that he had a bigger goal in mind?

Oh, for heaven's sakes, stop, she told herself sharply. This wasn't about marriage. It was about...well, who knew what it was about, she concluded, eyeing Duke warily. Anything was possible, especially with a man as unpredictable as Duke. She would probably laugh herself silly when she realized how far off the mark she'd been.

At the moment, though, trepidation was tearing through her at an astonishing clip. If she could have thought of any rational excuse, she would have bolted from the car in a flash. Heck, she would have packed her bags and moved out of Los Pinos to avoid having this conversation.

As it was, Duke was pulling into her driveway, cutting the engine and turning to her expectantly, obviously awaiting the invitation in for coffee. Dani swallowed hard and mumbled the invitation without much enthusiasm.

Duke regarded her with amusement. "Darlin', lighten up. This isn't about walking hand in hand to the gallows."

"Yeah, go tell that to someone who'll buy it," she muttered under her breath even as she led the way inside.

She flipped on every single light in the house as she passed through on her way to the kitchen. Forget cozy and romantic. She wanted illumination. She wanted it so bright, he would never mistake the ambience for an invitation. In fact, it wouldn't be bad if the lighting brought to mind a police interrogation room. Not that she'd ever been in one personally, but maybe Duke had.

She put the coffee on to brew, found a couple of old

mugs so he would understand that this wasn't a special occasion, poured some fresh sugar in the sugar bowl even though it was already half-full and put milk into a cream pitcher, despite the fact that they both drank their coffee black. When there was absolutely nothing else left to do, she finally sat down opposite him.

"Finished?" he inquired, not bothering to hide a smile.

She scowled, annoyed by his amusement. "Yes."

"Are you sure you don't want to dash off and check the mail or dust the living room?"

"Duke, will you just spit out whatever's on your mind and go? I have a splitting headache, and I have an early day tomorrow."

He was on his feet in a flash and moving behind her. She twisted to see what he was up to, but he rested his hands on her shoulders until she sighed and faced forward again.

"Duke! What do you think you're doing?"

"You said you have a headache," he explained patiently as he began to massage her temples.

Dani would have protested, but it felt too good. She could feel the tension beginning to ease even before his fingers began kneading the hard knots in her shoulders.

"No wonder your head's pounding," he observed. "You're tense."

"Well, of course, I'm tense. You've been dropping little hints all evening that you have something important to discuss. My imagination is running wild."

"Really? I'm fascinated. Just what sort of images have you managed to conjure up?"

"Never mind."

He chuckled. "Whoops, here come those knots again. They'd probably go away if you'd tell me what you've been thinking."

"They would go away if you would just say what's on your mind and get out of here," she countered.

"Tsk, tsk, that's not a very auspicious beginning," he taunted. "Maybe I'd better get into this another time, when you're not so cranky."

"Get into what, dammit? And I am not cranky."

He chuckled. "Yes, indeed, another time would be best. It'll keep."

Before she knew what he intended, he leaned down, brushed a brotherly peck across her cheek and headed for the door.

"Duke!"

"Night, darlin'. It's been fun."

"Duke Jenkins, if you walk out that door without explaining yourself, don't come back."

The threat was wasted. He was already halfway to the car by the time she finished. Since he gave her a jaunty wave as he pulled out of the driveway, she could only assume he wasn't feeling the least bit threatened.

"Well, damn," she muttered, staring after him.

As he drove home, Duke whistled cheerfully and congratulated himself on an evening well spent. He'd proved to himself once again that Dani wasn't nearly as immune to him as she wanted to be.

He could guess precisely which path her imagination had led her down. In fact, he had deliberately chosen his words just to point her in the right direction. Yes and no were answers to a whole lot of questions, most of them innocuous enough. But spoken with a little hint of seductiveness, they clearly hinted at very provocative queries to come.

After planting that particular seed in her mind, he'd been somewhat surprised that she'd allowed him in the house at all, given her avowed aversion to any kind of future with another single dad.

He had also been careful the past few weeks to stay away from White Pines or any other place where she was likely to be. Since any invitation always included Joshua and Zachary, he'd turned them all down. He'd wanted Dani wondering what he was up to, not remembering that he had two sons underfoot.

In the long run, he figured his strategy would pay off. In the short run, he was very close to losing his mind. How had he missed the fact that rearing two boys could be so incredibly challenging? Maybe not as challenging as exploring for oil, but a darned close second.

Maybe it was because they were twins, but Josh and Zack seemed to think as a single unit, conspiring to get into the most amazing amount of mischief just when he thought he had everything under control. Thankfully, they hadn't scared off Paolina, but he knew with every fiber of his being that the housekeeper was no substitute for a real mom. He intended to give them one or die trying.

It would have been a heck of a lot simpler, of course, if he'd picked one who was a little more amenable to the idea. Then again, courting Dani Adams was just about fascinating enough to take his mind off the tedium of all that paperwork her daddy piled on his desk.

10

After a restless night Dani stepped outside at mid-morning on Saturday to get the paper and discovered two little boys sitting on the front steps. She stared at Josh and Zack, then automatically looked around for some sign of their father.

"Dad's not with us," Josh said as if he, like his father, was capable of reading her mind.

"So I see. How did you get here?"

"Paolina brought us," Zack said.

Dani fought the panicky feeling that had been automatic from the moment she met these two wonderful, emotionally scary kids. "She just left you on my doorstep?"

"We came to buy cat food," Zack said. "Paolina said she'd get it at the grocery store, but the cats like the kind you have better."

Dani nodded as if the explanation made perfect sense, which it obviously did to them. "Well, then, I guess you'd better come in and choose the flavors you want."

"Anything but liver," Josh told her. "That smells yucky."

"Not to a cat," Dani pointed out.

Both boys looked startled.

"I guess you're right," Josh said. "And it's their dinner."

Dani grinned at him. "Exactly." She led the way into her pet supply room and pointed to the rows of gourmet cat food in cans and bags. "Can you two pick what you want on your own?" she inquired hopefully.

Zack gave her a shy look and, to her astonishment, slipped his hand into hers. "No, we want you to help. Okay?"

The warmth of that little hand tucked trustingly into her own brought on a flood of bittersweet memories. Every bit of instinct for self-preservation protested that she should make up a plausible excuse, walk away and leave the two boys to their shopping. One look into two pairs of hopeful eyes told her she couldn't do it.

"I'll help," she said grimly.

The process of choosing took far longer than it should have. They claimed they wanted to learn about every single ingredient in every single brand she carried. She distrusted their enthusiasm, but their sweet little expressions were so innocent she chided herself for being overly suspicious.

When they had filled a shopping bag with their selections and had added toys for each cat, they stood back and admired their purchases.

"I think you two have made excellent choices," she told them. "You've picked a good variety of very healthy cat food. Did you want me to send the bill to your dad?"

The two exchanged guilty looks.

"That's okay," Josh said. "We'll pay for it. I mean, not right this second, but soon."

Dani's suspicions stirred again. "Is this coming out of your allowances?"

"Heck, no," Zack said. "Dad's coming to get us when he gets finished at the office. He'll pay you."

Dani stared at them in astonishment. "Your father is coming here?"

Two heads bobbed.

"When?"

"After he gets done at work."

"Did he happen to mention when that would be?"

"Before lunchtime, I guess. He said we could all go out to eat together."

Why that sneaky, low-down, devious snake. Obviously, Duke had plotted to leave the boys with her for an entire morning. How could he? What if she'd been called away on an emergency? What if she'd simply been too busy to look after them? She regarded the two boys, who were waiting quietly for her response, and sighed. There was no emergency, and she wasn't too busy.

"Why don't we take the shopping bag into the kitchen, and I'll make us all some hot chocolate."

"All right!" Josh said.

"And cookies?" Zack asked, only to be shushed by his brother with a warning that he wasn't being polite.

"You're s'pposed to wait till you're invited," Josh said.

"That's okay," Dani told them. "Actually, I was just thinking about baking some cookies."

"Really?" Zack asked. "Chocolate chip?"

"Zack!" Josh protested.

Dani chuckled. "It's okay. Chocolate chip are my favorite, too. I always keep a package of the slice-and-bake kind in the refrigerator."

"We know how to do those kind," Zack said proudly. "Paolina lets us."

"Good, then you can help me," Dani said, taking the package out and searching for a cookie sheet and a knife that would do the job without being too dangerous for clumsy little hands.

The morning passed in a blur of hot chocolate, cookies, laughter and talk of dinosaurs and spaceships. She hadn't had so much fun since…

No, she told herself sternly. She wasn't going to go there. Not today. Today she was simply going to enjoy the fact that two little boys with incredible imaginations and their daddy's charm were sharing their lives with her.

Later she would try very hard not to let her heart break.

Duke surveyed the scene in Dani's kitchen and smiled. His little plot was working out very nicely. Left to their own devices, he'd known that Josh and Zack could climb over any wall Dani tried to erect between them.

He'd given Paolina very explicit instructions to make sure that everything went off without a hitch. She was to leave the boys at Dani's, then drive by twice over the next half hour to make sure they were inside. She had called him at the office to report that everything was *muy bueno,* very good.

Now that he had Dani guessing about his intentions, Duke had concluded that it was time to switch tactics once again. He intended to pester her like ants at a picnic. She'd been so sure she was in charge, that he'd accepted her terms for their relationship. He wanted to make certain she realized now that she'd been mistaken.

Today's unscheduled visit from Josh and Zack was just the start.

"Having fun?" he inquired as he knocked on the screen door and entered the kitchen.

Dani had a streak of chocolate on her cheek, marshmallow on her lips and fire flashing in her eyes. Her laughter faded at the sight of him.

"You and I need to talk," she said quietly. "Boys, can you put the rest of the cookies in the cookie jar for me?"

"Sure," they said at once, far more eagerly than they'd ever responded to one of Duke's directives.

As soon as she saw that they were doing as she'd asked, she walked into the living room. Duke followed, preparing himself for the barrage of questions he knew was coming.

"What on earth were you thinking?" she demanded the instant they were out of earshot of the boys.

"Excuse me?"

"I am not your baby-sitter."

"Of course not."

"I could have been out on a call."

"That was a possibility," Duke agreed. "Paolina was supposed to check to make sure you were here."

"I never spoke to Paolina. I found your sons sitting

on my doorstep, looking for all the world as if they'd been abandoned there."

"Naturally, you took them in."

"Well, of course I did. What was I supposed to do?"

"You could have called me to come and get them," he said mildly.

Dani stared at him silently, then some of the fight seemed to drain out of her. "Yes, you're right. I suppose I could have done that."

"Any idea why you didn't? I mean especially if having them here was a bother."

"It wasn't a bother, not like you mean."

He nodded at that. "Good. I'm glad."

"They're terrific boys. You know that."

"I think so." He shrugged. "Well, if that's all, I guess we'll be on our way. I promised to take them to lunch."

She actually grinned sheepishly at that. "I doubt they're all that hungry. We've eaten a lot of cookies. It probably spoiled their appetite."

"I don't suppose missing lunch will kill them." He paused and deliberately brushed a brotherly kiss across her cheek. "Thanks, again. How much do I owe you for the cat food?"

She stared at him, clearly flustered. Finally, she distractedly named an amount and accepted the cash. When he walked out the door, the boys in tow, she still looked as if she wasn't quite certain what had happened. Duke grinned all the way home.

Over the next few weeks he could see that the new approach was working better and better. Dani brightened perceptibly at the sight of him, then turned right around and pretended she couldn't stand to be near him.

He knew it was pretense, because he made a point of using any legitimate excuse at all to touch her.

A quick kiss of a greeting, a seemingly inadvertent brushing of their knees when they were cleverly and deliberately seated next to each other at the Adams gatherings he'd started attending again, a lightning-fast caress of her cheek as he said good-night. She trembled visibly at each fleeting contact. Color bloomed in her cheeks. Exasperation and yearning warred in her eyes.

Of course, the game was taking its toll on him as well. Some nights he went home so aroused, it took a jog around the house and an icy shower before he could settle down and have any hope at all of getting to sleep. When he realized he was tempted to start warming a pan of milk at bedtime, he knew he was in serious trouble.

Yes, indeed, the more Duke saw of Dani Adams, the more intrigued he was. He hated that no matter what he tried, she continued to look a little aloof, a little sad. In the midst of the wildest, noisiest family celebration, she kept mostly to herself. Not even Sharon Lynn's or Jenny's best efforts could penetrate her shell for long.

After the cookie-baking episode, she was more careful than ever, it seemed, to avoid spending any time whatsoever with his sons, so careful that it was clear she desperately wanted to gather them into her arms for hugs. Only a fool wouldn't recognize that she was a woman just made for mothering. It was in her eyes as she watched them, a longing so deep, so fierce that it reaffirmed Duke's determination to make her their mother.

The boys sensed those maternal instincts, too. They

gravitated to her at every Adams family event and though she was as skittish as a horse around a rattler, sooner or later she came around. Every single time.

Josh and Zack made her smile when no one else could. The smiles were cautious, tentative, to be sure, but they lifted Duke's spirits as much as any oil strike he'd ever made.

Dani seemed to be the only one who didn't get how much her warmth was valued. On some level, she clearly blamed herself for getting too caught up in the lives of those girls she'd ultimately lost. She thought she was the one who'd hurt them, when the truth was it was their father's cavalier attitude that had set them all up for anguish.

Duke would never make that mistake. He was a decisive man, always had been. Once he made a commitment, he stuck to it, for better or worse. He would have stayed married to Caroline, enduring the cold emptiness of the relationship if that had been what she wanted. Duty and honor were that important to him.

Now he wanted Dani Adams to become a significant part of Josh's and Zack's lives, a permanent part. The boys needed a mother's love. They needed Dani. And he would do whatever was necessary to get her for them. He owed it to them after the mess he'd made of his marriage to their mother. It was as simple and clear-cut as that for him.

His own feelings toward her were more complex. He enjoyed Dani's company. He wanted her in his bed. He had vowed to himself that he would always treat her the way she deserved to be treated. The only thing he couldn't promise her was love. He hoped that the things he could offer would be enough for a woman who understood the meaning and importance of family.

Thanksgiving was coming and he decided the holidays were the perfect time to step up his campaign, turn up the heat another notch, so to speak. Christmas would be the ideal, most romantic time to announce an engagement. He made that his goal and set up a strategic plan that corporate executives—Jordan included, he thought with a grim smile—would have envied.

Her family, bless them, cooperated by issuing an invitation for Thanksgiving dinner at White Pines. The message had been relayed by Jordan just that afternoon. Duke mentioned it to the boys when he got home that night, certain of their response.

"So, what do you think?" he asked.

"Cool," Joshua said. "Will there be turkey and dressing and pumpkin pie?"

"I imagine so," Duke said. He was fairly confident that this family would celebrate with old-fashioned excess when it came to their Thanksgiving feast.

"Will Dani be there?" Zachary asked.

"Of course."

"Are you gonna kiss her again?" Zack asked, proving that he was as adept as any Adams at sneaking up on people.

Duke held back a grin. "Maybe."

"Does that mean you and Dani are gonna get married?" Joshua asked. "I haven't got all this grown-up stuff figured out yet."

"Kissing sometimes leads to marriage," Duke conceded carefully.

"But what about you and Dani?" Josh persisted. "Are you guys gonna get married?"

Duke knew better than to set them up for disappointment. His plans were a little too iffy to make a firm declaration on the subject just yet, especially when anything he said was likely to be repeated. He could just imagine Dani's reaction to hearing the news of their impending wedding from someone else.

"We'll see," he equivocated.

More than once after a frustrating day behind his desk, he'd lain awake at night wondering if he really could get her riled up enough to marry him. He figured she was the kind of woman who was going to go down the aisle still denying that she was in love, especially with him. Persuading her otherwise might be challenging enough to make him forget all about bringing in another gusher.

If it turned out he was wrong about keeping his interest in Dani alive for all eternity, at least the boys would have a mom again. He would be free to get back to the kind of work he loved. Even as the unfairness and selfishness of that plan struck him, he tried to calculate how to make it work.

He felt Zack tugging on his sleeve to get his attention. "Then she would be our mom, right?"

"Yes, if it happens, she would be your mom. Would that be okay with you guys?"

Joshua shrugged. "I suppose."

Duke was startled by the less than enthusiastic endorsement. Had he read the signals all wrong again? "I thought you liked Dani," he said.

"I do, but moms go away sometimes," Josh said,

fighting tears. "It might be better if Dani was just our friend."

Holy kamoley, Duke thought. This was an angle he'd never expected. He gathered both boys close.

"Not every mom goes away," he said carefully.

He'd tried very hard not to blame their mother for running out. In fact, he'd bent over backward to shoulder most of the responsibility for driving her away. If she ever came back, he didn't want the boys to hate her for something for which much of the blame was his.

He struggled for an explanation that would console and offer hope at the same time. "We've talked about this before. Sometimes things happen between grownups that can't be helped. When it does, one of them goes away. That doesn't mean you shouldn't love them when they're around or treasure the good memories you have. You have to take risks or you'll go through life being very lonely."

"No way," Zack protested fiercely. "We've got each other. We'll never be lonely. We don't need anybody else."

"If that were true, would you be having such a good time with your new friends here in Los Pinos?"

Both boys hesitated as they considered that.

"I guess not," Josh conceded.

"Someday you're going to be a grown-up, and you're going to want even more than good friends. You're going to want somebody to love. I want you to believe that taking a chance on love is worth the risk, worth whatever hurt might happen." He grinned at them. "Because, you know what? Sometimes that risk pays off big time and lasts forever."

"Like with you and us," Joshua said.

Duke's eyes swam with unshed tears. "Exactly," he whispered. "Exactly like us."

And if he had his way, Dani would become a part of that tight-knit circle just as soon as he could make it happen. Despite what he'd just told his sons about putting everything on the line for love, the only thing he wasn't willing to risk was his own heart. He'd had years of evidence to analyze. He was pretty sure he didn't even have one.

On Thanksgiving morning Dani discovered the kitchen at White Pines in predictable chaos. Maritza, who'd been Grandpa Harlan's housekeeper practically forever, was trying her best to shoo everyone out, but lured by the scent of roasting turkey and pumpkin pie, no one was paying a bit of attention. Even Janet, whose lack of culinary skills was the stuff of family legend, seemed drawn to the one room in the house she usually avoided.

"Señora Janet, everything here is under control," Maritza declared again. "Please, you go and take the others with you. It is Thanksgiving. You should be relaxing and enjoying your company."

Janet made a token protest, offered to make the dressing and was soundly discouraged not only by Maritza, but also by everyone else as well.

"Ungrateful wretches," Janet said, laughing. She scowled at Jenny. "You especially. I expected more loyalty from my firstborn daughter."

"Hey, I grew up on your cooking for the first fourteen years of my life. The best I can say is that I survived it."

She turned to her younger sister. "Lizzy, you have no idea how grateful you should be that Maritza is here."

Janet threw up her hands. "Okay, enough. I'm going where I'm appreciated."

"I saw Dad out by the barn with Duke and the twins," Lizzy offered. "Dad is always eager to see you."

Janet gave them all a satisfied smile. "Yes, he is, isn't he?" she said as she slipped out the screen door.

Dani watched her go and wished she could follow. She was still putting up a valiant battle with her emotions, but she feared she was losing the war. Just the mention of Duke's name was enough to stir her senses alive. It really was absurd how little control she had over her reactions to the man. Worse, he knew it and he was deliberately plaguing her.

He never had gotten around to asking that all-important question that had brought him into her office a few weeks back. She'd been left to speculate and wonder and worry, even though he was suddenly underfoot everywhere she went. There hadn't been a doubt in her mind that someone would think to include him and the boys in today's celebration. Hearing that he was outside with her grandfather had made her pulse jump just the same.

"You could go, too," Jenny suggested mildly.

Dani stared at her. "Go where?"

"Out to the barn."

"Why would I want to do that?"

Jenny laughed. "Oh, sweetie, give it up. The only one not admitting that you're nuts about the guy is you."

Dani frowned. "One of these days, Jenny Running-bear Adams, you are going to fall head over heels in love with some man and I am going to lead the troops in making your life miserable about it."

"Not me," Jenny declared emphatically. "I don't have time to fall in love. Between lobbying in Washington and teaching, my plate is full. I'm perfectly content."

"Famous last words," Dani taunted. She glanced at Lizzy, who was listening in with an amused expression. "I say a year, tops. How about you?"

"First she has to meet somebody," Lizzy pointed out. "She never pokes her head into anyplace where she's likely to meet anyone interesting. She spends all her time surrounded by teenagers and lawyers."

"Watch it, baby sister," Jenny warned. "Our mother is a lawyer. She wouldn't appreciate you disparaging her kind."

"Everyone knows that Mom's an exception," Lizzy said loyally. "The ones you know are out for a buck."

"How would you know that? You've never met most of them."

"I hear you and Mom and Dad talking. How do you think I got to be so smart?"

Jenny chuckled. "Who says you're smart?"

"Daddy."

Dani and Jenny exchanged a look. "Of course," Dani said. "For a minute there, we forgot we were talking to Grandpa Harlan's best and brightest."

Lizzy scowled at her teasing. "I could tell you a few things…" she muttered.

"Such as?" Dani asked.

"You seem to forget that I worked for Duke all summer long," Lizzy taunted meaningfully.

Dani's heart seemed to lurch to a stop. "So?"

"I heard stuff."

"About?"

"Never mind," Lizzy said airily. "I'm going out where I'm appreciated, too."

She left her sister and Dani staring after her.

"What do you suppose she knows?" Dani asked, unable to mask her curiosity.

"Very little, I think," Maritza chimed in from the stove. "She is just talking big to get your attention."

"It worked, too," Jenny observed thoughtfully. "She mentioned Duke and your antenna shot up. Interesting reaction for a woman who claims the man doesn't matter to her."

"Oh, go to hell," Dani muttered.

"Young lady, you do not use such talk in my kitchen," Maritza said indignantly. "You are not too big for me to wash out your mouth with soap."

"Uh-oh," Jenny taunted. "You're in big trouble now."

"I'm going where I'm appreciated," Dani said.

"To the barn?" Jenny asked, her eyes twinkling.

"No. To find my father."

"Now there's the ticket. Run off to Jordan," Jenny taunted. "Don't expect him to side with you, though. He's like the rest of us. He's just waiting for an engagement announcement. He discovered that being a daddy was fun. Now he wants to try out being a granddaddy."

"He does not," Dani protested, though the claim made her very nervous. She suspected there might be some truth to it.

"Does, too."

"*Niñas,* stop it," Maritza ordered. "You will spoil the food with all this bickering. Be nice."

Dani laughed. "How often have we heard those words?" she asked as she wrapped her arms around Maritza and hugged her. "*Te amo,* Maritza."

The housekeeper's dour expression softened. "*Te amo,* Danielle. You are my own precious one."

"I thought I was," Jenny protested with a glint of pure mischief in her eyes.

"You, *niña,* are the thorn in my side, especially today. Now go. You both are in my way."

It seemed everywhere Dani went she was in the way. She tried the den, but Jordan, Cody and Luke were busy cussing a blue streak at the television. It appeared the Dallas Cowboys weren't delivering today.

Restless, it was probably inevitable that she would wander out to the barn. She swore it had nothing at all to do with Duke's presence out there. Everyone was there, after all. Not just the man who made her toes tingle and tempted her to forget every resolution she'd made about choosing more wisely the next time she fell in love.

She also swore that she wouldn't have gravitated directly toward him, if it hadn't been for Joshua and Zachary. They rushed over and each clasped a hand, drawing her straight toward their father.

"Tell her, Dad. Tell her about the horses you're gonna get us," Joshua said, practically jumping up and down with excitement.

Dani met Duke's gaze and felt that increasingly familiar jolt of excitement, the unmistakable tug that would have had a less stubborn woman throwing herself into his arms. She was almost used to it now. At least, it no longer left her thoroughly tongue-tied.

"If you're thinking of getting them horses, I gather they've passed the pet test?" she said to him.

"It's been months now, and the cats are still alive," he said dryly. "It's a small victory for responsibility." He regarded her speculatively. "You know, I'm going to need some help with this one."

"What kind of help?"

"Picking out the right horses, checking into their breeding, going over them to make sure they're sound. You're a vet. You'll be much better at that than I would be," he said, then added a little too casually, "Think you could carve out a little time and go with me to a horse sale?"

Dani was flattered that he trusted her judgment, but going off to a horse sale with him meant spending time alone, just the two of them. She suspected from the gleam in his eyes that finding the best animals for his money wasn't the only thing on his mind.

For weeks now Duke had done nothing to alarm her. He hadn't even given her more than a chaste peck on the cheek. Still, she was smart enough to realize that the growing lust she was feeling wasn't entirely one-sided. A few hours cooped up in a car and who knew what ideas he might get.

Not that she didn't trust him, she told herself. It was herself she didn't trust. The very sensible reasons she'd had for resisting Duke were fading, lost in a haze of pure longing that was deepening over time.

She forced herself to try once more to beg off. "Duke, I'm more than happy to give you some pointers, but I'd hate to be responsible for the final decision. It's your money."

"I'll be taken to the cleaners," he insisted. "They'll see me coming a mile away."

"Then take my father or Uncle Cody," she said, unsuccessfully trying to fight the note of desperation that was creeping into her voice. "Heck, Grandpa Harlan would love to go. There's nothing he likes more than a good horse sale and a chance to do some bargaining."

"I want your help," he insisted.

The man could match any Adams she knew for pure cussedness, she concluded with a sigh. "Why me?" she asked.

"You aren't scared to spend the day with me, are you?" he retorted.

Her temper flared with predictable speed at the taunt. "Of course not."

"You sure about that, darlin? You sound scared."

"Oh, for heaven's sakes, when is this sale?"

"Next weekend."

"Where?"

"Fort Worth."

It would be a long trip, but it could be done in a day, Dani reassured herself. They would be surrounded by hordes of people for most of that time. What could happen? Nothing, absolutely nothing. Not if she didn't allow it. Maybe it was time to put her resolutions to the test. She sighed.

"What time do you want to go?"

"I'll pick you up at five, so we'll have time to look the horses over before the sale starts."

She studied his face intently. His expression was pure innocence, but there was a glint in his eyes that suggested he was gloating. After all, he had gotten his way.

Again. Why shouldn't he gloat? She had the resistance of a limp noodle where he was concerned.

"Can we come, too?" Joshua pleaded.

As if he'd forgotten his sons' presence and the purpose of the trip to Fort Worth, Duke blinked and stared at Joshua for a full minute before shaking his head.

"No," he said flatly.

"But, Dad..." Zack protested.

"I said no," Duke repeated.

"The horses are for us," Zack argued.

"Yes, they are," Dani agreed, siding with the boys for her own less than honorable purposes. "They should have some say."

"Coward," Duke murmured just for her ears.

Since she couldn't deny it, she pretended she hadn't even heard. "Well?" she said. "Can they come?"

"No, indeed, they can't go," her grandfather said, stepping into the fray at the most inopportune moment possible. "I have plans for you two boys right here."

"But..." Joshua began.

"No buts," her grandfather said firmly. "No point in picking out horses, if you can't ride. While your daddy and Dani are off in Fort Worth, Cody and I will give you your first lessons."

To Dani's dismay, both boys reacted with enthusiasm. So much for her salvation. This time when she met Duke's gaze, there was no mistaking the triumph. Since Maritza wasn't nearby to reproach her, she told him to go to hell, too.

He laughed. "Been there, darlin'. This time I'm aiming for heaven."

11

It was pitch-dark outside, the kind of velvet blanket of darkness that made a person want to snuggle up next to a lover and light up the night with emotional fireworks.

Dani stood in the doorway, a cup of very strong coffee in her hands, and tried to dismiss from her thoughts the provocative image she'd just created. It was virtually impossible, especially since Duke seemed to be the lover crowded into that image with her.

It was barely four-thirty and she was already dressed and far too eager for their trip to Fort Worth. A dozen excuses for staying home had popped to the tip of her tongue since Thanksgiving, but she hadn't uttered a one of them. Either she was totally and unredeemably reckless or she was deluding herself about the power of the attraction between her and Duke.

When bright headlights cut through the darkness at the end of the block, her nerves kicked in. At this hour there was no question of it being anyone other than Duke. Since he was early, she could only assume he was as anxious as she was about whatever lay ahead.

She already knew that he'd made arrangements to drop Josh and Zack off at White Pines the night before. For some reason the evidence of his eagerness seemed to calm her just a little. He was usually so confident, so blasted sure of himself. It was nice to see a little hint of vulnerability for a change.

As he pulled to a stop, she stood her ground, watching, waiting to see what note he would strike when he greeted her. Casual and easy? Provocative? Maybe daring?

Her pulse skittered crazily as she anticipated his lips settling on hers for what he meant to be a cool, friendly greeting. Both of them knew by now that no amount of control or caution could tame a real kiss between them. It was why he'd deliberately dusted the air by her cheek and forehead for weeks now. Even innocent kisses had a way of turning stunningly sexual in an instant.

"Hey, darlin', are you ready?" he called out without leaving the car.

Fighting a ridiculous sense of disappointment, she forced a smile. "I'll be right there. Would you like some coffee for the road?"

He held up a covered mug. "Already have it. There's another one here for you, along with a bag of doughnuts fresh from the oven. I threw myself on Sallie's mercy over at the bakery, and she slipped me a few out the back door."

Dani had a hunch Sallie hadn't required much persuading. She was a sucker for a handsome face. Always had been, even though she'd been happily married to the same man for almost fifty years now. Sallie was every bit as much of a flirt as Betty Lou. Every man in town knew they could sweet-talk her into tucking an extra doughnut in the bag every now and again.

Dani took one last look at the cats' lineup of bowls in the kitchen to make sure they were all full, then grabbed her jacket and purse and locked the front door behind her.

When she reached the car, Duke leaned across the front seat and opened the door for her.

"No overnight bag?" he inquired.

Her alarmed gaze flew to his, but she managed to keep her voice even. "We're coming back tonight," she said firmly. "That was the plan."

"Well, of course, it is," he agreed at once. "But you know how unpredictable the weather can be this time of year. I've brought one. It never hurts to be prepared for plans to go awry."

"Ours won't," Dani stated grimly.

Duke grinned. "I'll be sure to pass along your conviction to the weatherman."

She studied him through narrowed eyes. "Do you know something about the weather that I don't?" she asked, cursing herself for not checking out the eleven o'clock news the night before or the weather channel this morning. For all she knew a blizzard could be headed for Texas, and they were driving straight into it. If getting stranded suited Duke's purposes, she wondered if he would bother to mention an approaching storm.

"Maybe I ought to check the weather channel before we take off," she said, reaching for the door handle.

"No need. They're just predicting a little rain around Fort Worth. It shouldn't be a problem," he said blandly, pulling out of the driveway before Dani had a chance to evaluate whether the rain presented a real danger.

"Just rain?" she asked.

He shrugged. "Unless the temperature drops."

She didn't like the way he was hedging or the way he was avoiding her gaze. "Maybe we should do this another time."

"Darlin', they're just calling for a little rain," he protested. "What's the worst that could happen? We'd have to stay overnight. We're both adults. That shouldn't be a problem, right?"

No, it shouldn't be, Dani agreed to herself. But it would be. She could feel it in her bones...and elsewhere.

"I don't know—" she began.

"Trust me, darlin', we'll be just fine. Now sit back and relax. Drink your coffee before it gets cold and try one of these doughnuts." He gestured to the bag on the seat between them. "There are jelly-filled, glazed and old-fashioned."

The bag was huge, big enough to hold at least a baker's dozen, though there were far fewer than that left. The assortment had clearly been plundered. Dani couldn't help grinning. "Just how many have you eaten already?"

"A couple," he said, then grinned guiltily. "Okay, maybe four. I never get to have doughnuts anymore. I'm trying to teach the boys to eat a healthy breakfast by setting a good example. I've eaten enough bran flakes in the last year to fulfill my fiber quota for two lifetimes."

"You know, an occasional doughnut won't kill any of you," Dani said. "Maybe if you ate them in moderation, you wouldn't be pigging out now."

"Darlin', I don't need a lecture on my eating habits from you."

"If you say so," she said, peering into the bag. The aroma of dough and sugar and raspberry jelly hit her smack in the face. She drew in a deep breath. "Oh, my."

"Downright intoxicating, isn't it?" Duke teased.

"Incredible," she murmured distractedly. All of her attention was focused on the choice she was about to make.

"You could have one of each," Duke said, clearly guessing her dilemma.

"I couldn't," she insisted and settled for the raspberry-filled doughnut that was still warm to the touch. Powdered sugar coated her lips. Jam settled in the corners of her mouth and left her fingers sticky. "Heavenly."

Duke glanced over at her, then sucked in a sharp breath. Pure lust darkened his eyes.

"What?" Dani demanded, her own breath catching.

"There are napkins in the glove compartment," Duke said in a choked voice.

"Why? Am I a mess?"

"Not exactly," he said. "But if you don't wipe away the sugar and jam around your mouth, I'm going to have to do it for you." His heated gaze clashed with hers. "I won't be using a napkin."

The image of his tongue searching out every little trace of sugar and jam slammed into her with the force of a gale. She fumbled badly as she tried to open the glove compartment and retrieve a napkin. Her hand shook as she tried to wipe away any trace of the doughnut she had savored.

"Too bad," Duke teased when she was done. "I was looking forward to helping."

"I'll just bet you were," she said. A change of topic was definitely in order. "Why don't you tell me what you have in mind when it comes to the horses. How much do you want to spend? Is there any particular type of horse you want?"

He chuckled. "Smooth transition. Don't tell me I was making you nervous."

"You weren't," she insisted.

"Liar."

She regarded him impatiently. "Duke, you asked me to come along today to help you buy horses. That's all I'm doing here."

"I know," he said.

She didn't trust that dutiful tone one bit. "I hope you do."

He sketched a cross over his heart. "Darlin', if you made yourself any clearer, I'd have a knot upside my head."

"Don't tempt me."

"Damn, but you're cute when—"

She scowled at him. "Don't say it. Don't you dare say it."

"You want me to be honest, don't you?"

"Of course, but—"

"That's all I'm doing. Telling it like it is."

Dani sighed heavily. "Why don't I believe that?"

"You have a suspicious nature," he suggested.

"My nature, as you put it, has been honed by experience."

"You're not comparing me to that Rob person again,

are you?" He didn't wait for her reply. "I'm disappointed. I thought we were way beyond that."

"Well, we're not," she grumbled. "You're sneaky and underhanded, just like he was."

"Me? Name one single sneaky, underhanded thing I've done."

Naturally, every one she came up with sounded petty, so she kept her mouth clamped firmly shut.

"Cat got your tongue?" he inquired.

"No the cat does not have my tongue," she snapped. "I'm just trying to be civil. Otherwise this is going to be a very long trip."

Duke's eyes were flashing with humor. "Hey, don't stand on ceremony on my account. Say whatever's on your mind and get it out of your system. I can take it."

She turned to face him. "Okay, don't say you didn't ask for it."

"I'm ready," he said, his expression stoic.

Suddenly, the list of his so-called sins seemed endless. She couldn't wait to enumerate them all.

"From the day we met you have been trying to disrupt my life," she accused. "You turn up everywhere I go like the proverbial bad penny. You've deliberately ingratiated yourself with my family. They all think you hung the moon. They're plotting and scheming on your behalf without the slightest regard for my feelings."

"That's not the way they see it," Duke pointed out.

"Well, of course, it isn't. They're a bunch of softhearted romantics. Grandpa Harlan is the worst of all. I thought I could count on my father being on my side, but even he seems to have joined the enemy camp. As for your boys, they have managed to slip past my best defenses."

His eyebrows rose at that. "Now there's a crime."

"Lay off. You asked me to say what was on my mind."

"So I did. Do go on."

"You don't listen to a word I say."

"I listen to every single word you say," Duke protested. "It's just that sometimes you and I may disagree on whether or not you mean what you say."

"Of course, I mean it," she practically shouted. "Do you think I'm just wasting my breath for the heck of it?"

Duke shook his head and regarded her with something she suspected was awfully close to pity. She felt like slugging him.

"Of course not," he soothed. "The logical, rational side of your brain means every word. I'm not so dense that I'd miss a thing like that."

"Then what's the problem?" she demanded.

He reached over and touched a finger lightly to the center of her chest. "That's the problem," he said gently. "Your heart and your brain aren't in sync. Sharon Lynn and Jenny see it. Your father and grandfather see it. Now, I may not understand a lot about women. I may know even less about emotions, but I do get one thing. When push comes to shove, it's what your heart feels that really matters."

Dani felt the very organ in question pump a little faster as if to confirm what he said. She'd been so sure that he couldn't see through her, so sure that she could keep her secret, forever if she had to. Then, *wham,* just like that it was all over. The truth was out or would be, if she confirmed his suspicions.

She just couldn't do it. She settled for lying, instead, in a valiant attempt to save herself—to save them— from making a terrible mistake.

"You're wrong," she said quietly, but emphatically. "You have it all wrong."

It would have been enough to convince any other man. Or at least any other man would have graciously accepted the lie and let things be. Not Duke. He just smiled knowingly.

"If you say so, darlin'."

"Don't use that patronizing tone with me," she said, fuming.

He seemed even more amused by the outburst. "Sorry," he apologized with a total lack of sincerity.

Dani shook her head and bit back another sharp retort that he would only find even more unconvincing.

"Hey, don't worry about it. We'll work it out."

"We will not work it out," she said, her teeth clenched.

"Sure we will. You may be an Adams, but I'm every bit as stubborn."

Now there, she thought dispiritedly, was the truth. The realization scared her to death.

Duke thought the drive had gone very well. Dani was so furious steam was practically spewing out of her ears. That was good. It meant he was getting to her, shaking her up, rattling her. Anytime now he would get her to make an honest admission of her feelings toward him. He'd thought for a minute she was about to blurt it out, but then she'd sucked in a deep breath and gone all stiff and silent on him. He could have told her that was every bit as telling, but wisely he didn't. She was in no mood to appreciate the observation.

He supposed he ought to feel guilty about backing her into a corner, but he needed her to acknowledge what she felt. So he had to move on to the next stage of his plan: getting her to say yes to a marriage proposal.

He glanced over at her as they pulled into a parking place behind the barns where the horse sale was being held. Her hands were clenched together so tightly in her lap that her knuckles were white. He had a feeling if he laid his hands on her shoulders, he would find knots of tension as big as Texas…right before she throttled him for touching her.

"Are you planning on speaking to me ever again?" he inquired lightly. "If not, exactly how are you going to communicate with me when you spot the perfect horse?"

Her lips twitched ever so slightly. "I was thinking of kicking you real hard in the shins."

He grinned. "That would get my attention, that's for sure."

"I wonder," she said.

His gaze narrowed. "What's that supposed to mean?"

"It means I'm not sure that a baseball bat to the head would get your attention unless you wanted it to."

"I am single-minded," he agreed. "You probably need to remember that."

"Believe me, it's not something I'm likely to forget," she retorted. "Now are we going to sit here all day or are we going to check out the horses?"

He went around the car and opened her door with a

flourish. "Lead the way, darlin'. There's nothing I like better than following along behind a pretty woman."

She scowled at the remark and, he noticed, made darn sure that she was always beside him and not in front of him. With brisk efficiency, she found the listings of the horses for sale and scanned the pages, checking several and crossing off twice as many.

"Let's go," she said, studying the arrangement of the stalls. "There's a pinto pony in number seventy-six that might be just right."

When they found it, Duke took one look at the skittish animal and concluded it had been rounded up wild and half-starved to death before being brought to today's sale. As Dani approached, fear darkened the horse's eyes and made them flare dangerously.

"Dani," Duke said very softly. "Careful."

She nodded, acknowledging the warning. Then she reached in her pocket for a lump of sugar and held it out. The pony shied away from her. Dani eased closer, murmuring nonsense until eventually the pony remained still when she approached. Duke's heart stayed in his throat the whole time. He was fairly sure he didn't breathe again until Dani backed out of reach of the horse's nervous hooves.

"That horse has been mistreated," Duke said angrily when she was beside him again. "You're lucky he didn't kick you."

"He's malnourished, that's for sure," she agreed, her eyes wide and shimmering with tears. "But he's beautiful, Duke. He's full of life."

"He's too skittish for the boys."

"He wouldn't be if someone cared for him," she argued.

"Dani, he's the first horse we've seen. Hold off on a recommendation until we've seen the rest that you've marked."

She faced him stubbornly. "He's going to stay on the list," she insisted. "You'll see."

Duke sighed, relieved that he'd borrowed a horse trailer large enough to carry half a dozen horses. He had a feeling Dani was going to be an easy mark. If he didn't agree with her selections, she would probably buy the others herself.

They looked over another eleven horses. Out of the even dozen she'd selected, she found four she thought were both sound and likely to go for the right price. Not counting that blasted pinto, of course. That made five she considered worth bidding on.

"Which one of us is going to bid?" she asked Duke when it was time for the sale to begin. "You should since it's your money we're spending."

"I'm sticking with you," he insisted. "You know the value of these horses better than I do. I'm liable to get carried away."

She regarded him doubtfully. "You don't strike me as the kind of man who'd get carried away at an auction."

"Why not?"

"Too hardheaded," she said succinctly. "You'd be more likely to set a figure and stick with it, no matter how badly you wanted the horse."

To be perfectly truthful, she was right, Duke admitted, but only to himself. At least that's how he always had been. Today, though, he had the feeling that he could very easily get caught up in Dani's excitement and lose his head completely. In fact, he was already more than half certain that they would be leaving with that pinto if he had to buy it for her himself. She hadn't stopped talking about it since they'd first visited the horse's stall. He had a feeling buying it would be the kind of outrageous gesture no one had ever made for her before. Maybe it would prove to be the clincher in his plan.

There were two palominos early in the sale, practically mirror images of each other. Duke knew that Dani was leaning toward them for the boys. He'd liked them himself. They appeared gentle enough.

In the guise of having her show him what she was looking for when she examined them, he'd gone over them himself and confirmed Dani's view that they were strong and sound. When he'd commented on just that, she'd regarded him with an odd expression on her face. He'd warned himself to be very careful. One more mistake like that would be his downfall. Dani was too smart not to catch on sooner or later that he knew exactly what he was doing. Then there was going to be big trouble. He was resigned to it.

In the meantime, though, he had her to himself for an entire day. She'd stopped being skittish hours ago. She'd even laughed at a few of his jokes and reached for his hand on one occasion, only to drop it like a branding iron when she realized what she'd done.

When the first of the palominos came on the block, the bidding was fairly light. Dani picked the horse up for well under the limit Duke had set. She flashed a look of triumph at him at the conclusion of the bidding.

"This is fun," she announced. "No wonder Grandpa Harlan loves horse-trading so much. I hope we can get the second one, too." Her eyes darkened with worry. "Or do you think the boys would rather have horses that don't look alike? Are they sensitive about the twin thing?"

Duke had never given the matter much thought. Even though they were identical, they'd never been dressed exactly alike or given the same toys. They had surprisingly individual tastes and interests. Their personalities were a blend of harmony and diversity. At times, they acted as one. At other times, they behaved like any other squabbling, jealous non-twin siblings.

"My hunch is the only way to avoid conflict might be to give them matching horses," he told her. "This is a pretty big deal. We don't want either of them getting the idea that the other's horse is better in some way you and I don't get."

Dani grinned sympathetically. "Figuring out how eight-year-olds think does have its moments, doesn't it?"

"I'm sure it has brought many a parent to his knees," Duke agreed. "Go for the other palomino."

"I agree. Maybe if they both weren't so beautiful, I'd go a different way, but they're gorgeous."

"You don't think this second one is going to have a problem with that left front foreleg, do you?"

She shot him a suspicious look. "What are you talking about?"

Careful, Duke warned himself. "It seemed to me his gait was a little off. You mentioned it yourself, didn't you?"

Dani scanned her notes. "I did write it down," she agreed, but she was clearly unsettled by his observation. "I don't think it's a problem, though. I've seen other horses like that do just fine. If it comes to that, it's a correctible problem with fairly minor surgery. If you wanted more than a riding horse, we should probably reconsider, but for Josh or Zack, the palomino will get along okay."

Duke nodded. "I'll trust your judgment."

The bidding for the second palomino was livelier than the first, proving that plenty of others were just as unconcerned as Dani about the horse's unusual gait. When they neared Duke's preset limit, Dani glanced over at him.

"Well?"

He grinned. "Go up, if you have to. The other one was a steal. It'll all even out."

"All right," she said and reentered the bidding frenzy with enthusiasm.

Naturally, she triumphed, Duke was holding his breath on the last round. Not that he couldn't afford to spend more. He could. He just wasn't sure the horse was worth it. The beaming smile on Dani's face, however, was worth every penny.

"That's it, then," he said when the bidding was done. "Mission accomplished."

"Not quite," she said.

"Let me guess. The pinto."

"I have to have him," she said. "He needs a good home."

"Do you have room in your backyard?" Duke inquired dryly.

She shot him a we-are-not-amused look. "There's plenty of room at Mom and Dad's," she said.

"And you get out there how often?"

"Do you really have to be so blasted logical?" she inquired testily.

Duke threw back his head and laughed at that. She grinned and admitted, "Okay, it's like the pot calling the kettle black. I want that horse."

Duke nodded. "I know. His number won't be up for a while now. Want to go grab a bite to eat?"

"Sure."

He led the way to a vendor selling hot dogs and soft drinks. Dani slathered her hot dog with mustard, relish and was debating over the onions when he caught her eye. She swallowed hard, then left the onions untouched. He figured it was tantamount to an admission that she knew before the day ended they would share at least one kiss, probably more.

They finished their meal and were about to go back inside, when Duke caught a glimpse of the dab of mustard at the corner of her mouth. All of the desire that had rocketed through him that morning when she'd been eating that doughnut came back now with twice the intensity.

"Wait," he said softly and reached for a napkin. Alarm flared in her eyes as he tilted her chin up. His thumb skimmed her lower lip, even as he gently wiped away the mustard with the napkin.

"Thanks." It came out as a breathless whisper.

"No problem," he said, though it was a lie. There was a very definite problem. He suddenly wanted nothing more than to drag her off somewhere and tumble her into a haystack or a bed or any other place that would be soft and accommodating.

As if the gods had heard his prayers, a flash of lightning split the sky, followed by a clap of thunder. The skies opened up and rain came down, first in huge, individual drops, then in solid gray sheets. Duke grabbed Dani's hand, and they made a dash back inside.

Fortunately, they'd been quick enough to avoid being soaked to the skin. Duke glanced over her. "You okay? We could leave if you're too wet. There's no point in catching pneumonia."

"Nice try, but I am not leaving without my horse," she said stubbornly.

Quite a few of the other serious bidders caught a glimpse of the storm and decided to flee before it got any worse. When the pinto's number was called, the hall was half-empty. Dani had only one competitor for the horse, and he was bidding with lackluster enthusiasm. He dropped out after only four rounds.

Eyes shining, Dani turned to Duke. "I stole him. I virtually stole him."

"I just hope the payback for your thievery isn't a broken neck," Duke retorted.

"A lot you know," she countered. "That horse is going to be the best investment I ever made."

"Obviously, you've never heard of stocks and bonds," he countered.

"Oh, give it up," she said finally and flashed a knowing smile at him. "Otherwise I might make you explain why it is that you claimed not to know anything about horses, when it's obvious that you know at least as much as I do. I might have taken classes in vet school, but you've spent time around horses, haven't you?"

Uh-oh, Duke thought. "You figured it out, huh?"

"Hours ago. Next time you decide to feign ignorance,

it might be a real good idea to keep your mouth shut," she advised.

"I was hoping you'd think I just happened to ask particularly intelligent questions."

"Not just intelligent questions, *well-informed* questions. There's a difference."

"Are you going to hold it against me?"

"Not if you'll tell me why you lied about knowing anything about horses."

"Isn't that obvious?"

"Not to me."

He reached out and touched a finger to her cheek. His gaze locked with hers as he confessed, "It was the only way I could come up with to get you alone for an entire day."

"Oh."

He smiled at that. Oh, indeed. He wondered what she'd think if she figured out he'd been praying to beat the band that this rain would turn to ice any second now so they would be stranded overnight, too.

As if to prove that he still had some pull with heaven, hail began pinging against the cars and trailers outside, making an unmistakable clatter.

Dani's eyes widened as she recognized the implication. "Hail?"

"Sounds like it."

"Maybe it'll pass," she suggested hopefully.

"Do you want to take that chance?" he asked reasonably.

She looked torn. Clearly, she was indecisive about which danger was the greatest—going or staying. She lifted her gaze to his and he could read those by-now familiar warring emotions, desire and panic.

"I'll trust your judgment," she said quietly.

As she said it, her gaze never wavered.

And Duke felt the full weight of responsibility settling on his shoulders. She was leaving more than their going or staying up to him, and they both knew it. He would also be the one to decide if tonight was the night they finally made love.

He could make her respond, make her forget her reservations about their relationship with just a kiss. It would be a simple matter to seduce her…if he dared. Whatever he decided, he would have to live with the decision forever after.

_12_

She could live with this, Dani told herself staunchly as Duke drove through the blinding combination of rain and sleet in search of a decent-looking motel. They were adults. Nothing was going to happen beyond getting a good night's sleep unless they both wanted it to.

Unless, of course, her hormones overruled her head, she thought grimly. Maybe she should play it safe and put up more of a fight to go straight back to Los Pinos. She glanced at Duke's tense expression. When he gazed over at her and gave her a quick smile, she felt her pulse zing dangerously. Suddenly, a tactical retreat seemed like a very good idea.

"Are you certain we can't get back tonight?" she asked, peering out the window at the leaden sky. "It looks as if it might clear up," she added with unjustified optimism based on a pinprick-sized patch of blue in the distance.

"Do you believe in the tooth fairy, too?" Duke inquired, not taking his eyes from the hazardous road.

"You don't have to be sarcastic," she said, but she could see his point. The road already had an inch or more of swirling water on it, more than enough to send a car off in a skid and dangerously close to enough to have it stall out. Despite that tiny bit of blue, most of the sky was filled with stormy, rain-filled clouds.

"Why don't you help me out by looking for a half-decent place to stay," Duke suggested. "I passed one motel a block back, but it looked like a dump."

Dani had seen it, too. To describe it as seedy-looking would have been a compliment. Duke would have had to drag her kicking and screaming into a place that crummy. "You drive. I'll look," she said resignedly.

It took another fifteen minutes before she spotted a motel with a Rooms Available sign lit and a small, cozy-looking restaurant attached. It wasn't exactly a luxury resort, but it would do. Perhaps even more important from her perspective, there wasn't the slightest suggestion of a romantic retreat about it, at least if taste was any factor at all. It was very much bright lights and gaudy ambience.

"How about that one?" she asked. "It looks clean."

Duke followed the direction of her gaze. His expression turned skeptical. "You don't mind the flashing neon and the water-bed option?"

"The water bed is just that, an option," she said firmly, even though her stomach turned flip-flops at the thought of climbing into one with Duke. "As for the neon, who cares what's flashing outside. We'll be asleep."

"Your choice," he said and swung the car into the parking lot. "I'll see what's available."

"Duke?"

"Yes?"

"Skip the water bed. I want an ordinary mattress."

"All to yourself?" he inquired, his tone light.

She thought about it for no longer than a heartbeat, but apparently that was long enough for him to interpret the message of uncertainty.

"I'll get two rooms," Duke said, taking the decision out of her hands.

If he was upset, he didn't show it. Still, Dani stared after him, already regretting her cowardice. Would it be so awful to steal just one night with this man?

The answer to that was a straightforward, unequivocal yes. One night would never be enough. Despite her very best efforts, he had gotten to her. She had ignored danger signs, alarms and warning bells. She had allowed herself to fall for him—and for his kids—but it wasn't going to work.

Not for lack of interest, of course. Duke wanted her. She wasn't mistaken about that. He also considered her good mother material. She had recognized that as well. But he didn't love her. There was a part of himself he always held back, even when he was flirting the most outrageously. In the end, that inability to love her wholeheartedly was all that really mattered. She wouldn't settle for less than the surrender of his heart.

Of course, she, too, was holding back, she reminded herself. It made them quite a pair.

She peered disconsolately out the window just in time to see Duke dashing back to the car. His clothes were soaked. Water dripped from his hair and ran down his face. He looked as if he'd just climbed from a shower with his clothes on. The image sent heat shimmering through her.

Duke, however, was shivering. "Bad news, darlin'. There's only one room left. We're going to have to share."

Dani's heart began to hammer. She couldn't demand that they search for someplace else. They'd passed almost every motel within miles of the horse show. They were either shabby or fully occupied. Duke was too soaked to be driving around anymore, anyway. Fate, it seemed, had stepped in.

"It has two beds, though," he said as he pulled up in front of the room at the very end of the row facing the street.

Dani blinked and stared, taken aback by the belated announcement. "What did you say?"

"Not to worry. It has two beds."

Relief washed over her, followed almost instantly by disappointment. The latter, combined with a healthy dose of frustration, made her cranky.

Reluctantly, she followed Duke, coming to an abrupt halt just inside the doorway. There were two beds, all right, both of them seductively huge. The motel might have an uninspired, gaudy exterior, but the rooms themselves were generously sized and decorated with expensive, but still garish taste. There was a lot of red, she noted, with a startling dash of purple thrown in. Through the open doorway she could see that the bathroom was tiled in a vivid pink.

Duke caught her expression and grinned. "If you think this is bright, you should meet Mrs. Perez at the registration desk. She's wearing an outfit that would blind anyone without sunglasses. She says everyone needs color in their lives. It cheers them up."

He crossed the room to stand in front of her. "Are you feeling cheered up?"

"Not exactly," she said, though she was rapidly getting

there. She made one last desperate pitch for sanity. "Are you absolutely sure we couldn't make it back home?"

Duke didn't appear to mind the question. He seemed to sense her need for reassurance.

"Absolutely," he said emphatically. "It's pouring rain, mixed with hail. Another hour of these plummeting temperatures and the roads will be sheets of ice. I don't want to take a chance skidding on the highway while I'm trailering three horses back home. We'll pick them up in the morning and get an early start. Maybe the weather will break by then."

"And maybe it won't," she observed. "Then what? You going to settle down in Fort Worth?"

"You ever known it to rain for months on end in Texas?"

"No, but I've never known a man to be scared by a little shower before, either."

"Darlin', we made the right decision. Mrs. Perez says a tornado touched down not twenty miles north of here. You can't see across the road. This isn't a little, inconvenient shower we can wait out. It's a full-blown winter storm and way too unpredictable to be on the road."

"Whatever you say."

The truth was she was having a full-scale attack of jitters. Ever since she'd gotten a look at those beds and all that provocative red, she'd felt caught up in an irresistible web of sensuality. In the pit of her stomach, she had that hovering-on-the-edge sensation that the room itself was just daring her to behave wickedly.

Given her own sadly deficient resistance, she told herself she didn't want to spend the night within fifty miles of this man, not with the spark of pure lust she'd been spying in his eyes these past months. Heck, in these past few minutes.

Worse, she suspected it was reflected in her own eyes. The man made her hotter than West Texas pavement in the midday August sun, she conceded as Duke went into the bathroom and turned the shower on.

He stuck his head out the door. "Sure you don't want to join me?" he inquired, regarding her hopefully.

"Very sure," she lied.

"I won't take long," he promised. "Then I'll put on some dry clothes and we can have dinner. The restaurant stays open until eight. Mrs. Perez says it has the best Tex-Mex in this part of town. Her husband's the cook."

"Could be she's prejudiced."

He winked. "I wandered in and got a whiff of what's on the menu. Could be she's right. The aroma was downright decadent. It made my mouth water."

There was nothing Dani liked better than fiery Tex-Mex. Maybe that heat would take her mind off the steam being generated in this motel room. "That'll give me something to look forward to, then," she said.

He grinned. "I thought spending the night all alone with me would be temptation enough," he taunted, then closed the door in her face before she could respond.

Why did he have to be right? she wondered with a wistful sigh. She didn't want to be attracted to Duke Jenkins. She sure as heck hadn't wanted to kiss him, the first time or the last or any of the times in between.

Okay, let's be honest here, she corrected. She had wanted to experiment with one little kiss, but she hadn't wanted to like it. She'd wanted to hate it. She'd wanted to be so turned off that she would never, ever be tempted to throw herself into his arms the way she was right this minute. In that state of mind how could she ignore the pull of those mammoth beds? One kiss now and it would be all over, except for the morning-after regrets.

She'd lost count of the exact number of times he'd managed to steal a kiss since they'd met. She just knew it was enough to make sure she craved them. She'd moved them straight to the top of her list of things to avoid at all costs, way, way above hot fudge sundaes.

Which just proved how totally and thoroughly perverse she was. She knew the pitfalls of a relationship with a man like Duke. Ironically, she had conceded now that he was nothing like Rob. He probably wouldn't dump her on a whim without the slightest consideration of his boys. In fact, he was very much a single father whose first obligation was always going to be to his sons. And at the moment, what he wanted most to give them was a mom. In fact, she suspected that at least fifty percent of his actions lately had been calculated to claiming her not for himself, but for them. Making her the substitute mom for his kids would create a strong bond, but not strong enough to withstand the lure of another woman he might someday decide he wanted all for himself.

Nobody knew the danger of playing with that particular fire better than she did. That didn't seem to stop her from shivering like a wisp of grass in the wind every single time he touched her. Thinking about him only a few feet away, naked, was enough to send shock waves through her.

He was going to touch her tonight, too. Any minute, in fact. She just knew it, knew it with the certainty of a woman who was head over heels in love and searching for signs and portents in every single glance and innocent caress.

He was going to brush one of those oh-so-casual kisses across her forehead. She was going to subconsciously moisten her lips and then, *wham,* his mouth was going to slant across hers, and there would be no stopping what happened next. Pent-up sexual frustration had a way of exploding sooner or later. This was definitely later, which meant the explosion was likely to be of atomic proportions.

Duke started his shower with the water as hot as he could stand it, hoping to chase away the chill that had cut all the way through to his bones. It didn't heat him nearly as fast as thinking about Dani being right outside the door, maybe resting on one of those impossibly huge beds.

He chuckled at the memory of her expression when she'd seen them. She'd looked flabbergasted, panicky and then, in surprisingly short order, wistful. He took the last as a very good sign.

Not that she wasn't sending out more mixed signals than an inexperienced Ham radio operator. He knew in his gut that it wasn't a question of her being indecisive. He figured she'd already made up her mind that she wanted to make love. She just hadn't figured out how to deal with the aftermath, the inevitable, unspoken questions that always tumbled through a woman's mind when she wasn't sure where a relationship was headed.

Duke figured he had enough answers for both of them. This wasn't going to be a one-night stand, if that's what she feared. It was simply going to seal their fate, tie up the deal like a signature on a contract. He would go home from Fort Worth with two palominos, one skittish pinto and a fiancée.

"Now, that's romantic," he muttered under his breath. "Tell her that and you can kiss marriage goodbye."

Fortunately, he'd had the foresight to plan the rest of their evening with more care. He'd done more than peek into that restaurant. He'd spoken to Mr. Perez and planned an evening that would bring tears to her eyes and, with any luck at all, melt her heart.

By the time they got to the restaurant, there would be a bouquet of fresh flowers to replace the artificial ones on the table. Instead of a dripping red candle in an old wine jug, there would be half a dozen thick white candles casting a glow from fancy silver holders. Mr. Perez said the family had brought many pieces of fine silver from Mexico, and they would be happy to share them on such a night. And, yes, he had the perfect bottle of champagne. Like his wife, Mr. Perez had the soul of a romantic. He'd understood immediately what Duke was after.

"Very big night, *sí?*"

"Very big," Duke had agreed. The most important of his life.

Just thinking about the dinner and his plans for after raised his body temperature to a shade under unbearable. Suddenly, he had to shut off the hot water and replace it with cold. Which meant he left the shower right back where he'd started, chilled to the bone and shivering.

He wrapped a towel around his waist and stepped back into the room to grab his clothes. At the sight of Dani sitting cross-legged in the middle of the bed, her eyes glued to the TV, he halted in his tracks.

"What the hell are you watching?" he demanded as he glimpsed bodies writhing on the screen.

"Cable," she said, her voice breathless and vaguely stunned.

Choking back a chuckle, he inquired lightly, "X-rated cable, by any chance?"

She nodded, but never looked away from the screen. Duke didn't dare follow her gaze for more than a flash. Too many images like the one on-screen, and they would never get out of the room for dinner.

Dani tilted her head to follow the unlikely angle of the action. "Can you imagine?" she murmured.

"Dani?"

"Hmm?"

"Turn it off."

Her head snapped up, eyes wide. "What?"

"Turn it off," Duke said in a choked voice.

"But why?"

She studied him intently. Duke recognized the precise instant when she noticed his arousal. Suddenly, she grinned impishly.

"It's very educational," she told him.

"Any education you need along those lines, I'll be glad to give you firsthand."

Color bloomed in her cheeks. That wistful expression flared in her eyes. She fumbled with the remote and turned the TV off. There hadn't been all that much talking going on in the movie, but the absence of even that much background noise left the motel room way too silent. Duke could practically hear the wheels in her brain turning as she tried to reach a conclusion about his intentions—and her own.

Now what? He heard the question as clearly as if she'd spoken it aloud. He wished the answer were half as clear. He could tumble her onto that bed right this second. The invitation was plain in her eyes.

But he'd had a plan, he reminded himself. A good plan. One that would win her heart, as well as her body. It didn't start with a quick roll in the hay, even if that would put an end once and for all to this awkward indecision that hung over them. She deserved a little wining and dining.

"I'll be dressed in a minute," he said, his gaze still locked with hers.

Before he could change his mind, he went back into the bathroom and slammed the door. Desire made his pulse race and left his fingers unsteady. It took him twice as long as it should have to drag on his clothes, run a comb through his hair and a toothbrush over his teeth.

He even pulled a bottle of that after-shave from his bag, the kind Josh and Zack thought all girls liked, and splashed on a little. He supposed there was something to be said for the spicy scent the boys had chosen for him one Christmas, but as far as he could tell, there was nothing wrong with plain old soap and water.

He gazed at himself in the mirror and shook his head. What was wrong with him? He was acting like a besotted schoolboy. If he wasn't careful someone would get the idea that he was in love. Of course, he knew better. With any luck, Dani wouldn't see through the charade and guess that he thought love was a fool's game.

Before he could have another bout with second thoughts about shortchanging her, he opened the door. "Ready?"

"As ready as I'll ever be," she said, "since I only have the clothes on my back."

"Just be thankful you didn't get drenched the way I did," he said. "Do you want to drive back up to the restaurant or make a dash for it? It's undercover most of the way."

"Dashing will be fine."

She meant it, too. She sprinted ahead of him so fast, he realized that she was every bit as nervous as he was about being alone together in that room.

Though the motel was fully occupied, they were the only two people in the dining room.

"I hurry everyone," Mr. Perez announced with a beaming smile. "I know this is very special occasion. A honeymoon, yes?"

Duke let the guesswork pass. He had a feeling there would be enough discussion about Mr. Perez's conclusions with Dani once they reached their table.

Sure enough, Mr. Perez had no sooner filled their glasses with champagne and vanished into the kitchen than she turned on Duke.

"Honeymoon?" she inquired sweetly. "Where would he get an idea like that?"

"I told him tonight was special, that's all," Duke declared. "He obviously drew his own conclusions."

"Conclusions that merited fresh flowers, candlelight and champagne, I see."

"Actually, those were my ideas."

Her eyes widened. "Really? Fascinating. Is the mariachi band warming up in the back?"

Duke chuckled. "Probably, but if it is you can thank Mr. Perez for it. I was content with the jukebox. It has some really terrific oldies on it."

She stared hard. "You checked out the jukebox, too?"

"Of course. You can't slow dance to just anything on a first date."

"Is that so?"

"Of course not. It has to be romantic, memorable."

"Just one question. When did this go from being a business trip to being a date?" She tilted her head and regarded him thoughtfully. "When you saw the beds, perhaps?"

Duke shook his head and regarded her solemnly. He reached across the table and brushed a tendril of hair away from her cheek, then followed the curve until he cupped her chin. "No. I got this idea the first time I laid eyes on you."

She didn't blink and look away as he'd expected. Instead, she smiled. It was like sunshine breaking through clouds. Duke knew in that instant that he was more than halfway to reaching his goal.

If the rest of the night went even one-quarter as smoothly as this, by morning there was no way she wouldn't say yes when he asked her to marry him. He would find a jewelry store, if he had to bribe the manager to open it on a Sunday morning, and insist on picking out a ring before they ever left Fort Worth. He wanted her well and truly committed to being his before they ever got back to Los Pinos.

"You're looking very smug all of a sudden," she observed.

"Not smug," he insisted. "Pleased. I can't tell you how much I've wanted to share an evening like this with you."

"Stranded in a storm with me smelling like a barn?"

"If you're trying to spoil the mood, forget it. You look beautiful, and you smell like flowers."

"That is flowers you're smelling," she pointed out. "Either that or the after-shave you have on."

"You don't like it? The boys promised me all girls loved it. They picked it out special."

Dani grinned. "The boys have been coaching you?"

"Just on a few of the finer points of courtship."

"Tell them they missed the boat on the after-shave. Soap and water suits me just fine."

"I'll shower again the minute we get back to the room," he offered.

She swallowed hard at the promise. Duke had a hunch she was mentally climbing into that shower with him. Suddenly, she regarded him with suspicion.

"You're playing with my head, aren't you?"

"Am I?"

"You bet."

"How, precisely, am I doing that?"

"You're deliberately planting provocative ideas."

He worked hard to hold back a triumphant grin. "You're having provocative ideas about the two of us?" he inquired innocently. "You can't possibly hold me responsible for what goes on in your head."

"Of course, I can. You're sneaky and devious that way."

"Ever stop to think that maybe you're the one with the wicked mind? You were watching X-rated cable, you know."

"That was an accident," she protested. "Once it was right there in front of my eyes I couldn't seem to look away, sort of like stumbling on a wreck on the highway."

"An interesting comparison."

She scowled at him. "I wasn't comparing sex and traffic accidents."

"Good, because they don't have a lot in common as far as I can see. Sex is a whole lot more fun, to say nothing of way less deadly, at least if it's done right. We could talk about it more, if you like."

"You're doing it again," she accused.

"Doing what?"

"Putting those images into my head."

"Darlin', it seems to me you just have a one-track mind."

She sighed heavily at that. "Maybe I do," she conceded. "But it wasn't true until I met you."

Duke barely contained a victorious shout. "Fascinating," he said quietly.

"To the contrary, it's actually pretty terrifying how badly I want you," she admitted.

She looked so lost and vulnerable that Duke wanted to scoop her up and comfort her…right before he seduced her. He settled for taking her soft hand in his and brushing his lips across her knuckles.

"Don't look so scared, darlin'. We're going to be sensational together."

For how long? He could practically read the unspoken question in her eyes. Because she needed to know this much—and he needed to make it very clear, he answered her unspoken question aloud.

"Stop worrying, darlin'. We're going to be sensational forever."

13

The entire evening had been calculated to destroy her unspoken resolve. That much was obvious to Dani as she slipped into Duke's arms for yet another slow dance.

What was less clear was why he had gone to so much trouble. After a couple of glasses of bubbly champagne and a few spins around the deserted dance floor, the answer was fuzzier than ever.

Okay, he wanted to seduce her. Nothing unclear or unexpected about that. But he also seemed determined to make the whole evening memorable.

Not that he had to worry with regard to the sex, she thought wryly. She was already anticipating making love with Duke so eagerly that he couldn't possibly think she needed additional persuading. There wasn't a doubt in her mind that he would make love with the same passion with which he tackled everything in his life.

No, he seemed to be after more than her surrender in bed. Champagne, candles, fresh flowers, they all added up to a man on a romantic mission, a forever kind of mission.

"Stop thinking so hard," he advised, regarding her with amusement.

Her gaze snapped up to clash with his. Was the man psychic or what? "I just wish I could figure out what you're up to," she said a little wistfully.

"Who says I'm up to something?"

"You do. Every now and then this vaguely guilty expression flits across your face. What's that about?"

He shrugged. "I can't imagine. I don't feel the least bit guilty about anything."

"Not even luring me to Fort Worth with a storm on the way?"

He chuckled at the accusation and executed a tricky spin designed to rob her of the ability to speak.

"Are you giving me credit for controlling the weather?" he inquired lightly as she tried to get her equilibrium back.

"No, just taking advantage of it."

"Darlin', a wise man takes advantage of all life's opportunities."

"So whatever plotting has been going on in that head of yours began when the first drop of rain fell earlier this afternoon and not a moment before?" she asked skeptically.

He did look vaguely uncomfortable at that. "Not exactly."

As one song ended and there was a pause before the next, she took the opportunity to look him in the eye. "When exactly did this particular opportunity present itself?" she inquired.

"Does it really matter?"

"It does to me. Let's just call it a test of faith."

"Meaning?"

"Meaning, I want to see if you have enough faith in me to tell me the truth."

He stared hard at her, as if searching for loopholes. Dani kept her gaze unblinking.

"Okay, okay," he finally mumbled. "When the boys started talking about wanting to learn to ride, I saw an opportunity to get you alone for a while. Just for the day, though."

"Not overnight?"

As the music began again, he grinned unrepentantly and swept her back into his arms. "No," he insisted, "this is just a bonus."

Dani couldn't help it. She chuckled. "There now, that wasn't so difficult, was it? See how honesty pays?"

"I suppose that depends on whether you ask the Perezes to let you bunk with them or come back to our room with me." His gaze locked with hers. "So, Dani, it's the moment of truth. What's it going to be?"

She should have left him dangling, held off on an answer until dessert just to torment him, but she couldn't do it. "I suppose, since you've gone to so much trouble…"

His lips began a slow curve into a smile. "The room?"

"The room," she agreed softly.

"Now?" he inquired with ego-boosting eagerness, already heading back to their table for the check.

She grinned and shook her head, then deliberately pulled out her chair and sat. "Settle down, cowboy," she advised. "This is one opportunity that doesn't need to be claimed in a rush."

For a while there Duke's heart had been in his throat. Dani had seen straight through him, guessed all—well, almost all—of his devious little secrets and, he'd been almost certain, had been about to bring his whole scheme crashing down around his head. That she hadn't was testament to the depth of her feelings. He wondered if she even recognized how revealing her reactions had been. He doubted it. She would hate that he could see into her heart, especially since she'd worked so hard to hide all the soft spots.

Comforting himself that his goal was all but certain, Duke settled back in his chair and forced himself to relax. It wasn't all that difficult. He simply set out to enjoy the play of candlelight across her face, the shimmering of gold it set off in her hair. He relished the hitching of her breath whenever his fingers chanced to graze hers.

In fact, he discovered that the slow build of anticipation had its own reward. It had been a long time since he'd felt the kind of insistent, gut-deep hunger for a woman that he was feeling for Dani by the time they clasped hands and walked slowly back to their room.

The temperature hadn't dropped nearly as precipitously as had been predicted. The rain had softened to little more than a gentle shower, leaving the air cleansed and crisp.

To his amazement, Dani stepped out from under the shelter of the covered walkway and tilted her face up to the sky. A fine mist settled on her skin, leaving it as dewy as a spring morning and a hundred times more appealing. She held out her arms as if to embrace the night. The gesture was so totally unselfconscious, so gloriously uninhibited and happy that Duke found himself joining her, getting soaked for the second time that night. He hardly even noticed.

"Isn't it wonderful?" she murmured, meeting his gaze.

"It's wet," he observed, concluding that she was definitely a little tipsy.

"It reminds me of 'Singing in the Rain,' one of my all-time favorite movies," she said, looking nostalgic.

He recalled the specific scene vividly. "Gene Kelly dancing in the street," he said with a smile. "Are you planning to launch into song or dance any second now?"

"No," she said with a wistful sigh. "I can't sing and I can't dance."

"Who says?" he protested. "No one's grading you out here. Come on, darlin'. Go for it."

He encouraged her by whistling the first few bars of the song. She did a little skip, then something vaguely resembling a tap routine. She was no Gene Kelly, that was for sure, but her face was glowing and her eyes were sparkling under the twinkling display of neon that splashed color across the damp pavement.

"You, too," she insisted, grabbing his hand.

"I'll sing," he offered instead, belting out what he considered to be a credible rendition of the movie's title song. He grabbed her off her feet and twirled her around for the sheer exhilarating fun of it. It was, if he did say so himself, quite a finale.

Or, perhaps, an extraordinary opening, if the main

production was yet to come. Either way, he was well and truly caught up in the storyline.

Especially when her body slid slowly down his as he lowered her feet back to the ground. Eyes wide, she met his gaze evenly, then slowly, so slowly that his body throbbed with the anticipation of it, she lifted her hands to his cheeks and framed his face. When she stood on tiptoe and kissed him, he was more or less convinced that the whole state of Texas shook.

"Oh, baby," he whispered raggedly, when he could catch his breath at all. "That was a real show-stopper."

She grinned at him, her expression very feminine and very smug. "Come along. I'm not waiting around out here for the applause. Something tells me it'll be a long time coming, and I have better things to do."

"Really? You turning brazen on me, darlin'?" he inquired hopefully.

"I'm thinking about it," she said, leading the way to the doorstep of their room.

Duke decided he was enjoying her seduction far too much to race right inside. Instead of opening the door, he leaned down and stole one more kiss, a real barn burner of a kiss.

It was Dani who eventually dragged her mouth away from his and stared up at him with dazed eyes. "Inside," she murmured. It came out as part command, part plea.

Duke nodded. "Fine by me."

"Open the door, then."

"I think I'll leave that up to you."

Her gaze faltered. "But you have the key." Alarm flared for a second in her eyes. "You do have the key, don't you?"

"Sure do. It's in my pocket. Anytime you want to slide your hand in there and get it," he suggested provocatively, "we can go right on in."

She regarded him with amusement. "Think you're real smart, don't you?"

He feigned a disinterested expression. "Smart enough."

"Okay, mister, let's see if you can take what you dish out," she said, offering her own challenge.

The glittering dare in her eyes made Duke vaguely uneasy. He braced himself for the torment of her touch. It would be interesting to see just how far she would go to prove which of them was the more clever.

"Which pocket?" she inquired with mild curiosity, after a visual survey of the alternatives.

When he would have replied, she touched a silencing finger to his lips. "Never mind. I think I'll just take my time and figure it out."

She stepped in very close, until her breasts were pressed against his chest and her warm breath was fanning across his cheek. Her arms circled his waist and she very, very slowly ran one hand up the curve of his backside until she reached the top of his pocket. Duke's blood began to hammer in his veins.

She searched that pocket so thoroughly and with such lingering, devilish caresses he thought for sure his heart would burst.

Then, when he was sure that his jeans couldn't possibly be any more uncomfortable, she did the exact same thing all over again with the other back pocket.

"Not here," she finally concluded, regarding him gravely. "Now where could that key be?"

Duke was totally incapable of replying. Maybe if he could have, maybe if he'd snatched the darn thing out himself, he could have saved himself from the wicked probing of his remaining pockets.

She slid her hands up his chest, examined the pockets in his shirt with care, finally satisfying herself that the key was elsewhere. He was breathing hard when she was done.

Then she moved on to the front pockets of his jeans. Deft fingers managed to skim far more than the depths of those pockets. With some sort of uncanny intuition she had managed to save the one that actually held the key until last. By then he was relatively certain that his body was one caress away from coming apart.

As she slowly and triumphantly removed the key, he stepped back so fast he almost tumbled off the curb. "Satisfied?" he muttered.

"Not yet," she said, giving him a saucy smile. "You?"

"Definitely not yet."

"Well, then, I guess we should go inside before we make a spectacle of ourselves."

Duke regarded her curiously. "What just happened here?"

"I'm pretty sure I proved that I know how to get you all hot and bothered," she said with obvious satisfaction. She opened the door and stepped inside, then gave him a head-to-toe survey that could have melted steel before adding, "It remains to be seen if you can do the same."

He shook his head. "Darlin', don't you know how dangerous it is to issue that kind of a challenge to a man as close to the end of his rope as I am?"

"No," she said, then added innocently, "Perhaps you should show me."

Duke stepped inside and slammed the door so hard behind him, it rocked on its hinges. Dani grinned at the impatient gesture.

"Careful there. If we want any privacy, we need that door right where it is."

"Very amusing," he said and reached for her.

She put up very little resistance when he tugged her into his arms and settled his mouth over hers. There was nothing careful or tentative about this claiming. He was a man possessed. He wanted to taste her, to make very sure she knew that from this night on she belonged only to him.

Duke had never felt this demanding need for a woman. Not that he hadn't enjoyed sex. He had the usual appetite for the feel of a soft body beneath his own, for being surrounded by slick, moist heat.

But this hot, urgent passion seemed to run deeper than that. It was as if he needed to prove that beyond the teasing and the provocation, beyond the flirting and kisses, there was more. For the first time in his life, he felt as if he were putting some new part of himself on the line.

Perhaps his heart.

His pulse hitched at the thought. But not even the terror that should have followed would have been enough to get him to walk out of this room tonight.

Oddly enough, though, the panic never came. He would have to figure out why later.

In fact at the moment, as his fingers made short work of buttons and snaps, then skimmed over bare flesh, all he felt was the exhilaration of a man who was right where he wanted to be, with the woman with whom he belonged.

Forcing himself to drag in a deep, calming breath, he slowed down. He lifted Dani off her feet, then placed her on the bed as reverently as he'd ever touched anything in his life.

Dani returned his gaze with a hooded, smoldering look of her own. He was relieved by that, glad that there was no evidence of the lost, vulnerable woman he had met a few months ago. Whatever she felt for him in her heart, she was meeting him tonight as a strong, decisive woman, the kind of woman he'd seen evidenced in her work. Maybe, he thought, he'd played some small part in giving her back her confidence.

His gaze danced over her, then took a slower, lingering survey. She was so lovely. Small and delicate in many ways, there was a surprising, but unmistakable strength about her. He followed the subtle definition in her arms, stopped to savor the gentle sweep of a shoulder, then moved on to admire the generous curve of her breasts. He trailed a finger down that soft slope to a tip that was as hard as a pebble beneath his touch, then repeated the action on her other breast until she gasped with pleasure and her eyes drifted closed.

When his mouth closed over one sensitive peak, her eyes flew open and her hands tunneled through his hair as if to keep him there.

Duke was far from finished, though. Each breast was but a stopping point on his journey of discovery. He wanted to know every inch of her, to discover textures and tastes and secret pleasure spots. He wanted her to remember every second, every caress.

"Duke?"

He stopped his intimate examination of a sensitive spot on the inside of her thigh and met her gaze. "Yes?"

"Look at me," she pleaded softly. "Look at me and make love to me. I want you inside me now."

"In a minute, darlin'. I'm not quite through with my survey."

"Your survey is making me crazy," she confessed.

He hid a grin. "That's the general idea."

"But I want to make you crazy, too."

"Oh, baby, you do," he vowed. He reached for her hand. "Here, feel." When he placed her hand over the hard shaft of his arousal, a slow smile spread across her face. Confidence returned. Her gaze met his boldly.

"If that's the case," she said, "then let's go for it."

"We're not racing a clock, are we?"

"I just thought it would be good to seize the opportunity," she pointed out.

Duke chuckled. "Like you told me, this opportunity isn't going anywhere. In fact, we're just now starting to take full advantage of it."

He set out to prove to her the exquisite torture of slow, deliberate caresses and deep, bone-melting kisses. She was slick with perspiration and writhing against the sheets by the time he knelt between her thighs and slowly entered her.

The moist, welcoming heat claimed him as surely as he'd set out to claim her. She was slick and tight and eager. The movement of her hips was timed perfectly to him as if they'd learned this rhythm in another lifetime and only in each other's arms. He was all but certain it had never been like this before.

Duke was struck by the stunning thought that this was what people meant when they referred to soul mates. That had always been an elusive concept to him, the idea that destiny chose two people and saw to it that they came together for eternity.

But as their bodies melded, as wave after wave of stunning pleasure washed over them, he began to wonder if he hadn't been a little too quick to dismiss the notion.

When Dani's cry of release shimmered around him, it was all he could do to hold back a triumphant shout. She was his now, as surely as if she'd already said yes to the proposal he had yet to make.

As for him, if he looked very, very closely inside his heart, he had a feeling he might discover that he was just as much her captive. To his astonishment, rather than being panicked by that, all he felt was a sort of intense, heady relief.

Dani stretched languorously. She had never felt better in her life. As long as she didn't allow a lot of doubts to start crowding in, she would be just fine. Better than fine. She would be magnificent.

There was one sure way to see that doubts remained at bay. She slid across the mattress and tucked herself up against Duke, pausing to admire the hard planes and angles of his body. There wasn't an ounce of spare flesh on him. And the man generated enough body heat to warm all of Texas. Her inquisitive, probing hands slid across his belly, then down. He moaned softly, then came wide-awake with a start. After a moment of obvious disorientation, he regarded her with amusement.

"What are you up to?" he inquired.

"Isn't that obvious?"

"Explain it to me, anyway."

She grinned. "Just checking to see if this was one of those rare times when opportunity knocked twice."

He regarded her balefully. "Twice? I'm fairly certain I recall it knocking several times during the night."

"That was then. This is now."

He studied her face intently. "Trying to keep the regrets at bay, by any chance?"

Dani stared at him in shock. Was she so obvious? "Why would you ask that?"

"Because I know you better than you think I do." He grinned that lazy, sexy grin that destroyed her defenses. "Come on now, no regrets."

"Easy for you to say. This doesn't solve anything between us, Duke, not really."

"I'm perfectly willing to make it legal," he said. "Just say the word."

She stared at him. His expression was neutral. Clearly he didn't intend to give away whether he was serious or not. "You want to marry me?" she asked, spelling it out so there could be no mistake.

"You didn't think this was some casual, one-night stand for me, did you? I'm not that kind of man." He shook his head with exaggerated sorrow. "Never mind. I'll prove it to you."

"There's no need."

"Of course, there is. You can't marry me, if you don't trust me."

Warning signals that had apparently been on the blink for too many hours were recharged now. They were clanging like the very dickens. "I'm not going to marry you, period," she insisted, even though the pull of the idea made her limp with longing.

"We'll see," he said smugly.

Dani sighed. "Duke, we're consenting adults here. This doesn't require a proposal to make it okay."

"Never said it did." He shot her a chin-up, defiant look. "I'm asking you to marry me just the same."

"No," she said again, though her stomach was as jittery as if she'd said yes.

"Why not?" He met her gaze evenly. "And don't try telling me you don't love me, because I'm not buying it."

"Well, aren't you the cocky one?" she retorted. "Just because we made love doesn't mean I'm *in love*."

"Nope," he agreed solemnly. "That's not proof all by itself."

"Then would you mind telling me where you got such a cockamamie idea?" Maybe then she could see to it that she never, ever did anything similar again.

"You women have your intuition," he said. "We men have other ways."

"Such as?"

"Darlin', I'd be going against the code if I gave it away."

"Code? What code? Gave what away?" she asked, thoroughly exasperated.

"It's a guy thing."

She stared at him incredulously. "It's a guy thing? Well, this is a girl thing." She climbed out of bed and draped herself in the bedspread, figuring that delivering her tirade stark naked would take a little of the sass out of it. "I am not now nor do I ever intend to be in love with you. I will not marry you."

Duke didn't seem to be the least bit distressed. "We'll see."

Dani marched off to the bathroom and slammed the door behind her. When it was closed, she leaned heavily against it.

"Well, damn," she murmured.

How was she supposed to fight a man who was offering her the very thing she wanted most in the world: Marriage and a family every bit as strong as the one into which she'd been welcomed as a child.

By telling herself a thousand times a day that he didn't really love her, she reminded herself. The only hitch to that was the fact that last night, in his arms, it had felt an awful lot like he might be loving her back.

14

Duke recognized an ambush when he saw one. Jordan had asked him to drop by Dolan's and pick up a package for him while he was out to lunch. It should have occurred to him that Sharon Lynn would have been more than happy to have the blasted package delivered.

So, because he wasn't thinking straight, hadn't been thinking straight ever since he'd returned from Fort Worth, he walked into the drugstore as innocent as a lamb. There, clearly just waiting for him, were both Sharon Lynn and Jenny. They perked up visibly at the sight of him.

Duke sighed. Everyone had maintained a polite, if clearly expectant facade right through Christmas and New Year's. Now, since no ring or engagement announcement had been forthcoming, apparently Sharon Lynn and Jenny had been designated by the family to get to the bottom of what had gone on between him and Dani on their trip and what was likely to go on between them from now through eternity.

"Afternoon, ladies," he said, figuring he could bluff

his way through the conversation or else run like hell. Since the latter wasn't a real option, he decided he'd better brazen it out.

"Hey, Duke, come on and join me," Jenny suggested, patting the stool beside her.

"I really need to get back to the office," he said, flashing her a smile. "Jordan just asked me to pick something up for him while I was out grabbing lunch."

She regarded him skeptically. "Have you actually had lunch yet?" she asked with typical Adams directness.

He sighed. "No."

Sharon Lynn beamed at him. "Well, then, no more excuses. Uncle Jordan can wait a few more minutes. Sit right down. What'll it be? A hamburger? Grilled cheese? BLT?"

Duke wondered which one would be the quickest to prepare and gulp down. "Grilled cheese," he said.

"Fries with that?"

Fries would take too long, especially in the quantity Sharon Lynn served them up. They would have to be eaten one by one. "No, not today."

"And to drink? Coffee?"

No way. He would have to wait for coffee to cool. "Just water," he said.

Apparently, his nervousness was transparent. The two women exchanged an amused glance. He, in turn, regarded them suspiciously.

"Okay, what are you two up to?" he asked.

"Nothing," Sharon Lynn claimed.

"Absolutely nothing," Jenny concurred.

He scowled in Sharon Lynn's direction. "When are you and Kyle Mason setting a date?" he inquired, hoping to divert her attention from his love life by focusing on hers.

She grinned. "The date's set. First Saturday in June. He finally got around to proposing in the middle of college football on New Year's Day. The man's timing is impeccable. Now there's no way I can doubt how much he loves me. He actually stopped watching the Aggies for a full fifteen minutes." She grinned and waved her ring under his nose. "I hope you'll be there."

"Of course." So much for that tactic, he thought, turning to Jenny. Before he could ask, she held up her hand to stop any inquiry he was planning.

"No love life. Not interested. No time," she declared.

He grinned at her vehemence. "And how does Harlan feel about that?"

Sharon Lynn chuckled as Jenny heaved a heavy sigh. "Grandpa isn't too thrilled with her attitude," Sharon Lynn confided. "In fact, I'd say she is on his personal to-do list. Get Jenny a husband, right up there in big, bold print."

"Oh, go suck an egg," Jenny retorted.

Duke regarded her with amusement. "Let that be a lesson to you. If you don't want anyone meddling in your love life, stay out of theirs."

Jenny's gaze narrowed. "Meaning?"

"Meaning I could very easily join forces with your father," Duke warned.

Both women hooted at that, which wasn't quite the reaction he'd been hoping for.

"You poor man," Jenny said. "Don't you realize that you and Dani are way, way above me on his list? In fact, I'd say at the moment you two are his number one priority. He's always preferred to hedge his bets and go with a sure thing. I'm way too speculative at the moment."

Duke sat, silently absorbing the news. He waited for the panic to set in, just as he had over and over again in that motel in Fort Worth. It didn't come. In fact, in a curious way, he was relieved that he had allies, powerful allies. He'd felt surprisingly disappointed and disgruntled when Dani had flat-out turned him down in Forth Worth.

Why was that? he wondered, trying to think back over the past few months. He was a bright man. Surely, he could analyze this thing with Dani from start to finish and reach a logical conclusion.

It had started as a game. Duke was willing to admit that much, even though it didn't say much for him. Then it had moved on to a game he was playing for his sons' benefit.

Now, much to his amazement, he realized that the stakes were totally personal and very, very important. He'd gone and fallen in love with the woman. He tried to imagine his life without her, and he couldn't. All he saw was a bleak and empty future, the exact kind of future he'd once considered his due for all his sins.

Lately, though, he'd had a taste of brighter possibilities and he knew he would never be happy unless he did everything in his power to make them happen. He wanted more than a mother for the kids. To his astonishment, he'd discovered that what he wanted most of all was a wife. He wanted a woman who could make his heart leap simply by walking into a room. He wanted a woman who listened and teased and taunted. He wanted a companion, a friend and a lover.

He wanted Dani.

Of course, realizing what was in his heart was a snap compared to convincing Dani what was in hers. He looked from Sharon Lynn to Jenny. Both women were studying him with blatant curiosity.

"I'm not your problem, ladies," he declared, summing up in a nutshell the conclusion he'd just reached.

"Explain," Sharon Lynn said, her elbows on the counter and her chin cupped in her hands as she regarded him intently.

"It's Dani," Jenny concluded without waiting for his reply. "She's holding out."

"Seems to be," he agreed.

"Why?" Sharon Lynn asked. "Have you told her how you feel?"

"I asked her to marry me."

Jenny didn't seem the least bit surprised by that. She waved her hand impatiently. "That isn't what Sharon Lynn asked. Have you told her how you feel?"

Duke hesitated to admit that he was just coming to grips himself with the fact that he was in love with her. In the natural, old-fashioned order of things, he supposed he should have reached that conclusion before he hauled her into bed. He definitely should have reached it before proposing.

"Sleeping with her isn't an answer," Jenny said, stunning him into silence. "Proposing marriage is nice, but that's not enough, either."

"In other words, have you mentioned that you love her?" Sharon Lynn prodded more specifically.

Duke cleared his throat.

Jenny sighed. "No. The answer's no, isn't it?" She

glanced at Sharon Lynn. "Men are such idiots. Now do you see why I'm content to live my nice, peaceful existence without one?"

Sharon Lynn rolled her eyes. "Women like you always fall the hardest," she warned. "I can hardly wait."

"Oh, shut up. We're not talking about me," Jenny said, turning away from Sharon Lynn and facing Duke squarely. "Now what do you intend to do to get this marriage business with Dani straightened out before she does something crazy like going back with that awful Rob Hilliard?"

"Hilliard?" Duke demanded tightly. "What the hell does he have to do with anything?"

"He's been calling again," Sharon Lynn said. "He brought the girls by over the holidays. Dani cried for an hour after they left."

That was all news to Duke. Bad news. He had warned the guy to stay away. The only way to ensure that happening, though, was to get Dani to marry him. Unfortunately, though, he was fresh out of ideas. Aside from acknowledging that what he was feeling these days was love, he was forced to admit that he was stymied. Finding oil where it shouldn't be was a breeze compared to this.

"I was hoping you two could make a suggestion," he said, throwing himself on their mercy. Something told him he could trust them. They both had Dani's best interests at heart. "You seem to have all the answers."

"Now you're talking," Jenny said approvingly.

"Something dramatic," Sharon Lynn said.

"Something simple," Jenny countered. "Dani would be embarrassed by dramatic."

Duke thought of Dani's performance in the motel parking lot, not her singing and dancing, but that sexy slip-sliding game she had played for the room key. She was not half as demure as Jenny apparently thought she was. He thought maybe dramatic would be for the best. Kelly had shared some of the more outrageous things Jordan had done to win her heart. Perhaps he should try a few of those on her daughter. Maybe Dani would be charmed by the nostalgia of it, if nothing else.

"Thanks for the help, ladies," he said, climbing off the stool. "I think I'll take it from here."

"But we haven't come up with a really good plan," Jenny protested.

"And you never even got your sandwich," Sharon Lynn said.

"That's okay. You've provided plenty of inspiration," he assured them, grinning at the self-satisfied smirks they exchanged.

"Keep us posted on your progress," Sharon Lynn pleaded.

"Sweetheart, if there's any progress, I'm sure you won't need me to drop by and fill you in. With an Adams involved, word will spread like wildfire."

Ever since her return from Fort Worth, Dani had been dragging around, her mood despondent. She'd been snapping at Maggie at the clinic until the poor girl had threatened to quit unless her boss's mood improved.

"You need a man in your life," Maggie said. "In my opinion, you're frustrated."

Little did she know, Dani thought sourly. She'd never been less frustrated in her life, sexually speaking. Emotionally, however, was another thing entirely. Rob's impromptu little visit with the girls hadn't helped, either. They'd all been in tears by the time he packed them up again and took off, her refusal to reconsider their relationship ringing in his ears.

Apparently, word of her crummy attitude was spreading, too. Everyone in the family was watching her as if they expected her to break out with chicken pox or maybe hives at any second. They were hovering, their expressions alternately sympathetic and hopeful. Well, the whole blasted lot of them could go jump in the creek, she thought miserably. Their lives weren't on the line. Hers was.

Duke's proposal echoed in her head at the most inopportune moments. Memories of the way his hands had molded and shaped her body with intimate precision, drawing ragged sighs and heartfelt gasps, left her feeling so hot and bothered she was tempted to turn the air conditioning on, even though it was barely freezing outside.

It would be so easy to say yes, so uncomplicated to cave in to Duke's pressure. If, of course, he'd pressured her. Instead, the man was nowhere to be found. She'd even dropped in on her father at work, hoping to catch a glimpse of Duke. Of course, it had been lunchtime, she consoled herself. He'd probably just slipped out for a sandwich.

She declined Jordan's offer to take her out somewhere and wandered down to Dolan's herself. Sharon Lynn and Jenny had been huddled together at the counter, their expressions guilty as sin when they spotted her.

"You just missed Duke," Sharon Lynn said a little too brightly.

"Was he here for lunch?"

The question drew another guilty look. Sharon Lynn shrugged. "Not really. He was running an errand for Uncle Jordan."

"I see," Dani said and slipped onto a stool. "Can I have a hot fudge sundae, please?"

"Now?" Sharon Lynn said as if it were the most scandalous request she'd ever heard. "In the middle of the day?"

Dani scowled at her. "Do you have a problem with that?"

"No, of course not," her cousin declared and rushed to scoop up the ice cream. She added extra hot fudge and enough whipped cream to clog the arteries of half the population of Los Pinos.

She and Jenny watched uneasily as Dani silently ate every single bite.

"Man trouble?" Jenny inquired eventually.

"Who, me?"

"Yes, you," Jenny said impatiently. "What's with you and Duke?"

"Nothing," Dani said, noting the amused look the two exchanged. "Okay, what's up? Do you know something I don't?"

"Not a thing," Jenny responded.

"Absolutely nothing," Sharon Lynn concurred.

Dani didn't believe either one of them. There was some sort of scheme afoot. "I hope you're not interfering in this," she said, regarding first one, then the other intently.

"Absolutely not," they assured her dutifully.

"Because if I find out that you have been, I will…" She couldn't think offhand of anything quite dire enough.

"What?" Sharon Lynn prodded, an impudent, teasing glint in her eyes.

"Yes, what will you do?" Jenny inquired, clearly fascinated by the threat.

"I will deliver entire litters of kittens to your doorsteps in the middle of the night," she warned.

"You do that anyway," Jenny said. "White Pines is crawling with them."

"So's our place," Sharon Lynn agreed. "Dad's still trying to figure out how you manage it."

Dani sighed at the failed threat. "Okay, forget the kittens, but I will make you pay. Remember that. And I will do it when you least expect it."

She slid off the stool and headed for the door. She was pretty sure she heard them chuckling when they thought she was too far away to catch them at it. There really were times when having a family that knew you so well could be a nuisance, she thought as she barely resisted the urge to slam the drugstore door behind her.

Since the clinic was already closed for the afternoon, she decided to take a drive out to White Pines. Not that she couldn't expect more of the same taunting from Grandpa Harlan, but at least he usually managed to impart some wisdom along with his teasing.

She found her grandfather in the paddock along with Cody and one of the hands. They were going over a horse that appeared to be lame. She would have offered to check him out herself, but Cody knew every bit as much as she did about this kind of thing. She had some expertise, of course, but small pets were her forte. She was called in to treat large animals only when the vet in the next town couldn't be reached.

Waving to the men, she went into the stables and saddled up the pinto, which had turned out to be a surprisingly quick learner once it concluded that no one here was likely to harm it. He'd put on weight and no longer had that wild look in his eyes.

"You're my pal now, aren't you?" she whispered as he nuzzled her pocket for one of the sugar cubes she invariably kept there for him. She took out two. "Here you go."

Maybe a good, long ride was what she needed. It would clear her head.

The bottom line, she concluded as she raced straight into the wind, was that she wanted desperately to trust her heart. She wanted to admit that she had fallen in love with Duke, but how could she? She kept coming back to the boys.

She knew from her own experience with Jordan that being a stepkid could be just fine, better than fine. But Jordan and her mom had been committed to each other for years, even though it had taken him a long time to recognize what was in his heart.

She and Duke didn't have that same long history. There was every chance that they would fail at making a relationship work. She had thrown herself heart and soul into her relationship with Rob and look at what a mess she'd made of that. They'd even had a four-year foundation to build on. By comparison, this thing with Duke had been a whirlwind courtship.

She was so lost in thought that her grandfather had ridden up beside her before she was even aware he was in the vicinity. He dismounted and walked over to sit beside her on the fence rail.

As his warm gaze settled on her, she saw the worry lines that were clearly etched in his forehead. "You okay, kiddo?"

"More or less."

"Problems with Duke?"

"Nothing but problems," she conceded. "Ever since we came back from Fort Worth, he's been avoiding me. Other than a glimpse or two in a crowd here over the holidays, I never even saw him."

"Maybe he's just giving you time to think."

"I suppose."

He cupped a hand under her chin and forced her to look at him. "So, when are you going to put that boy out of his misery?" he demanded. "He's going around looking like a lovesick puppy and you don't look one bit better. It's time to fish or cut bait, darlin' girl."

"Oh, please," she muttered. "Duke Jenkins couldn't look pitiful if he took acting classes for a lifetime."

"It's true. Jordan says he can't keep his mind on work, either. That's a sure sign a man's in love."

"You know what happened with Rob," she reminded him. "The girls still haven't gotten over it. How can I take that chance again? It wouldn't be fair to Joshua and Zachary, especially since Duke can't even bring himself to admit he has any feelings for me at all."

"Have you admitted you're in love with him?"

The question made her pause. "No," she conceded eventually.

"The way I hear it, he has asked you to marry him. Is that true?"

"Yes, but—"

"But what, darlin' girl? No man asks a woman to marry him and takes it lightly."

"He hasn't said he loved me. We can't start off a marriage like that."

"Maybe he just has a hard time getting the words out, same as you."

"Maybe," she conceded, considering the possibility for the first time. Duke wasn't the sort of man who would want to risk rejection by putting his heart on the line, not with a woman who'd already turned down his marriage proposal.

"Let me ask you something else. Are you going to love those kids of his one bit less if you don't marry their papa?" he inquired slyly.

Dani heaved a sigh. It was true. Despite her very best intentions, she adored Joshua and Zachary. They were a never-ending delight. Just like their father. If she held her ground, if she refused to marry Duke, would the hurt be any less than it would be at some future date that might never come? No, she concluded thoughtfully.

She grinned at her grandfather. "You're a very smart man, you know that?"

"Well, of course, I am. It's about time somebody around here acknowledged it. Go on, gal. Tell the man. Somebody's got to jump into this thing feetfirst or we'll never get the show on the road. Seems to me like no Adams has ever been chicken to take a chance when something really mattered to them."

"I could drown," she pointed out, even though her mind was already made up.

"Not a chance, Dani girl. I've seen the way the man looks at you. He'll be there to catch you. There's not a doubt in my mind about that. Not a single doubt."

Dani wished she could be as sure, but in the end, it didn't really matter. Rob had taken the control of her destiny out of her hands. For way too long now, she had assumed that someone else would have to prove themselves before she would ever dare to put her own heart on the line. That wasn't any way for an Adams to live.

She gave her grandfather a fierce hug. "Thank you."

"For what?"

"For making sense. For being you."

"Don't thank me. Just be happy. That's all the thanks I'll ever need from any of you."

15

D**espite** the resolve he'd reached after talking to Sharon
Lynn and Jenny, Duke knew he was only a heartbeat
away from giving up in pure frustration. Dani had made
her feelings plain enough in Fort Worth and after. How
many times could a man ask a woman to marry him
without making a total fool of himself? He had a hunch
he was already way beyond the limit. He could go to
his grave someday consoling himself that he'd tried.

It was thinking about all the lonely days from now
until then that had him vowing to give it one more valiant effort. A last hurrah, so to speak. Something worthy of Kelly and Jordan Adams's daughter.

Of all the legendary tales he'd heard, he liked the
one about the airplane dropping rose petals best. It was
dramatic, romantic and appealed to his sense of the
outrageous.

Working up his courage, he walked into Jordan's office a few days before Valentine's Day and asked if the
small company plane was available.

"You need to check out a site?" Jordan asked, barely

glancing up from his work. "You don't need to ask, you know that."

Duke cleared his throat. "Actually, this is personal," he admitted, earning Jordan's immediate attention.

"Really? Does it have anything to do with Dani?" His gaze narrowed. "I won't have an elopement. If the two of you get married, it will be right here with all the family around."

"Actually, getting a quick yes and hauling her off to Vegas might be the safest way to go," Duke responded thoughtfully. "But the truth is I don't need the plane so we can elope. She hasn't budged off 'absolutely not, never' yet."

"I see," Jordan said, his disappointment plain. "Then why do you need the corporate jet?"

Duke bit back his embarrassment and said, "Remember the rose petals?"

That brief mention was enough to bring a smile to his boss's face. "Oh, yes," he said, then shook his head. "Didn't work, though. Kelly was a stubborn one."

"I have to try something," Duke insisted. "This is the best I can come up with."

"I suppose it's worth a shot. Dani always did love that story. She was furious she wasn't around the day I did it." He grinned. "The jet's yours. When are you going to do it?"

"Valentine's Day."

Jordan nodded. "Nice touch."

Duke spent days making the rest of the arrangements. Dani had been surprisingly agreeable to the date. He hadn't had to do any clever persuading at all.

In fact, he realized after he'd hung up, that she hadn't even asked what he had in mind.

Just the same, he had every detail worked out. He was going to take her out for an expensive, romantic dinner, then suggest a drive. If the weather cooperated, there would be a bright moon and lots of stars. Just in case, he intended to pop half a dozen romantic CDs in the car, along with a bottle of champagne. He was tempted to drag the boys with him when he went to pick out the ring, but he feared he would only be setting them up for disappointment if his scheme failed and Dani continued to refuse to marry him.

He spent Valentine's Day in one business meeting after another. None of them had gone well. His mind hadn't been on business. He'd finally had his secretary cancel the last two meetings on his calendar. He'd gone home and paced the floor in relative privacy. Only the cats had been there to regard him sympathetically. Five-thirty finally came.

This was it, then. He put on his best suit, tucked the ring into his pocket, made one last call to the pilot to make sure the plane was set and drove over to pick Dani up promptly at six-thirty.

He stood on her doorstep and stared at her in open-mouthed shock. She looked gorgeous in some sort of red velvet dress that skimmed her shoulders and hugged her waist. A single diamond winked at her throat, drawing his attention to the creamy expanse of bare skin exposed where the dress plunged to a deep V.

"You look…" Words failed him. She didn't help him out. She just kept her gaze fixed on his, waiting. "Spectacular," he said finally.

"Thank you."

He had to drag his gaze away before he reached out and followed the neckline of that dress with his finger. Only then did he notice the huge picnic hamper at her feet.

"What's that?"

"Dinner," she explained, watching him nervously. "I thought we could have a picnic."

He stared at her in astonishment. "In February?"

That drew a defiant jut of her chin. "Why not? It's a beautiful night."

"It's also forty degrees."

She'd apparently considered all of his likely arguments and readied responses. "We can eat in the car, turn the heater on," she said at once.

"And die from inhaling all that carbon monoxide."

She actually laughed at that. "Trust me. We're not going to die."

He thought of his own dinner reservation, then dismissed it. What the heck. Since he'd long since given up on trying to deny her anything she'd set her heart on, he drove to the place she designated, shared the gourmet meal she'd brought along and sipped the champagne she'd provided, ignoring his own bottle which was chilling in the back seat. All the while he regarded her with mounting suspicion.

"What are you up to?"

"What makes you think I'm up to something?"

"Experience."

"You think you know me so well, don't you? Well, you don't, Duke Jenkins. I am just as capable of impulsive, spontaneous actions as the next person."

"Oh, really?" he said just as he heard the sound of a small plane flying low overhead. He glanced up in time to identify Jordan's corporate jet. At least something was going according to plan.

Then he took another look and his mouth dropped open. Trailing in its wake wasn't a cascade of flower petals, but a banner lit with what appeared to be colorful, twinkling Christmas tree lights.

"What the heck?" he muttered. A banner and lights weren't part of the plan. Maybe they'd been Jordan's idea. He glanced over at Dani and noted that she was watching his reaction expectantly. Maybe this particular trick had been up her sleeve.

"Did you have something to do with this?" he asked.

She shrugged, her expression innocent. "Read the banner."

He sighed as he thought of all those rose petals going to waste, but this was definitely better. If she was taking the initiative, it had to mean they were finally making real progress.

He leaned out of the car and tried to read the banner as she'd requested. He really did try, but it was pitch-dark except for those tiny twinkling lights and the plane was circling so fast it was making him dizzy. He had a hunch, though, he could figure out the gist of it. If he was right, it wasn't a message he wanted to get from a banner. He wanted to hear the words from the woman next to him.

"I can't quite read it," he said. "Maybe you'd better spell it out for me."

"You can't read it?" she asked, craning her neck out the window on her side to see for herself. When she pulled back into the car, her expression reflected pure disappointment. "Well, damn."

Duke reached over and forced her to face him. "What's it say, darlin'?"

She swallowed hard and tried to evade his gaze. Finally, after what seemed an eternity, she looked him square in the eyes. She began to speak, cleared her throat and tried again.

"It says 'Will You Marry Me?'" she said in a nervous whisper.

A rush of pure joy swept over him. He barely managed to contain a triumphant shout.

"What was that? I couldn't quite hear you."

She scowled at him. "Will you marry me or not?" she demanded testily.

Duke figured he'd pressed his luck just about as far as he could. "I'm not like you. If you were hoping I'd turn all wishy-washy now that the shoe was on the other foot, it's just plain too bad, because the answer's yes. I'll marry you tonight, if that's what you want?"

"You will?" She seemed startled by the response and more than a little intrigued. "Tonight?"

To hell with Jordan's warning about an elopement. "If that's what you want," he said.

"I do. I mean, yes. Please. Right this minute."

"Any particular reason you're in such a rush?"

"I'm afraid I'll have second thoughts," she admitted candidly.

"About loving me?"

"No," she said at once. "Never that."

"Then what?"

"About taking such a huge risk on the future."

"Darlin', life is all about taking risks. If you don't take a few, you're not really living at all." He cupped her face in his hands. "Besides, there's no risk involved here at all. Nobody's ever going to love you the way I do. This is forever. You have my guarantee."

"You love me?" She sounded dazed.

"Took me long enough to figure it out, but yes, I love you, Danielle Adams. Always will. I promise."

"Forever's a long time," she said, but she was smiling at last.

"Not half long enough for the two of us."

"Don't you mean the four of us," she teased.

"Or five or six," he amended. "There's not enough trouble in the world that you and I together can't handle it. Agreed?"

She stared into his eyes, then slowly nodded, a smile on her lips. "Agreed."

Just then Duke noticed the first rose petal flutter down against the windshield. It was followed by another and then another. He postponed the kiss he'd had in mind and gestured outside.

"What on earth?" Dani murmured, poking a hand out to catch one of the petals. Her eyes widened when she realized what she'd captured. "Rose petals? Red rose petals?"

"Everybody said I needed to do something dramatic to capture your heart," he said. "This was my last shot."

"You planned to propose to me again tonight?" she asked. "I did all this for nothing?"

"Not for nothing," he assured her. "It just proved what an incredible pair we'll be. We both came out here tonight with the same idea."

She regarded him intently. "If you were planning this, where's the ring?"

"Who says I have one?"

"Forget it, Duke. You're too arrogant not to have one tucked away somewhere. Where is it?"

He winked. "In my pocket," he taunted.

A grin spread slowly across her face. "You know, there's nothing I enjoy more than an old-fashioned treasure hunt."

"And as I recall, you're very, very good."

She smiled. "Yes, I am, aren't I?" And then her clever hands went in search of that diamond.

Duke figured what happened next was the part of the engagement celebration they would keep to themselves. Some family legends just weren't meant to be shared.

* * * * *

Read on for a sneak peek of
The Cowboy and His Baby
part of the 2-in-1 anthology Winter's Proposal
from #1 New York Times *bestselling author*
Sherryl Woods!

1

Damn, but it was cold, Cody Adams thought as he chased down the last of the herd of cattle he was rounding up. Texas had never been this frigid, not even in the middle of January. He was surprised half the livestock hadn't flat-out frozen in the harsh Wyoming winter. They'd lost a few head of cattle, but nothing like what he'd anticipated the first time the temperatures had dropped below zero and the snow and ice had swirled around him.

The bitter cold and the frequent blinding snowstorms did serve one useful purpose, though. They kept him so busy—kept his brain cells so frozen, for that matter— that he hardly ever thought about home. He'd freeze his butt off and suffer frostbite on most any part of his anatomy for the blessing of a blank memory. He didn't want to think about Texas or his family. Most of all, he didn't want to think about sneaky, conniving Melissa Horton and the way she'd cheated on him.

It had taken him a long time to block out the image of his longtime girlfriend wrapped in his best friend's arms. Even now, more than a year later, that terrible, gut-wrenching moment sneaked up on him when he least expected it and reminded him that that kind of pain might hide out, but it seldom went away.

With the last of the herd rounded up and dusk falling, Cody gestured to one of the other hands that he was leaving and headed back toward the small but cozy line shack he'd insisted he preferred to the bunkhouse. He'd claimed it kept him closer to the cattle for which he was responsible, but the truth was, he craved the isolation.

For a man who had been a very social creature back in Texas—okay, a notorious flirt—it was quite a change and, for the time being, a welcome one. It was the only surefire way he could think of for staying out of trouble and avoiding the sort of heartache that falling for some woman just about guaranteed.

His boss, impressed by the fact that for years 28-year-old Cody had been running White Pines, his family's ranch back in Texas, hadn't argued with his idiosyncratic decision. Lance Treethorn had insisted only that a phone be installed so he could reach Cody on business. He was the only one with the number. He rarely used it. Cody dropped by the ranch house often enough to stay in touch.

On the tiny porch Cody stomped the snow off his boots, gathered up an armload of firewood and went inside. Within minutes he had a fire roaring and had shucked off his skeepskin jacket. He stood in front of the blaze, letting the heat warm his chilled body. Unfortunately, it couldn't touch the cold place deep inside him.

He'd been standing there for some time, lost in thought, when he noticed the stack of mail sitting on the table in the kitchen area of the one-room cabin. It was sitting atop a foil-covered pan that he suspected from the sinful, chocolaty aroma, contained a batch of freshly baked brownies. He grinned and ripped off the foil. Sure enough, brownies. Apparently, Janey Treethorn had been by again.

The fifteen-year-old daughter of his boss had a giant-size crush on him. Thankfully, though, she was painfully shy. She limited her overtures to dropping off his mail, always with a batch of brownies or his favorite apple pie. In the summer it had been fresh fruit cobblers. She was usually careful to stop by while he wasn't home. On the one occasion when he'd caught her, she'd blushed furiously, stammered an apology for intruding, and fled on horseback before he could even say thanks.

Unable to resist, he grabbed one of the brownies and ate it as he sorted through the few pieces of mail she'd left, putting the bills aside to be paid later. A small blue envelope caught his attention. Turning it over, he recognized his sister-in-law's handwriting.

As always, when anything came from a member of his family, his heart skipped a beat. Letters were rare enough to stir a pang of homesickness each time one arrived. Jordan's wife had been dutifully writing to him once every two weeks or so from the moment she and Jordan had gotten married. For a man who swore he wanted nothing to do with anyone or anything back home, it was downright pitiful how he looked forward to Kelly's chatty letters and the family gossip she shared with such humor and telling insight. This one was more than a week overdue. Since the others had come like clockwork, he'd been trying not to admit just how worried he really was.

He could tell right off there was something different about this one, too. It was stiffer, more like a card than a letter. He grabbed a second brownie, then carried Kelly's latest correspondence with him back to his chair in front of the fire.

When he ripped open the envelope, a tiny square dropped out of the card inside. He grabbed for it instinctively and found himself staring at an infant swaddled as tight as a papoose in a blue blanket. He caught himself grinning at the sight of that tiny, red, scrunched-up face.

So, Jordan was a daddy, he thought, amazed by the shaft of pure envy that shot through him. He'd known the baby was due any day now. Kelly had kept him apprised of every detail of her pregnancy, including his older brother's bemusement at the natural childbirth classes she'd insisted he take with her. He wondered if Jordan had made it through the delivery or if he'd fainted at Kelly's first big-time contraction.

He closed his eyes against the tide of longing that rolled over him. He was missing so damned much, he thought, once again cursing Melissa for the betrayal that had made staying in Texas where he belonged impossible.

He was missing seeing his other brother Luke and his wife Jessie's little girl grow. Angela had turned two back in December. Kelly had sent a picture of her with her face streaked with icing and her fist in the middle of the chocolate birthday cake with its two, fat pink candles. He'd tucked it in his wallet, along with the snapshot of Kelly's daughter from her first marriage, Dani, a little con-artist-in-training who could persuade penguins to buy ice, if she was of a mind to. Now he opened his wallet and inserted the tiny picture of this latest addition to the family.

He stared at the brand new baby one last time and wondered if he'd ever see him. He'd been named Justin James, according to the information on the birth announcement.

"We're going to call him J.J.," Kelly wrote in the note accompanying the card. "We can't wait for you to see him. Jordan swears he hasn't slept a wink in the past week. I don't know how that can be, since I'm the one up every time the little monster screams in the middle of the night. I haven't noticed Jordan pacing the floor alongside me. I think he's been sleeping with a pillow over his head deliberately, so he can claim he never hears J.J. crying. He swears he only wakes up after I've already left the bed. The silver-tongued devil says it's missing me that wakes him. He thinks a line like that will make me more sympathetic to him. Fat chance.

"No, seriously," he read on, "your big brother has been a huge help. I think he's a little awed by father-hood…or maybe it's just that mountain of diapers he's expected to wash every night."

Cody chuckled at the image of his button-down brother, the big-time oil company executive, changing diapers and warming bottles. Maybe he was taking to it better than any of them had anticipated, including Jordan himself.

"We're scheduling the baptism for the end of the month and we expect you to be here," the letter con-tinued. "No excuses, Cody. It's time to come home."

It's time to come home. Kelly's words echoed in his head, taunting him, reminding him that nothing would ever make this beautiful, sprawling Wyoming ranch into home. Lance Treethorn was a kind, decent man. He'd become a good friend. His daughters were real little an-gels and they treated Cody like one of the family. Even so, it wasn't the same. Not that a little thing like being homesick mattered. Even though his heart ached for the life he'd left behind, he knew he could never go back. He'd rather eat dirt than get within a hundred miles of the traitorous Melissa ever again.

It had been over a year since he'd left Texas, eighteen months to be exact, but not even time had cured him of the rage that had sent him away from everyone and everything dear to him.

Mention Texas and he didn't think of his beloved White Pines, didn't think of his parents or his brothers, much as he loved them all. The only image that inevitably came to mind was of Melissa Horton. Sometimes not even an entire bottle of the best liquor in the store could blot out the memories of the woman who'd betrayed him with his best friend.

Even now the vision in his head of Melissa was so vivid he could practically feel the silky texture of her skin and the soft flow of dark auburn hair through his fingers. He could practically smell the sweet summer scent of her.

But along with the sensual memories came the blinding rage, as powerful now as it had been on the day he'd left Texas for good. Accompanying that rage was the anger and frustration of realizing that he was, in part, responsible for what had happened. Maybe if he'd told her he loved her, she wouldn't have turned to Brian Kincaid in the first place. Maybe if he'd had a clue just how much she mattered to him, instead of taking her for granted, he wouldn't be lying awake nights aching for her. He'd been a fool. She'd been a cheat. Quite a pair, the two of them. Maybe he deserved to be this miserable. She certainly did, though he had no idea if she was. She could be happily married to Brian now, for all he knew.

Before he'd realized what he was doing, he'd ripped the note inviting him to the baptism of Jordan and Kelly's baby to shreds. He couldn't allow himself to be tempted back, not even by something as important as this. He would not go back to Texas. Not now. Not ever.

The decision was firm, but it left him feeling heartsick and more lonely than he'd ever felt in his life.

He was almost glad when the ring of the phone shattered the silence. He grabbed the receiver gratefully.

"Hey, boss, what's up?" he said, knowing it would be Lance Treethorn on the other end of the line.

The widowed father of three young girls, Treethorn had his hands full with trying to run the ranch and raise his daughters to be proper young ladies. He'd succeeded with the oldest. Janey was as prim and proper and dutiful as a father could ever want, but the two younger ones, ten and twelve, were terrors. Cody didn't envy the thirty-five-year-old man trying to get them raised and married without calamity striking.

"We got the herd rounded up today," he told Lance. "We only lost one more to the cold."

"Thanks, Cody, but I didn't call for an update."

Something in Lance's voice triggered alarm bells.

"What's wrong?" he asked at once. "Are there problems with the girls?"

"No, it's nothing like that. We're all fine, but you had a call here at the house." "I did?" He'd given the Treethorn number only to Jordan, with a direct order that it never be used except for a dire emergency. He knew his brother would never break that rule. His heart thudded dully as he waited for whatever bad news Jordan had imparted.

"Call home," his boss told him. "It sounded pretty

urgent. Your brother asked how quickly I could get a message to you. Obviously Jordan still doesn't know you have a phone in your cabin."

"No," Cody admitted, grateful that his boss had never asked why he insisted on having such a buffer between him and his family. Lance was the best kind of boss, the best kind of friend. He was scrupulously fair. He lent support, but never asked questions or made judgments. There had been no hint of criticism in his voice when he'd commented just now on Cody's decision to keep his private phone number from his family.

"I'm sorry he bothered you," Cody apologized anyway.

"You know damned well it's no bother. I just hope everything's okay at home. Give me a call if there's anything I can do to help."

"Thanks, Lance."

Cody hung up slowly, thinking of the tiny picture that he'd placed in his wallet only moments earlier. Had something happened to Justin James? Or to Kelly? Why else would Jordan call? Damn, but he hated being so far away. What if... He allowed the thought to trail off.

"Stop imagining the worst and call," he muttered out loud, finally forcing himself to dial his brother's number, knowing that this call, whatever it was about, would shatter whatever distance he'd managed to achieve from his past.

Jordan picked up on the first ring. His voice sounded tired and hoarse.

"Hey, big brother," Cody said.

"Cody, thank God. I was worried sick you wouldn't get the message for days."

Jordan, the most composed man Cody had ever known,

sounded shaken. The alarm bells triggered by Lance's call were clanging even louder now. "What's wrong?"

"It's bad news, Cody. Real bad."

Cody sank onto a chair by the kitchen table and braced himself. The last time Jordan had sounded that somber was when their brother Erik had been killed in an accident on Luke's ranch.

"Is it Dad?" he asked, hating even to form the words. Harlan Adams was bigger than life. He was immortal— or so Cody had always tried to tell himself. He couldn't imagine a world in which Harlan wasn't controlling and manipulating things.

"No, he's fine," Jordan reassured him at once, then amended, "Or at least as well as can be expected under the circumstances."

"Dammit, Jordan, spit it out. What the hell has happened?"

"It's Mother," he began, then stopped. He swallowed audibly before adding, "She and Daddy were out riding this morning."

He paused again and this time Cody could hear his ragged breathing. It almost sounded as if Jordan were crying, but that couldn't be. Jordan never cried. None of them did. Harlan had very old-fashioned ideas on the subject of men and tears. He had set a tough example for them, too. He hadn't shed a single tear when Erik died. He'd just retreated into stony, guilt-ridden silence for months after the loss of his son. The rest of them had coped with their grief dry-eyed, as well. If Erik's death hadn't caused Jordan's cool, macho facade to crack, what on earth had?

"Jordan, are you okay?" he asked.

"No. Mother took a bad fall, Cody."

Cody felt as if the blood had drained out of him. Hands trembling, he grabbed the edge of the table and held on. "How is she? Is she…"

"She's gone, Cody," Jordan said with a catch in his voice. "She never woke up. She was dead by the time the paramedics got to the ranch."

"My God," he murmured, stunned. Forbidden tears stung his eyes. Ashamed, he wiped at them uselessly. They kept coming, accompanied by a terrible sense of loss. "Are you sure Daddy's okay? Why aren't you with him?"

"Luke and Jessie are over at White Pines now. Luke's got the funeral arrangements under control. Kelly and I will be going over right after I get off the phone. I wanted to stay here until you called back. How soon can you get here?"

Cody noticed his brother asked the question as if there were no doubt at all that he would be coming home. "I don't know," he said, struggling between duty and the agony that going home promised.

Disapproving silence greeted the reply. "But you will be here," Jordan said emphatically. "I'm telling Daddy you're on your way."

Cody rubbed his suddenly pounding head. "I don't know," he repeated.

"Look, this is no time to be indulging in self-pity, little brother," Jordan snapped impatiently. "Daddy needs you here, probably more than he needs any of the rest of us. He'll need you to take up some of the slack at White Pines while he pulls himself together. He's always depended on you. Don't let him down now."

Cody said nothing.

Jordan finally broke the silence with a sigh. "We're scheduling the funeral for Saturday," he said. "Be here, Cody."

He hung up before Cody could reply.

Cody sat in the gathering darkness, silent, unchecked tears streaking down his cheeks. He had no choice and he knew it. Mary Adams might not have been the kind of warm, doting mother a child dreamed of, but Harlan Adams had worshiped her. He could not let his father go through this kind of grief without all of his sons at his side. It was the kind of loyalty that had been ingrained in him since birth. As badly as he wanted to pretend it didn't matter, he knew better. Nothing mattered more at a time like this.

He took some small comfort in the odds that said he would probably never even see Melissa. He doubted she would have the nerve to show up at the funeral. She certainly wouldn't have the audacity to show up at White Pines afterward. It would be okay. He could slip in and out of town before temptation overtook him and he sought out so much as a glimpse of her.

At least, that's what he told himself on the long, sad drive back to Texas after he'd cleared his departure with Lance. He'd chosen to drive to delay his arrival as long as possible. Maybe to come to grips with what had happened in private. He'd spend a few days with his family to grieve. A few days to do whatever he could for his father. A few days to spoil his nieces and hold his brand new nephew. A few days to soak up enough memories to last a lifetime.

With all that going on, Melissa would be the last thing on his mind.

The very last thing, he vowed with grim determination as he finally turned into the lane to White Pines.

He slowed his pickup and looked around at the land that he loved, the land he'd hoped one day would be his since Luke's mile-wide independent streak had sent him chasing after his own dream and his own ranch and Jordan was only interested in oil.

Even in the dead of winter, it was starkly beautiful, at least to him. He was home and suddenly, despite the sorrow that had drawn him back, he felt at peace for the first time since he'd driven away more than eighteen months before.

Melissa Horton took a break from her job behind the lunch counter at Dolan's Drugstore and perched on a stool with the weekly newspaper and a cup of coffee. Her attention was riveted to the story of Mary Adams's tragic riding accident.

The 55-year-old woman had always been incredibly kind to her. Melissa had figured Mary pitied her because she'd been mooning around Cody for most of her life. Once Mary had even tried to give her some advice. It had turned out to be lousy advice, but Melissa was certain Mary had thought she was doing her a favor.

Mary had sat her down one afternoon over tea and told her that Cody was taking her for granted. Not that that was news. At any rate, Mary had claimed that the only way Melissa would ever win him would be to make him jealous. Tired of being ignored except when it suited Cody, and taking the well-meant advice to heart, Melissa had tried to do just that by going out just once with Cody's best friend.

What a disaster that had been! Had she chosen any-one else, maybe the plan would have worked, but she'd foolishly selected the one man she'd figured wouldn't get hurt. Brian had known her heart belonged to Cody. He'd known their date meant nothing, that it was only a ploy to shake up Cody. He'd even tried to argue her out of it, warning her it could backfire, but her mind had been made up. She had risked everything, certain that Mary Adams was right. She'd seen it as the only way to get Cody to finally make a commitment to her.

She should have guessed that Brian understood Cody even better than she did. Every time she thought of the anger and hurt in Cody's eyes that night, it made her sick to her stomach. He had stared at them for the space of one dull, thudding heartbeat. He'd looked not at her, but through her. His gaze riveted on Brian, he'd said, "A hell of a friend you turned out to be."

He had spoken with a kind of lethal calm that had been more chilling than shouted accusations. Then he'd turned on his heel and walked away. He had taken off the next morning and never once looked back.

For the past eighteen months she'd had no idea at all where he was. Brian hadn't heard from him, hadn't expected to, for that matter. She hadn't had the cour-age to ask Cody's family for information. Her shame ran too deep.

There had been times when she'd considered being in the dark a blessing. It had kept her from chasing after him, from destroying what few shreds of pride and dig-nity she had left.

Now, though, she had no doubts at all that Cody would be coming home. She might have driven him away with her betrayal, but his mother's death would surely bring him back.

Had he changed much? she wondered. Had he lost the flirtatious, fun-loving nature that had charmed her and half the women who'd crossed his path? Would she have to live with regrets for the rest of her life for turning him into a bitter, cynical man?

"No good'll come of what you're thinking," Mabel Hastings advised, coming up behind her to peer over her shoulder at the front page of the newspaper.

"How do you know what I'm thinking?" Melissa asked defensively.

Mabel shook her head, her tight gray curls bouncing at the movement. When Mabel had a permanent, she meant it to last. She'd been wearing the exact same hairstyle as far back as Melissa could remember. It did not suit her pinched features.

"I been reading you like a book ever since you set eyes on Cody Adams way back in junior high school," Mabel informed her huffily. "You seem to forget how many times you sat right here at this very counter making goo-goo eyes at him."

Melissa chuckled despite her irritation at the unsolicited interference. "'Goo-goo eyes'? Mabel, exactly how old are you? A hundred, maybe? Not even my mother would use an expression like that."

The older woman, who was probably no more than sixty, scowled at her. "Don't matter what you call it, the point is you've been crazy about that boy way too long and just look where it got you."

Melissa sensed the start of a familiar lecture. Listening to it was the price she paid for having a job that paid enough in salary and tips to keep her financially afloat and independent. She didn't have to take a dime from her parents.

"Okay, I get your point," she said, trying to avoid the full-scale assault on her sense and her virtue. "Drop it, please. I probably won't even see Cody."

She was bright enough to know it would be far better if she didn't. Her life had taken some unexpected twists and turns since he'd left, but it was settling down now. She was at peace with herself. There were no more complications, no more tears in the middle of the night over a man who didn't love her—at least, not enough—and no more roller coaster ups and downs.

No way did she want to stir up old memories and old hurts. One look into Cody's laughing brown eyes and she couldn't trust herself not to tumble straight back into love with him. She'd clearly never had a lick of sense where he was concerned.

Now, though, the stakes were way too high. Now she had more than her own heart to consider. She had someone else to protect, someone more important to her than life itself—Cody's daughter, the child he didn't even know he had.

* * * * *

The Cowboy and His Baby
By #1 New York Times *bestselling author*
Sherryl Woods, available now wherever
MIRA Books are sold!